A KISS IN THE DARK

The soft, comforting kiss Rio had thought to bestow singed his lips like a branding iron. Courtney's mouth was both the promise of heavenly attainment and the hell of unattainable satiation. One kiss was a joyous torment. A million kisses would never be nearly enough.

With a low groan, Rio released her arms to slide his hands down her back, pressing against her delicate spine to urge her closer. A sighing whisper fluttered through Courtney's parted lips to tease his mouth and senses as her pliant body melted and flowed into his.

Muttering a curse against his own weakness, Rio crushed her soft lips with his hard mouth, drinking the essence of her like a man with an uncontrollable thirst. She was wild strawberries, and warm honey, and sweet, exotic, forbidden fruit. Defying reason, Rio nibbled hungrily.

Driven by need, he slid his lips from hers to test the satiny texture of her cheeks and ears and the secret spot behind the delicious lobe. Courtney's whimper of pleasure as she curled her arm around his taut neck caused a flare of pain in his loins.

"Oh, you are beautiful, Courtney," he murmured into the curve of her neck as he trailed a string of kisses from her ear to her arched throat. "And you are every inch a woman—never doubt it."

Books by Joan Hohl

COMPROMISES
ANOTHER SPRING
EVER AFTER
MAYBE TOMORROW
SILVER THUNDER
NEVER SAY NEVER

Published by Zebra Books

NEVER
SAY
NEVER

Joan Hohl

Zebra Books
Kensington Publishing Corp.
http://www.zebrabooks.com

ZEBRA BOOKS are published by

Kensington Publishing Corp.
850 Third Avenue
New York, NY 10022

First Printing: October, 1999
10 9 8 7 6 5 4 3 2 1

Printed in the United States of America

CONTENTS

Dear Reader,

I have always believed that love stories—tales of the trials and tribulations of men and women finding each other and the true loves of their lives—were favorites, told perhaps by roving troubadours and, who knows, possibly even around fire pits in prehistoric caves, long before the advent of the printed words of romantic fiction.

I love reading these stories; I love writing them.

I wrote the two stories presented in this volume, *Morgan Wade's Woman* and *Night Striker,* early in my writing career in the 1980s, under the pseudonym Amii Lorin—a name I created by combining the names of my two beautiful daughters, Amy and Lori, who were, and are, and will always be the the enduring lights of my life and my proudest production.

These stories focus on two cousins and the strong men they fall in love with. You will note, I'm sure, that the stories were written in a certain style, as dictated by the marketplace at that time. I could have made changes—but why when, in essence, these stories are vintage, timeless stories of love and romance?

I sincerely hope you enjoy reading them as much as I enjoyed writing them.

Happy reading,
Joan Hohl

MORGAN WADE'S WOMAN

Chapter One

Sam pushed through the doors of the tall building that housed the offices of Baker, Baker, and Simmes, Attorneys-at-law, and stood tapping her foot impatiently on the sidewalk. Where was her driver? She was only vaguely aware of the admiring glances turned her way by men passing, both on foot and motorized. She had only to step onto a public street at any time to receive these glances and, quite often, to her disgust, remarks as well.

That Samantha Denning was a strikingly beautiful woman there was no doubt. She stood five feet eight inches in her slim, stockinged feet. She was very slender, with long perfectly shaped legs and softly rounded curves exactly where they belonged. Her face was a perfect oval, the skin fair, with creamy pink cheeks, and a short, straight nose above full red lips that covered perfectly shaped white teeth. Dark brows arched gracefully over large, deep-green eyes, the lids heavily fringed with long, dark lashes. But what one saw first was her hair. Thick, long, wavy, not quite red, but more the color of highly polished, expensive mahogany. It seemed, when it hung loose, to have a will of its own. Subdued now in a coil around her head, it offset perfectly the severely but expensively cut hunter green suit she wore. With a black leather tote bag and black stack-heeled boots, her somewhat somber look was the only concession she would give to mourning clothes. They were none too effective, however, as a few curly tendrils at her temple and in front of her ears had escaped their combs and danced merrily on her face in the soft spring breeze, defying the impression of the dark suit and black accessories.

Samantha tapped her foot even more impatiently as, glancing at the narrow platinum watch on her slim wrist, she thought, *Damn, where is that man?* Looking up, she saw the sleek midnight-blue Cadillac glide to a stop opposite her at the curb. Before she took the few steps required to reach the car, the driver had jumped out of the front seat and was holding the door to the back open for her. As he touched her elbow lightly to help her enter, she said crossly, "Where have you been?"

"Sorry, Miss Sam, but the traffic's pretty heavy," he murmured. She glanced out the window to note the truth of his excuse, realizing she had been so deep in thought while she waited she hadn't even noticed.

"Yes, I see, I'm sorry I snapped, Dave. I'm going home now."

Dave smiled to himself as he pulled the powerful car into the stream of traffic. It was like her to apologize for snapping at him. She was self-willed, haughty, and imperious most of the time with her family and friends, but rarely ever did she speak sharply with the employees.

Dave had been with the Dennings fifteen years now, he as chauffeur and his wife, Beth, as a cook. They respected Mr. Denning, liked his petite, delicate, second wife, and were fond of her young half-sister Deborah. But they both adored Sam, this rebellious, redheaded firebrand, from the day she had come to the big house on Long Island to stay. Dave smiled again as he drove the car expertly through midtown Manhattan toward home, remembering that day seven years before.

What an uproar the house had been in, Mrs. Denning wanting everything perfect for the first meeting with her stepdaughter. Even Mr. Denning's normal reserve seemed about to crack as he and Dave waited for her plane to land. They had expected a shy seventeen-year-old and what they saw walking toward them was a queen.

She had said lightly and unself-consciously, kissing his cheek, "Hello, Father," and then had turned as Mr. Denning said in introduction, "This is our driver, Dave Zimmer."

He had been wearing the usual gray uniform and he chuckled to himself now as he remembered the way her eyes had looked him up and down.

"Not mine, not dressed like that at any rate. I'd as soon drop dead as be seen being driven by a liveried chauffeur."

That said, she'd given him the most beautiful smile he'd ever seen and added, "Please, Mr. Dave, could you not wear your everyday clothes if you have ever to drive me?"

He had been lost from that moment. It had been about the same when they had reached the house. Within ten minutes she had overawed her tiny stepmother and equally small half sister and enslaved the rest of the employees. She had ruled the roost ever since.

He had heard the story years ago, how the quiet, reserved Charles Denning had gone to England on a business trip and returned four months later with a ravishingly beautiful wife from a wealthy British family. Being a wealthy man himself, he had bought the huge house on Long Island for her. But nothing seemed to content her, not her husband or the house or even the daughter she bore eighteen months after their marriage. She missed her friends at home and refused to make new ones in her husband's homeland, referring to them all as gauche. When Samantha was two, she fled to her family, taking the girl with her. Though Charles Denning had fought for custody of his child, his ex-wife's family was powerful and he had to be satisfied with a few visits during those years.

Immediately on Samantha's mother's death, he had instructed his lawyers to notify the family that Samantha was to come to him. She had been back at school in Switzerland when she received the news and requested he allow her to finish her schooling and go ahead with plans made to do her tour of Europe with an American girl she'd been friends with in school for years. Her father had acquiesced to her request but had sworn that when he finally had her home he would keep her there.

Sam leaned back against the plush upholstery, looking completely calm and relaxed. Inside she was fuming. How could he do this? Why? She went over it again in her mind, the meeting she had just come from and what had precipitated it.

They had gathered in the library the afternoon before. Her stepmother, Mary, calm now from the tranquilizer her doctor had given her, her half sister, Deb, still looking pale and a little lost, Deb's fiancé, Bryan Tyson, and Sam. Mr. Baker had asked them to assemble at three for the reading of the will. The reading had gone along smoothly without interruption with Mr. Baker's voice droning on about bequests for the employees; then he went on to the family. He went into great detail about what was to be left to Deb and Bryan after their marriage. Sam was very surprised as she learned of the enormity of her father's estate and was deep in thought when Mr. Baker said her name and proceeded with her father's wishes concerning her.

At first Sam stared at him, stunned, then almost sprang from her chair.

"I will not do it. I'll contest the will."

Mr. Baker coughed slightly. "My father thought you would react this way," he replied, "so he instructed me to ask you if you could see him in his office to discuss this tomorrow morning at ten?"

"I'll be there," she said grimly and left the room, not waiting to hear the rest of the will. She had gone to her bedroom to pace the white fur rug, unseeingly touching furniture and the lovely things she had collected over the years. The beautiful room, all white and gold, failed to give her the soothing feeling it usually did. She had been thoroughly agitated and wondered how she could stand it till the morning.

Again, she went over that meeting of an hour ago. Both young Mr. Baker and old Mr. Baker (he had to be in his eighties, although he looked twenty years younger) had been there. Mr. Baker the elder had come directly to the point.

"Miss Denning, I see no way you can possibly break your father's will."

He was watching her hands, beautiful hands with long, slender fingers, the nails gracefully oval-shaped, covered with pink polish.

"I don't see why. The terms are ridiculous."

"Not at all, Miss Denning, and not at all unusual."

Well, they certainly seemed so to her. She heard again in her mind Mr. Baker's voice yesterday as he read the stipulations to her inheritance.

1. If she married an American citizen by the day she was twenty-five (just five months away) she would receive the sum of five million dollars, to be controlled by the husband and Mr. Baker, with a generous monthly allowance for her own personal use.
2. If in five years time the marriage was still intact, the control of the money would revert to herself and her husband jointly.

3. If the marriage was dissolved within said five-year period, the money would revert back to her father's estate, leaving her with a much smaller monthly allowance.

4. If she chose not to marry within the stipulated time, she was to have a small monthly allowance and a home with her stepmother until such time as she did marry or died.

"I'll forfeit," Sam had declared. "I still have my inheritance from my mother." She knew that amounted to approximately two hundred thousand American dollars.

"I'm afraid not, Miss Denning," Mr. Baker murmured. "You see, before your mother died, she changed her will, leaving your father in complete control of your inheritance, and that money is included with your father's."

Sam sat staring at him, speechless. He then went on to explain why he thought she would be unable to break the will, as her father had certainly been in a sound mind when it was drawn up, also his reasons for so stipulating. Oh, Sam knew his reasons. First, he had thought her too headstrong and concluded she needed the firm hand of a husband to control her. Second, he wanted her to make her home permanently in the States, thus the stipulation she must marry an American citizen. The fact that he had set her twenty-fifth birthday as a time limit probably meant he thought the sooner she was safely married the better.

Mr. Baker told Sam that her father had changed the age limit three times in as many years and had given instructions to have it changed again one month before Sam's birthday. His death negated those instructions.

Sam had left the lawyers' office with her mind in turmoil. Now she was almost home and still had not sorted out her thoughts very well. The amount of the inheritance alone staggered her. Five million dollars! Notwithstanding the strings attached, it was an enormous amount of money.

Perhaps she should have expected it, for Deb's share was an equal amount. Yet she would not have been hurt or felt left out if she'd have received much less. She had spent a total of nine of her twenty-four years with her father; Deb had been his from birth.

The Cadillac turned in and along the curved driveway slowly, and Sam looked up at the house. It was a beautiful house, an anachronism really, and the cost of maintaining it was staggering. Yet her father would not give it up. He had loved it, and had considered the money well spent.

Sam entered the house and went directly to the small sitting room in search of her stepmother, thinking how unusually quiet the house had seemed since her father's death. She found both Mary and Deb there, sitting close together, talking quietly. Sam sat down in a chair near them, dropped her bag onto the floor beside her, and said, "It seems it would be useless for me to contest the will." Her voice was low and her eyes had an almost lost look.

"Oh, my dear," her stepmother murmured, reaching her small hand out to her. "Please believe I knew nothing of these conditions in your father's will. If I had, I would have tried to dissuade him. They are quite impossible."

"I know, but I don't think it would have helped anyway. He was determined, in his own mind, to tie me down and keep me here." Then, in a stronger voice laced through with anguish, she added, "Didn't he know how much I'd come to love him and this country?" Her voice dropped to a whisper. "Didn't he know?"

Mary and Deb looked at each other helplessly a moment. They had never seen Sam like this. They had seen her angry often; she and her father had gone into battle regularly and they suspected both thoroughly enjoyed it. They had seen her cool and disdainful. But never had they seen this hurt, vulnerable look.

"Samantha," Mary said softly, "you needn't feel you

must fulfill these conditions. I'd be happy to supplement your allowance with some of my own."

Sam's voice caught slightly as she replied, "Thank you," and picking up her bag stood up and said as she walked quickly to the door, "I'll be in my room if you want me, Mother."

Mary called, "Sam," but Sam was already across the hall and on the stairs. Mary turned to Deb with tears in her eyes. "Go to her."

Deb followed Sam up the stairs and into the bedroom. Standing uncertainly inside the door she asked, "Would you like some company?"

Sam smiled at her gently. "Of course, Poppet, sit down, we can talk while I change." Deb sat on the bed and watched as Sam pulled her boots off, slipped off her skirt and jacket, walked across the room to the closet that completely filled one wall, and hung her clothes away neatly.

Deb's eyes went over her half-sister admiringly as she stood there in nothing but panty hose and bra. *What a beautiful thing she is,* Deb thought, and wished again, as she had many times before, that she had met Sam's mother. Deb did not envy Sam anything, except, perhaps at times, her height. Like most petite people she sometimes longed to be tall. But as far as looks went, Deb was honest enough with herself to admit she was not lacking in that department. With her dark hair and very fair skin, she was a lovely woman. Deb also realized that the love she had for this tall sister who had come into her life when she was just thirteen bordered on hero worship.

Pulling the combs out of her hair, Sam walked to the white and gold dressing table, sat down, and picking up her hair brush, began brushing her hair in long slow strokes. Set free, her rich auburn hair hung in deep waves halfway down her back. Deb watched her for a short time, her eyes dark with compassion. "What are you going to do, Sam? Do you know?"

Sam's eyes lifted and met Deb's in the mirror. "I really haven't a clue, Poppet. It's quite a bind."

Deb knew how deeply upset Sam was, for the British accent was heavy. Generally there was just a tinge of it in Sam's speech, becoming thick only when she was very angry or upset.

Pensively Sam added, "My first thought was to find a job, but then, what sort of work could I do?" She paused before adding, "You realize, love, I've been extensively and expensively educated, all of which prepared me to do nothing of use. I can ride, swim, play tennis, and golf with the best. I'm also a fair decoration in any room or gathering. None of these things will earn me a dime." She sighed. "Oh, I suppose I could apply for a post as a salesclerk, but who is going to hire the daughter of Charles Denning once they know?"

Deb didn't answer, understanding Sam was sorting it out for herself as well as explaining her options.

"That leaves marriage within five months," Sam went on, "or depending on your mother. The allowance father stipulated in the case I fail to marry in five months' time is less than I've been receiving since the day I first came to this house to live."

"And your mother's inheritance—" Deb began.

"Is tied up with Father's," Sam finished.

"Is there no one you could marry?"

"Oh, there are quite a few I could marry." Sam waved her arms airily. "I must have had at least five proposals of marriage within the last two years, but you see, Poppet, I have no wish to marry any of those men. The idea of spending five days, let alone five years, with any one of them gives me the horrors."

Sam laughed lightly as she walked to the closet and withdrew a white terry robe. "I'm going to take a long hot bath before lunch; maybe that will relax me some. Will you ask Mother to hold lunch a few minutes?"

"Of course." Deb smiled to herself as she left the room. Sam had stopped calling her stepmother Mary and began calling her Mother after their father's death of a heart attack just a week before. The suddenness of his death had shattered his wife and Sam had seemed to take a very protective attitude to both Mary and Deb.

Sam slid her body down into the warm bubbly water and sighed deeply. She wondered now, as she did so often of late, whether she could be an emotional cripple of some sort. She knew she had normal physical urges because she had felt, at times, an almost hurtful, aching need. Yet whenever any of the young men she knew, and there were many, tried to make love to her, she froze. She could respond only lightly to a good-night kiss, and it worried her a little. What she had told Deb was true—the idea of marriage to any of them horrified her. She really didn't know what to do.

Sam woke the next morning to spring sunshine streaming in her windows and a letter postmarked Nevada on her bedside table. "Babs," she said softly, pushing herself into a sitting position as she slit the envelope open. She hadn't heard from her best friend for two months, when Babs had called to tell her her second son had arrived. Sam scanned the pages quickly. Babs began with sincere condolences for all of them, then went on to rhapsodize on the virtues of her youngest. She then came to the most important part of her letter:

We are having the christening next week and, darling, both Ben and I so want you to be Mark's godmother. You could, of course, stand by proxy, but it would probably do you good to get away for a while at this time, and I do long to see you. Please say you will come. Give my love to the family.

Babs

Sam let the hand holding the letter drop into her lap and mused on it. Should she go? The urge to run had been on her since she'd left the Messrs. Bakers' office. Here was a place to run to. Here was someone to run to. She'd not fallen asleep till very late the night before worrying over what she should do and had reached no decisions. Perhaps talking it over with Babs would help. She had a way of putting things into their proper order of importance. Laughing all the while, Sam thought now, shaking her head and smiling. Sam then sat up straight, swung her long legs off the side of the bed, and picked up the receiver of the white phone that sat on the gilded white and gold table next to her bed. She called her travel agent and made plane reservations for the following Wednesday, then sent a wire to Babs informing her of her arrival day and time.

The big jet was airborne and the seat belt sign blinked out. Sam unfastened her seat belt, moved her seat back, closed her eyes, and relaxed. She felt good and looked it. She hadn't missed the admiring glances sent her way, both in the waiting room, and as she boarded the plane. She was wearing a cream silk fuji long-sleeved blouse with a matching tie at her throat and a soft wool pants suit in a deep shade of cocoa that set off her almost red hair to perfection. She carried no purse but instead had slung over one shoulder a large soft leather satchel. Comfortable matching low-heeled pumps completed the look.

When she had packed her suitcases she hadn't been quite sure what to take with her. The weather in the East had been unseasonably mild for early March, so she had laid out lightweight clothes. Then on reflection she had put some back into her closet and added a few heavier things. She did not know what the weather was like in the part of Nevada where Babs lived.

Sam smiled slightly to herself with the thought of Babs. Babs of the laughing eyes. Oh, the scrapes Sam had had to extricate her from while they were in school. Babs had an impish streak and had been forever in hot water. Nothing serious, but zany things, usually involving their teachers or later, when they were older, young men. She was bubbly and full of fun and mischief, and to Sam, always cool and composed, fell the task of smoothing the rippled waters. They had become fast friends when they were both twelve years old. The friendship had deepened and matured as the girls grew. They had made the grand tour after leaving school and when Sam had gone to her father in Long Island, Babs had returned to her family in Nevada.

They had been to Europe and Asia together since, and Babs made several shopping trips a year to New York. Then three years ago on one of her trips East, Babs had told Sam she was getting married, almost immediately, to Benjamin Carter, a name Sam had heard often over the years. Babs had assured Sam that she was very much in love, but as she was also very pregnant, couldn't Sam go back to Nevada with her right away and be her maid of honor? Sam went.

Sam had liked Ben Carter on sight. He was a tall, quiet, good-looking young man, and he blatantly adored Babs. The wedding had been a hasty and, as everything involving Babs, hilarious affair, the only off-note being the man whom Ben had wanted as his best man was out of the country and unable to make it back in time for the wedding, much to Ben's disappointment.

Sam had spent just four days in Nevada, and had not seen Babs again until she had made a five-day shopping trip to New York last August. She had told Sam she was buying a new maternity wardrobe, as she was three months pregnant. They had had a wonderful five days together, making their home base the apartment on the East Side that Sam's father kept for the convenience of the family whenever they had extended stays in the city. She and Babs had torn around shopping all day and had seen a few shows in the evening. Yes, it would be good to see Babs again.

The sign flashed on, Sam fastened her seat belt, then the wheels touched down, and the big plane rolled to a stop. The Las Vegas terminal was, as usual, very busy and Sam stood hesitant a moment. On hearing Babs call her name, she turned to see her and Ben hurrying forward. She smiled as Babs gasped breathlessly, "Oh! We were afraid we were late, we just this minute landed." Ben and Babs lived in the copper regions of the state and kept their own plane for easier mobility.

Babs would always be Babs, and she almost flung herself into Sam's arms, giving her a warm hug. When she stepped back she exclaimed, "It's positively demoralizing for anyone to look as ravishing as you do, Sam . . . how are you?"

"I'm perfectly well, thank you," Sam said, smiling. "You look lovely yourself," she added, her cool eyes going over her friend's slightly full figure. "The extra weight looks good on you."

"Oh, I gained too much carrying Mark." Babs smiled ruefully. "I've still got some to take off."

"You've been saying that for two months," Ben chimed in, but his voice was gentle, and the look he gave his wife caused an odd twist inside Sam.

"Welcome, Sam," he added, putting one arm around her shoulders giving her a light squeeze. "Babs is right, you look terrific."

"Hi, Ben, and thank you, sir," she answered, slipping her arm around his waist to return his hug. "You both look wonderful to me."

Ben laughed. "Now if we can adjourn this meeting of the mutual admiration society, suppose we stop blocking traffic and get out of here."

The women laughed and started moving, Sam asking Babs about the children. That set Babs off, and she went into a discourse about her offspring, talking nonstop, with Sam barely able to get a word in edgewise, while Ben took up Sam's case and led them outside to find a taxi. Finally Babs came back to earth to say, "We're going to spend the night in Vegas, and fly out to the house in the morning. Okay?" Sam barely had time to smile and nod as Babs rushed on. "I haven't really had a night out since Mark was born and this darling man here has said he is going to buy us a lavish dinner and let me gamble all night if I wish."

"Up to a financial point," Ben said softly, lovingly, as his wife snuggled even closer to him in the back of the cab.

They're so completely, unself-consciously in love, Sam thought and again felt that twist inside, hating to admit to herself that it was envy. She had always wished only the best for Babs but she could not help thinking if there had been a Ben somewhere for her she would not have this stupid mess she found herself with now. Then she gave a mental shrug, deciding firmly to enjoy her visit with the Carters.

The taxi deposited them at the MGM Grand and Sam looked around curiously as Ben registered for them. It was almost too much to take in at once. The hotel was fantastic, but what caught Sam's attention was the number of people about. It was the middle of the afternoon and everything was crowded.

Babs, watching Sam's face as she looked around, laughed. "You think this is something, wait until tonight." Sam just smiled and still glancing around followed Ben and Babs as they were shown to their rooms. The room was beautifully impersonal, in the manner of good hotels everywhere.

Used to staying in the best, Sam nodded her head, glancing around in satisfaction.

They had decided, while still in the cab, to let Sam rest after her flight, and meet for dinner at seven. Babs stated firmly that she intended to nap, as she fully planned to make a night of it.

Sam opened her suitcase, removed the things she'd need for the evening and gave her teal silk chemise a shake before hanging it up. She then sank into a warm, scented tub. She felt sleepy, she didn't know why, but every plane flight lasting over an hour always left her feeling this way. She was glad Ben and Babs had wanted to stay over. She had never been in Vegas. When she'd come before, she hadn't left the airport, but had gone from one plane to a much smaller one, and flown straight to Babs's parents' home. Sam was curious, as nearly every one of her friends had been to Vegas at least once and had been astonished at finding Sam had not.

Her bath finished, Sam slipped a nightie over her head, called the desk to request a wake-up call at six, and slid between the sheets. She felt deliciously relaxed and wondered idly whom Babs had asked to stand as godfather as she drifted into sleep.

Sam left her room a few minutes before seven, to find Babs and Ben right outside her door. Her eyes went over the two of them appreciatively. Babs was still something to see, even with the added pounds. Small and very fair, with almost white-blond hair and dark-brown brows and lashes on a lovely face with flawless skin, she had a small, pert nose and big brown eyes that forever danced merrily. She was dressed in a softly tailored midnight blue jacket and pants, and looked decidedly delectable. Standing next to her, Ben looked even taller than his six feet and very handsome in the smoky grey suit that matched his eyes. A black sueded tab-collar shirt set off his good looks and shock of sandy-colored hair.

Babs's eyes went over Sam slowly, taking in the combination of teal dress, red hair, and flawless skin. Brown eyes laughing, she gave a small pout.

"Oh, Sam! Any woman that looks as gorgeous as you should be outlawed."

Chapter Two

What a night! They had dinner and Babs did some gambling at the MGM but she would not stay in one place. They hit the Sands, Caesars, and other casinos, and while Babs and Ben stood at the tables or played blackjack Sam wandered through the rooms. Sam didn't gamble, but she assured her friends she was completely happy just watching. And watch she did. She was fascinated. She had been to all the posh casinos in Europe but never had she seen anything like this. The magnificence of the decor in the different hotels was worth seeing, but what absorbed Sam were the people. All kinds of people, from all over the world, from the very elegantly dressed to the almost (but not quite) down at heel. Many looked to Sam as if they hadn't slept for days, and the very air seemed to be charged with the excitement of a living thing.

Except for a light tinge of color in her cheeks and an added sparkle in her green eyes, Sam looked as always as she drifted in and out of the rooms—cool, composed, her bearing almost regal. And in a town full of almost unbelievably beautiful women, eyes followed Sam wherever she went. Male eyes avidly; female, enviously.

She had a wonderful time and when Ben announced that they must leave, she was surprised to see it was light outside. They dashed into the MGM to get their valises and to change, and then taxied to the airport. Within an hour Ben was circling Vegas and heading the Piper toward home, and Babs was strapped into her seat fast asleep. It was a short flight and soon they were at the house.

Sam exclaimed her delight over the large, rambling ranch house set in beautifully landscaped grounds, as Ben grinned at her. "Our mine might not be as grand as the Ruth, but it keeps the wolf from the door." Sam grinned back. She knew that copper was not the only thing Ben's family had, but timber and cattle, and different industries as well.

The house was designed in a U-shape with hallways leading off the large foyer. Babs linked arms with Sam, leading her down the hall to their left to a large airy room, one wall of which was practically all glass. Sam looked around at the light Danish furniture, the deep rose carpet, pale pink walls, and dusty pink draperies drawn open at the wall. "What a lovely room, Babs," she murmured, walking to the glass wall to gaze out at what was obviously the back of the house. A beautiful lawn dotted with shrubbery and trees in early soft green bud, due to the unseasonably warm weather, greeted her eyes. At the base of the lawn to her left was a kidney-shaped pool with a patio surrounding it, and across from it to Sam's right was a tennis court. Also to Sam's right but closer to the house sat several umbrellaed tables with lawn chairs placed around them. Altogether it was a lovely view. Sam turned back to Babs with a soft smile. "You have a beautiful home, Babs."

Babs nodded in agreement, obviously pleased. "Now come see the most beautiful of all." She led Sam back along the hall near the end where Sam surmised the family bedrooms were and into the nursery. A young girl of approximately seventeen sat in a rocking chair, reading to a chubby, towheaded toddler and Sam could see an infant asleep in a crib against the wall. On seeing Babs, the boy cried "Mommy," slid off the girl's lap, and ran into Babs's arms. She swung him up to her, turning to Sam, "Benjie, this is your Aunt Sam," and to Sam proudly, "Ben Jr." Sam took a chubby little hand into her own, smiled, and said quietly, "Hello, Ben Jr. I hope you and I will be great friends."

Benjie stared at her with huge brown eyes a moment; then with a beautiful smile breaking his face, he stretched out his arms to her, gurgling, "An Sam."

Laughing, Sam took him into her arms, enjoying his sweet, clean smell, while Babs looked on proud and delighted at her son's easy conquest.

"A charmer, just like his father." A voice came from the doorway, and Sam glanced up to see Ben, his face reflecting his wife's pride.

"He certainly is," Sam laughed. Her eyes went back to Benjie. "Would you like to show me your new brother?" He nodded, his face becoming eager as he turned in Sam's arms and pointed a small finger at the crib. Sam walked to the crib and looked down at the small duplicate of the child in her arms. Before she could say anything, Benjie's small finger moved to his lips and he whispered, "Baby seep." Laughing softly, Sam turned to a beaming Babs and said, "I envy you." It was not a casual compliment, it was true. Sam had felt a shaft of pure envy go through her as she gazed at the sleeping child, and had felt surprised and slightly shocked. Never being around small children much, she had never experienced their enslaving charm. She was completely captured.

Babs smiled at the young girl who was now standing by the rocking chair. "And this is Judy Demillo, my house-keeper's daughter and the baby's nursemaid, among other things. Please be very nice to her, for we must keep her happy." She grinned teasingly. "I could not possibly cope without her."

While Babs was speaking, Sam studied the girl. She was a beauty, very slender, with dark hair and brows and big dark eyes set in a thin, heartshaped face. Her skin had a creamy magnolia texture that was probably the envy of all her friends.

"Hello, Judy." Sam extended her hand, smiling gently, thinking the girl had the look of a timid doe.

"How do you do, Miss Denning." Judy returned Sam's smile shyly. Her small hand was as soft as a baby's, her voice was light, sweet. "Shall I take Benjie now?" Sam gave the boy a quick hug before handing him to Judy.

"I want a shower before lunch," Babs declared, turning toward the door. "And I imagine you do too, Sam." As they left the room Sam smiled at Judy and blew a kiss to Benjie from her fingertips.

Back in the hall Babs went to a door directly across from the nursery. "Lunch in two hours, Sam, and don't fuss. Wear jeans or whatever you're comfortable in. I'll come for you a few minutes early and show you around the house."

Babs knocked on Sam's door an hour and a half later. Sam had unpacked her suitcases, had a quick shower and a short nap, which had taken the edge off her tiredness. Now, dressed in putty-colored slim chinos and a hunter-green boatneck shell, her face devoid of makeup, she looked lovely, if a little pale. Babs had a slightly drawn look herself. She was in blue jeans and a white knit top, which stole all color from her face. She had a fuzzy look around her eyes, which told Sam she had also had a nap. "I'm not used to the night life anymore." Babs laughed tiredly. "I think I'd better have another nap before dinner, if I don't want to fall asleep at the table." As they strolled down the hall, Sam yawned, then grinned apologetically. "I think I'd better do the same."

Sam loved the rambling house. As they went from room to room she noted that the keynote here was comfort. The furnishings were expensive, but casual, and some pieces, Sam's practiced eye told her, were priceless. Yet everything blended perfectly, giving the house a warm, relaxed atmosphere. The contrast between it and the elegant house in Long Island was astonishing. Again Sam felt that odd twinge in her chest, thinking, this is a home for a family, a house for raising children and sharing love, a reflection of the contentment Babs and Ben shared.

Babs saved the kitchen for last. Although Sam's love of cooking would greatly surprise anyone who knew her, other than her own family, Babs knew of it better than any other person. She had followed in Sam's wake into the kitchens of private homes and restaurants for years, standing back, watching Sam beguile and coax recipes from master cooks and chefs. Babs knew of the notebooks full of recipes Sam had collected from all over Europe. Now she watched, a smile on her lips, as Sam stood entranced in the middle of the large, spotlessly clean, fully equipped room. She led her to the small, slim, dark-haired woman preparing lunch at the stove.

"Sam, this is my housekeeper, Marie Demillo."

"How do you do," Sam smiled, looking closely at Marie. "I see where Judy's beauty came from."

"Thank you, Miss Denning," Marie beamed. They chatted a few moments, Sam voicing appreciation of the well-kept kitchen, Marie appreciating Sam's appreciation. Lunch was a slow, relaxed affair, Sam and Ben bantering back and forth like longtime friends. Babs smiled contentedly. The man she loved and the friend she had always adored were fast friends. She was completely happy.

They had their coffee in the living room sitting comfortably in the big roomy chairs. Babs, glancing at her husband, murmured lazily. "When can we expect Morgan, darling?"

"I talked to him while you had your nap, and he said to tell you he promised to be here for dinner."

"I don't believe it!" she exclaimed. "Then he'll be here a few days with us. That man could certainly do with a rest." As Ben nodded, Babs caught the look of mild inquiry on Sam's face. "Ben's best friend, Morgan Wade," she explained. "He'll be godfather to your godmother for Mark. As a matter of fact, he's Benjie's godfather too." She paused a moment before chiding, "Come to think of it, you'd be Benjie's godmother, too, if you hadn't been traipsing around Vancouver or wherever at the time."

"I'm sorry now that I was away." Sam grinned at Babs. "I would have loved to have been Benjie's godmother." Searching her memory, she frowned. "Morgan Wade, the name sounds familiar. Have I met him?"

"No, I don't think so," Babs mused. "Of course not, he was to be Ben's best man but he couldn't get here in time for the wedding, remember?"

Sam smiled and nodded but thought grimly, *Some wretched friend if he couldn't have made a better effort at the time, considering the swiftness of air travel.* She had thought the same at the time of the wedding, but then, as now, said nothing.

Ben leaned forward, offering coffee refills to the women as he said, "I hope you'll like Morg, Sam."

"Morg's like an older brother," Babs chimed in, then lifted her eyebrows at Ben. "How old is he? Thirty-two, thirty-three?"

"Three," Ben replied, and went on, laughter in his voice, "I dogged his feet like a puppy while I was growing up."

Sam's eyebrows went up in question. Babs supplied the answer. "Morg's a cattleman, has an immense spread upstate. His ancestors were headed for California, got as far as Nevada, and liked what they saw. They settled and the Wade spread has been here ever since. All of them cattlemen, till Morg's father, George. He was a maverick. A friend got him interested in photography while he was still a teenager and he was lost to ranching forever.''

Ben took up the narrative. ''The ranch came to him when Morg was about fourteen, and he installed a manager, allowing himself freedom to accept assignments all over the world, mostly wildlife. As he and my father were close friends, Morg came to us whenever George took on a new assignment. He was with us through most of his teens, seeing his father only at holidays and summer vacation.''

''And he's a throwback.'' Babs laughed. ''A cattleman to the core. He loves that spread with a passion. Hates to leave it; that's why I was surprised when Ben said he'll be here today, three days before time. I wouldn't have been at all surprised if he'd have arrived Sunday morning, just in time to go to the church.''

Ben lay back in his chair, his legs stretched out, his eyes looking back on memories.

''Old Morg even tried to opt out of college,'' he reminisced, ''but his father finally convinced him that a well-rounded education was necessary, even to a rancher. He worked like hell during his college years, went every summer, did the work of four years in three and still graduated near the top of his class. His father died in Africa of one of those rare things we'd never even heard of while Morgan was in his senior year. Then it was my father who had to talk to him like a Dutch uncle to keep him in school.''

Babs again took up the story. ''As it turned out, the manager George had hired had not been a good one. When Morgan came home from school at age twenty-one, he found the ranch run down and finances fairly well depleted. And he's been working like a fiend the last twelve years to build it up again. Practically lives on the land, being in the house just about long enough to eat and sleep, if that. Even though he has the best housekeeper this side of St. Louis."

"I don't believe that." They were the first words Sam had uttered in the last half hour.

"Oh, but it's true," Babs laughed, "and Marie would be the first one to tell you that Sara Weaver is a gold mine. She came out here from the Pennsylvania Dutch country with Morgan's mother, Betty, when she married George. And as Betty died in a car accident when Morgan was two, Sara is the closest thing to a mother Morg has ever known." She glanced at Ben. "Except maybe your mother."

Ben nodded. "Yes, Morg's fond of Mother but he was in his teens when he came to us and by then he was Sara's."

"She must have missed him during those years," Sam put in, and again Ben nodded. "And I know he missed her. When he finally came home to stay, even with the money so tight, he redid the ranch house for her."

Babs piped in, "You should see his kitchen, Sam, it'd blow your mind."

Sam stared at her in disbelief, this from a woman whose kitchen would blow any cook's mind. Babs laughed gaily and held up one hand.

"Honest injun, it's something else. Marie turns green at the mention of it."

"Then I shan't mention it," Sam promised softly. Babs stood up, stretching and yawning. "I'm going to spend some time with the kids before I go for another nap. Want to join me, Sam?"

"I certainly do," came the reply from an equally drowsy Sam. As they left the room they both smiled fondly at Ben, already half asleep in his chair.

They spent the next hour in the nursery and Sam was given the honor of feeding Mark his bottle. As she held the tiny baby in her arms, Sam again experienced that small shaft of envy. He was so small, so very beautiful, and for the first time in her life Sam wondered what it would be like to have a child of her own. When the boys were put down for their naps, Sam and Babs made for their own beds.

In her room Sam drew the draperies over the glass wall, pulled her top over her head, then slid out of her sandals and pants. Stretching out on the bed in her bikini panties and bra, she was instantly asleep. The late afternoon sun-rays, the glare muted by the draperies, crawled up the bed, waking Sam when they touched her face. She glanced at the clock by the bed quickly, remembering Babs's parting words: "Dinner at eight, cocktails in the living room at seven-thirty."

It was not quite six, so Sam lazed another half hour, not quite asleep yet not fully awake, before she rose to get ready for dinner. She had a long, warm bath, the water scented with salts, and as she soaked she wondered idly what Ben's friend would be like. Shrugging her shoulders carelessly, she stepped out of the tub, patted herself dry, slipped into a lacy bra and briefs and made her face up lightly. After pulling a simply elegant fitted linen sheath in a subtle shade of lilac over her head, she slid her feet into soft leather sandals. As she brushed her hair, she decided to wear it loose this evening. Giving one last flick with the brush, she looked into the mirror, decided she'd do, and left the room.

Although it was past seven-thirty when she entered the living room, she found it empty, and hesitating only a moment, she made for the kitchen, pausing in the doorway to ask, "May I come in, Marie?"

"Of course, Miss Denning," came the reply from Marie, standing at the sink washing vegetables.

"Sam."

"Miss Sam," Marie emphasized.

"Done." Sam walked across the room to stand looking down over Marie's shoulder and added, her voice eager as a child's, "What's for dinner?"

Marie turned a smiling face up to Sam, "Mr. Morgan's a steak man, so I'm broiling Delmonicos on the charcoal grill outside. The foil-wrapped potatoes have been in the coals for an hour already. With that you'll have broccoli hollandaise and a tossed salad."

"Dressing?"

"My own."

"Hmmm, I can't wait," Sam laughed. "And dessert?"

"We'll let that be a surprise."

"Sounds super." Sam smiled, retracing her steps out of the kitchen. She heard voices as she neared the doorway to the living room. On entering, she paused and three heads were turned toward her. For a few moments she had the unreal feeling of a stop-motion effect and was unaware of the picture she made, framed in the doorway. The moment was broken as she stepped out of the frame into the room, and at the same time the three people came to their feet out of their chairs.

Babs walked over to Sam, a vision in a fuchsia cocktail dress, her voice teasing, "We had just decided you were still asleep, and I was delegated to go tip the bed." Sam shook her head lightly and replied softly, "I was in the kitchen with Marie."

"I should have known," Babs laughed.

In the few seconds that this exchange lasted, Sam was sizing up the man standing beside Ben. He was, she judged, at least six feet two inches, perhaps six feet three inches tall. Broad-shouldered, narrow-hipped, long-legged, and slim almost to the point of gauntness. Feeling the short hairs on her nape bristle, Sam thought, *That's the most dangerous-looking male animal I've ever seen.* On the heels of that thought she felt a tiny curl in her stomach which she recognized, in some shock, as fear. Fear? Then she was standing in front of him, hearing Babs say simply, "Samantha Denning—Morgan Wade."

Lifting her eyes, Sam was struck, as if from an actual

blow, by the direct, riveting stare from the coldest black eyes she had ever seen.

It seemed the curl grew inside her as she automatically answered "Mr. Wade" to his "Miss Denning," spoken in a disturbingly soft voice. She was fighting an alien sense of panic, his eyes still on her, as she nodded yes to Ben's "Martini, Sam?" The eye contact was broken when Morgan turned to Ben's query to refill his glass, and Sam sank thankfully into a chair.

Sam sat very straight, almost rigid, on the edge of her chair, her face composed, if somewhat pale, showing nothing of the turmoil in her mind. With growing amazement, she wondered at her reaction to this man. Instant dislike she'd have understood. She had experienced that at times. But fear? Yes a very real, if small, jolt of fear. That she had never experienced before. It was almost as if, in some way, he was a threat to her. She heard Babs's chatting and smiled in her direction. What was she talking about? Sam hadn't the vaguest idea. When Morgan turned back to her to hand her her drink, Sam saw his eyes glitter briefly at her barely whispered "thank you." Hearing the slight tremor in her own voice, she mentally pulled herself up short thinking, enough of this nonsense. Feeling a slow anger beginning to burn inside, she lifted her chin. As she did, black eyes again struck hers, but this time the glance bounced off eyes as cold, as hard as the emerald they matched in color. And as the sun strikes sparks from the stone, her glance struck sparks of challenge. She saw his own glint in acceptance. She had thrown the glove. He had picked it up.

Warfare silently declared, voices slowly penetrated. Something was being said on their roles at the christening, and she made herself relax against the back of the chair, hearing Babs say, "Okay with you, Sam?" Again she smiled and nodded. She would have to question Babs later on this point. Was what okay with her? Sam hadn't the least clue.

Ben asked Morgan Wade something about the ranch, and the conversation switched to ranching in general. Putting a look of interest on her face, Sam sipped at her drink and studied him over the rim of her glass.

He sat lazily in his chair, his long legs stretched out, crossed at the ankles. His arms formed a triangle, elbows on the chair arms, holding his drink with both hands in front of him. His hands were big, the fingers long and slender, and Sam felt a small shiver skip down her spine on seeing his right index finger rub and caress the rim of his glass. She shifted her gaze to his clothes—a lightweight suit, expensive, in a rich brown that almost matched his skin color, with an ecru shirt open at the throat, the sight of which also disturbed her vaguely.

Again her gaze shifted, upward, to his face, not quite in profile as he looked at Ben, who was speaking. Decidedly good-looking, almost devastatingly so, saved from being handsome by the almost harsh bone structure. The jaw firm, hard, the nose longish, but straight, well-defined, hard lips, the cheeks high, and overall the tanned skin stretched tight, smooth, with shallow hollows under the cheekbones adding to the look of gauntness. Hair as black as his eyes, thick and glossy, growing a little long to curl at the collar and behind the ears. Full black eyebrows, with a slight arch, and the longest, thickest black eyelashes Sam had ever seen on a man.

Babs interrupted the men's talk with "Dinner, bring your drinks" and they drifted into the dining room. It was a disaster. Sam found herself sitting directly across the table from Morgan and every time he spoke, whether to her or to the others, she felt her anger and resentment grow. It wasn't what he said, but the tone in which he said it. In fact, she was hard put to remember what was said all evening. She only knew that by the end of it, she had labeled Morgan Wade as that blasted arrogant cowboy.

She tried to do justice to Marie's dinner, but only pushed

it around on her plate with her fork. The surprise dessert, which turned out to be an exceptional mousse, she barely touched. When Babs questioned her on it, she pleaded fatigue for the loss of her appetite. Having done so, she used fatigue again to excuse herself shortly after they had finished their coffee in the living room. There was no demur, but she caught the arched brow and mocking look Morgan gave her as he wished her a quiet good night. In her room she thought in agitation she would be unable to sleep, but she fell asleep at once.

Sam wakened to bright, spring sunshine and a feeling of well being. Stretching in contentment, she laughed and chided herself on her feelings of the night before, telling herself, he's a man like every other, a little full of his own importance, but certainly no threat to her. She would make an effort to be pleasant in the face of his arrogance and in four days time they would both be gone. He to his ranch, and she to Long Island.

That settled, she had a shower and dressed quickly in flat sandals, jeans, and a pullover. She brushed her hair, pulled it back, twisted it, and pinned it to her head with a long barrette. Feeling famished, she left her room in search of breakfast. She found Babs alone at the breakfast table, and was informed that Ben and Morgan had left an hour ago on business of their own. The knowledge dismayed her not at all. The morning passed swiftly. Sam made periodic trips to the nursery, falling more in love with the two boys every time.

The men were back for lunch, and Sam felt relief as Babs again ran over the procedure to be followed at the church two days hence. Sam, changing the conversation, determined to stick to her earlier resolve, told Ben and Morgan what she and Babs had done all morning, and in turn, asked what they had been up to.

Morgan cast her a quick, surprised look, a question in his eyes; then, as if he understood her purpose and agreed with it, he answered her, his voice deep and pleasant. Sam almost sighed audibly in relief. Maybe, just maybe, they would get through the next few days without coming to blows.

They again took their coffee into the living room, the men following slowly behind the women. Sam was already seated when they strolled into the room and as she glanced up, her breath caught at the appearance Morgan made. His slim length alone was arresting. He was wearing a white cotton shirt that was a glare against his dark skin as he walked through a ray of sunlight shining into the room from the french doors. The shirt was tucked into skin-tight jeans that rode low on his hips and across his stomach, which was not just flat but almost concave, causing his belt buckle to tilt forward slightly at the top. Both men were in stocking feet, as they had been riding and had removed their boots before entering the house.

After their second cup of coffee the men excused themselves, claiming work, and Babs, drawing her mouth into a mock pout, complained of being neglected. The pout changed to delighted laughter as Morgan, passing her chair, reached down and ruffled her hair. "There isn't a man alive who could neglect you, gorgeous," he drawled as he sauntered from the room, his entire form a picture of unconscious grace. Sam moved uneasily in her chair.

Babs turned to her, laughter still in her voice. "What a charming liar that man is." The tone of her voice told Sam the deep affection she had for him. Sam resolved again to keep it light; she would in no way have Babs hurt.

Babs poured herself more coffee and, settling back, cradled her cup in her palms with a sigh. "Well, finally, now we can have a long talk." She proceeded to inquire after Mary and Deb, asking if the wedding was still on for October and then, gently, of Sam's father's death. Sam answered her questions, then told her the details of her father's will.

Babs sat staring at her a moment, the look on her face

one of sheer disbelief. After long seconds she exclaimed, "My God, Sam! That's pure Victorian."

"I know," Sam smiled. "I had exactly the same reaction."

"What are you going to do?" Babs asked as everyone else had who heard the conditions of the will.

"I haven't the foggiest, love," Sam said wryly. "I simply do not know."

"Unreal," Babs murmured, "positively unreal."

"Quite."

The subject was dropped as they decided to visit the boys. As they left the room, Babs's head still shook in wonder.

They had been with the boys perhaps an hour when Ben and Morgan came in. Sam had been sitting with Benjie, who, on seeing Morgan, slid off her lap to run toward him, little arms outstretched, shouting, "Unca Mog, Unca Mog." Bending down, Morgan caught the child under the arms, swung him off his feet, and tossed him into the air over his head, teasing. "What's up, hotshot?"

Sam caught her breath at the rough handling of the child, releasing it slowly when Benjie squealed, "Ben is," just as big hands seemed to pluck him out of the air. Benjie piped excitedly, "Again, again," but Morgan shook his head. "Not today, chum, let's have a look at your brother." Walking to the crib, Benjie repeated the words he'd said to Sam the day before, "Baby seep."

"Then we'll be very quiet," Morgan whispered as he reached the crib and stood looking down. Then, his voice tone normal, "Playing possum, he's wide awake."

Sam drew her breath in sharply and held it as suddenly she saw his arm tighten around Benjie's small bottom and bending, slide the other arm under Mark. Straightening slowly he turned, the baby securely caught against him. Sam expelled her breath on a rush, hearing Babs laugh.

"It shook me the first time I saw him do it, too, Sam."

Morgan gave her a wicked grin, delighted in knowing he'd frightened her—twice. Still grinning, which made a lie of his words, he drawled mockingly, "I'm sorry if I shook you, Miss Denning."

Before Sam could retort, he turned to Judy, "Did I frighten you too, beautiful?"

Sam watched color stain Judy's cheeks thinking, *Babs is "Gorgeous," Judy's "Beautiful," and I'm Miss Denning. I guess that'll keep me in my place.*

"You couldn't frighten me, Morgan," Judy laughed, the color deepening in her face.

She's got a crush on him, Sam decided, watching the color mount in Judy's cheeks. Shifting her gaze, she studied Morgan's smiling face, his teasing eyes. This one, she thought, is used to female adoration—very used to it. For some strange reason the thought was unsettling.

A short time later Babs announced, "Nap time." To Benjie's cried "not yet" Morgan replied in mock sternness, "Sack out, wrangler," and handed him to Judy and Mark to Babs. Kisses were given and received, and Sam, Ben, and Morgan left the room, Babs calling, "I'll be out in a minute."

Sam headed for her room but was stopped by Ben's invitation. "Come have a drink, Sam." She hesitated, but then followed them into the living room.

Ben started for the liquor cabinet but was stopped by Morgan's hand on his arm. "Sit, I'll get it." Without asking, he mixed a martini for Sam and a virgin Mary for Babs. Then taking two more glasses he put an ice cube into each, filled the glasses halfway with Jack Daniel's, and handed one to Ben. Moving to stand in front of the fireplace, he took a long, appreciative swallow of his whiskey.

Babs came into the room, dropped into her chair, picked up her drink, sipped, and murmured, "Hmm good. Benjie's a love, isn't he?" She asked the room in general, which brought a laugh from them all. The talk was light and easy for a time. Then, refilling his glass, Morgan moved to the doorway with a casual "I'm for a bath." Ben soon followed, claiming a nap wouldn't hurt either.

Sam and Babs sat quietly for a time, sipping their drinks. Suddenly Babs sat up, looked at Sam with an odd expression on her face and exclaimed. "Of course! That's the answer, Sam, Morgan."

"Whatever are you talking about?" Sam asked lazily.

"You can marry Morgan," came the jolting reply. Sam's eyes flew wide, and her voice rose slightly.

"Have you gone mad?"

"Not yet," Babs answered serenely. "It's the perfect solution to the will, Sam."

"Really Babs?" Sam began. "But I don't see . . ."

"Of course it is, Sam," Babs interrupted. "You need a husband within five months, right?" Sam nodded. "Yet you have no wish to marry any of the men who have already offered." The nod was more emphatic. "You think they'd want a regular marriage? A normal male-female relationship?"

"I know they would."

"Okay," Babs went on. "You get a husband. No demands. Morgan gets a wife with money, which he needs."

"It couldn't work," Sam stately firmly. "In the first place I hardly know the man." She held up her hand as Babs started to interrupt. "And in the second place, although he may need money, he doesn't strike me as needing a wife overmuch."

"That's where you're wrong," Babs denied. "He can hardly step off the place but that the females are falling all over him, trying to drag him down the aisle. And he is simply not interested. Oh, he's had his flings, as a matter of fact quite a few, but he is too wrapped up in that ranch to be bothered with a wife."

"But then why do you think . . ."

"That's the beauty of it, Sam. This way, with a wife, he

gets a modicum of immunity from the felines, without the demands of a more, er, normal marriage. And what does your barely knowing him have to do with it? Will you think, Sam? You could use the house, a place he spends very little time in, as a home base and travel around to wherever you please. As long as you touch home for a short stay occasionally, in this day and age, who could call that a separation?''

She paused to draw breath, but before Sam could say anything Babs went on. ''At the end of five years, you get a quiet divorce and go your separate ways: Morgan financially in the black at last and you with, I'm sure, the bulk of your inheritance intact.''

''Oh, Babs, I don't know, you make it sound as if it almost might do.''

''What else is there?'' Babs insisted. ''It would be lovely if you could fall in love, but really, Sam, if in all these years you haven't met Prince Charming, I somehow can't see him tooling down the pike in his Maserati within the next few months.'' Babs grinned impishly at her.

Sam grinned back. ''I can't either, but, good God, how would one go about it? I mean really, one can't just walk up to a comparative stranger and declare, 'I say, would you care to marry me for my money?' ''

Babs giggled and Sam had to smile, but added, ''I mean it, Babs, I couldn't do it.''

''You don't have to,'' Babs told her, ''I'll explain to Ben and he'll talk to Morgan.''

''Do you really think?''

''I do.''

Sam hesitated long moments, then sighed. ''All right, I don't like it, but I don't see any other way short of sponging off Mary.''

Babs knew that was the deciding factor.

Chapter Three

As she dressed for dinner, Sam felt nervous to the point of being sick. She should not have told Babs to go ahead. If that arrogant cowboy mocked her offer, she'd leave at once for Long Island, christening or no christening. No, she'd hit him first, then she'd leave.

She had made up her face carefully and now, standing in front of the closet, she decided, since the evening was cool, to wear a longsleeved chocolate chenille dress, one of her favorites. Giving herself a last glance in her full-length mirror, she lifted her shoulders in resignation, then left the room.

Dinner went smoothly, Ben and Morgan carrying most of the conversation, discussing the merits of different breeds of cattle, much to the disdain of Babs. For her part, Sam was happy to remain quiet and concentrate on forcing her food down. Back in the living room, with coffee cups in hand, the talk centered on various activities of their mutual friends. As soon as Morgan had set his cup down,

Ben excused the both of them, to a surprised look from Morgan, and they again left the room.

Sam got up and circled the room, only to sit down again with a sigh, upon which Babs shot her a look and stated firmly, "You need a drink." Babs then proceeded to make half a pitcherful of martinis. She poured out one and handed it to Sam, who downed it in four fast swallows.

"Good grief, Sam, relax. You do much more of that and you'll be flat on the floor."

Sam shrugged and refilled her glass, but she sat back into her chair, drawing her feet under her, and sipped at the drink. Babs launched into a discussion of clothes and from there to her children. The time seemed to drag and Sam, pouring her third drink, was beginning to fidget when they heard the men returning.

Morgan went directly to the Jack Daniel's, but Ben stopped inside the doorway saying softly, "I think Benjie is calling for us, Babs." Babs literally jumped out of her chair, glanced at Sam, and left, Ben right behind her.

Sam sipped her drink, watching Morgan warily. He dropped the cube into the glass, then splashed the whiskey over it and turned. As he walked slowly to Sam, she had the urge to run, and kept her seat out of sheer will power. Morgan looked completely at ease. He stopped a few feet from her, still silent. His eyes on her, he lifted his glass and took a long swallow. She could tell nothing from his face or eyes and was having trouble keeping her fingers from trembling, when he lowered the glass. His soft tone sent a shiver down her arms. "I hear you want to make a trade."

"A trade?" she whispered, thinking she sounded rather stupid.

He gave a short nod and stated bluntly, "My name for your money." She bristled, but forced herself to answer, "Yes.

"When?"

"Why, I don't know, there's my family and . . ." she faltered.

"No, as soon as legally possible," he cut in adamantly.

"But, really—" she began, but he cut her off again.

"I want to get back to the ranch, and do you really want your family here? How long do you think it would take them to get wise? Better to let them think you've had a whirlwind affair that ended at the altar. Right?"

"I suppose so."

"Good. Bargain?"

"Bargain," Sam answered weakly.

"Okay," he said briskly. "Tomorrow we'll go into town and apply for a license and do whatever else has to be done. Then as soon as we can, we'll get married and go home."

"Whatever you say," Sam murmured faintly, wondering if she was going to be sick as she gulped at her drink.

At that moment Babs stuck her head around the doorway. "All right if we come in?"

Morgan laughed, white teeth flashing in his dark face. "Of course, it's your house."

They talked for over an hour, Ben and Babs advising them on what must be done. Then Sam rose, stating, "If we're having an early start, I think I'll turn in," and left the room quickly. Babs caught up to her in the hallway outside her room and putting her hand on Sam's arm whispered, "Are you all right, Sam?"

"Of course," Sam assured her. "It's just . . . everything's happening so fast."

"I know, but I think it'll work, really," Babs urged.

"I hope so." But Sam's voice didn't sound very hopeful.

The next three days blurred together for Sam. She woke Saturday morning tense and headachy, telling herself she couldn't go through with it, she'd have to beg off somehow. The headache and most of the tension drained away under a shower. Calmer now as she dressed, she thought hopefully, *Perhaps Morgan is having second thoughts*. It may be quite easy to call it off. They might even joke about it.

She stepped out of her room to see Morgan closing the door of his own directly across the hall, next to the nursery. Before she could open her mouth and without even a good morning he said almost curtly, "I was just going to knock on your door. Breakfast is ready. Ben and Babs just sat down." Glancing at his watch impatiently he went on, "We better get moving."

"Mr. Wade," Sam started, but he broke in dryly.

"Don't you think you'd better call me Morgan, Samantha? The days of a wife calling her husband mister are long gone." Taking her arm he propelled her down the hall to the dining room, she practically running to keep up with his long-legged stride. She was breathing quickly when she reached the table and not only from the trip down the hall. She was emotionally shaken as well. Her only clear thought being, *I'm not going to be able to stop this*. With a rising sense of unease she turned to Babs, who had just wished her good morning, ready to plead, you've got to get me out of this. Babs, not waiting for Sam's return greeting, went on. "We're going into Ely with you. Ben has some things to look to, and unless you have a white dress with you, you and I have some shopping to do."

"A white dress! What for?" Sam repeated in surprise, catching the quick, sharp-eyed look Morgan threw at her.

"What for?" Now it was Babs's turn to repeat. "Why, to get married in, silly. Do you have one with you?"

Before Sam could answer, Ben, laughing softly, said, "I don't think our bride is altogether awake yet." Thinking *I don't think your bride's all together, period*, Sam answered Babs, "No, I don't have one, but I don't think it necessary to wear white." Morgan and Babs spoke simultaneously.

"I don't see why not."

"Of course it is."

"But . . ." Sam started.

"Samantha," Morgan interrupted sharply, "I know I said I'd like to do this as fast as possible, but I didn't mean we shouldn't do it right."

"Exactly," Babs stated firmly.

Sam's hands fluttered, turning palms out, and she gave in with a barely audible, "All right, we'll shop." Taking a roll from the bun warmer in the middle of the table, she sat crumbling it onto her plate. Feeling Morgan's eyes watching her, she glanced up.

"You'd better have some breakfast."

"I'm n-not really h-hungry," she stammered. Blast it, she'd never stammered in her life. "Coffee and juice will do."

"Then drink your juice," he ordered. Picking up the coffee carafe, he filled her cup and then the mug in front of him.

Anger burned through her at the tone of his voice. As if he were speaking to a child! She emptied the juice glass and placed it carefully on the table, observing coldly, "You're not eating."

At her words he cocked an eyebrow and smiled mockingly. "I ate over an hour ago. Unused to the good life, I get up early."

Babs chuckled. The burn deepening inside her, Sam turned and watched, in some disgust, as Babs polished off her bacon and eggs with sickening gusto.

Excusing herself, Sam left the table, hurried to her room, brushed her teeth, applied a light coat of lipstick to her mouth, grabbed her handbag, and joined the others, who were waiting for her beside a very dusty Chevy Blazer parked in the driveway. Settling herself in the back with Babs, Sam could barely keep her nose from wrinkling. The inside of the vehicle was every bit as dusty as the outside. At that moment Morgan slid behind the wheel and caught her reflection in the rearview mirror. As if he read her mind he drawled, "May as well have the heap washed while we're in Ely."

The heap being all of six months old, Sam had to assume he referred to all vehicles as heaps. Pulling her eyes from his mocking black ones, she stared sightlessly out of the window. The drive into Ely didn't take long enough for Sam. In fact none of the things they had to do seemed to take long. From filling out the marriage license form to speaking with Babs's pastor and arranging to have him marry them in his study on Wednesday morning at ten. Babs had insisted on the last, stating emphatically that a dusty civil office just would not do. With a mounting feeling of having won the battle but lost the war, Sam went along with everything decided, voicing no preference.

They separated, agreeing to meet again in two hours time for a late lunch; the women to shop, the men to follow their own pursuits, the nature of which Sam hadn't the vaguest idea. Except of course, the cleaning of the Blazer.

Sam did not buy a dress. She found nothing she liked, admitting to Babs the fault was not in the shops or the merchandise. They had seen some lovely things. She was, as she told Babs, simply not with it. She shopped for the boys instead, to voiced disapproval from Babs.

Joining up with the men again, they entered a small coffeeshop. Morgan and Ben chose a booth and sat across the table from Sam and Babs. After giving their order of four cheeseburgers and coffees to the waitress, Babs told the men of the failure of the shopping trip.

Ben laughed, giving his wife a fond, teasing look. "Somehow that doesn't surprise me. I don't know a woman who can suit herself shopping inside two hours." Babs made a face at him but didn't answer. Sam, glancing up at Morgan, gave a small sigh. He wasn't laughing. Quite the opposite, his face had gone still, his mouth a hard, straight line. He sat silent while the waitress served their meal but as soon as she had walked away, he spoke to Ben, his eyes steady on Sam's face.

"May I use your plane Monday?"

"Certainly," came the prompt reply from Ben around a mouthful of burger. "Where are you headed?"

"Vegas. I'll fly the girls in early in the morning and Sam may take the day to shop. Hopefully she can suit herself there." This last on a decidedly mocking note.

Sam nearly choked on her burger and was about to protest, but catching the danger signals flashing from Morgan's eyes, changed her mind, thinking she could veto the plan later. Babs disabused her of that thought almost at once. "Oh, Sam, what luck, two trips to Vegas in the same week." Sam managed to give Babs a weak smile, then turned to frown at Morgan thinking, *All right, your point again, cowboy, but I swear I'll buy the first damned white dress my eyes land on, even if the wretched thing's a rag.*

They left the coffeeshop and made their way to the Blazer, which, Sam discovered, minus its coat of dust, was a lovely deep green. On the way back to the house Sam and Babs managed a halfhearted conversation, and once there, they went directly into the boys' room. Benjie squealed with delight at Sam's presents.

Sunday flew by for Sam. She was up early, helping Marie with the last-minute preparations for the buffet lunch to be served to the relatives and friends Babs had invited to the christening celebration. Then it was time to leave for the church. Sam held Mark throughout the service, he sleeping contently through it all. They drove directly back to the house, a long line of cars behind them.

Confusion reigned. The guests overflowed the house. Sam, silently giving thanks for the fair, mild weather, kept on the move. Steering clear of Morgan, she circulated, being greeted like a long-lost daughter by Babs's parents and younger sister, getting reacquainted with Ben's parents, and stopping to talk and laugh with people she had met at Babs and Ben's wedding. If she came upon a group that included Morgan at the time, she went right on by, but she was not unaware of the number of young, pretty females who seemed to hang on him, or of his deep, somewhat disturbing laughter that rang out frequently.

Sam had been on her feet, except for the time spent in church, for over sixteen hours and she had had too much champagne, she admitted to herself ruefully, when she sank gratefully onto her bed sometime after eleven. Pushing everything out of her mind she was asleep at once.

She woke slowly to a light tapping on the door. Before she could talk herself into moving, Babs poked her head inside, calling, "Wake up, sleepyhead. Morgan said to tell you go hit the deck, he wants to leave in an hour." On the verge of saying "Tell Morgan Wade to go to hell," the sight of Babs's happy, laughing face stopped her and she murmured, "Be with you in thirty minutes."

Grumbling to herself that he was some kind of flaming idiot, she showered and dressed in an effortlessly chic charcoal matte jersey wedge dress. As she slid onto her chair at the table, she raised her eyebrows in question at the two empty places where Morgan and Ben usually sat.

Babs, sipping her coffee, her breakfast finished, stated, "They ate earlier. Ben's gone, had some people to see. Morg's changing his clothes, be with us in a minute."

"Aren't we the favored ones?" Sam purred acidly, attacking the dish of grapefruit in front of her, unaware of the quick, concerned look Babs gave her.

She was still jabbing listlessly at the fruit when Morgan strode into the room looking vital and alert in khakis and a cadet blue linen jacket over a crisp white poplin shirt that, Sam grudgingly admitted to herself, looked terrific.

Without sitting, he poured himself coffee and stood drinking it, watching Sam quietly a few minutes before chiding softly, "No breakfast again." It was a statement, not a question. Sam, not bothering to answer or even look up, lay down her spoon, pushed her plate away, and lifted her cup to stare moodily at her coffee before sipping it.

Babs laughed a little nervously, knowing Sam's temper when aroused, and implored Morgan, "Have a care, Morg, Sam's still tired and a bit testy this morning."

Black eyes glinted with devilment and his tone was sardonic as he cooed, "Poor baby."

Sam jerked to her feet, her face a mask of cold hauteur. "If we must have this shopping trip, then let's do so and have done with it."

The flight was too short for Sam's taste. She sat enjoying the panorama below her, occasionally asking questions of Babs, ignoring Morgan, which didn't seem to bother him in the least.

In Vegas they parted company, agreeing to meet for lunch. Sam did buy the first white dress she saw, simply because it was perfect—a sheath with ballet-length sleeves and a cowl collar that stretched from one shoulder tip across her throat to the other, draping down the back and revealing the upper half of her lovely shoulders and back. She chose soft white leather pumps and a matching clutch bag and declared herself outfitted, much to the delight of Babs, who decided to shop for herself as they still had an hour before meeting Morgan.

They left Vegas right after lunch, returning in time to play with Benjie before his nap. They idled the rest of the day away and Sam excused herself early to go to bed.

Sam's tension grew steadily Tuesday until, late in the afternoon, she had to force herself to laugh and reply lightly to Babs's concerned questioning.

"One doesn't get married every day, pet."

"I know," Babs replied. "But do you realize, Sam, you've barely spoken to Morgan for two days. I know this isn't a love match or anything, but you could try to be civil."

Chastising herself for her boorish behavior in her friends' home, Sam made an effort to hold her end of the conversation at dinner. Later in the evening, as she poured her fourth martini, she decided she was running out of banalities when Morgan, stretched out lazily, rose to his feet in a fluid move, strolled across the room to her, and plucked her drink out of her hand.

"Walk outside with me for a while, there's something we have to discuss." Giving Babs and Ben a brief "excuse us," he led her from the room. He waited at the dining room for her to get a wrap, then they went through the sliding glass doors in the dining room and onto the soft grass. He strolled toward the tennis courts and said suddenly, his voice harsh, "What the hell are you trying to say with the booze?"

Caught off guard Sam stammered, "W-what?"

"Babs told me you're a very light drinker," he rasped. "Yet that drink I took from you was your fourth. Yesterday it was wine. As a matter of fact you've been belting it away since Friday. If you're having second thoughts, you don't have to drink yourself insensible, just say it and we'll drop the whole thing."

"I don't understand."

"I think you do. Do you want to call it off?"

"No, of course not," she answered quickly, too quickly.

"There's no *of course* about it," Morgan grated. "You better be sure, Samantha, very sure, before it becomes a fact. An irrevocable fact."

She thought his phrasing a bit odd, but again answered quickly, "I am."

He said nothing for some time, then, "All right, but let me suggest you lay off the booze and get some rest. We've got a long day tomorrow, starting early and ending late." Grasping her forearm in his big hand, he started back to the house.

Sam was speechless. Who did this man think he was? No one had ever presumed to tell her she had had too much to drink or when to go to bed. Angry now, she snapped,

"What do you think you're doing?" For, going through the dining room, he bypassed the living room, and was practically dragging her down the hall to her room. His fingers tightened painfully as she tried to stop and pull her arm free. She was shaking in fury when he stopped at the door to her room. Grasping her other arm he held her still and, bending over her, said softly, "Calm down and stop acting like a spoiled child. You're so uptight you're about ready to go off like a firecracker." His voice held laughter as he ended, "Get some sleep. You want to be a beautiful bride, don't you?"

"Oh, you—" Sam began, only to gasp as, dipping his head swiftly he brushed his lips across hers and whispered, "Good night, Samantha." Pushing open the door he gave her a gentle shove into the room and pulled the door closed firmly behind her.

Sam stood inside the door, still, rigid, her hands tightly fisted at her side. *I must be mad,* she thought wildly. *Why didn't I stop this when I had the chance? It can't possibly work, he has nothing but contempt for me and I hate him.* She was uncomfortably aware that her mouth tingled from that brief brush of his and her arms felt hot where his hands had held her. She felt a very real fear. *I must stop this,* she thought desperately.

But she didn't. It was over quickly. She stayed in her room until it was time to leave. Babs brought her coffee, which she drank, and toast, which she ignored. She dressed and paced the room until Morgan knocked on the door with a quiet, "It's time to go, Samantha." Sam hesitated, stepped back, then lifting her chin, walked to the door and opened it to stand straight and still as his eyes went over her body, then back to hers.

"You look lovely."

"Thank you." Her face was perfectly composed, her voice icy. She walked past him and down the hall to Babs, waiting at the door. The drive into town was uncomfortable, Morgan and Babs eyeing Sam warily. If someone had asked Sam to describe the pastor's study five minutes after leaving it, she would have been unable to do so. Yet the brief service was vividly imprinted on her mind. Morgan's voice, deep, firm, repeating, "With this ring I thee wed, with my body I thee worship, with all my worldly goods I thee endow," as he slid a narrow platinum band on her finger. Her own voice low but clear, repeating the same vows and placing a ring, the larger twin to her own, on his finger. The ring, hastily handed to her by Babs, was a complete surprise to Sam. Even as she slid it into place she could not believe he'd leave it there. He simply did not come across as the type of man who would advertise his marital status. But then, Sam still had a lot to learn about Morgan Wade.

When the pastor said, "You may kiss the bride," Morgan brushed her lips as he had the night before and then Babs and Ben kissed her. Minutes later they were back in the car. They went directly back to the house as Marie was preparing what she called a wedding luncheon for them. Ben drove and, as they had entered the back seat, Sam sat as close to the door panel as she could, giving a short nod, but not even looking up as Morgan said, "Excuse me," when he stretched his long legs across to her side of the floor, bumping her foot with his.

Without speaking, Sam sat staring out the window, seeing nothing, unaware that her fingers twisted at her ring, or of black eyes watching her, anger building in them. What she was aware of was the same tingling feeling on her mouth that she had felt the night before.

Marie and Judy were waiting to toast the newlyweds with champagne when they returned to the house. Sam didn't know whether to laugh or cry, and she felt sorry for Judy, whose eyes, whenever they touched Morgan, grew sad and forlorn. Drawing Babs aside Sam asked, "Will there be time for me to call home before lunch?"

"Of course," Babs answered with a small laugh, as Benjie had joined the group and was jumping up and down in noisy excitement. "Use the phone in Ben's study, it'll be quiet there."

Sam entered the study, then turned in surprise as Morgan followed her into the room, closed the door and leaned back lazily against it. "I'd like some privacy, if you don't mind," she snapped.

"I do mind," he replied flatly. "I'm staying."

She glared at him, but he returned the look coolly, not moving. Turning her back to him sharply, she perched on the edge of Ben's desk, reached for the receiver, and dialed the Long Island number. Beth answered.

"This is Sam, Beth. Is Mary about?" Then to Beth's inquiry of herself, "I'm fine. How are you?" Beth told Sam she was also fine, then asked her to hold on as she went in search of Mary. A few minutes later Sam heard Mary's gentle voice. "Hello, Samantha? Is something wrong, dear?"

Forcing her voice to lightness, Sam answered, "Not at all, just the opposite." Breathing deeply, she closed her eyes. "I was married this morning." Silence.

"Sam, are you joking?"

Sam, hearing the note of concern in Mary's voice, plunged on. "No, darling, I'm not joking, we just returned from the church a few minutes ago."

"But, my dear, who? Do I know him?"

"No, you don't know him, Mother. I just met him myself." She managed a light laugh. "Swept me off my feet. His name's Morgan Wade, a friend of Ben's, little Mark's godfather. He's a rancher here in Nevada," she added quickly before Mary could ask what he did.

"Sam, is this wise?" Mary's soft voice was tinged with suspicion.

"I don't know," Sam said gaily. "Is it ever? I don't much care, I'm in love." She was amazed she didn't choke.

"Are you truly?" Mary asked hopefully.

"Yes, Mother, truly," she affirmed, uncomfortably aware of Morgan leaning against the door.

She was not prepared for Mary's next question. "May I speak to him, Sam?" Without thinking, she turned a frantic face to him. As if he'd heard Mary's voice, Morgan walked across the room, and took the receiver from her hand. Sam was amazed at the gentleness of his tone.

"Hello, Mrs. Denning, this is Morgan."

Sam watched him as he listened and when he spoke again his voice was warm, seemingly sincere. "Yes, I know it was very fast. But I assure you it will be all right."

Again he listened then answered, "No, we can't come east just now. This is a very busy time for me at the ranch." There was a pause. "I appreciate that fact, and I promise you I'll bring Sam east as soon as I can. Yes, of course." Another pause, then, "Hello, yourself, how are you?" His tone was lighter and Sam knew he was now talking to Deb. She knew Deb's question had been, "How is Sam?" by his answer: "Sam's fine." His tone grew teasing, "In fact she's beautiful, isn't she?"

Oh, brother, Sam thought, his tongue should fall out of his head. She heard him say, "Of course you may," then he handed the receiver to her and walked back to the door.

Sam thought to forestall Deb's questions by saying "Hello, Poppet, will you do a favor for me?"

"Of course, what is it?" Deb answered.

"Well, call the Messrs. Baker and inform them of the situation. Tell them I'll send copies of the marriage certificate right away." Before Deb could answer, she added, "And would you pack a few of my things and send them to me?"

"Yes, what do you want me to send?"

"I'll e-mail you a list. Now, I really must go, love, as Babs is holding lunch for us."

"But, Sam," Deb protested.

"I'll call you from the ranch in a few days and answer all your questions, but right now I must run, as Morgan is starting to glower at me. Kiss Bryan for me. Bye for now." Sam hung up quickly.

"Neatly done." Morgan's voice came softly. "Was I glowering?"

Sam chose to ignore him as she walked to the door. He didn't move. "Let me pass," she snapped.

"Not just yet, I have something to say."

Sam felt a shiver run down her spine. Gone was all warmth from his voice. It was cold, hard, and it matched his face.

"I've had enough of your sulkiness, Samantha. Now you'll either shake yourself out of it, or I'll do it for you."

"How dare you—" she began, but he cut in roughly, "I dare one hell of a lot and if you want to find out how much, keep pushing. You had your chance to back out and didn't. So put a smile on that beautiful face, for we are leaving this room now and joining our friends for lunch and you'd better behave like the lady you're supposed to be, or believe me you'll wish to heaven you had."

Sam stood stiff with anger a few seconds, but his reference to Babs and Ben had hit home. She was being unfair to them. She thought, with shame, of the uneasy glances both had given her all morning. Turning to him with a half smile she murmured, "You're quite right, shall we declare a temporary truce?"

"No, Samantha," he shook his head firmly. "Not temporary, it will have to be a permanent one. This bargain of ours can't work if we don't."

Lunch went well, Sam not missing the look of relief on Babs's face at her thawed attitude. As Sam kissed and hugged Babs, Ben, and Benjie and said good-bye to Marie and Judy, Morgan stashed their suitcases in the Blazer, promising Babs he'd bring Sam to visit soon. They drove the first twenty miles in silence and Sam jumped when Morgan asked suddenly, "Who's Bryan?"

"What?" Then, remembering her phone call, "Deb's fiancé. Why?"

He shrugged in answer, changing the subject. "Sara will have supper ready for us when we get home."

Home? She was going to a house she'd never seen, with a man she didn't know. Home? Her home was in Long Island. She said none of this out loud. Instead she raised delicate brows. "Sara?"

"Sara Weaver, my housekeeper."

"Oh, yes, Babs mentioned her," Sam murmured. "She knows about us?" He glanced at her quickly and nodded, then turned his eyes back to the road. A good driver herself, Sam had been watching him and decided he drove expertly, his big hands easy on the wheel. But as he also drove very fast, except for a few quick glances shot at her, he kept his eyes on the road.

Suddenly he slowed the vehicle, pulled it off to the side of the road, and brought it to a stop. Sam looked at him, startled. "Something wrong?"

"No." Reaching around to the back seat he produced a Thermos bottle. "Marie supplied us with coffee, we may as well stretch our legs and drink it." Pushing his door open he got out and walked around to her as she slid out her side.

Standing together, he leaning against the hood, they drank coffee from plastic cups and he said casually, "You seemed surprised that I'd called Sara." Sam nodded. "I had to give her some warning." At her questioning look he added, "She's house proud, probably been cleaning the place ever since I called her." He laughed ruefully. "If I'd have sprung you on her without giving her time to do her thing, she'd have had my hide nailed to the kitchen door."

"I see," Sam said, then asked hesitantly, "Does she know the circumstances?"

He grinned, his eyes laughing at her. "As to sleeping arrangements?" Sam felt her face grow hot and she looked away from him nodding. The beast was laughing at her, she could hear it in his voice.

"No, I simply told her what room to get ready for you. She didn't like the idea very much." His voice went dry. "I explained that within the social stratum in which you were raised, it is not at all unusual for a husband and wife to have separate rooms. She accepted that grudgingly."

Sam looked up at him in amazement. Accepted grudgingly? An employee?

He read her face and the easy, relaxed look on his own became hard, his voice cold. "Understand this, Samantha, Sara is not the hired help. She's family."

Sam, who had started to relax as they talked, stiffened, not from his words, but his tone.

Misunderstanding her withdrawal, he went on. "If Sara dislikes you, she'll still tolerate you because you're my wife. But if she likes you, she'll probably adopt you and be ordering you around and fussing over you before the weekend's out. Either way you will treat her with respect." Turning, he jerked the door open. "Let's get moving."

She got into the Blazer without looking at him and sat rigid, staring straight ahead. She wanted to explain that she did understand his feelings in regard to Sara, had understood since Babs had told her of it. But his cold face stopped her.

He slid under the wheel, tossed the Thermos onto the backseat and put his hand on the key, but didn't turn it. Swearing softly, he turned angrily and grabbing her shoulders forced her to face him. The hardness vanished from his face when he saw hers. Her eyes held a hurt look and her lips trembled slightly. His eyes hung on her mouth a long moment before glancing up to her own. "I didn't mean to sound harsh, but I had to make it clear that I will not have Sara hurt." His tone had softened. "Do you understand?"

"You love her very much, don't you?" Sam whispered, wondering at the small twinge of pain she felt inside when he answered simply, "Very much." He let go of her suddenly, as if just realizing he was still holding her. "Jacob too."

"Who's Jacob?"

"Sara's husband. Didn't Babs mention Jake?" At the brief shake of her head, he explained. "When my father and mother got married, Sara stated firmly her Miss Betty was not going to Nevada without her." Sam nodded, indicating she knew this. "At the same time, Jake stated equally firmly that Sara wasn't going without him. They were married three days after my parents."

"What does Jake do?"

"Name it. The place would fall apart without him." He grinned at her easily, relaxed again. "In fact, if my father had left him in charge when he went traipsing the world, instead of hiring that damned manager, I'd have come home to a much different situation."

His eyes looked back through the years a few seconds, then he gave a short laugh. "Mainly Jake keeps the place in order and takes care of anything that grows." At her raised eyebrows he added, "He was a farmer in the Pennsylvania Dutch country, and I wouldn't be surprised if he could make a fence post grow."

She laughed, the tension gone again. Smiling, he started the engine and pulled onto the road. The big vehicle ate up the miles with Morgan's foot on the gas pedal. Sam, growing tired, rested her head back and fell asleep. She woke when they stopped. Opening her eyes slowly, she asked, "Why are we stopping?"

"We're home."

Sitting up quickly, she looked up to see Morgan watching

her, his body slightly turned toward her, his left forearm resting on the steering wheel. She looked around in confusion, not fully awake, and saw they were parked on a drive in front of a garage. The house was to the left of it, a breezeway connecting the two. She opened her door and stepped out awkwardly. Massaging the back of her neck, she looked the place over as Morgan took their valises from the back.

The house was a rancher, built in the shape of an L with a smooth lawn surrounding it. In the distance off to the left, Sam could see the ranch outbuildings and a white-railed corral. A flagstone walk ran from the driveway to the front of the house. Morgan led Sam along it to the front. As they neared the door, it was flung open to reveal a full-bodied woman of medium height with a smile on her plain, unlined face.

"Welcome home, and congratulations, Mr. Morgan." She fairly beamed at him, then turned expectantly to Sam. "Thank you, Sara," Morgan said, turning to Sam. "Samantha, this is Sara Weaver—Sara, my wife, Samantha"

Sam put out her hand. "How do you do, Sara?" Sara grasped Sam's fingers in her broad, work-roughened hand. "I'm fine and I hope you'll be happy here, Mrs. Wade."

"Sam," Sam replied automatically. Sara said almost the same as Marie had done just one week ago. "Mrs. Sam."

"All right, Sara," Sam laughed, looking around as they moved into the room.

They were in the living room, and the door they had come through was in the corner of it. The front wall had a large bow window with a deep window seat onto which big, plump walnut cushions were tossed. Two comfortable-looking leather chairs with a low table between them were placed in front of the windows. On the far left wall was an archway leading into a hall and in the far left corner were a long matching leather sofa fronted by a generous coffee table fashioned with rustic charm from natural wood. On the right wall, Sam had noticed as she entered an archway through which she'd glimpsed the dining area. And in that wall between the archway and the back wall was a large, stone fireplace in front of which was another coffee table and two huge chairs with matching ottomans. The floor was hardwood with kilim rugs scattered about, and the ceiling was open-beamed, the beams darkly gleaming against the flat white plaster between. The room was all in warm Southwestern shades, and it was as inviting as a pair of warm arms. But what drew Sam was the back wall, like the one in her room at Babs's—it was entirely glass, with sliding doors which led, as Sam saw as she walked up to them, onto a broad porch with outdoor furniture casually placed. Three steps led off the porch to a flagstone walk set in the lawn which sloped gently fifty feet to a shallow bank with a rock garden. Three stone steps down the bank the lawn leveled off, smooth and flat as a putting green and at the base of it a flagstone patio encircled a kidney-shaped swimming pool, its water now reflecting the last long rays of the late afternoon sun. This was Sam's favorite time of day, when those last golden rays bathed everything in a deep, warm glow, softening even the most harsh of outlines. *How perfect to have my first look at this time,* Sam thought fleetingly, and turned back to the two people who had watched her silently the last few minutes. Her eyes alive with pleasure, she turned to Morgan. "It's beautiful, Morgan."

"Yes," his voice echoed her softness. No stiltedly polite "thank you" or overly casual "glad you like it." Just simply, "yes."

Turning to Sara, her eyes still glowing, Sam sighed, "How I envy you this house."

Sara understood. Sam had acknowledged her place in the house. Sara granted Sam's own with, "I happily give it to you." As had happened so many times before, Sam had entered and conquered. Sara was hers. Morgan stood, a small smile tugging the corner of his mouth, as the bond was forged between the two, so different, women.

"Now come with me, Mrs. Sam," Sara said briskly, moving to the suitcases inside the door. "I'll show you your room. You'll want to wash up, and supper's ready to be served."

Morgan also reached for the suitcases. Sara, snatching Sam's up, scolded, "I'll take that, Mr. Morgan, you get cleaned up yourself, if you want to eat." Sam laughed, as Sara added, as if to a grubby little boy, "Don't you dare come to the table in those jeans."

The idea of anyone speaking like that to that big, arrogant, black-eyed devil amused Sam greatly and she had trouble controlling her face as Morgan replied dryly, "Samantha's wearing jeans."

"Well, they're different somehow on a lady. Don't you dare, Morgan," Sara tacked on warningly, forgetting the Mister.

Morgan laughed out loud, shaking his head as he watched Sara lead Sam across the room to the arched hallway.

It was a short one, some twelve or fourteen feet, Sam thought, leading into another at a right angle. There was a door on each wall and Sara nodded to the one on their left. "Mr. Morgan's office." Eyeing Sam, she indicated the one on the right. "*His* bedroom."

They turned to the right at the joining and Sam saw a much longer hall, realized this part of the house was the downward stroke of the L. A few steps along the hall and Sara stopped, opened a door on the left, and waited for Sam to enter. Sam's breath caught and she stood quietly a few seconds glancing around. The room was done completely in white and shades of blue: the deep-piled carpet in azure, the walls and ceiling in pale sky and the draperies at two large windows on the far wall and bedspread in a soothing shade that reminded her of the ocean on a summer day. The woodwork and furniture were in spotless white. Sam loved it.

"I hope you'll be comfortable here." Sara looked around doubtfully. The idea of a husband and wife not sharing the same room obviously did not sit well with her.

Sam, smiling slightly, murmured, "I don't see how I could help but be, it's a lovely room."

"And here's your bathroom," Sara added, walking across the room to the left. She opened the door to reveal a sparkling interior complete with large, deep tub. *It's as if someone knew what I love,* Sam thought.

"Now don't bother unpacking," Sara said, going to the door. "I'll do that later. You wash up and come right in for supper."

Sam smiled as the door closed with a snap, remembering Morgan's warning that if Sara liked her she'd be fussing and ordering her about. Laughing softly, she went into the bathroom. Apparently Sara liked her.

Chapter Four

Sam stood staring out through the glass wall at the late afternoon sunrays bouncing and dancing off the pool's water. She didn't really see it, as she was deep in thought. She had been here ten days now, and so far things had gone much more smoothly than she had anticipated. She saw very little of Morgan, as he was gone by the time she got up in the morning and seldom returned to the house before seven. Then he'd come striding through the house to his room to have a quick shower and change in time to sit down to dinner at seven-thirty. After dinner he'd sit with Sam in the living room long enough to drink his coffee and then, going to the liquor cabinet built into the wall between the dining room archway and the fireplace, he'd drop the inevitable one ice cube in a short, fat glass, splash Jack Daniel's over it, murmur "excuse me" and go into his office. Sam would not see him again except for a quick glance into the office when she said good night on her way to her own room a few hours later.

He had told her the first evening after her arrival that

he'd leave the office door open a bit in case she had any questions as to where anything was. Sam had replied lightly, not looking up from her book, "That's quite all right, don't bother. I'll ask Sara if I need anything." She'd looked up in shock when he said quietly, "Sara does not sleep in the house, Samantha. She and Jake have their own small place on the other side of the garage."

"But, I thought—" she began. He cut in, his eyes wicked, the corner of his mouth twitching in amusement. "There's nothing to be afraid of, I'll be here." Laughing softly under his breath, he'd gone to his office.

Sam had not slept well those first few nights, but on finding that once in her room she heard nothing, not even Morgan going to his own room, whatever time that might be, she had shaken off the uneasy feeling and had slept well since.

On her first day at the ranch Morgan had not worked, at least not on the property. He had wakened her early, tapping on her bedroom door insistently until she'd groaned, "Yes, what is it?"

"Roll out, Red," he'd ordered. "My men will be expecting to meet you this morning. You have twenty-five minutes, so you'd better get moving."

Still groaning, Sam had bitten back some very nasty words as she dragged herself off the bed. Twenty minutes later she'd strolled into the kitchen, still half asleep but looking perky in jeans, a heavy knit pullover, and a soft suede jacket.

Morgan's eyes had skimmed over her coolly before shifting to the wall clock. Handing her a cup of coffee, he'd said, "That'll have to do for now. We'll eat later."

Sam had gulped down the hot brew, then followed him through the still, pink dawn to the outbuildings she'd spotted briefly the day before. A small group of men stood, hats in hands, waiting for them. With surprising abruptness

Morgan made the introductions, then turned away from her to give the men work instructions.

Feeling dismissed, wondering at the hot shaft of pain the feeling caused, Sam walked to the corral fence, breath catching at the sight that met her eyes. Standing inside the corral, elegant head arched high, bathed in the first sharp rays of morning sun, was the most beautiful golden palomino Sam had ever seen. As if recognizing she had a captive audience, the mare tossed her head and danced delicately to the corral fence, allowing Sam to stroke her long nose.

"She's a beauty, isn't she?"

Not having heard Morgan walk up to her, Sam jumped at his softly drawled voice.

"Yes, she is," Sam sighed, hand dropping to her side.

"She's yours."

With a small gasp, Sam spun around to stare into his strangely watchful face. "But—"

"To ride," Morgan inserted softly. "When I have the time to take you out." Before she could ask him when that would be, he added, as if he had read her thoughts, "After you've become accustomed to the house—and me."

How many times since then had she gone over his words trying to determine exactly what he'd meant? Sam asked herself now. He had not mentioned taking her out again and pride demanded Sam not ask him.

Sam blinked her eyes and saw that the daylight was just about gone. She knew she should go bathe and dress for dinner, but instead she stood still, wondering how Morgan would react to Sara's dinner surprise.

She and Sara had become quick friends, chatting easily and comfortably on any subject that came to hand. Though shocked at the idea when Sam first mentioned it, Sara had given in to Sam's pleading to help with the housework as she found time hanging on her hands. Sara had assigned Sam light duty, as Sam called it, admonishing her sternly not to let Morgan find out about it. Sara considered Sam, to Sam's deep amusement, too much a lady for heavy housework. But two days ago Sam had managed to invade Sara's kitchen.

On Thursday, Jake had carried the large cardboard carton containing the things Sam had asked Deb to pack and send her into Sam's room. Sam had liked Jake at first meeting. Not much taller than his wife, he was broad in the shoulders, strong as an ox and gentle as a kitten. His wife bossed him around outrageously and he loved it, as did his boss.

"Here are your things, Mrs. Sam," he'd called to her through her bedroom door. Sam had flung open the door with an "Oh, thank you, Jake. I imagine you were all getting a trifle tired of seeing me in the same clothes all the time."

"Oh, I don't know about that." He gave her a shy grin. "I think you always look pretty, no matter what you wear," he complimented as he left the room. His tone was that of an affectionate parent. Jake had adopted Sam too.

Sara had come into the room to help Sam unpack the bulging carton. Touching things lovingly, exclaiming in delight, she had put the beautiful clothes, shoes, and handbags in the closet, placed books in the case by the bed and CDs next to Morgan's in the rack in the entertainment unit built into the wall on the other side of the fireplace. Then her eyes lit up when she realized what was in the notebooks at the very bottom of the carton. Sam's recipes were her passport to Sara's kitchen.

They had sat, drinking coffee, at the kitchen table every moment Sara could spare since. Sara studied the recipes, Sam translating the ones in French, and just yesterday had declared she would try one on Morgan, with Sam's help of course. "Do we dare?" Sam had asked impishly.

The meals Sam had eaten since arriving had all been delicious and perfectly prepared, most with a decidedly German flavor, some strictly American. But due to the wide variety of foods Sam was used to, quite a few of which she had cooked herself in the big kitchen in the house in Long Island, she was well ready for a change.

"Oh, Mr. Morgan's been around," Sara had returned airily. "I wouldn't be surprised to find he'd tasted most of these at one time or other." Sam, considering Morgan's unconcerned attitude to whatever was placed before him at the dinner table, forbore to comment.

They had studied and discussed the different recipes when Sara finally chose a Viennese cream torte, probably hoping, Sam thought, they wouldn't have to face the music till the end of the meal.

Now she turned sharply as Morgan strode into the living room. His brows shot up as he glanced at his watch before his eyes skimmed over Sam's jeans and ribbed top. "Aren't you changing for dinner?"

"What time is it?" she asked, her own eyes taking in his stockinged feet, dusty jeans and shirt, and the broad-brimmed Andalusian hat he had brought home from a trip to Spain that he wore low on his forehead. "Seven-thirty," he supplied and laughed softly as she cried, "It can't be," making a dash for the hall, his long stride right behind her.

She had a swift shower, hurried into her panties and bra, applied makeup lightly, and brushed her gleaming curtain of hair. Sliding her feet into strappy sandals, she pulled a delicate rose-print camisole dress from her closet and over her head. She gave her hair a last smoothing with the brush, then, tossing the long, heavy hair back off her shoulders, left the room.

Morgan turned from the liquor cabinet, a drink in each hand, as Sam entered the living room. He watched her as she walked across the floor to him and she felt her chin lift and her back stiffen as he studied her. His eyes were insolent as they went over her face and hair; moving down her body and back up again, to linger long seconds on the neckline of her dress where it plunged deeply between her breasts. She felt her face grow warm at his appraisal and in retaliation coolly raked her own eyes down the length of his body. That he looked unnervingly attractive she had to admit to herself. His black hair curled at the nape of his neck, shiny and still damp from the shower. His lean tanned face, the cheeks smooth, gleamed with a freshly shaven look. His black brows rose over eyes amused at her survey. His cotton twill shirt was startlingly white against the dark skin of his throat and the chocolate brown flat-front corduroys that fit snugly on his slim hips and down his long legs. When her eyes lifted to his, his voice held mocking laughter. "Enjoy the view?"

Anger flashed from cold green eyes and she replied icily, "Just another man."

His laughter was derisive, his voice low. "And for five million dollars you expected more, is that it?"

Sam went rigid with fury. Barely able to control her voice, she seethed, "How dare you!"

He answered softly. "I think you'll find out before too long, Samantha, that I dare anything." The amusement had left his voice and his face was deadly serious. Sam felt a small twinge of fear. Before she could answer he put in smoothly, "Shall we have our dinner?" He strolled into the dining room, leaving her to follow him.

She seated herself across from him, refusing to look at him, and forced herself to smile at Sara as she served dinner. The dessert took on more significance as they ate silently, and Sam was sorry she'd ever asked Deb to send her the notebooks. Finally Sara sat the torte in front of him and stepped back, an anxious look on her face, waiting for him to taste it. *Good Lord*, Sam thought, *one would think she was afraid he'd beat her if he didn't like it.*

One eyebrow raised, he looked first at Sara, then at Sam before tasting it. "An excellent torte, Sara," he complimented quietly. "I don't recall you serving this before."

"Thank you, Mr. Morgan." Sara's voice was tinged with pride. "You're right, I haven't made this before. It's one of Mrs. Sam's recipes and she helped me make it."

"No kidding," Morgan answered sardonically. "I hadn't realized Mrs. Sam was so domesticated." He smiled gently at Sara's confused look, which turned to relief at his smile. Smiling happily, she left the room.

Sam glared at him across the table as he calmly ate his dessert. When he had finished, his eyes again slowly raked over her. "My heavens," he mocked, "all this and she cooks too."

They drank their coffee in silence, Sam's eyes smoldering, Morgan's amused. As soon as he put his cup down, he stood up, poured his whiskey, and went to his office. Tonight he did not excuse himself.

Sam carried the coffee tray to the kitchen and complimented a beaming Sara. At her suggestion they try another recipe soon, Sam voiced a vague, "Yes, well, we'll see," and hastily left the room. She went straight to her bedroom, not bothering to say good night to Morgan as she passed the office door. Once inside her room she kicked off her sandals and sat down at her small desk to write to Deb.

She had written four lines in twenty-five minutes when she threw the pen down and stood up. Pacing back and forth in agitation, she thought, *Damn that cowboy for annoying me like this, what is the purpose of it?* She couldn't think of any reason and, giving up, decided to read, hoping that would calm her, and glanced about for her book. Not seeing it, she went back into the living room in search of it and was drawn to the wall of glass by the shimmering glow of moonlight. Standing still, transfixed by the dance the moonlight was doing on the pool's water, she didn't hear Morgan come up behind her. She jumped, then spun around sharply at his softly whispered words. "Still mad, Redhead?"

Her voice was a hiss through her teeth. "I detest being called Red."

He laughed, low in his throat, and caught her off guard saying, "That's a beautiful dress." She was groping for a retort when he bent his head, brushed her lips with his own, as he had done twice before, and whispered. "And you're a beautiful woman." His mouth brushed hers again and, one big hand going around her neck under her hair, the other around her waist, he pulled her to him. His mouth pressed down on hers, his lips forcing her own open. Sam went still in his arms a moment in shock, but his hard, demanding mouth seemed to be robbing her of strength. She couldn't think, felt oddly light-headed, and without her willing it, her arms slid up around his neck, her body went soft against him. His arms became hard, coiled bands that pulled her tightly against the hard length of him, robbing her of breath.

His mouth left hers, went to the curve of her neck, sending tiny shivers down her spine. The hand at the back of her neck slid to her arm and grasping her firmly drew her back away from him as his lips trailed along the neckline of her camisole to stop and caress the soft skin at the V between her breasts. His other hand slid sensuously over her hip.

Sam felt like her body had been set on fire. Desperately trying to fight a confusing urge to surrunder, she gasped, "Morgan, you must stop."

Lifting his head, he bent low over her. His lips almost touching hers, he said fiercely, "I must not stop. I want you, Samantha, and I'm going to have you. Now." With those words he clamped his mouth on hers passionately, his lips bruising hers. All resistance went out of her and she clung to him feeling she could no longer stand up. Feeling her go limp against him, Morgan bent and scooped her up. Holding her tightly in his arms he carried her into his bedroom.

* * *

Sam lay tightly against Morgan's body, her head resting on his chest. She couldn't move, for although he was asleep, his arm still held her. She had made one tentative attempt to move away once and the arm had tightened. Now she pressed against him almost afraid to breathe. She didn't want to wake him. She wept silently.

He had been an expert lover, if a little rough at first. When she had cried out in pain, he had become very still. His voice an incredulous whisper, he exclaimed, "My God, Samantha, I had no idea!" Her outcry had not stopped him, but he had become gentle, almost tender, his hands, his mouth, caressing, building in her a hunger almost as great as his own. Her cheeks burned now, remembering how she had surrendered, willingly, eagerly, to his possession of her, making her his. But she had been his, she admitted to herself now, the damp, matted hair on his chest soft against her cheek, from the beginning. From the minute she had walked into Babs's living room and had felt the impact of his black eyes on her, she had been his.

She shivered and his arms tightened. She didn't want to love him. She thought of Ben, tender, affectionate, his eyes warm with love when he looked at Babs. That was the kind of man she had wanted to love. Not this hard, unfeeling, cold-eyed cowboy who laughed at her mockingly. That he wanted her physically, he had just proven. Seemingly tireless, he'd drawn her to him again and again, murmuring softly of a hunger that gnawed, a thirst that raged. In a mindless vortex of pleasure created by his caressing hands, his exciting mouth, Sam had floated in an unbelievably beautiful state of sensual sensation, until sheer exhaustion caught him, sent him into a deep sleep. No, she didn't want to love him, yet she faced the fact she was his. She did love him. She wept silently.

Sam woke slowly and stretched languidly, feeling completely relaxed and free of tension for the first time in weeks. Opening her eyes fully, she stiffened, shame flooding through her as she remembered the night before. She was alone, the house was very quiet, and she knew by the bright sunlight shining through the window that faced the porch, the only window in the room, that it was late in the day. Good Lord! Had she slept most of the day away? She had been exhausted till she had finally slept. The blackness of the room had changed to a pale gray. Now, the room in bright light, she looked around. She had not been in Morgan's bedroom before, not even when Sara had shown her the house. The bed she was lying in was huge, the biggest bed Sam had ever seen in her life, and at this moment was quite rumpled, a fact which made Sam's face warm. The walls and ceiling between the open beams were white, the furniture dark walnut. The carpet and matching draperies were a rich hunter green. Through the open bathroom door she could see that room was in black and white tile; even the towels were black and white. No frills, almost Spartan, definitely a man's room.

She jumped out of bed suddenly, thinking, I've got to get out of here, and her cheeks flamed again. She had not a stitch on. Her dress and undies lay draped on the white chair in the corner, and she knew Morgan had picked them up, for when he had removed them the night before, they had been dropped carelessly in a heap on the floor.

Snatching them up and holding the dress against herself she opened the bedroom door cautiously, peeking out. Seeing the hall empty she dashed for her own room, sighing with relief as she closed the door behind her.

The salty drops mingled with the water as Sam stood numbly under the jet spray of the shower. She had to go, she decided, and it tore at her heart. Not to be near him, not to see him—the thought was almost unbearable. But she knew she had no choice, for how long would it be, if she stayed, before those mocking black eyes, filled with contempt, told her he knew how she felt?

Sam moved back and forth in the room packing her suitcase. She'd take only what she needed. Sara could send the rest of her things east later. She knew Sara was not in the house now, as she always had Sunday free after preparing the noon meal. And it was now after five. Sam had no idea if Morgan was in the house or not, as she had not left her room after fleeing his.

She went into the bathroom to collect her toiletries and stopped in her tracks as she came back into the bedroom. Morgan was leaning lazily against the bedroom door-frame, his thumbs hooked through two of the belt loops on his close-fitting jeans. The breath caught in Sam's throat. *What a magnificent male animal he is,* she thought. *Like a huge cat, at ease, relaxed, yet giving the impression of being ready to spring in an instant.* She felt a slight shiver as she watched him. His eyes went over her clothes and valise on the bed, the open closet door and bureau drawer. Then his cool glance came to rest on her. His voice was unconcerned.

"Running away, Redhead?"

Sam had control of herself now. She had had her cry, and in a cool, composed voice she answered, "I'm going home"

One black eyebrow arched and he drawled, "Really, I thought you were home." Before she could say anything he went on, "How are you going to explain your sudden appearance alone? Don't you think it will sound a little strange if, after assuring them you were in love, you tell them that after two weeks of marriage your husband raped you?"

Without stopping to think Sam gasped, "But you didn't," then stopped, shocked at her own denial.

Morgan laughed softly. "I know, I just wanted to make sure you did."

"I won't stay here," Sam snapped angrily.

"Why not?" Black eyes went over her slowly and Sam felt herself grow warm. She had not dressed after showering, but had slipped on a terry robe, belting it tightly. She moved away from his look, her bare feet silent on the carpet as she went to place her makeup bag in the suitcase. "You know why," she flung over her shoulder.

"Yes," he answered dryly. "Because you thought you'd bought yourself a man's name, and now you find the man came with it."

"How dare you," she breathed indignantly. "We made an agreement, a marriage in name only."

"I warned you last night, Redhead, I dare almost anything."

"I told you not to call me that," Sam said hotly, but he went on as if he hadn't heard her. "And I made no such agreement, not when Ben first talked to me about it or when you and I discussed it later. If there were terms and conditions, it seems you forgot to tell me at the time, and it's a little late now." He paused, then added gently, "I'm sorry if I hurt you last night, but I had no way of knowing of your—er—virginal state."

"What kind of girl did you think I was?" Sam cried.

"I thought you were a woman," he snapped sharply. "My God, Samantha, you're going to be twenty-five soon. I didn't think any young woman reached that age and remained innocent today and I'll call you Redhead or anything else I damn well please."

Sam's cheeks were hot, and she opened her mouth to protest, but he hadn't finished. "I said I'm sorry I hurt you and I mean that, but I'm glad I was the first." Sam lowered her eyes so he could not read them as she thought, *I'm glad too.* Turning from him, she walked to the closet and reached blindly toward her clothes. Her hand stopped, became still, as his voice, hard now, lashed at her. "So you're going to run, throw it all away, because you haven't the guts to grow up."

Sam spun around, glaring at him. "What do you mean, throw it all away?"

Morgan's eyes were as cold as his voice. "I mean there'll be no polite little visits every now and then, so you don't lose the money. I'll divorce you, Samantha, and you can live off your stepmother until you find a man who'll marry you under your conditions. Or you might fall in love, if you're capable, and the physical side of it won't be so abhorrent to you."

"You really are a beast," she whispered.

"Maybe so," he said, his voice flat. "But that's beside the point. It's up to you. You can go or stay. But make no mistake, if you stay, what happened last night will happen again regularly." His voice hardened. "You can hate my guts for the next five years, but you'll stay put, I'll see to that. There will be no little side trips alone. If you want to go anywhere, it will be with me. And don't think I can't keep you here—I can." At the look which had come into her face as he spoke, he sighed in exasperation, rasped, "What the hell did you expect, Samantha? Did you really think we could live in the same house for five years without sex? Or did you suppose I'd keep a girl friend somewhere and drive back and forth after working fourteen hours a day?" She opened her mouth to answer him, but he went on harshly. "If you go now, it will be final. So make up your mind. What's it going to be, go or stay?"

Sam's eyes were wide, unbelieving. "You want an answer now? This minute? You won't give me time to think about it?"

He had moved into the room as he talked and now he stood, not more then two feet in front of her. His face was expressionless, his voice rough. "I've given you two weeks to think. As a matter of fact you should have thought it out before you married me. If you'll remember, I asked you if you had second thoughts the night before we got married. You assured me then that you didn't. You've had more than enough time, Samantha. What's it going to be?''

Sam turned away so he couldn't see her face. *He means it,* she thought wildly, *he'll divorce me. I won't see him again.* He had said, not knowing how she felt, she might fall in love. But she knew, somehow, deep inside, there would never be another man for her. It would be hell, she knew, if she stayed. Not being able to show her love, having him use her body to relieve his physical needs. But it would be worse not to be near him, not to see him at all. In a small, tired whisper she said, "I'll stay." Without a word, he turned her around and pulled her into his arms.

Chapter Five

Spring fever, lovesickness, Sam had both, and though she readily gave in to one, she silently riled at the other. What had she ever done to deserve Morgan Wade? The mere thought of his name set off a tingling reaction throughout her system that left her weak, longing for the sight of him.

From the time she was fourteen, Sam had been besieged by admirers. Some coaxed, some pleaded, a few even begged for a chance to make her care for them, but Sam had blithely gone her way, untouched, unmarked by any of them. The idea that, of all the men she'd known, this lean, long-legged cowboy could ignite her senses to the point of near madness, was a very bitter pill to swallow. For Morgan didn't coax, and Morgan didn't plead, and most emphatically, Morgan didn't beg. Morgan demanded. The fact that she gave in without demurs to his demands was the confidence-shattering self-knowledge that Sam riled against.

Sam slowed the mare to a walk and drank in the sweetness of spring on the land. *Being the complete idiot I am,* she thought wryly, a small smile of self-mockery twisting her lips, *I not only allow myself to become enslaved to the man, I go off the deep end for his land as well.* Bringing the horse to a complete stop, Sam idly stroked the mare's beautifully arched, golden neck, her eyes pinpointing the ranch buildings. When he had had the palomino cut out of the corral for her, Morgan had warned her not to lose sight of the buildings when she rode alone. Green eyes flashing rebelliously, Sam had turned on him angrily, but he cut off her hot protest before she could voice it.

"I mean it, Samantha. I don't want you riding out alone. I don't have the time, nor can I spare the men, to launch a search for you if you get lost. Which you probably would." Morgan paused, black eyes hard with determination. Then, seeing the disappointment she couldn't hide on her face, his voice gentled. "I'll take you out when I get the time." A teasing light entered his eyes. "If you're a good girl, Redhead, maybe we'll ride out on Sunday."

They had, and from that first ride across his property, Sam was a goner. Morgan's manner, though teasing, was easy, relaxed, as he showed her the land he so obviously loved. The mountains, with their color shadings at different times of the day, the Indian paintbrush, larkspur, and other spring flowers all had their effect on her. Whether it was the countryside or her guide, Sam wasn't quite sure, but for the first time in her life she felt as if she were home.

As spring faded into summer, and that too wore on, Morgan seemed to work even harder. He looked tired. The smooth skin over his cheeks and jaw grew tight and drawn and his hard slim body became even harder. When he held her at night the muscles in his arms, shoulders, and thighs felt like corded steel. He was drawn to a fine, tough edge and he frightened her a little at times.

Over coffee one evening in late spring Morgan casually

told Sam he was thinking of buying a plane, a Lear jet, and just as casually asked her what she thought of the idea. Surprised, and flustered that he'd even bother to ask her, Sam had told him stiffly to do what he thought best, then watched in dismay as his eyes went flat and expressionless. With a sharp nod of his head he'd left the room, murmuring cryptically, "I always do."

He'd bought the Lear and Sam hoped the plane, enabling him to get around faster, would give him more time. It hadn't. If anything, he seemed to have less.

Unsure of her position in their strange relationship, Sam asked few questions and Morgan volunteered little information. But she did learn, from the few things he did say, and the off-chance remarks made by Sara and Jake, that his interests did not lay wholly in the ranch as she had thought. He was in partnership in ranches in South America and Australia, owned interests in mines in Nevada and Africa, and was involved in other ventures in the States and Europe. She saw little more of him now than she had in the first two weeks of their marriage. He spent most of his time, the evenings he was at home, in his office, usually on the phone. If she had thought at first he had married her with the idea of her money making his life easier, she knew now how wrong she'd been. She had never known a man who worked harder. She felt a deepening respect for him, and she loved him to the point of distraction.

Most nights, when he was home, they slept together. He coming to her room when he'd finished in his office, usually very late. Other than the first time, she had spent only one night in the huge bed in his room.

It had been a particularly lovely night in late spring and Sam, curled into one of the big chairs in the living room, was reading. Morgan had been in his office not much more than an hour when he sauntered into the room and up to her chair. Bending over, he plucked the book from her fingers and as he dropped it to the floor, his voice was low, almost raw.

"It's too nice a night to waste, Redhead."

Scooping her into his arms, he'd carried her to his bedroom. Sam liked it there in that big bed. For some strange reason she felt more his wife in his bed. He had not taken her there again.

Her tears still wet his chest before she slept, but no longer from a feeling of shame. She honestly admitted to herself that her own physical need of him matched his for her. She wept now from frustration and fear. Frustration at having to wear a mask, hiding her true feelings from him. Fear that his own seemingly insatiable appetite for her would slacken and she'd find herself alone at night as well as in the daylight.

She was alone too much and now, in early August, it was beginning to show. She was losing weight. She ate very little when Morgan was home and hardly anything when he wasn't. Sara fussed over her to no avail. She simply was not hungry. Not for food.

Time was heavy, the days too long. The small jobs Sam found to do, the light housework, a small amount of cooking, puttering in the small garden Jake had helped her lay out, did not take nearly enough time. She went riding, but though she had always before enjoyed riding alone, it had somehow lost all appeal. She swam and sunbathed, her normal light tan turning to a deep golden color. She read. She paced. She wanted to scream. She grew tense and strained and was consumed with jealousy. Morgan was away often. He'd tell her casually the night before he left that he'd be away a few days. A few days often stretched into a week. She was positive there was another woman, possibly more than one. She knew that with a man like Morgan, handsome, charming when he chose to be, with a look of complete sensual masculinity, the women would gravitate to him, unable to keep their eyes or hands off him. When he was away, she hated him fiercely.

Sam had been away from the ranch only twice in the almost four and a half months she'd lived there. And for a young woman who was used to tearing around the world at the merest suggestion, the confinement was not easy to live with.

On a Friday evening not long after he had bought the jet, Morgan told Sam he had to fly to San Francisco in the morning. That statement alone surprised her as he never bothered to tell her where he was going, just that he was. After a small pause her surprise changed to an almost childlike excitement when he asked her if she'd care to go with him, adding that she could do some shopping while he took care of his business and then they could have dinner, perhaps see a show, and fly home Sunday morning. Sam forced her voice to sound calm, not wanting to appear overeager, and said she'd enjoy that, as she did have some shopping she could do. At the odd look that flashed quickly across his face, she had wondered miserably if he'd hoped she'd refuse. Nevertheless she had enjoyed the trip. Morgan was relaxed, charmingly attentive, which Sam attributed to their being in public, and seemingly quite willing to take Sam anywhere she wished to go.

Sam had shopped for hours but bought only a few things. A pair of riding gloves, two silk shirts, and a pair of terribly expensive white jeans that she couldn't resist, even though, when she'd pulled them on in the fitting room, they fit as though they'd been painted on her. She'd been completely happy with her day and was amused, on entering the hotel room, to find Morgan already there, one brow raised at her few packages.

"It took you this long to buy that?"

She hadn't offered to show him what she'd bought, sure he wasn't in the least interested, and after a few long seconds he'd shrugged, dropped onto the bed, said he was going to grab a nap before dinner, and fell promptly asleep.

Their dinner on the Wharf had been superb, the show excellent, and on returning to their hotel room, Morgan's lovemaking ardent. Sam had returned to the ranch content. Her contentment didn't last long, however, as Morgan was away most of the time the next few weeks.

At the beginning of June, when Morgan was again away, and Sam was in what she'd always thought of as her bad time of the month, she thought that although she loved it, if she didn't get away from the house she'd go mad. On the spur of the moment she decided to visit Babs for a few days. Although they talked often on the phone, Sam had not seen Babs since her wedding day. She knew the silver gray Jaguar that Morgan had bought, again consulting her first, was in the garage. She had heard Morgan ask Jake the night before if he'd drive him to the small airfield where he kept the plane, as he wanted to go over some papers on the way, and she'd heard Jake put the car in the garage when he'd returned.

Hurrying into the kitchen, she told a startled Sara to go home and take care of Jake as she was going away for a few days, then had left the room on the fly before she could question her. She had thrown some clothes into her suitcase and left before she could change her mind. She was not concerned about driving the Jaguar—she had driven powerful cars ever since she became old enough to drive. What did nag at her was Morgan's words the day he'd given her the choice of go or stay. "If you go anywhere it will be with me." With a snort of impatience at herself, she shook off the feeling of unease and decided firmly she would enjoy herself. She had, although the warm, family atmosphere in Babs's home left her with a lonely, hurt, ache inside.

Morgan came home the day after Sam did. Waiting, like a coward she thought, for the right time to tell him where she'd been, he caught her off guard, as glancing up at her across the dinner table he said softly, "Have a nice vacation, Samantha?" Unable to believe that either Sara or Jake had said anything to him, Sam stammered, surprised, "H-how did you—?"

"You really should have filled the tank, you know," he cut in, his voice like silk. "That Jag eats up the gas." His voice rapped, "Where did you go?"

"To see Babs," she'd snapped, resenting his tone. "We all missed you," she added sweetly, then wished she hadn't, as she saw his eyes narrow.

He stared at her silently a few moments, his eyes glinting warningly. When he spoke, his voice was a threat.

"Next time you want to see Babs, tell me, and if I can take time off we'll go together, or invite them here. Don't go off by yourself again." At the flash of defiance in Sam's eyes he added, much too softly, "I mean it, Samantha."

The spark of fight went out of Sam, and she looked away from him. Why? Oh, why, she thought in self-disgust, did she allow this man to intimidate her like this? She had never in her life retreated from a man before. She didn't like the feeling.

That had been over two months ago, and although Morgan had not gone away as often in the last few weeks, Sam saw very little of him They ate dinner later, as he stayed out as long as the light held, coming in dusty, his shirt sticking to him in dark wet patches. He slid into Sam's bed earlier than before too, sometimes, but not often, not even making love to her, just taking her into his arms and falling into a deep sleep within minutes.

Sam worked in the morning sun, fitfully pulling weeds in the herb garden behind the kitchen. Morgan had gone away two days before, the first time in weeks, and Sam was feeling moody and as surly as the weather. It had become mucky and close the day before, storms threatening which so far had not materialized, and Sam was hot and sticky and lonely.

She jumped up, pulling the gloves from her hands, on hearing the roar of the Jag as Morgan pulled into the drive. She was around the house and halfway to the car before he cut the engine.

She made herself slow down as she walked to the car, watching him hungrily as he unfolded himself from the driver's seat, then reach back inside for his suitcase. As he turned to her, she felt a stab of pure jealousy, positive he had been with another woman. The lines of strain were gone from his face and he looked rested for the first time in weeks.

He grinned at her, and she almost believed he was glad to see her. "This weather's a bitch isn't it?" Arching a brow at her sweat-soaked shirt and grubby knees below her shorts he added, "What in hell are you doing working in this heat, you crazy redhead? Why aren't you in the pool?"

Sam frowned at the word *redhead,* though she felt an icicle thrill go down her spine. She would never admit it, but she loved the sound of it on his lips. It had become, for her, a substitute for the endearments she never heard.

"You work in the heat." She kept her voice as light as his, not wanting to sour his good mood.

He laughed softly and dropped an arm over her shoulder as they walked toward the kitchen door.

"I wouldn't if I didn't have to," he lied.

The look Sam shot at him called him a liar and he laughed again softly, easily, and the stab of jealousy tore deeply into her. What was she like? Sam tormented herself with the thought. This woman who could make Morgan look and act like this.

He lifted his arm from her shoulder and opened the kitchen door for her to proceed him into the house. Inside he stood still for a second, looking around the empty, silent room. Then he turned sharply to Sam and her heart sank. His face had gone stiff, his eyes hard, and his soft, laughing voice of a moment ago now had a raw edge.

"Where's Sara?"

"She went into town with Jake to do some shopping," Sam answered as lightly as she could.

"You're alone here?" The edge was sharper.

Sam turned away biting her lip. *You don't have to worry, I won't run away,* she wanted to snap, but what she said was, "I don't mind, I like being alone."

"I know." His voice had an odd inflection that Sam couldn't understand. "And what about lunch?"

"Morgan, I am completely capable of preparing my own lunch, for heaven's sake." Sam felt let down and exasperated and now her own voice had an edge.

"I'm aware of that fact."

For some reason Sam didn't understand, his manner had changed again, he was relaxed, his voice light and teasing. "What I'm wondering is, are you prepared to make mine as well?"

"Well, of course!" The face she turned to him wore a surprised look at the abrupt change in him. Would she ever understand this man? Glancing at the clock and noting it was only ten-thirty she asked, "Are you hungry? Do you want lunch now?"

"No, I'm not hungry—for lunch." Then he surprised Sam even more by adding, "Suppose you give me a half hour or so to check any messages Sara left on my desk while I've been away, and then we'll have a swim together before we have lunch."

Sam's face looked even more surprised. He'd said it casually, as if they swam together regularly, when in fact they had never shared the pool. She answered quickly, forcing her voice to stay light, "All right, I'll have a shower while you're in your office." And she walked ahead of him out of the kitchen.

Standing under the shower, Sam felt the curl of excitement that had started with Morgan's words building inside. *Don't be a silly child,* she told herself softly, but she couldn't stop the feeling of happiness that washed over her. She felt almost grateful to that unknown woman who had sent Morgan home in such a relaxed mood. She had stepped out of the shower and was wrapping a towel around herself as she thought this and she became perfectly still. *I must surely be going mad,* she thought now, the feeling of happiness dying. The idea that she was thankful to another woman for any small crumb of pleasure Morgan might offhandedly offer her made Sam feel sick. A picture of herself six months ago flashed through her mind. Samantha Denning, laughingly turning her lips away from the mouths of the men she'd gone out with, coolly turning down their offers of marriage, frigidly telling them to keep their hands to themselves when they had reached out to touch her. And now, Samantha Wade, who trembled in the arms of this tall hard-eyed man, whose own arms slid around his neck eagerly as her mouth hungrily accepted his. *Oh, God!* she thought now. *Why should love be like this?* And she felt, for the first time, a measure of compassion for the men who had pleaded with her to marry them.

She stood there quite still, dripping on the bathmat for a long time, and was jerked into movement by a short rap on her bedroom door as Morgan called.

"Hurry up, Redhead, I'll see you in the pool."

Sam quickly blotted herself off and twisted her hair back as she walked into the bedroom. Taking a long barrette from her dresser, she fastened the silky red mass to the back of her head, then stepped into the bottom of her bikini and gave a sign of dismay, for it hung on her hips. Shaking her head slightly, she reknotted the material, taking in the slack and put on the skimpy top, noting she had to tie that more tightly than before also. She turned to the full-length mirror on the closet door and gave herself a long, critical look. She was not happy with what she saw. She was much thinner, her collarbone and pelvic bones sticking out prominently. She had a dark, bruised look under her eyes and her face had a drawn, strained look. She grimaced in distaste, then turned sharply away, not wanting to look on the pitiful woman reflected there.

Sam stood at the side of the pool, watching Morgan's sinewy, powerful arms slice through the water. As he reached the far end and turned, he saw her and shot back across the pool. Placing his hand on the edge he lifted himself smoothly from the water. He stood in front of her, legs slightly apart, and brushed the shining black hair from his face. Standing still, his eyes raked over her. His voice soft, almost silky, chided, "You look like hell, Redhead, how much weight have you lost?" Reaching out his hand, he trailed his forefinger along her collarbone. "Haven't you been feeling well?" His voice sharpened as his hand moved to grasp her shoulder. "You're not pregnant, are you?"

Sam winced as his fingers dug into her soft flesh. "Of course not," she gasped, wondering at the strange look that sped across his face. "And I'm perfectly well, I've just been minding the heat, I guess." Wanting to change the subject she added quickly, "Doesn't it ever rain here?" It worked, for he laughed, then drawled, "Not much." Looking up at the black clouds moving in the distance he added, "Even though it looks like it might before too long. So let's get our swim while we can." With those words he grabbed her hand and grinned at her squeal as he leaped into the water pulling her with him.

They swam side by side for some time, he matching his strokes to her shorter ones. When she stopped to catch her breath, he slid his big hand around her neck and drew her to him. His mouth close to hers, he whispered, "Let's get out of here, Redhead, I'm hungry." He laughed softly as she gasped and pulled away from him muttering, "Oh! Men!"

Sam stood in her room patting herself dry with the huge towel draped around her and turned swiftly on hearing her door open. Morgan sauntered into the room and Sam turned her back to him feeling her face flush as she clutched the towel firmly to herself. He was wearing nothing but a towel draped loosely about his lean hips and she went tense and rigid as he came up behind her, his arm coiling around her waist. Sliding under the edge of the towel and moving it aside, his hand caressed the smooth, still damp skin underneath. As she felt him lower his head, slide his lips along the sensitive skin on the side of her neck, Sam said breathlessly, "I thought you were hungry?"

His mouth close to her ear, he murmured in amusement, "Yes, but I didn't say what I was hungry for, Redhead." Giving her towel a quick hard tug he dropped it onto the floor as he turned her around into his arms. "There are those who eat," he purred, "and those who eat."

Her body stiff, Sam decided firmly that this time she would not respond, but her decision wavered when his mouth found hers, his lips hard, demanding, urgent. In the next instant, as she felt his tongue search for and find her own, she sighed and went soft against him, her arms going around his neck, her fingers digging into his hair. He drank even more deeply of her mouth and his arms tightened, the one dropping to her hips, flattening her body against the length of his, letting her know his need of her.

Later, much later, Sam stood at the stove in her robe, watching the eggs she had just poured into the pan. Morgan sat stretched out on a kitchen chair, looking relaxed and somewhat smug. She could feel his eyes on her back, and she jumped at the sound of his voice, low and deep.

"One of the messages on my desk was to call the lawyers Baker."

Sam spun around, her brows raised in question.

"Don't scorch our lunch, kid."

"But what did—?"

"It will wait until we eat," he interrupted.

Sam turned the omelet onto a plate and set it on the table next to the molded salad she had made early that morning. Seating herself, she turned to Morgan, questioning, "What did the Bakers want?"

"Mmm, you really are a terrific cook, Redhead." He put another forkful of eggs into his mouth.

"Morgan." Her voice was low, tinged with warning.

His eyes stared blandly into hers as he slowly chewed and swallowed, the corner of his mouth twitching in amusement as he watched the green eyes start to spark with anger. Just as she was about to explode, he said calmly, "It seems there's a question concerning our finances and they'd appreciate my going to New York to straighten out the problems."

"Are you going?" she asked softly, hesitatingly.

"I suppose I might as well, as Mr. Baker strikes me as the type who would just keep calling until I did," he answered offhandedly.

Sam nodded slowly, pushing the food around on her plate disinterestedly. *He'd said I, not we, but I.* She looked down at her plate and asked softly, a little fearfully, "May I go east with you, Morgan?"

He looked at her silently a few minutes, then his voice mocked. "Have you been a good girl, Samantha?" His eyes gleamed with deviltry as he watched her jerk upright in her chair.

Green eyes blazing, she sputtered, "Really, Morgan, I'm not a child, I'll be twenty-five in a few days and you have no right to speak like—"

He cut in sharply, "Calm down, Redhead, and eat your

lunch, you're thin enough." He paused, then went on, "That's right, you'll be celebrating a quarter century in a few days." He laughed at the look she threw him. "Now be nice, kid, and I'll think about it while you get my dessert. You do have dessert for me?"

Sam nodded, afraid if she opened her mouth she'd scream at him. She went to the refrigerator and removed the rich creamy rice pudding Sara had made the day before. She served him, then sat stiffly in her chair, poking at the jelled salad in front of her.

"Eat your salad," he ordered, then continued, "The pudding's very good. Aren't you having any?"

She shook her head, her lips tightly compressed. He was deliberately tormenting her, she knew, but she refused to give him the satisfaction of answering him back. Morgan finished his pudding and wiped his mouth with his napkin. As he tossed it onto the table he said seriously, his face expressionless, "I'll make a bargain with you, Samantha."

Sam looked at him, not answering at once. What was he up to now? she wondered. "What sort of bargain?" she asked finally.

"I'll take you east with me, even stay a week or so in Long Island for you to spend your birthday with your family." Sam caught her breath, but he was going on. "On two conditions."

"What conditions?" Sam breathed, almost afraid to ask.

His eyes held hers, his voice was completely without emotion. "One, tomorrow morning you move your things into my room and, as of tonight, you sleep in my bed. I'm pretty damned tired of crawling out of your bed and trotting to my room to dress every morning." Sam felt her face flame, but his eyes held hers, which widened as he added. "Two, there'll be no more tears, late in the night, every time I make love to you."

So he hadn't been asleep as she'd thought. She hesitated a second and he said impatiently, "Well, will you bargain?"

She managed to break the hold of his eyes and lowering hers, she whispered, "Yes."

He pushed his chair back, stood up, and walked around the table to her. Taking her by the shoulders, he lifted her from her chair. He bent his head, kissed her hard, then, lifting his mouth from hers, said softly, "It's a bargain sealed. Can you be ready to go by the end of the week?"

Again she whispered, "Yes."

Nodding almost curtly he removed his hands and left the room.

Chapter Six

Sam rested her head against the seat of the rented car and sighed in relief. She had forgotten what New York in August was like.

"Tired?" Morgan glanced at her, then returned his eyes to the highway.

"Not really," Sam settled more comfortably on the seat. "The air-conditioning feels lovely after the heat outside the airport."

He nodded, not looking at her, his eyes steady on the highway, a driver's nightmare with its usual Monday morning traffic heading into New York. Sam lowered her eyelids and looked at him through her lashes, studying him a moment. With his weight loss over the summer the sharply defined lines of his profile were intensified. The skin stretched firm and smooth over the high cheekbones and strong, hard jaw. The color of his skin exposed on his face, throat, and hands had deepened to a rich copper. Sam felt her face grow warm, remembering that except for a lighter swath around his hips, the rest of his body was the same dark color. And she wondered, a little uneasily, when and where he had acquired that color on his long straight legs. The more pronounced leanness had not detracted from his looks. If anything, he was more handsome than when she had first met him.

Morgan felt her eyes and, as one brow inched slowly upward, he drawled, "Something?"

Sam cast about in her mind in confusion and grabbed at the first thing that entered her head. "I—I was just wondering what everyone will think of you." She called herself all kinds of an idiot as she watched the corner of his finely defined lips twitch in amusement.

"I've been meaning to talk to you about that, Redhead." The soft drawl heavier, he added, "I suppose, when we get to Long Island, like it or not, we'll have to play the role of newlyweds."

"Yes, I know." Sam wondered how she had managed to keep her voice so cool. His choice of words had hurt, even though she felt relief wash over her at them. She had become more tense and nervous about this every day since she had agreed to his bargain six days ago. The added days had not helped. Morgan had not been able to get away at the end of the week as he'd planned and had told Sam the trip east would have to wait.

Sam turned her head away from him and closed her eyes, letting her mind drift back over the last six days. She had kept her part of the bargain, and as the threatened storm had finally broken that night, was glad to huddle close to Morgan in the big bed. She had never been afraid of storms, but somehow out there in the space between the mountains, it had seemed so much more threatening. The thunder had rumbled angrily, the lightning cracked long and sharp, brightening the bedroom with its fierce but cold light. Sam had clung to Morgan, feeling safe in his strong, hard arms and ignored the silent laughter that shook his broad chest.

The first few days had not been too bad. She and Sara had been busy, first with transferring Sam's things into Morgan's room, Sara's face telling Sam plainly she thought the move right and proper, then straightening the now empty room. After Thursday night, when Morgan informed her they could not leave until Monday, the tension started to build inside her. She had called Mary and Deb to tell them they were coming, then had had to call them back telling them of the change in plans. She had become steadily more tense, afraid that for some reason or other they would not be able to leave, and if they did, what would be the reaction of her friends and family to Morgan. Then this morning, before daylight, she had awakened to Morgan calling her name softly and had opened her eyes to find his face close to hers as he whispered, "If you're going with me, Redhead, you'd better get moving. I'm leaving in one hour." She'd jumped from the bed and ran to the bathroom, his laughter following her. The flight east had been smooth and uneventful. Morgan flew the jet exactly as he drove the car, expertly.

Sam, bringing her thoughts to the present, opened her eyes and felt a thrill of excitement seeing they were close to the city. Morgan had an appointment with the Messrs. Baker which, Sam noted glancing at her watch, he would make just in time. She planned to do some shopping, her weight loss being such that few of her clothes fit properly. Sam decided she'd look for a special dress, as Mary was planning a belated wedding party and birthday celebration for Friday evening. The thought caused her pain. This was her twenty-fifth birthday. Morgan had forgotten. She gave herself a mental shake. Why ever did she think he'd remember?

They reached their hotel and dispensed with the rented car. In the large room Morgan asked if she needed money, which she didn't, told her he had to go or he'd be late, said he'd see her whenever, and left.

Sam went into the bathroom to freshen up and looked at herself in the mirror. She didn't like what she saw. Her hair pulled back into a French braid made her face look even thinner than it was. Something had to be done, she decided. She walked quickly to the phone and called her hairdresser. She knew the shop was always closed on Mondays. She also knew he was usually in the shop on Mondays, and was not surprised when she heard his smooth, clear voice answer, something he never did when the shop was open, as he paid a receptionist a very high salary to do it for him.

"Charles?" Sam said, not waiting for a reply as she knew it was him, "Samantha Wa—Denning."

"Samantha," Charles purred. "Wherever have you been, darling? I haven't seen you in ages."

"I've been away, getting married," she answered evenly, and smiled at his reaction.

"What in the world did you want to do that for? Oh, well, no matter, what can I do for you, sweetheart?"

Sam smiled again at the way the endearments rolled off his glib tongue. She knew that many people had doubts about Charles's masculinity, but she had none. If she had ever had any, they had been dispelled the day she found herself alone, not by accident she was now sure, with him in the shop and he'd tried to seduce her in the beautician's chair. She'd had a fight on her hands that day, but she'd won it. He had accepted his defeat graciously, and they were good friends.

"My hair's a sight," she laughed, "and there's a big to-do the end of the week." Sam inserted a pleading note, "Charles, you must help me."

She heard him chuckle softly. "You know I'm closed Monday, you beautiful baggage, but come around and I'll see what I can do with that red mop."

"Thank you, Charles, you're a love." Sam heard him chuckle again as she replaced the receiver. Six hours later

Sam stepped into the hotel elevator and pushed the button for their floor. She felt tired but good, and although she carried only one package, she had spent a lot of money, having all but one outfit sent to the address on Long Island. She smiled to herself as her hand went up to her hair, the long slim fingers sliding into the loose curls. She loved the cut Charles had given her. She laughed aloud softly, remembering his words as he'd stood back to look at her and admire his own work. "Lord, Sam, you're a beautiful creature. That cut gives you a wild, free look. Why did you do an idiotic thing like get married?"

Her face sobered, *Wild and free.* Well, she certainly hadn't been too wild lately, and she'd never be free again.

She walked into the room and stopped, closing the door softly behind her. Morgan sat sprawled lazily in the chair by the window, reading the *Times*, his long legs stretched out in front of him. He looked up as she entered and went dead still, the paper held motionless. She endured his scrutiny as long as she could. Somehow she managed to keep her voice cool. "Do you like it?"

He folded the paper and dropped it on the floor, his eyes on her, before answering, his voice deep. "You look like a redheaded witch. Are you?" Before she could say anything, he added, "You must be. Cast a spell too. I can feel it doing strange things to me already." His voice went lower. "Come here, Samantha."

"Morgan, I'm hot and tired, I—"

Even lower. "Come here."

"I'm starving, I want my din—"

Almost a whisper now, and a definite warning. "Samantha."

Sam walked across the room slowly, dropping the package and her handbag on the bed as she passed. She stopped in front of him and as his hand went to her waist she saw something flash in the late afternoon sunlight coming through the window. His hand drew her down to her knees on the floor between his legs then, taking her left hand, he removed a ring from the end of his finger and slid it along hers till it touched the narrow band of platinum already there. Her eyes widening as she stared at it, she exclaimed. "That's the most beautiful thing I've ever seen!"

The large emerald-cut emerald, set in platinum with two diamond baguettes on either side, looked almost too heavy for her slim hand. The deep, clear color of the stone matched the eyes she lifted to his. "Morgan, what—?"

"Happy Birthday, redheaded witch," he murmured.

"I—I don't know what to say," Sam stammered.

He leaned back in the chair; his hands, clasped on her waist, drew her up to him, against him. His mouth an inch from hers, he whispered, "We'll think of some way for you to thank me."

"Are you hungry?" The words were spoken softly when Sam opened her eyes. She turned her head to see Morgan, fully dressed, sitting in the chair by the window.

"Famished," she murmured, her voice blurred with sleepiness. She closed her eyes again. She felt absolutely hollow. She had been looking forward to dinner with longing as she returned from shopping yesterday, and she hadn't had any. Morgan had said he'd think of some way for her to thank him, then had proceeded to show her exactly where his thinking led. As on the first night, he'd been tireless, and she had wondered at the almost desperate urgency of his lovemaking. When, finally, he'd stretched out on his back and drew her into his arms, pulling the covers over them both, she was exhausted, all thoughts of food gone.

"What time is it?" She yawned. Her eyes flew open as he drawled, a hint of laughter in his voice, "Nine-thirty."

"Nine-thirty! Why didn't you wake me? Dave will be here

with the car at eleven.'' She sat bolt upright, then blushing, clutched the sheet around her nakedness. Morgan laughed out loud and she sat glaring at him. He returned her stare, the corners of his mouth twitching. Sam could see he had no intention of either turning around or leaving the room and her voice became a plea, ''Morgan, please.''

He shook his head and grinned at her. ''You have one hour and thirty minutes to get yourself dressed, fed, and ready to leave this hotel by the time the car gets here. But first, you must get from that bed to that bathroom and I'm quite comfortable where I am, thank you.''

His grin widened as, eyes flashing, she snapped, ''Damn you,'' lifted her chin, threw back the sheet, jumped from the bed and ran for the bathroom.

They walked through the hotel doors just as the midnight-blue Cadillac slid alongside the curb. Dave jumped out to open the door to the back seat, his eyes going over Sam anxiously before, growing guarded, he turned to Morgan.

Sam hurried across the pavement, looking cool and lovely in the pale pink Empire-waist dress and matching sandals she had bought the day before. Stretching out her hand to him she said softly, ''Hello, Dave, how are you?''

''I'm fine.'' He clasped her slim hand firmly a moment, his eyes warm. ''Welcome home, Miss Sam.''

Morgan stood tall and quiet behind her and, a little breathless, she introduced them. ''Dave, this is my husband, Morgan Wade.'' Turning her head slightly to Morgan, she smiled coolly, and added without a catch, ''Darling, our driver and friend, Dave Zimmer.''

Morgan was silent, his face expressionless. In confusion Sam turned back to see Dave's eyes study Morgan briefly before extending his hand, Morgan's arm shot past her and as his hand clasped Dave's he said, a small smile twitching his lips, ''I assure you, Dave, I'm taking very good care of her.''

"Yes, sir, Mr. Wade."

They settled themselves on the back seat and Dave's face, as he slid behind the wheel, told Sam he was satisfied. With a few quiet words, Morgan had acquired a follower.

Sam was tense, and although Morgan had not even blinked when she had called him darling, she was worrying over what attitude he'd assume when meeting Mary and Deb. She glanced at him quickly. He looked healthy and full of vitality and altogether too handsome in a khaki linen jacket and white oxford shirt open at the neck, the white contrasting sharply with the deep tan of his face and throat. *The wretched man hasn't even the grace to look tired,* she thought peevishly, and felt her cheeks grow warm remembering the night before. Catching her look, Morgan arched a brow and grinned wickedly at her as if he'd read her thoughts.

Her tension mounting, Sam gave a sigh of relief, wanting to have it over with, when the big car turned into the drive and slowed to a stop in front of the big house.

"Very elegant," Morgan said softly, stepping out of the car and turning to help Sam before Dave had cut the engine.

As Sam stepped from the car, the front door opened and a small, dark-haired figure ran lightly down the steps and in a soft, lilting voice cried, "Sam," as she hurtled herself into Sam's arms.

Sam hugged her half sister, then held her away from her, laughing softly. "Poppet, you're looking positively radiant."

"Oh, Sam, I've missed you so much. It's seemed like ages," Deb said softly and Sam felt the breath catch in her throat, for Deb had tears in her eyes. Then Deb turned, an unsure look on her face, and tilted her head way back to look at Morgan, who had stood quietly watching. She put her hand out slowly. "Morgan?"

Morgan took her hand into his, and Sam was astonished

at the look of tenderness on his face as he said gently, "I've never had a sister, Deb, but if I had, I'd want her to be just like you, small and dark and captivating." He paused, then added, "Will you be my sister, Deb?"

Sam watched, some of the tension inside her lessening, as the unsure look on Deb's face changed to one of enchantment. "I'd love to be your sister, Morgan," Deb answered, a radiant smile curving her lips.

Stepping forward, Morgan let go of Deb's hand to scoop her off her feet and into his arms, kissing her soundly on the mouth.

"Don't enjoy that too much, Deb." The pleasant warning came from Bryan as he came slowly down the steps.

Morgan set a laughing Deb back on her feet and she turned to Bryan, who came to a stop next to her. "Darling, this is Morgan and as he is my new brother, you must be nice to him."

"As long as he doesn't make a habit of kissing you," he answered dryly, looking up at Morgan, who stood a good four inches taller than he did. The two men eyed each other silently a few seconds, each taking the other's measure, then seemed to reach a decision simultaniously as both grinned and put forth a hand.

"Bryan."

"Morgan."

Bryan turned to Sam and Morgan saw the same warm look in his eyes that he'd seen in Dave's as he murmured almost the exact same words. "Welcome home, Sam."

"Hello, Pet." Smiling, Sam walked into his outstretched arms.

Morgan's voice was as dry as Bryan's had been a few moments ago. "As long as you don't make a habit of that, Bryan."

Laughing easily together, the four mounted the steps and entered the house. The feeling of ease left Sam abruptly when, once inside the large hall, Deb said, "Mother's waiting in the small sitting room, Sam." Arm in arm, she and Bryan walked in the direction of that room.

Sam's steps faltered and without saying anything or even looking at her, Morgan took her hand, entwined his fingers in hers and drew her along behind the other couple.

"Settle down, Red," he drawled softly. "I promise I won't let you down. Be a good girl and your family will be as ignorant of our deception when we leave as they are right now."

Sam shot a startled, uneasy glance at him, but they were at the sitting room doorway before she could form a reply.

As they entered the room, Mary stood, hands out-stretched, saying in her sweet, cultured voice, "Samantha, darling, I can't tell you how good it is to see you and have you home again."

Morgan loosened his hold. Steps hurrying now, Sam went to Mary, put her hands in hers and, bending, kissed her soft cheek. "And it's wonderful to be here with you, Mother." Then, turning, "Here's Morgan."

Her stepmother was delicate and sometimes seemed a trifle vague, but everyone in the house knew that very little escaped her attention. So Sam held her breath as Morgan, bending over the petite woman, enclosed her tiny hand in his large one. "I'm happy to meet you, finally, Mrs. Denning. May I call you Mary?" On her nod, he continued "Though I could hardly believe her, you are every bit as lovely as Sam said you were."

Mary's cheeks pinked becomingly. "How charming you are." Her eyes dancing, she added, "And I'm afraid a bit of a rogue."

Morgan grinned, his black eyes laughing. "You won't tell anyone, will you?"

Mary's soft, sweet laughter floated through the air. "I hardly think that will be necessary, my dear. Now, I'm sure you both want to freshen up. Samantha, dear, you're in your own room, of course. Take Morgan up and join us for lunch whenever you're ready."

Sam closed the door gently behind her, watching Morgan as he sauntered into her room, his eyes missing nothing. "Thank you," she whispered.

He turned slowly, his eyes pinning her to the door. "What for?"

"For being so nice to them. They're very important to me."

His voice was very low. "I know that. It was easy to be nice to them, they're very nice people." His voice took on an edge. "For God's sake, Sam, what did you expect me to do?"

She shrugged helplessly; despite his words earlier, she had been worried. "I don't know, but I was afraid." Her breath caught; she could say no more.

His eyes mocked her, his voice was impatient. "I know that too. Five months and you don't know me at all, do you, Redhead?"

She straightened, moving away from the door. She was home, in her own room and she was determined, no matter how much she loved him, he would not intimidate her here. "I know you as well as I care to," she said coolly, walking to the bathroom. Her hand on the doorknob, his laughing voice stopped her.

"It won't work, Samantha."

Sam felt a small shiver trickle down her stiff spine. Forcing her voice to remain cool, she snapped. "I don't know what you mean."

His laughter deepened, as did his voice. "No? I think you do. Planning to put me in my place while we're here, aren't you? You won't, but have fun trying, Redhead, because I'm going to enjoy watching you."

She spun around, her eyes blazing and without taking time to think, bit out, "You really are an arrogant bastard, aren't you?" She stopped, appalled at herself.

He was across the room in a few strides, gripping her shoulders painfully, his eyes and voice hard with anger.

"Is that how you think of me?"

"Morgan, I'm sorry."

"Don't ever be sorry for saying what you think to me. I'm your husband and regardless of what you think of me, we have a bargain and you'll stick to it." The anger seemed to drain out of him and dropping his hands to his sides he said calmly, "We don't want to keep your family waiting too long for their lunch." Pulling the bathroom door open for her he added, "Don't be too long—darling."

Sam's hands shook as she washed her face and applied fresh makeup lightly. She was more frightened of him when he was cool and calm than when he was angry.

Sam's nerves grew taut over the next few days. She felt like she was living with two different people. When they were alone in the bedroom, Morgan was reserved, withdrawn. He barely spoke to her and for the first time since he'd carried her to his bed and made her his, he didn't touch her at night. When they were with other people he was charming and attentive, the endearments coming smoothly and easily from his mouth.

Mary and Deb had told no one they were coming, wanting to have Sam to themselves for the few days before the party. Sam and Morgan spent those days horseback riding with Deb and Bryan or lazing by the pool, for all the world like a happy family group.

By Friday morning Sam felt slightly sick with apprehension. Morgan would be meeting her friends for the first time at the party and she wondered nervously what they would think of him and, more importantly, what he would think of them.

Sam found herself alone soon after breakfast, Mary and Deb having gone shopping for some last-minute items for the party. Morgan was gone when she woke and hadn't returned for breakfast. Restlessly she paced her room, then, grabbing up her purse, she left the room and ran down the steps. She'd go for a drive. Always before, whenever she was upset, she drove alone, and it had always soothed her, calmed her down. She hadn't driven her car since coming home, hadn't even looked at it, and now as she left the house by a side door and hurried along the graveled walk to the row of garages in back, she was eager to get behind the wheel again. Although she knew that Dave would have kept her car in perfect running condition, it would probably do it good if she gave it a good run.

Hurrying along, head bent, Sam was deep in thought, remembering the last time she'd had to let off tension by driving alone. She'd quarreled bitterly with her father. Over what? She couldn't remember, but she remembered leaving the house in anger and driving, much too fast, for over an hour. When she'd returned, the anger was gone and she'd calmly gone to her father and smoothed over their argument. Two weeks later he was dead and she was thankful now that she'd—

"Going somewhere, Redhead?" Morgan's voice cut across her thoughts, and she stopped, startled, looking up quickly. He stood leaning against the Cadillac parked in front of the garage.

"I didn't hear the car," Sam said in confusion. He'd been riding and Sam's eyes ran the length of him. He wore flat-heeled riding boots and his long legs and slim hips were encased in tight black jeans. A white shirt open at the throat, sleeves rolled to the elbow, was an assault on the eyes in the bright morning sunlight. Within seconds every detail about him registered in her mind. The gold watch gleaming against the dark skin on his wrist, the narrow platinum band on his finger, the crisp black hair, the ends given a silvery look by the sunlight. His eyes were hidden from her by wire-framed sunglasses, and his mouth, sensuous, the lips perfectly outlined, which could become suddenly straight and hard, now curved in mild amusement.

Sam took him all in and was shattered emotionally. As she moved, began walking toward him, she admitted to herself that the only thing on this earth she wanted was to walk up to him, slide her arms around that slim waist, fasten her mouth to his and feel the long, lean hardness of his body against hers. Her thoughts brought her up short, and she eyed him in resentment. Why, why, of all the men she'd met, did it have to be this one? This cowboy who looked at her in contemptuous amusement.

"I've been here awhile." His voice was pure silk. "And I asked you a question."

Anger burned through her. Who the hell did he think he was? Her voice frosty, she said, "I'm going for a drive."

"Dave driving?"

"Of course not! I'm taking my car." Sam ground her teeth as she watched one black brow arch above the rim of his sunglasses.

"I'll go with you," he said softly.

"No," she almost shouted the word at him.

The tone lowered, became a soft purr. "I said I'll go with you."

Sam glared at him, then stormed into the garage, slid behind the wheel and backed the shiny blue Miata out of its stall.

Now both brows peeked over the glass rims and as Morgan folded himself into the seat next to her, he murmured, "Nice little toy you have here."

She smiled sweetly at him. "I hope you're comfortable— darling."

Morgan grinned at her and in fury she tore along the drive and onto the road and for the next thirty minutes drove like the demons of hell were tailgating her. He sat silent until she had ripped back up the driveway and into the stall, stopping the car a bare half inch from the back wall. Watching her, his attitude one of complete boredom, he removed his sunglasses, held them by one earpiece between thumb and forefinger and gently swung them back and forth. "Feel better now, Redhead?" he drawled. Bending and leaning to her, he kissed her lightly on the lips.

His utter indifference exploded the already seething anger inside her. Sam didn't think, she reacted. Her hand flew up and across his face, then back to her mouth. In horror at what she'd done, she watched his eyes and face go hard. The red mark of her fingers growing on his check, he said coldly, "You're behaving like a very spoiled little girl, Samantha, and I'm getting a little sick of it. Be very careful you don't twist the tiger's tail too hard, or you're liable to find you've started something you can't finish."

Sam sat rigid as, without looking at her again, Morgan slid his body out of the car.

Although she felt rather sick, with nerves fluttering in her stomach, Sam managed a small salad at lunch, but begged off dinner, claiming a headache, promising Mary she'd have a nap before the party. In fact she did fall asleep after swallowing two aspirin and stretching out across the bed. She woke to find Morgan already showered and getting dressed. Without a word she entered the bathroom, taking an extra long time over her bath and applying her makeup until, relief washing over her, she heard the bedroom door close behind him.

She entered the now empty bedroom, stepped into lacy white briefs and gold evening sandals. She brushed her hair into deliberately wild and disordered curls around her face. She sprayed herself lavishly with a light, spicy perfume and, with more than a little trepidation, she went to her closet and removed her new dress, putting it on quickly before she could change her mind. Why had she bought it? she wondered, as she studied her reflection in the long mirror. It was not her usual style at all.

Of white silk charmeuse, it contrasted perfectly with the beautiful golden glow her skin had acquired over the summer. But, she reflected, the slip dress style with slim spaghetti straps revealed much too much skin. The cut of the dress gave her waist an even smaller look, and from the waist the material fit perfectly over her hips and fell straight to the floor, giving her a long, leggy look.

Sam shook her head slowly at her reflection. No, Morgan was definitely not going to approve. Glancing at the clock, she realized she was already late, so with a small shrug of her shoulders, she straightened her back, lifted her chin, and left the room.

Morgan was the first person Sam saw as she came slowly down the broad, curving staircase. He stood talking to Mary and some of Sam's friends, and as if he sensed her there on the stairs, he looked up, then went completely still. She saw a flicker of surprise go across his face and his eyes widen for an instant before narrowing. His reaction had lasted only seconds, but Sam knew he was angry, very angry. She continued to move down the stairs, her breath catching in her throat, as she watched Morgan murmur a few words to Mary and start toward her. He had taken a few strides, then stopped short, his face going hard, as a deep, caressing voice was raised above the normal tones of the other guests. "Sam, my love, if you intended to make an entrance, you've certainly succeeded. You look positively ravishing."

Sam saw Morgan turn sharply and walk away before she turned, at the bottom of the stairs now, and smilingly placed her hands into the outstretched ones of the owner of that deep voice.

Jeffrey Hampton was as handsome as ever. Tall and fair, his light hair gleaming in the brightly lit hall, he stood smiling at her, his eyes bright with admiration. Leaning to her, he kissed her gently on the mouth and said softly,

"It's great to see you again, angel, it's been a very dull summer with you not here."

Sam laughed up at him, but said in a stern voice, "Jeffrey Hampton, that's an awful thing for you to say, in view of the fact that you became engaged this summer."

"Oh, that," he shrugged lightly. "What has that to do with the fact that I still love you madly and missed you?"

Sam frowned. "Jeff, behave yourself." But she had to smile again at the quick impish grin he gave her. She had turned down his proposal of marriage twice, but even so had continued to go around with him. He was a charming, delightful companion and they had fun together.

Now she couldn't help comparing him with the man she'd married. As always, he was elegantly dressed, tonight in what looked like Armani in a dark blue that set his fair looks off very stylishly. As Jeff cupped her elbow with his hand and led her into the large room off the hall cleared of all furniture and full of laughing, talking people, she realized she hadn't even noticed what Morgan was wearing.

She glanced around quickly and saw him across the room standing in front of the fireplace, looking completely relaxed, with one arm resting against the mantelpiece, drink in hand, looking down at the young woman speaking to him. Sam's eyes went over him and, as before, the look of him did strange things to her legs and made her breath catch in her throat. His black evening clothes were perfectly cut to his long, lithe frame and, along with his tanned skin and black brows and hair, gave him a slightly satanic look. His white shirt and flashing white teeth, as he suddenly smiled, looked startling against all that darkness. Her eyes shifted to the woman he'd smiled at—Jeff's newly acquired fiancée, Carolyn Henkes.

Sam had never liked Carolyn overmuch and now, as she watched her flutter long, pale-gold lashes up at Morgan, she decided she liked her even less. That Carolyn was a beauty, Sam would not deny. With long white-gold hair that framed a beautiful pink and white heart-shaped face, out of which gazed large cornflower-blue eyes, she was as lovely as an exquisite china doll and, Sam knew, just as brittle. She could be delightful and sweet, but equally biting and vicious if she thought her interests were threatened. Morgan, Sam noted with dismay, seemed captivated by her.

She heard Jeff chuckle close to her ear and knew his eyes had followed hers as he whispered, "It would seem my intended is quite taken with your somewhat overpowering husband."

A few minutes later, as the music started, Sam felt Morgan's arm slide around her waist, heard him drawl softly, "I think we're to have the first dance—darling." He led her to the cleared area at the end of the long room. His appearance was that of the happy, devoted bridegroom as he drew her into his arms and bent his smiling face to her. But Sam felt cold apprehension go through her, for every muscle in his body was tense with anger and his voice, in her ear, whispered harshly, "What the hell are you trying to prove with that dress?"

Chapter Seven

Some six hours later Sam entered her room and stood rigid, fists at her sides, her back to the door. She knew an angry argument was about to follow her and, sighing deeply, she moved into the room, kicking her sandals off as she went. The plush beige carpeting felt good to her tired feet and she stood still, in the center of the room, curling her toes against the soft fibers. She felt tired and slightly light-headed. She had eaten very little all day and had had far too much champagne, as she had seemed to acquire an almost unquenchable thirst after that first dance.

The party had been torment for her. Morgan had barely talked to her after that first dance and yet he had managed to give the impression of their being the happy newlyweds as he moved about the room meeting her friends. He had danced with all the women and stood and talked with all the men, occasionally giving her one of his devastating white smiles. But his eyes did not smile and Sam could see the fury glittering in them across the width of the room.

She had not been the one at his side, making the introductions. Carolyn, smiling up at him and hanging onto his arm like a growth, had performed that duty for her, occasionally casting Sam a smug, malicious glance.

Jeff had been her shadow all evening. As she had moved about, forcing herself to talk and laugh with her friends, he had become increasingly more familiar, dropping his arm first about her shoulders, then around her waist. Each time he danced with her his hand grew more bold, caressing her braless back. Sam had quietly told him warningly to stop. Jeff had laughed at her and, taking her hand, had drawn her through the french windows into the garden. The garden had been transformed into a make-believe place of moving lights and shadows by the strings of patio lights draped from tree to tree for the party. There were couples dancing on the grass just outside the doors and Jeff kept moving deeper into the garden along the hedge-lined path away from the glow of the lights. He had stopped suddenly and, without a word, pulled her into his arms and kissed her.

Sam stood passive a few moments. Jeff's kiss, as always before, was pleasant, but it struck no response from her. When she didn't respond, Jeff's lips became more demanding and Sam pulled herself free and walked away from him, deeper into the shadows. She had walked a short distance when she stopped, then, turning quickly, hurried back to Jeff, and in a voice barely controlling her anger, told him she wanted a drink. He didn't argue, thinking her anger directed at him, but followed her quietly into the house.

Sam brought the wineglass to her lips, amazed at the intensity of her feelings. Her hands were shaking and she drained the glass quickly and put it down before anyone noticed. Pain tore through her as a picture of what she had seen flashed across her mind. Carolyn, smiling face upturned, one arm stretched out, fingers touching his cheek. Morgan, white teeth flashing in his dark face as he bent over her, his big hands closing on her shoulders. It had taken every ounce of will power Sam possessed to turn away and walk back to the house. She had wanted to scream and fly at Carolyn's face with her nails. Somehow she managed to get through what was left of the evening without giving herself away. Now, as she stood absolutely still in the middle of her room, her nails dug into her palms and she felt her back stiffen. She had been sure he saw other women when away, but to actually see him, here!

Sam froze as the door opened, then closed quietly. The long silent moment drew her nerves taut and she spun angrily at his softly grated, "Get that goddamned rag off before I do it for you."

Her mouth open to argue, the words died in Sam's throat when she looked at him. The look of him frightened her. He leaned lazily against the door, and she thought wildly that he looked like some huge cat ready to pounce on her. She had never seen him this angry and, although his voice had been soft, she could see he was fighting to control himself. His face seemed carved in stone and his eyes, which could look hard and cold as black ice, now blazed at her in fury.

Sam found her voice and even managed to keep it cool. "You have no right to speak to me like that."

His purred answer drew fingers of ice down her spine. "You have thirty seconds."

Sam stared at him. This didn't make sense. All this fury over a dress? She lifted her head even higher, cool green eyes matched her tone, giving away nothing of the unease she felt. "Morgan, I don't think I understand what this is all about."

"No?" Eyes narrowing, he moved toward her. Her pose of cool indifference seemed to unleash the heat inside him. The purr took on a very rough edge. "Then I'll tell you what it's all about. That dress is an open invitation to all comers." As she opened her mouth to protest, he snarled harshly, "Don't interrupt. You're my wife, Samantha, my woman, you use my name. And what wears my brand is mine. I don't share my wealth."

All composure gone, voice rising Sam cried, "Wears your brand? Morgan, I'm a person, not part of your stock."

"I never said you were, but that ring you wear is my brand and as long as you wear it, you're mine." Voice low, menacing, he added, "And if your pretty boyfriend ever puts his hands on you again I'll drop him. Now get that damn dress off."

Sam winced as if the words he rapped out at her actually struck her. Turning her back, she put trembling fingers to the small zipper at her side and tugged. The dress slid from her to the floor, forming a circle around her feet. In defiance, she stepped outside that circle and kicked the garment across the room. Standing straight and stiff, the lacy panties her only covering, she heard a low humorless chuckle behind her and, eyes wide, watched his jacket, shirt and tie arch through the air and land on top of her gown.

"No," Sam whispered, her shaking hand reaching for the nightgown lying across the foot of the bed next to which she stood.

Morgan's hand closed around her wrist; his voice was a harsh whisper in her ear. "Did you enjoy the feel of pretty boy's hands and lips, Samantha?"

His words hurt. A picture of him bending over Carolyn flashed through her mind, and that hurt even more. She wanted to hurt back, and giving no thought to her nudity, she wrenched her arm from his hand and turned on him hotly. "You bloody beast. How dare you? Jeff's an old friend and he loves me. He's gentle and considerate and I should have married him when he asked me." She was lashing out blindly, not pausing to think, trying to inflict on him a small measure of the pain she had felt tear through her in the garden. "I'll see him whenever I wish and if I want to go to bed with him, I shall. He at least doesn't want my money." Pulling his rings from her finger, she threw them at his face. "And you can take your brand and you can—"

The words died on her lips for, after throwing the rings, she had tossed back her head and seen his face. Real fear crawled through her stomach as his hands gripped her shoulders painfully. "You redheaded witch," he gritted between clenched teeth. "You try and put horns on me with Hampton and I'll take him apart—slowly. Do you understand that?"

Sam nodded dumbly, unable to take her eyes from his savage face, fighting the panic growing inside. Releasing her shoulders he stepped back. "Pick your rings up and put them on. Now."

It was a command, and without question she hurried to obey. But a spark of defiance made her say as she straightened, sliding the rings into place, "May I please go to bed now?"

The grin he gave her was wicked as, cupping her chin in his hand, he bent his head to hers and said mockingly, "I thought you'd never ask."

Sam jerked her head away as his mouth touched hers. "No, Morgan, it's late and I'm very tired, I want—"

"Too bad." His words cut across hers like a steel blade. "I warned you to be careful not to twist the tiger's tail too hard. You had to see just how far you could go, didn't you, Red?" He pulled her against him, his mouth hard, demanding, hurting hers.

The sound of his voice, his unbridled rage, frightened Sam and she fought him. She kicked him, hit out with her hands balled into fists and she tore at his hair.

His face grim, set, he picked her up and dumped her onto the bed. She lay sprawled, gasping for breath, her eyes wide with shock, watching him as he stripped off the rest of his clothes. Rolling over she tried to jump from the other side of the bed, but Morgan dropped down beside her, and his arm shot out and around her waist, dragging her back against him. She fought like a wild thing, twisting and arching her body away from him, hitting, kicking. She cursed him in a raw, breathless hiss and he laughed at her. Twice she was rewarded for her efforts when she heard him grunt in pain, deep in his throat. Once when her nails raked across his cheek, again when her teeth drew blood from his shoulder. She couldn't win and she knew it, but she also knew she'd put up a good fight, for his dark skin glistened as wetly as hers and the hair around his face was as damp as her own. She lay quiet, finally, drawing great gulps of air into her lungs, her eyes still rebellious and stormy on his.

"You're really beautiful, Redhead," he whispered as he lowered his face to hers. Then, his lips brushing hers "And a magnificent adversary, but you lose." His mouth took hers in a kiss that robbed her of all breath and all reason. It was full daylight before he moved away from her to lay on his back breathing deeply, his eyes closed.

Sam lay beside him, the back of her hand pressed against her mouth, fighting, in vain, against the tears that rolled down her temple and into her hair. She was filled with shame and disgust, but with herself, not him. That she loved him she'd faced months ago, but how deep, how intense within her that love went was borne upon her now.

His lovemaking had been almost savage, and she'd been lost from that first kiss. She'd matched his savagery with her own, obeying his commands willingly, eagerly. There was not a spot on her body that his hands and mouth did not now know, and she'd trembled in delight at their knowing. He'd bid her own to explore him, and she'd gloried in their knowledge. Yet he'd as much as told her she was a possession, part of his property, to be used when he needed, like his house, or his plane, or his horse. She felt wounded and lacerated almost beyond endurance.

He turned his head and looked at her, then sighing deeply, in what she was sure was disgust, he left the bed and went into the bathroom. She heard the water running in the shower just before she fell asleep.

When she woke it was midafternoon and she was alone. She lay for some time reliving the night before, then, with a deep sigh, she got up. She wanted nothing as much as she wanted to pull the sheet over her head and never leave her bed again.

Before showering she stood and studied her nude form carefully in the mirror. Again she sighed. She was beginning to have an angular look. She had always been slim, but now, with the weight she'd lost, she looked almost skinny. But this fact she barely noticed, for all she saw were the bruises Morgan had left on her. It had been a fierce battle. Morgan had not been playing with her. Even her legs had not escaped the marks from his hands. At the thought of those hands she twisted around and went into the bathroom.

Sam had dressed in jeans and a long-sleeved shirt and was sitting at her dresser brushing her hair when Morgan came into the room carrying a tray. Her eyes, guarded, wary, met his in the mirror. Lifting the tray in a wry salute, he arched a brow, murmured sardonically, "From Beth, with orders to eat all of it." He walked across the room and set the tray on the table by the windows, then stretched out in the chair next to it.

"I'm really not hungry." Sam went back to her brushing.

"It's two o'clock, you've eaten practically nothing for over twenty-four hours, Samantha. Come over here and eat something." His voice held a lazy drawl. It also held an order.

Flinging the brush down, she spun around, eyes blazing, ready to argue. The sight of his face stopped the words in her throat. He lay back in the chair, eyes closed, looking incredibly tired. He had a pinched, drawn look, the welts her fingernails had made red and angry looking across his cheek.

She had seen him after weeks of working fourteen- and sixteen-hour days, and he had never looked like this. *What are we doing to each other?* she thought tiredly. All fight and anger drained out of her. She walked to the table and sat in the chair across from him. The tray held a pot of coffee, two fat mugs and a covered plate, which held bacon, eggs, and two toasted English muffins dripping with butter.

Sam filled both mugs with coffee and sat watching Morgan, gnawing on her lip. He had obviously been riding, as he wore boots, jeans, and a blue chambray shirt, the sleeves rolled up to his elbows. "Your coffee's getting cold." She said the words softly, not sure if he'd fallen asleep. At the sound of her voice he slid his body up in the chair and opened his eyes, one brow going up in question at the look on her face. She lowered her eyes, stammered "I— I'm sorry about your face."

The soft laugh had the sound of bitterness, not humor. "You're some tigress, Redhead." He nodded at the tray "Eat something, Samantha, then I want to talk to you." Reaching a hand to the tray, he murmured, "May I?" He picked up a piece of the muffin at her nod.

He sat munching the muffin, watching her as she forced down a piece of bacon and some of the eggs. When she sat back in her chair, her mug cradled in her hands, he said, "Finished?" Sam nodded, watched his fingers smooth over the welts on his cheek. "I told Mary I rode too close to a tree branch. So if anyone asks, you know what to say. Unless, of course, there's someone you'd like to tell the truth to."

"Morgan, please."

He smiled slightly at the note of reproach in her voice and went on. "Well, then, Mary tells me we've received quite a few invitations, beginning with a dinner dance at the club tonight and varied other things right through the weekend. You had remembered that this is the Labor Day weekend?'' At her brief nod he continued. ''I told her, for my part, she should accept any of these invitations she wished, but I'd send you to confer with her on the matter. Okay?''

''Yes, of course.''

He drank his coffee, held the mug out for her to refill it, before going on. ''Now the important part. I like your family very much, Samantha, and I see no reason why we should worry them with our marital difficulties. So I suggest we call a truce. At least for the remainder of our visit.''

''You mean to take me with you then, when you go home?'' Her voice was low, but she had managed to keep it steady.

Morgan had bent his head to his mug, but at her words his head jerked up, his eyes going hard and cold. ''Are you trying to tell me you're not going with me?'' Before she could answer, he added, his voice very soft, ''Maybe you're thinking of ending this marriage.''

The last thing in the world I want is to end our marriage, her mind cried. Aloud she replied carefully, ''I thought, perhaps, you were thinking along those lines.''

He looked at her a long time through narrowed lids before answering shortly, ''You know that's impossible under the circumstances, don't you?''

''Yes,'' she whispered.

He gave her a strange look, then rapped, ''All right then, do you agree to a truce?'' When she again whispered, ''Yes,'' he stood and completely surprised her by bending over her and brushing his lips across hers. Straightening, he began to unbutton his shirt. ''Do you have any plans for what's left of the afternoon?''

''Yes. I have a friend who runs a boutique not far from

here and I thought I'd run over and do some shopping. Why? Did you have something you wanted to do?"

He threw her a wicked grin. "Yes, I'm going to take a shower and have a nap until it's time to dress for dinner Too bad you can't join me."

"In which?" Sam retorted.

His grin widened. "In both. Are you going to be shopping for something to wear tonight?"

"Yes, why?" She eyed him warily, thinking their truce would be short-lived if he tried to tell her what to buy.

He was tugging his shirt from his jeans as he answered. "Get something in white. Although I didn't approve of your dress last night, I have to admit that with the tan you've acquired you look pretty terrific in white." Without waiting for her to comment, he turned, pulling his shirt off, toward the bathroom.

Sam's eyes widened when she saw his back, for, although they were longer, the red, angry-looking welts crisscrossing his back exactly matched those on his face. How could she have done something like that? she thought as a small gasp escaped through the fingers that had flown to her mouth.

On hearing her gasp, Morgan turned quickly. "What is it?" Sam's eyes widened even more at the ugly mark her teeth left on his shoulder.

He frowned and his voice sounded concerned. "Sam, what is wrong?"

"Oh, Lord, Morgan, your back—your shoulder. Do you think you should have a tetanus shot?"

With that he laughed aloud in real amusement. "No, I don't, my redheaded tigress. I get T shots regularly and I doused myself with antiseptic this morning and I will again after I've showered, so stop looking so scared. Run along and enjoy your shopping." Still laughing softly he turned and strode into the bathroom.

Sam did enjoy her shopping. After a short consultation with Mary, during which she agreed to all plans for the

weekend, she and a very willing Deb made the short run
to the small shop. She and Jean, the woman who ran the
shop, spent a few minutes catching up on news of each
other, Jean exclaiming over Sam's ring, then the three
women got down to the serious business of clothes for
Sam's slimmer figure. She bought pants and a few skirts,
tops, and three dressier outfits, one in white, even though
she'd told herself she wouldn't. Then telling Jean they'd
see her at the club, they went back to the house and right
to their rooms, as it was time to get ready for dinner.

Morgan was still sprawled out on the bed asleep when
Sam got back and her eyes kept straying to his sleeping
face as she moved around the room quietly, hanging her
clothes away. Relaxed, his face had lost the tight, drawn
look and in turn seemed less grim and hard.

She slid silently into the bathroom and was standing in
panties and bra in front of the bathroom mirror, some
fifteen minutes later, making her face up, when the door
opened and he leaned against the frame, watching her.

Raising the eye shadow applicator to her lid, she lifted
her eyes, caught the look on his face reflected in the mirror, and repeated his words of that afternoon. "What is
it?"

He stretched out an arm and his fingertips touched
gently at the large, purpling bruise on her arm. Then his
hand dropped to her hip where another bruise was partially
covered by her panties. Giving a light tug at the elastic, he
exposed it in all its colorful size. His eyes went over her
slowly, noting all the marks on her. As his eyes came back
to her face, he raised his finger to her cheek, gently caressing it. His voice deep and husky with emotion, he said,
"And you were concerned about me!" His other hand
lifted her arm and drew her toward him as he bent his
head. Pressing his lips gently to the bruise on her arm he
murmured, "I'm sorry, Sam, I had no right to do this to
you. You have my word that it won't happen again."

Taken completely by surprise by this gentleness he'd never shown to her before, Sam's reply sounded cold and stiff. "All right, Morgan, now we'd really better get ready as it's getting late."

"Of course." His hands dropped and he stepped back abruptly.

She noticed, for the first time, that he was already partially dressed, lacking only shirt, tie and jacket. Scooping up her makeup she slipped by him. "I'll leave you to shave."

She had finished her makeup and was struggling with the long zipper at the back of her gown when he reentered the room. Standing as if fascinated, he watched her a few seconds, until she snapped in agitation, "Don't just stand there for heaven's sake, help with this blasted thing." His lips twitching, he walked up behind her and with one tug closed the zipper. Stepping back he ordered, "Turn around."

She turned around slowly as he took in the white sheath. It was simply cut and fitted snugly, with long close-fitting sleeves and a low, square neckline, but not too low. The fitted skirt had a modest back vent.

"Very nice. Now stand still," he murmured, going to the dresser and taking a case from the top drawer. As he walked back to her, he opened the case and removed a necklace from it, then, flipping the case onto the bed, he stood behind her and clasped the chain around her neck. Sam went to the mirror and stared at the large diamond-encircled emerald that hung at the end of the platinum chain.

"But why?"

"Call it a belated wedding gift." He shrugged, went to the closet, pulled out a white shirt, muttered brusquely, "Now say thank you and get the hell out of here, so I can get dressed." Hesitantly, she went to him, gave him a quick kiss, mumbled "thank you," and hurried from the room, not understanding him at all.

The evening passed pleasantly enough, the only sour note as far as Sam was concerned was Carolyn's obvious interest in Morgan, and the fact that Morgan seemed to return that interest. Even Deb, who had decided Morgan was just about perfect, looked from one to the other, then to Sam with raised eyebrows.

During the next few days Sam felt the admiration and respect she already had for Morgan growing steadily. She knew he worked very hard, giving little time to relaxation and games, and yet, in the company of wealthy young men who made games their vocation, he adjusted quite well. He joined Bryan and two others in a round of golf and finished with a score only slightly higher than Bryan's, who was considered by far the best golfer in the district. He played a hard, fast game of tennis, with a serve that shot across the net like a missile. Sam had once before witnessed his swimming ability, the powerful strokes propelling his body swiftly through the water. She now found he could surf well and sail a small boat expertly. But it was when he stepped into the saddle that he put them all in the shade. All of her large group of friends rode well, the women as well as the men, but with Morgan, it was a part of his life. He seemed to become one with any horse from the moment he mounted, and no matter how difficult the animal, left no doubt as to who was the master.

They went to casual luncheons and cookouts and a formal dinner party at the home of Jeff's parents. At a wild, late-night poolside party Morgan stunned Sam by cutting in on Jeff and executing perfectly some very intricate dance steps. As the days slid by, Sam found herself becoming more and more withdrawn and rigid, for every time she'd look around for Morgan, she saw Carolyn hanging on his arm, and the look of concern growing in Deb's eyes. Deb,

Sam knew, might be crazy about her new brother-in-law, but she adored Sam and she was worried.

They were at the breakfast table the Thursday following Sam's birthday party when Morgan was called to the phone. He took the call in her father's study, which he had commandeered as his own, making long phone calls and doing an endless amount of paper work whenever he had a few free minutes and late into the night. As before he put in sixteen-hour days.

He was in the study about ten minutes when he came out, barked "Sam" and went up the stairs two at a time.

Sam finished her coffee, lifted her shoulders in an I-don't-know to the questions in Mary's and Deb's eyes, and followed him up the stairs. When she entered their room she stopped cold. Morgan had their cases open on the bed, and was packing his own.

"What—" she began, but he cut her off.

"Something's come up, Samantha, that needs my personal attention. We've got to leave. I've already phoned to have the plane ready. I'll take you home, grab a few things I need, and take off." He turned back to the open dresser drawer.

Sam didn't move. When he turned around, hands full of clothes, he raised his eyebrows at her.

"How long will you be gone?" she asked softly.

"A week, ten days maybe," he shrugged. "I'm not sure. Why?"

Making up her mind suddenly, she answered, "Couldn't I stay here?" Before he could protest she hurried on. "Deb's wedding isn't too many weeks off, you know, and we have gown fittings and shopping to do. Morgan, we don't even have a wedding gift for them yet. Couldn't you come back here when you've completed your business?"

He looked at her hard and long before answering. "All right, Samantha, but don't shop for a wedding gift till I get back; we'll do that together. And, Redhead, behave yourself while I'm away." He laughed at the startled look she gave him. "Now come help me pack so I can get moving." It seemed he was gone in no time, and Sam was left with a strange, empty feeling.

The following day Sam and Deb were having lunch at the club when Jeff dropped into the chair next to Sam and said in mock forlornness, "Would you ladies allow a deserted man to join you for lunch?"

"Of course," Sam smiled "But why deserted?"

His eyes danced devilishly. "My beloved left yesterday afternoon to visit with an aunt in Maine and I'm on my own for a week or so. And, as I understand you're also on your own, I was thinking perhaps, we could be on our own together."

Sam had not missed the sharp look Deb had turned on her when Jeff said Carolyn had left so soon after Morgan and she felt slightly sick, but she managed to keep her voice light. "Sorry, Jeff, but Deb and I were just now making plans. You see, we have hours of shopping and fittings for the wedding and it's going to be a rush to get finished before Morgan gets back."

His handsome face wore a look of disappointment. "Oh, well, some days you can't win any of them."

Somehow Sam got through lunch, even managing to laugh at Jeff's mild jokes, but she drove home in silence, refusing to acknowledge Deb's worried glances. At the house she went straight to her room to pace back and forth with one thought. Had Morgan taken Carolyn with him? It seemed too much a coincidence, their leaving within a few hours of each other.

With a soft knock Deb entered, said hesitatingly, "Sam, darling—" but she got no further as Sam whispered, "Don't ask, Deb, please."

Sam was miserable. Although she went shopping and had fittings and oohed and aahed over incoming wedding gifts, one thought tormented her. Is he with her? She

alternated between anger with and love for him and felt
disgust with herself for her own weakness. She ate less than
usual and lost more weight. She felt numb inside while
maintaining an outward composure. She heard nothing
from him.

Two weeks after Morgan left, Deb told her quietly that
Carolyn had returned. Two days after Morgan came home.

In Mary's sitting room in front of the others, he drew
her into his arms and kissed her. But once alone in the
bedroom, he looked her over critically. "What kind of
hours have you been keeping, Redhead?" he growled.
"You look like hell."

"Thanks a lot," Sam snapped. Put out because he was
looking so well, she slammed out of the room. They had
almost three tense weeks together before he was gone
again, not to return until the week before Deb's wedding.

Sam hadn't been feeling well since the middle of Sep-
tember, and when she began being sick to her stomach in
the morning, then missed her second period, she faced
the fact that she was pregnant. She had mixed feelings
about it. She wanted Morgan's baby very badly, but she
was beginning to believe he wanted out of their marriage.
By the time Deb's wedding was over, they were barely on
speaking terms, though they put on a good front in public.

The day after the wedding Morgan told her to pack.
"We're going home. I have to go to Spain tomorrow."

"How long will you be gone?" she asked as she had
weeks before.

His eyes and voice cold, he answered, "Ten days, possibly
two weeks. Why? Aren't you coming with me again?"

"No, I'm not." At the look of anger that came into his
face she added quickly, "I'm going home, Morgan, but I
want to drive."

"Are you crazy?" he snapped. "I've seen you drive,
remember? You'll come with me."

Growing angry herself now, Sam took her stand. "I do

not, as a rule, drive like that and I think you know it. I want my car.''

"For God's sake why?" he grated, his eyes furious. "You have the Jag and the wagon at the ranch."

She held firm and to keep herself from shouting at him, she said through gritted teeth, "Morgan, I want my own car and I'm driving it to Nevada."

His eyes held hers a long moment, then he turned away sharply. "Do as you wish, I couldn't care less." Without another word he packed and went, this time with no pretense of tender leave-taking. It seemed to Sam that all hope went with him. She had a horrible feeling of certainty that their strange relationship was over.

Chapter Eight

That night Sam lay wide awake, her mind working furiously. Morgan had said he'd be gone about two weeks. It would take her, at most, a few days to drive to the ranch. If she waited until next week to leave, she'd be subjected to Deb's probing, concerned glances. Yet, if she left tomorrow or the following day, she'd have a week of Sara's sharp-eyed scrutiny. Neither prospect held much appeal.

Aunt Rachael! The name sprang into her mind out of the blue. Sam had received several letters from her favorite aunt, coaxing letters, asking her when she was coming to visit. On the spur of the moment Sam decided to fly to England and stay with her mother's sister for a week. And Morgan Wade could just go hang.

Arrangements were quickly made and two days later, much to the surprise of her family, Sam was on her way to England. On the plane the thought, belatedly, struck Sam that Morgan had never told her what the Messrs. Baker had wanted. With a shrug she dismissed it, too busy concentrating on not being airsick to worry about it now.

Rachael Crinshaw, tall, elegant, her auburn hair still glowingly beautiful, was waiting for Sam at the airport. After the general confusion of luggage collection and customs, they followed Rachael's chauffeur to her Mercedes.

When she was settled into the car, Sam let her head drop back wearily against the seat.

"Are you all right, Samantha?" Rachael asked in quick concern. "You are absolutely white and, to be perfectly honest, you look like a stick with material draped around it. I realize the fashions call for slimness, but don't you think you've carried it a bit far?"

"I'm fine, Aunt Rachael." Despite the tiredness dragging at her spirit, Sam smiled. "I haven't been dieting. The summer was so hot and humid I simply had no appetite. I'm sure I'll regain the weight now that summer is finally over." *In fact,* she thought wryly, *I'm positive of it.*

"Well, I should hope so," Rachael chided gently. "Really, dear, you look absolutely haggard. I fully intend supervising your meals while you're here. I can't imagine what that husband of yours is thinking of to allow you to reach this degree of—of gauntness."

"Oh, really, Aunt Rachael," Sam laughed a little unsurely. "Morgan has no control over what I eat. You, of all people, should know how I'd react if a man tried directing my life down to the food I put into my mouth."

At least the Samantha her aunt had known would never have allowed a man to direct her life, Sam thought ruefully, memories of the number of times Morgan had done just that making her squirm with discomfort.

Sam greeted the sight of her aunt's tall, imposing house with a sigh of relief. She was so tired her eyelids felt weighted with lead. Why was she always sleepy lately?

"If you don't mind, Aunt Rachael," Sam said, the minute they stepped into the large, formal hall, "I think I'd like to go right to my room and have a nap before dinner."

"Good idea." Rachael eyed her sharply. "I want to see

some color back in your cheeks, my girl. Now, go along with Claude and have a good rest. Dinner at seven, as usual.''

With a wan smile Sam followed her aunt's very correct butler up the stairs. When she came down again three hours later, Rachael ran a critical eye over her, before declaring, ''Much, much better. You are still pale, but the tight, pinched look is gone. Really, my dear, I had no idea they led such a wild existence in Long Island. Indeed, I understood your stepmother, Mary, was a shy, timid woman.''

''Oh, Aunt Rachael!'' Sam laughed. ''Mary is a shy, timid woman and I love her dearly.'' Sam went on to briefly outline the activities that had been planned for her and Morgan. ''Quite a few were held outdoors and, as I mentioned earlier, the heat really bothers me. I assure you I am fine.''

Finally convinced, Rachael smiled warmly. ''Good. I've been very busy since you called, Samantha. As I know how flying makes you sleepy, I planned a quiet dinner tonight, but I've invited quite a few of your friends for dinner tomorrow night.''

''Oh, but Aunt Rachael—'' Sam began, the idea of not only having to act well when she felt so washed out, but also appear as the happy bride, daunting.

Her aunt didn't let her finish her protest. ''You haven't been over here in ages, darling, and all your friends want to see you. Several in particular.'' Her brows arched expressively. ''I reminded them that you are now a married woman.''

The dinner party turned out to be much more of an ordeal than she could have anticipated, even though it started out well. On awakening that morning she had been pleasantly surprised to find no sign of the gripping nausea or wracking sickness that had dogged her mornings for the past few weeks.

She and Rachael spent a leisurely, relaxing day, Sam wondering at times about the almost smugly self-satisfied expression that periodically played across her aunt's face. As Rachael was not forthcoming about the reason for her inner pleasure, Sam went to her room to dress for dinner in a bemused, questioning frame of mind.

Her question was answered the minute she stepped into her aunt's large drawing room, for one figure seemed to stand out from the several guests already gathered there.

"Duds!"

Sam's cry of delighted surprise brought all heads around to see her run across the room and into the outstretched arms of a tall, husky, sandy-haired man.

"Duds! How in the world did you get here? You look marvelous. I thought you were in Australia?"

The man's arms, tightening in a bear hug, cut off the overlapping string of Sam's words.

"Slow up a bit, darling." Clear blue eyes, bright with laughter, gazed into green. "One question at a time, please. But first"—his strong face split into a grin—"let me return the compliment twice over. You look delicious. Let's have a kiss."

Sam's mouth was caught in a deep, warm kiss which she returned unhesitatingly, without restraint. Dudley Haverstone, or Duds as Sam had christened him, was the only young man she had ever been able to truly relax with. From her fifth year, when her mother had married Dudley's father, Duds had been her older brother, her teacher, and her tormenter.

"Hmm, you taste delicious too," Duds murmured when he'd released her lips. Although his tone was serious, his eyes teased her as they'd always done. "And you had to go and get yourself tied to the formidable Morgan."

"You know Morgan?" Sam gasped, eyes widening.

"Doesn't everyone?" Duds drawled before adding, "Well, perhaps there are a few who don't."

"But, Duds, how do—"

"Enough about the cowboy," Duds cut her off. "I want to hear about you." Taking her arm, he drew her toward the far end of the room, calling over his shoulder, "If you'll excuse us, Aunt Rachael? Sam and I will rejoin the party in a few minutes."

With an indulgent smile Rachael waved them away before turning back to her guests.

"I missed you, Sam." They were sitting close together on an elegantly covered love seat, hands clasped. All traces of his former teasing tone were gone from Duds's voice. His eyes studied Sam's face minutely. "Little sister, why are you so thin?" Real concern tinged his tone, and the beginning of anger. "Is he giving you a hard time? Or have you heard the rumors already?"

"Rumors?" Sam's throat closed with alarm, a stab of fear jabbed at her stomach. "What rumors?"

"Oh, bloody hell," Duds groaned softly. His hands tightened almost painfully on hers. "Forget I said that, love."

"What rumors, Duds?" Sam's voice had steadied, gone cold.

"Sam, don't," Duds pleaded. "It's only rumors, after all. I'm sorry. I—"

"Duds, please, tell me." Neither Sam's face, nor her tone revealed the anxiety she was feeling. "I'd rather hear it from you. I haven't talked to anyone but Aunt Rachael since I arrived yesterday and even if Aunt Rachael had heard something, she wouldn't tell me. You know all the people who are going to be here tonight. You also know there will be more than one willing to enlighten me."

Duds grimaced, but before he could say anything Sam hurried on. "Duds, help me. If I know what to expect, I can handle it."

"You're right, of course," Duds sighed, then his voice went hard, frustrated. "He has been seen, several times

the last week or so, with the same woman. A few times in
Italy and, a couple of nights ago, here."

"Here!" Sam couldn't hide her astonishment. "Morgan
is in London?"

"You didn't know?" Duds eyes sharpened on her face.
"You didn't come over to join him?"

Sam's head was shaking before he'd stopped speaking.
"No," she whispered, "I thought he was in Spain."

"Spain? Then what was he doing in Italy?"

"I don't know," Sam laughed shakily. "I know very little
of Morgan's business, Duds." She paused, telling herself
to leave it at that, but she had to ask. "Do you know who
the woman is?"

"No, love," Duds answered softly. "And neither did my
informant. Sam, I think I'd better also tell you that the
woman seemed very sure of herself and that he was being
very attentive. At least that's the story I got."

A change in the buzz of conversation at the other end
of the room caught Sam's attention and, glancing up, she
felt her breath catch painfully at her throat. As if their
speaking about him had conjured him up, Morgan stood
in the wide doorway, looking cool and relaxed and shatteringly handsome in a silver-gray hand-tailored suit that,
if possible, made his hair and eyes look even blacker.

With deadly accuracy those eyes honed in on Sam,
paused a moment on her hands tightly clasped in Duds's
before lifting to pierce hers, black fury raging in their
depths.

"Morgan, darling, you're late."

Her aunt's melodious voice reached Sam's disbelieving
ears and, shock waves rippling through her, she watched
in astonishment as Rachael hurried across the room to
him, lifted her cheek for his kiss. Did Rachael know him
too then? Apparently, for Morgan murmured something
that made her laugh, brushed a becoming tinge of pink
across her cheeks.

Somehow Sam managed to conceal the tension mounting wildly inside. Looking cool, almost remote, she fought down the urge to run as Morgan nodded an encompassing greeting to the others before sauntering across the long room to where she sat with Duds.

Duds was on his feet before Morgan was halfway to them, right hand extended, left hand still clasping Sam's.

"Hello, Morgan, it's been a long time." Duds's voice, though friendly, held a note of wariness. "I'd heard you were in town."

"Dudley." Morgan's hand gripped Duds briefly. "When did you escape from the bush?"

"A week ago," Duds smiled fleetingly. "Although I only actually arrived in London two days ago."

"I see. The day before Samantha did." His voice was smooth, his tone even, and yet Sam felt a chill freeze her spine. When he turned to her, Sam felt the full impact of his eyes. The width of the room had not deceived her as to his emotions. For all his cool demeanor, Morgan was in a towering rage. Bending slightly over her, he caught her chin in his hand, lifted her face to his.

"Hello, darling. Have a nice flight?" His silky tone sent a shiver feathering down her arms, momentarily closed her throat. "You're a little pale, Redhead," he jibed knowingly. "Still sleepy?" Before she could answer, he brushed her lips with his, then released her and turned back to Duds. "Flying always makes Samantha sleepy, you know." One arrogantly cocked eyebrow dared Duds to admit he did.

Claude's intoned, "Dinner is served," saved Duds from committing himself and he sighed with relief. Sam rose to slip her hand around the arm Morgan angled at her.

"I thought you said you had business in Spain," Samantha murmured as they followed the other guests to Rachael's elegant dining room.

"A last-minute change in plans," Morgan replied quietly. "The meeting was switched to London."

Meeting with whom? And what where you doing in Italy? The unspoken questions lit a flame that burned away her shock at seeing him and replaced it with anger.

"And I thought you said you were driving to the ranch." The soft, silky words were murmured close to her ear as Morgan held Sam's chair for her, giving a good impression of gallant solicitude.

"A last-minute change in plans." Sam's smile was saccharine.

"Morgan, you take the head of the table," Rachael commanded pleasantly, "and, Dudley, you sit there, next to Samantha."

Sam breathed a sigh of relief. Her aunt's order to Morgan prevented his retaliation, even though the glittering glance he gave her before moving to the end of the table warned that he was not going to forget this.

To Sam's amazement most of her friends were acquainted with Morgan. *How had he met them? When?* In growing confusion she listened to the easy flow of conversation, somehow managing to remain cool as she answered questions, while at the same time avoided the black, amused eyes.

"Why aren't you eating?" Duds murmured. "Has he upset you? I mean by showing up so unexpectedly?"

"Yes," Sam answered honestly. "Duds, I don't understand this at all. Everyone seems to know him. You know him. How?"

"As far as everyone else goes, I haven't the foggiest," Duds answered slowly. "I met him in Australia several years ago. Not long after I went out there, as a matter of fact. You didn't know he has interests out there?"

"Yes, of course I knew," Sam answered quickly. "But— why didn't he tell me he knew you?"

"Possibly because he didn't know of our relationship, love." He smiled reassuringly. "I haven't seen him since your marriage and there was never a reason to mention you before." Duds paused, then laughed softly. "You and I, being the awful correspondents we are, could probably have gone through three mates before the news caught up to us."

Sam's soft laughter mingled with his. It was true, she hated to write letters and she knew Duds hated it too. Glancing up, the laughter died on her lips as her glance was caught, held by two chips of black ice. Sam felt a chill creep along her spine as Morgan lifted his wineglass in a mocking salute to her. Lifting her chin, she forced herself to meet his cold stare until he sipped at his wine, then she deliberately turned her face to Duds.

"How ever did he meet Aunt Rachael?" she asked Duds quietly. "Do you know?"

"Yes, I do. She told me he presented himself to her several months ago, while he was on a business trip here in London." He paused, then his face lightened. "And that may answer your first question. Perhaps Aunt Rachael introduced him to your friends at that time."

Sam was convinced he was right. It was exactly the sort of thing her Aunt Rachael would do. But why hadn't she told her Morgan was in London? Sam sighed, thinking, *because she wanted to surprise me.* That was also exactly the sort of thing she'd do.

The seemingly endless dinner finally did end and they moved into the drawing room. Sam, her mind still reeling from the sudden appearance of both Morgan and Duds, felt a throbbing begin at her temples that very quickly grew into a full-scale hammering. The way every female in the room fawned over Morgan upset Sam even more. *And he loves every minute of it,* Sam thought furiously.

Loving him, hating him, Sam watched as Morgan, so effortlessly, set her so-called friends' hearts and imaginations on fire. His long, lean body propped indolently against the mantelpiece, white teeth flashing in his dark-skinned handsome face, his soft, lazy drawl tickled their ears and delighted their senses. Sam could feel the sensuous aura he exuded surround her as well and in desperation she fought against it. Head pounding, she riled against the circumstances that had brought her to this moment. At the same time she wanted to scream at Morgan that he had no right to amuse himself with other women while she carried his child. The fact that he was unaware of her pregnancy did not even penetrate her inflamed consciousness.

No one in the room, not even Duds, who knew her so well, was aware of the rage tearing at her mind. With an outward coolness that was almost tangible, Sam masked the pain and anger that seethed below the surface.

Longing for nothing more than two aspirins and a bed, Sam nearly groaned her relief when the door closed on the last of the guests. Turning back into the wide hall, Sam blinked and glanced around quickly. Morgan seemed to have vanished into thin air. Duds forestalled Sam's asking her aunt where Morgan had gone.

"Come have a nightcap with me, Sam. You look like you need one."

Sam followed Rachael and Duds back into the drawing room and accepted the drink she didn't want.

"I'm driving down to the house at the weekend." Duds sipped his brandy, his eyes studying Sam closely. "Why don't you two come with me? You look exhausted, pet. A few days in the country air would put some color back into your cheeks."

"I don't know, Duds," Sam murmured. "But I don't think—"

"Samantha, will you come up here, please?"

Morgan's voice, quiet and authoritative, cut across Sam's words. She stiffened at his tone, then shrugged; well, at least she now knew where he'd disappeared to. With a cool, "Excuse me," she left the room and went up the wide stairway. The pain in her head that had eased somewhat in the last few minutes began pounding away at her temples again as she walked into her bedroom.

Morgan stood in the middle of the room clad only in very brief shorts, his evening clothes tossed carelessly onto the bed. Her hand still clutching the doorknob, breath catching painfully in her throat, she watched as he stepped into a pair of brown brushed denims, drew them up his long, muscular legs and over his slim hips. After tugging the zipper closed, he glanced up, his eyes cold and remote.

"It seems I've said this so often I feel I should have a recording made to save time," he attacked, "but, anyway, I'm flying to Spain tonight. When are *you* going home?"

He sounded angry and fed up. The pain in Sam's head stabbed viciously.

"My return reservation is for Monday night."

"Cancel it." Morgan's tone was as cold as his eyes. "I'll be back Saturday. You can fly home with me."

Rebellion flared hot and fierce inside Sam. Arrogant devil, whom did he think he was speaking to, his girlfriend?

"I can't do that," she snapped icily. "I've just accepted an invitation from Duds to go down to the house for the weekend." The decision made, Sam vowed nothing Morgan said could make her change it.

"The house?" His tone was mild, much too mild.

"Duds's house, in Kent." Somehow she matched his tone. They could have been discussing the weather. "The house I grew up in." Black brows shot up in question. "Duds is my stepbrother, Morgan." Sam answered the silent question.

For some reason Sam couldn't begin to understand, the knowledge seemed to anger Morgan even more. His eyes narrowed; his voice took on a savage edge.

"Is that why he has this protective—proprietorial— attitude about you?"

His tone and words startled Sam. He sounded jealous. Morgan? Jealous? For one brief instant hope flared wildly inside Sam. It died as quickly. No, not Morgan. But Morgan had pride in abundance. She could hear his grating voice of weeks before. *You're my wife, Samantha, my woman. I don't share what's mine.* And that was it, in a nutshell, Sam thought, defeated. She was Morgan Wade's woman. His pride demanded she remain exclusively his woman until *he* decided to change the status quo.

Pain that far superseded the throbbing in her head ripped through Sam. She went hot, then cold. What about her pride? What had become of the cool, poised Samantha Denning who had effortlessly turned away from any hint of involvement with any man? And now this one man, this—this cowboy who had sold his name, dared to question her? Searing anger mingled with the pain.

"Duds is like a brother to me," she finally snapped. "His attitude has always been protective."

"How nice for you," Morgan drawled nastily. "You can tell him to relax his guard, find his own woman to protect." His voice lowered with menace. "You have a protector."

"That's going to keep you rather busy, isn't it?" Green eyes cool, Sam faced him unflinchingly. At the question in his eyes, she smiled, purred. "I hear you have a friend."

"I have many friends." His glittering black eyes held hers evenly.

"I mean a special lady friend." A flash of irritation surged through her as his lips twitched in amusement. The beast, it had taken every ounce of composure she possessed to say that calmly and he thought she was funny.

"Samantha," he drawled, "if you want to know if I've taken a mistress, why the hell don't you ask me, instead of pussyfooting around?"

Sam's stomach lurched sickeningly. Suddenly afraid, not wanting to hear him admit it, she shrugged, turned to leave the room. Closing her eyes, she lied through her teeth. "I really couldn't care less. I'm going to spend the weekend in the country. Have fun, Morgan, *wherever* you're going."

"Samantha."

Sam's hand froze in the act of turning the knob, his deadly calm tone causing her blood to run cold. She hadn't heard him move, yet his warm breath fluttered over her hair. Her breath caught in her throat when his arm slid around her waist and drew her back against his hard body. His voice, soft and caressing, made his actual words more terrifying. "If I find out he as much as touches you, I'll kill him, pseudo-brother or not."

A picture of Duds's strong face, cold and still, robbed forever of its happy grin, rose in Sam's mind. *Dear God, he means it,* she thought sickly. A shudder passed through her too-slender body and, as if he could read her mind, Morgan underlined, "I mean it, Samantha. So be a very good girl while you're enjoying the country air and I'll expect you at the ranch within two weeks. Now get out of here so I can finish dressing."

Sam fled, first the room and two days later, the city. Her weekend in the country was not altogether successful.

Duds tried repeatedly to draw her out of the self-protective shell she'd built around herself. Again and again, obviously growing more frustrated each time, he begged her to open up. He began his assault on her defenses the afternoon they arrived at the house. Rachael had retired to her room to rest before dinner while Sam and Duds strolled through the house, reacquainting themselves with the familar objects.

"Hullo! Look at this, Sam."

They were in the playroom, so named because both Sam and Duds had disparaged the word *nursery*. Sam was perched on the broad windowsill, a sad smile on her lips, paging through a much read, dog-eared book of fairy tales. Glancing up at Duds's quiet exclamation, the smile softened reminicently. Her smile was reflected on Duds's plain face as he gazed down on a scruffy rag doll.

"Carmen!"

At Sam's whispered cry he lifted his eyes to hers, his eyes growing as impish as on the day they'd christened the doll.

"Ridiculous name for such a ratty-looking thing," he teased, tossing the doll to her.

Sam caught the doll, clutched it possessively against her breasts. "But that's exactly why we gave her such an exotic name, because she was so ratty." Sam's eyes clouded over mistily. "Don't you remember, Duds?"

"Yes, love, I remember."

As he walked across the room to her, his face set in somber lines. When he stopped before her, one hand came up to smooth away a stray hair that lay over her cheek.

"Sam, my pet, you worry me." Duds's voice was low, heavily edged with concern. "You're looking almost as ratty as that doll. God, if he's hurt you—" He sighed. "Can't you tell me what the trouble is?"

"Oh, Duds, it's so good to be with you again." Sam's eyes grew wistful. "I hadn't realized how much I'd missed you until I saw you again."

"Sam, my love," he chided. "You are avoiding the question."

"I know." Sam's attempt at a laugh fell flat. "I'm a big girl now, Duds. I must solve my own problems." Jumping up, she walked quickly to the door. "Come along, big brother, we haven't seen half the house yet and Aunt Rachael will be expecting her dinner soon."

After dinner Duds declared they all needed a walk in the garden. Aunt Rachael declined, but insisted Sam join him. Even though Sam knew what was coming, she went along with him.

"Look, darling, I don't want to be a nag," Duds began the minute they'd started along the path to the rose garden. "But I can see Aunt Rachael is nearly frantic about the way you've changed. Let us help you."

"Stop badgering me, Duds," Sam scolded. "If I thought there was anything either of you could do—" She stopped, Morgan's words clear in her mind. *I'll kill him, I mean it.* Sam shook her head. "But there isn't any way you can help me."

Sam slept very little that night, tossing and turning in the canopied bed that had been hers until she was seventeen. She longed for Morgan's wide bed beneath her, and Morgan's slim frame beside her. Duds's large, beautiful house was no longer home. Even the memories of her happy childhood here seemed hazy and unreal. With a sigh of regret Sam faced the fact that there was only one place on earth that she would ever feel at home in. And that was beside Morgan, no matter where he was. And that was the one place there was no real welcome for her.

During the following two days she spent long hours in the saddle, sedately, because of her condition, following the routes she'd ridden hundreds of times as a young girl. But now the countryside she'd so loved passed by unseen. Her mind's eye, filled with the memory of a long, lean body, along with glittering black eyes and a hard, sensuous mouth, was closed to the scenery around her.

Sam managed to avoid being alone with Duds again until Sunday evening. After dinner they went into the sitting room where a cheery fire crackled invitingly. Duds kept them entertained with stories of his life in Australia and informed them he'd be going back within the month.

"I don't know quite how it happened or when," he said softly, a faraway look in his eyes. "But suddenly I knew that I wanted to spend the rest of my life there." Then to the amazement of Sam and Rachael, he added, "I'm going to sell this house. That's one of the reasons for my being here now."

It was not yet eleven when Rachael stood up and said

she was going to bed. Sam, curled up in the large chair
that had been her stepfather's favorite, slid her legs to the
floor with the intention of following her. Duds's hand on
her arm stopped her.

"Samantha, are you pregnant?" he asked bluntly as soon
as Rachael was out of hearing.

"What gave you that idea?" Sam hedged.

"Aunt Rachael." Duds eyed her seriously. "She's been
observing you closely, as I'm sure you're aware of, and she
told me this afternoon that she's convinced you are."

Sam's eyes shifted to the dying flames in the fireplace.
For a few seconds she was tempted to lie, tell Duds her
aunt was wrong. Sighing deeply, she shrugged her shoulders lightly. What was the point in denying it? Her answer
whispered through stiff lips.

"Yes."

She heard an echo of her sigh, then a muttered curse.

"That bastard."

"Duds, please." Sam's eyes swung back to his pleadingly.

"But how dare he treat you like this?" Sam had to bite
back the words that Morgan dared almost anything. "Why
isn't he with you now?" Duds's tone held indignant fury.
"He must see how frail you look."

"He doesn't care," Sam choked.

"What the bloody hell do you mean, he doesn't care?"
Duds exploded. "He doesn't care about you? He doesn't
care about his child? What?"

"He doesn't care about me," Sam whispered. "And he
doesn't know about the child."

"Doesn't know?" Duds repeated blankly, then, decisively, "Don't tell him."

"What? But I have to tell—"

"No." He cut in firmly. "You do not have to tell him
anything." He grasped her hands, held them tightly.
"Divorce him—marry me."

"Duds!" Sam's eyes flew wide in surprise. "What are

you talking about? You don't love me—at least not that way."

"No, not that way," he admitted. "But I do love you and I can't go back to Australia with you looking like this. Your eyes would haunt me." His fingers squeezed hers painfully. "Love, come with me. Let me take care of you. You and your child."

"No, Duds," Sam shook her head. "Morgan would—" She was about to say Morgan would come after them, would very likely carry out his threat. Duds's angry words cut across hers.

"Morgan would deserve to lose his child, his actions convince me of that." He frowned. "You know, I liked him. From the first day I met him, I liked him. Liked and respected." He frowned again, then shrugged. "Strange, my first impressions of people are usually correct." Again he shrugged, more strongly this time. "No matter. The hell with Wade. Come with me, Sam. I promise I'll take as much care with your baby as I did with you."

"I'm sure you would." Rising swiftly, Sam lifted her hand to caress his beloved face. "But I can't let you." When he would have protested, she slid her fingers over his lips. "Sweet, sweet Duds. Somewhere, either out in the outback or wherever, there is someone for you. You'll never find her with me and Morgan's offspring hanging around your neck. Besides, he does really have a right to know about his child. I must go back and tell him."

"And if he still doesn't care," Duds groaned around her fingers. "If he doesn't even want it. Then what? What will you do?"

"I don't know," Sam confessed tiredly. "But I can always stay with Mary. She's been very kind to me, Duds. Kinder than you'll ever know."

Not for anything would Sam ever tell Duds or her aunt the reason Morgan married her. Or Mary's offer of support on hearing the terms of her father's will.

"Sam, please." Duds's voice held real pain. "Won't you reconsider? I tell you I can't go back and leave you like this."

"Yes, darling, you can," Sam insisted. "You must. I will be all right. With or without Morgan I will be all right."

Sam only wished she felt as much conviction as her forced tone implied. Later, as she undressed for bed, she stared blankly at her trembling hands. Would it ever end? she thought despairingly. Or would the pain of loving him go on and on until all thought ceased?

Their return to London on Monday morning was made in strained silence. Rachael and Duds insisted on seeing her off and when, finally, Sam boarded the big jet, she did so with a feeling of anticlimax. What awaited her at the end of her flight? Sam was afraid even to face the question, let alone try to answer it.

Chapter Nine

Sam's drive cross-country took much longer than it should have. She stopped to stroll around whenever a city or small town appealed to her. Although it was mid-November and much of the fall foliage was gone, there were still spots where the blaze of color was breathtaking. She wandered through big stores and small shops and even bought a few pieces of heavier clothing, for the nip that had been in the air a week ago was now more of a bite. She told herself she would be a fool not to take advantage of this opportunity to see something of the country. For although she had spent a good deal of her time traveling, it had been mainly in other countries and she'd seen very little of the States. She also knew she was lying to herself. She was putting off, to the last possible minute, her meeting with Morgan.

She longed to see him and yet she was afraid. So afraid, in fact, that she had almost decided not to go at all. She was not sure she could bear to hear the words "I want a divorce."

It hadn't been an easy decision. After returning to Long Island she told herself she must think it out calmly and unemotionally, and she had. For two days she thought of nothing else. She had decided she'd divorce Morgan, stay where she was loved, have and raise her baby alone. Mary would help her. She had found herself thirty minutes later frantically packing a suitcase, asking Mary to have everything she owned shipped to the ranch, saying hasty good-byes to everyone, and jumping into the Miata telling herself grimly she was going home, whether Morgan liked it or not.

All the way across country she had argued with herself. Did she have the right to use their child and her money to hold on to a man who didn't want her? But then, Morgan had told, no, ordered, her to return to the ranch, and didn't he have the right to at least know about his child, have that child born in his own home?

She arrived at the ranch midmorning over a week after leaving Long Island. She was tired and stiff and mentally exhausted, but Sara's warm welcome helped chase some of the weariness. There was no sign of Morgan and Sam wondered if he had returned from Spain, only to leave again for someplace else.

She called Mary to let her know she had arrived safely, and then decided to call Babs. At the sound of Sam's voice Babs cried, "Sam, darling, when did you get back?" Her voice warm with affection, Sam answered, "Not much more than an hour ago. How is Benjie?"

Babs and Ben had not been able to go east for Deb's wedding, as Benjie had become ill. Now Babs laughed. "Oh! The imp's bouncing around like a kangaroo again. It turned out to be only a mild throat infection, but Sam, I just couldn't leave him."

"Of course not. How is everyone else?"

"Perfect," Babs enthused. "I'm so glad you got home in time for the party, Sam."

"What party?"

Babs's voice held a touch of exasperation. "That Morgan, didn't he leave you a message or anything?"

"Well, I don't think he knew just when I'd get here." Sam hedged. "I didn't know myself. Have you talked to Morgan?"

"Talked to him," Babs exclaimed. "He's here. Or, that is, he was here and he'll be back. He drove to Vegas to pick up a friend of ours, but he'll be back later today."

"I see," Sam said quietly.

"When are you coming down?" Babs's voice had an odd note now.

"I don't think—" Sam began.

"Well I do," Babs said firmly, then her voice grew. urgent. "Sam, I think you'd better go throw a change of clothes, a nightie, and a dinner dress into a bag, get in your car, and come down here."

"Babs."

"I mean it, Sam. I'll look for you in a few hours. Bye now." Before Sam could say another word, Babs hung up.

Oh, what now? Sam thought. *And when did Morgan get back from Spain?* Deciding to find out, she went into the kitchen and asked point blank, "Sara, when did Mr. Morgan get back?"

"Why, over a week ago, Mrs. Sam," Sara answered. "He left again yesterday morning. He didn't say where he was going, never does, but he did say he'd call and let me know when he was coming home."

"He's at the Carters'," Sam told her. "And I'll be leaving in a few minutes to join him, so please don't bother about lunch. And we will call and let you know when we'll be home." Without waiting for any questions from Sara, she left the kitchen and not much later, the house.

It was midafternoon when Sam pulled into the Carters' driveway. She was pulling her bag from the back of her car when Babs ran to meet her. "I'm glad you came," Babs panted. "I'm going to take you right to your room so we can talk." With those words Sam found herself hurried through the house to the room she had slept in eight months before.

As Sam removed her jacket, she forced a light laugh into her voice. "Now then, pet, what's the mystery?" But she grew still at the look of concern on Babs's face and her exclaimed, "Sam, are you ill? You're so thin."

"No, of course I'm not ill," Sam was quick to assure her.

"But what is it then? Something's wrong with you. Is it Morgan?" At the look on Sam's face she added, "You love him, don't you?"

"Desperately," Sam whispered, then sank tiredly onto the bed.

"But I don't understand. What's the problem?" Babs demanded.

Sam sighed. Maybe it would help to talk to someone and who better than Babs? "It's very simple, pet, he doesn't love me. In fact, he can hardly bear the sight of me."

"That I don't believe," Babs snorted. "And as for him not loving you, don't you think if you had a, well, a more normal relationship?"

"You mean, if I slept with him?" Sam asked softly.

"Well—yes."

"Oh, Babs, I've slept with him since two weeks after we were married. You know him. Can you imagine him having it any other way?"

Babs laughed ruefully. "No, as a matter of fact I can't. He's quite a man."

"Yes." It was a simple statement.

"And it still didn't jell?"

Sam shook her head briefly and Babs went on. "I don't understand it. I always thought you two were perfect for each other." Sam looked at her sharply and Babs shrugged. "All right, I admit it, I've been trying to get you two together for years. I could have cried when Morgan couldn't get here for the wedding. I had it all planned. Then when you told me about your father's will, oh, Sam, I never dreamed you'd be hurt like this."

"Well, it's no good crying over it now and besides which you haven't heard the worst yet." Sam hesitated just a moment. "I'm pregnant, Babs."

"And he's still cold to you?" Babs was incredulous. "Why Sam, Morgan loves kids."

"He doesn't know," Sam said quietly.

"Well, you must tell him at once," Babs replied sharply. Her voice hardening, Babs added, "That should take care of her highness."

"Her highness?" Sam asked blankly.

"Stacy Kemper," Babs offered. "That's how I always think of her—the mercenary bitch." She laughed at Sam's startled look. "I know that's not like me. But with this one, I really mean it. She's the reason I insisted you come down. She's also the reason Morgan drove to Vegas."

Sam's eyebrows went up in question, even though she wasn't quite sure she wanted to hear any more. "As you know," Babs explained, "we've all known each other forever. Well, Stacy was one of the group, and for a while there it looked as if she really had her hooks into Morgan. That is until it became apparent that Morgan intended putting everything back into the ranch and not on her back. She took off with and married the first man with money that asked her, without bothering to say a word to Morgan. All of a sudden she was gone. We heard about her marriage later from her very embarrassed parents. I don't know how deeply it affected Morgan, for as you know, he doesn't let anything show."

Sam nodded, but remained quiet, waiting. Babs continued, "We heard a few years later that she had divorced her husband and taken up with an Italian shoe merchant or some such and then, last night, out of the blue, she phones me and invites herself here for a visit. She said she'd heard we were having a party tomorrow night and that she'd love to come. Believe it or not, Sam, I was speechless for a minute. Well, what could I say? So, of course, I said we'd be glad to have her. Then she said ever so sweetly that as she was without transportation at the moment, could someone come to Vegas for her? And as Ben had to be away most of today on business, Morgan offered to go. And I don't like it, Sam, I don't like it at all.''

Sam didn't like it either, although she said nothing. An Italian shoe merchant—and Morgan had been seen with a woman in Italy. A coincidence? It was hardly likely. Had he brought this woman, this Stacy, back with him? That seemed much more likely. Yet he had told her to come back to the ranch. What sort of game was he playing? First Carolyn, now this Stacy person. *Damn him, damn him, damn him,* Sam's mind cried furiously. Should she leave? Not wait to suffer the humiliation of being introduced to his ex, and now current, lover? Babs made the decision for her as, jumping to her feet, she picked up Sam's jacket and bag and said firmly, ''Come with me.'' She flung the door open and marched across the hall, to fling another door open and drop Sam's things onto the bed.

Sam glanced around as she entered the room and stopped dead. Morgan's suitcase lay on a bench at the foot of the bed; his brush and comb rested on the dresser.

''Really, Babs,'' she began, only to be cut off by a very determined-sounding Babs.

''Honey, I don't know how Morgan feels about you. I don't know if he feels anything for her. Hell, I don't know how he feels about much of anything, the clam. But in my house husbands and wives sleep together, not husbands and friends.'' At the look of pain on Sam's face she added with force, ''Oh, Sam, at least make a fight of it. Don't run away.''

Sam stayed.

She spent the rest of the afternoon getting reacquainted with Benjie and an amazingly bigger Mark. Ben got home just in time for dinner. Morgan didn't. Ben seemed genuinely happy to see Sam and kept the conversation going throughout the meal.

A few hours later Sam sat curled into a chair in the living room. She had just opened her mouth to continue her description of Deb and Bryan's wedding for Babs and Ben, when she went rigid.

Babs glanced swiftly at Ben and then at Sam. They had all heard the sound of the Jaguar as it came up the drive.

Sam was well aware that Babs had filled Ben in on the situation, and she had a moment of pure panic. *I shouldn't be here,* she thought. They had all been friends in one way or other and the last thing in the world Sam wanted was to bring dissension of any kind into this obviously happy home. Before she could unfreeze herself enough to move the door opened and Morgan strode into the room followed by a woman a few years younger than himself.

Sam barely looked at the woman, for her eyes fastened on Morgan. The night was cold and he was dressed in a heavy tan sheepskin-lined jacket, collar up. Along with black leather driving gloves, boots, and the inevitable black Andalusian hat, he looked rugged and knee-weakeningly masculine. On seeing Sam he stopped in his tracks and she thought she saw an odd look on his face, but it was gone in an instant. He reached up to pull his hat off, his face expressionless, as he moved into the room, closer to her. She was glad she was sitting down, for there was no mistaking the look in those black eyes. He was angry, very angry. As he shrugged out of his jacket, he said in a voice even and smooth as silk, "Well, Samantha, when did you get home? And how did you get here?"

Sam hated when his voice took on that silky tone. Lifting her chin, she answered coolly, "I got home this morning and I drove here in my own car. It's parked in the garage. And I'm fine, thank you," she tacked on, reminding him he hadn't asked. Very slowly she turned her head to look pointedly and haughtily at the woman who had walked up to stand beside him.

She saw the corner of his mouth twitch. In what? Amusement? Annoyance? She was too busy studying the woman to figure out which. She was, without doubt, beautiful. Hair and brows as black as Morgan's with startling red lips in a perfect matte white face. Her eyes a blue so pale as to be almost colorless. But she had, Sam thought, the look of—what? The word *predator* jumped into Sam's mind.

Morgan's smooth voice drew her attention. "Samantha, this is Stacy Kemper, an old friend. Stacy, my wife."

"Hello, Samantha." Stacy's teeth flashed white. Her voice was pure honey.

Sam did not rise or extend her hand. With only a hint of a smile touching her lips, she nodded slightly and murmured frostily, "Miss Kemper."

In a capsulized instant Sam's cool, green eyes recorded the reaction of the other four. Ben's face revealed his surprise. Babs seemed to be having a great deal of trouble keeping a straight face. Stacy withdrew her hand slowly, a look of wariness in the pale blue eyes. And Morgan? Morgan's reaction baffled her. Although he had stiffened at her arrogant iciness, his black eyes, locked on hers, glittered with an emotion she couldn't quite define. He was either extremely amused or flat-out furious. But which? Sam had a sudden overwhelming urge to run for her life. Sheer willpower kept her motionless in her seat, her eyes steady on his.

After what seemed half a lifetime, but was actually only seconds, Morgan released his visual hammerlock. Turning away with a casual ease that mocked the tension his eyes had generated so easily in Sam, Morgan tossed his jacket and Stacy's coat onto a chair and grinned at Ben and Babs.

"Stacy informed me, not ten minutes ago, that she was dying for a drink." His lazy drawl shattered the stillness that had held them all motionless and galvanized Babs into action.

"Of course," she exclaimed, jumping to her feet. "What a rotten hostess I am. Ben, will you get the drinks while I hang up their coats?" As if she realized she was speaking much too fast, Babs stood stock still, looked directly at Stacy, and said slowly and distinctly, "It's been a long time, Stacy. How are you?"

Studying Stacy with an outward composure that required every ounce of willpower she possessed, Sam didn't even hear her response to Babs or, for that matter, any of the ensuing conversation until a laughing remark from Stacy penetrated her concentration.

"I suddenly just could not win." The malicious gleam of satisfaction in her pale-blue eyes contradicted the rueful pout on her lush red mouth. "The dice had gone absolutely stone cold for me." Calculating eyes flickered over Sam and the rueful pout smoothed into a smug smile "If Morgan hadn't been there to cover my losses, well, I just don't know what I'd have done."

Blind fury turned Sam's eyes into chips of green ice. Whose money had he used to cover Stacy's losses with? And how had she repaid him? By allowing him to cover her as well? The questions stabbed painfully at Sam's mind and the green ice chips swung to Morgan in accusation.

One black brow arched elegantly; he returned her stare blandly, lips twitching tauntingly.

Fed up, sick to her stomach, Sam excused herself and left the room. Morgan did not follow her.

She just made it to the bathroom. After her stomach had relieved itself of her dinner, she cleaned her face, brushed her teeth, then stood irresolutely in the middle of the bedroom, Morgan's bedroom, wondering what to do. Surely, she finally decided, Morgan had not entertained the idea of having Stacy warm his bed while he was in his best friend's home? With a shrug she slipped between the sheets. Her last conscious thought was, what would he think when he found his wife in his bed?

Sam was not to know, for she fell into a deep, exhausted sleep. She half awoke during the night, feeling chilly, and without thinking burrowed under the covers closer to the warm body beside her. She was only vaguely, if pleasantly, aware of a feeling of warmth as Morgan's arms slid around her, drew her even closer against him. She didn't remember it in the morning, but she knew he had slept beside her, as his pillow still held the impression from his head. And she sadly decided she'd dreamed the sound of his voice, almost a groan, in the night, whispering her name.

Stacy had not yet put in an appearance, Ben had finished eating and left the table, and Sam and Babs were sipping their second cups of coffee and discussing the new fall clothes, when Morgan walked lazily into the dining room. He poured himself coffee, reached across the table to pick up a piece of bacon Sam had not eaten from her plate, cocked a brow at her, and drawled sardonically, "And how did you leave your—ah—friends, Samantha?"

Sam decided she disliked this sardonic tone as much as his silky one. Looking at him coldly, she answered in kind, "With much difficulty, I assure you." Rising slowly, she turned her back to him and left the room thinking, *and so the battle is joined—again.* The next day passed smoothly enough as Sam saw little of Morgan or Stacy.

Sam was left alone to dress for the evening, as Morgan had finished dressing and left the room while she made up her face in the bathroom. She had brought with her a dress she had bought, with the coming holidays in mind, on her drive west. After slipping it on, she carefully brushed her hair, then, stepping back, viewed the results critically. The dress, of deep-green velvet, was simply cut, with close-fitting long sleeves and bodice snug to her still small waist.

The neckline plunged in a V to a point between her breasts. The full skirt came to an inch above the floor. She went over to the dresser, removed the black case, flipped the lid, picked out the emerald ring she'd removed before starting her trip, and slid it onto her finger. Then she lifted out the pendant and fastened the chain around her neck. The emerald, which rested just below the base of her throat, glowing warm and rich against her now pale gold skin, seemed to reflect the exact color of her eyes and the circle of diamonds glinted with light. Giving a quick nod of satisfaction, she left the room. She intercepted Babs in the hallway between the dining and living rooms.

"Good grief, Sam," Babs, wide eyes fastened on the emerald pendant, whispered in an awed tone. "That's the most fantastically beautiful thing I've ever seen. Did you knock over Cartier's or something?"

"That's just the half of it, pet." Laughing softly, Sam held out her hand, moved it slightly so the light got caught in the large stone on her finger.

"Wherever did you get them?" Babs breathed hoarsely.

"The ring was a birthday present," Sam replied reluctantly. "The pendant was a belated wedding gift."

"Who from, for heaven's sake?" Babs dragged her eyes from the ring, lifted them to Sam's face, and added. "An oil-rich Arab sheikh?"

"I don't know any Arab sheikh, oil rich or otherwise," Sam murmured. She hesitated, then said even more softly, "The gifts were from Morgan."

"And you, my dear peabrain, claim he doesn't care for you?" Babs's already wide eyes widened even more. "Don't you know only a man in love with his wife will buy jewelry like that for her?"

All that long evening Sam clung to Babs's words, determinedly pushing away the thought that the gems were purchased with her money.

Entering the living room, Sam came to a stop at the barrage of greetings called to her by the dozen people gathered there. Stacy, beautiful in an ice-blue sheath that gave her a deceptively fragile look, stood watchfully by the liquor cabinet, but there was no sign of Morgan. Babs laughingly joined Ben as the cry went up for a belated wedding toast and, as they refilled glasses, Sam fought a rising unease. Where was Morgan?

"We can't have a toast without the bridegroom." The protest was registered by a tiny brunette whose name escaped Sam at the moment. "Where is Morgan, anyway?"

"Right here, Karen."

The lazy drawl, so close behind her, sent a shiver down Sam's spine. The hand that curved around her waist drew her close to his side, turning the shiver to a tongue of fire.

The toast was given, then Sam felt his fingers tighten against her side as Karen chided, "Well, for heaven's sake, Morgan, kiss the bride."

Startled, Sam glanced at him quickly, saw the devil dance in his eyes as he lowered his head to hers. His lips touched hers briefly and yet even in that fleeting instant he reasserted his ownership. With a muffled gasp of shock, Sam felt the tip of his tongue, hard as the tip of a stiletto, pierce her unwilling mouth. Her eyes shot angry green sparks at him when he lifted his head.

Hating herself, hating him, Sam watched in amazement as his eyes went flat before he turned back to the guests, a deceptively relaxed smile on his face. Drawing her with him, he sauntered into the room, his tone languid as he responded to the renewed calls of congratulations.

When the well-wishing was finally over, the punishing hold on Sam's waist was removed and Morgan left her side. Moving casually, as though his only interest lay in refilling his glass, he joined a pouting Stacy, still standing sentinel by the liquor cabinet.

At any other time Sam would have enjoyed the party.

Babs, Ben, and Morgan's friends accepted her as one of their own. They had known previously of the closeness between Sam and Babs, and the fact that she was now Morgan's wife seemed to delight them. The conversation was easy, most times amusing. The food was delicious. Sam was miserable. Although Morgan was careful not to be too blatantly attentive to Stacy, the smug, self-satisfied expression her beautiful face wore dashed all the secret hopes Sam had harbored in her heart as she'd driven west. She kept up with the chatter and badinage until shortly after three and then, unable to bear any more, she excused herself and went to her room.

Within minutes she was crawling into bed, tormenting herself with the question of whether Morgan would spend what was left of the night in their room or Stacy's. But at least the torment was short-lived, for as the night before, she was asleep as soon as her head touched down on her pillow.

Chapter Ten

The sound of Morgan's voice nudged her awake. Forcing her eyes open, she dully registered two facts. He was fully dressed and was holding a steaming mug of coffee in his hand. He watched her silently as she sat up and rested her back against the headboard.

"I'm going home this morning, are you going with me?" His voice was flat and even as he handed her the mug.

Sam sipped gingerly at the hot brew before answering. "Yes." His next words turned her insides to ice.

"Good. We have some talking to do, Samantha, and I'd prefer to do it in private."

She gulped her coffee too quickly, the hot liquid making her cough and, reaching out swiftly, he plucked the mug from her hands. Watching her, he drank from the mug, then handed it back after she'd caught her breath, wiping her eyes with the back of her hand. "I can't actually go with you, I have my car."

"I remember." His voice held the tone of a parent talking to a dim-witted child. "I'll follow you in the Jag."

"All right. What time do you want to leave?"

She emptied the cup and he took it from her. "More?" She nodded as, glancing at his watch, he told her, "It's eight-thirty. I'd like to be ready to go in an hour. Marie's getting breakfast now."

Sam's voice was startled. "But we can't leave without seeing Babs and Ben."

"I have no intention of doing so," he replied patiently. "But they'll probably be up by then. Now you'd better get moving. I'll get your coffee." He walked to the door and stopped, hand on the knob, when Sam said, "Morgan, I told Sara we'd call."

"I called her last night," he answered without turning. "And told her to stay home today, take the day off, as we wanted to be alone." He opened the door and went through, closing it softly behind him.

Had his voice been mocking? she asked herself, pulling her nightgown over her head as she leaped from the bed. Deciding it was, she grabbed underwear from the dresser drawer and dashed into the bathroom and under the shower.

She walked back into the bedroom ten minutes later to find Morgan sitting in the chair by the window sipping her fresh coffee. She felt suddenly shy of him seeing her in nothing but panties and bra and turning away quickly stepped into jeans and pulled a bulky knit sweater over her head. When she turned around to face him, he handed her the mug with a twisted smile. "Breakfast is just about ready, you'd better pack." He placed her bag on the bench at the foot of the bed and flipped the lid open as Sam collected her makeup and toiletries from the bathroom. She packed the few things she'd brought with her quickly and, as she was carefully folding her green velvet dress, Morgan said softly, "That's a lovely dress, Samantha, it suits you."

Sam stood still in shocked speechlessness a moment

before answering, her voice sounding wooden to her own ears. "Thank you. I think that's everything." But she stole a glance at him as she closed the lid and was surprised to see the bleak look was quickly gone from his face.

He got her jacket and picked up her suitcase, then stood waiting at the door while she put on her boots.

As Sam left the room, she heard voices from the nursery. Telling Morgan she'd join him in a few minutes, she went in to say good-bye to the boys. She talked a few minutes with Judy, then, with a tug at her heart, gave good-bye hugs and kisses to Benjie and Mark. She left the nursery quickly and walked down the hall to the dining room noticing her suitcase sitting next to Morgan's at the front door.

Morgan was filling two plates from the covered dishes on the sideboard, so she slipped into her chair and sipped her juice. When he placed her plate in front of her she bit back the protest that rose to her lips. How in the world would she eat all that food? she thought, eyeing him warily. Nevertheless she tried.

He had finished, poured himself a second cup of coffee, and was watching her steadily, when Babs and Ben joined them.

"I see you're all set to take off after you've eaten." Babs filled her plate and sat down, saying lightly, "You weren't going without saying good-bye, were you?"

"Of course not," Sam cried.

"I'd have come in and tilted your bed," Morgan added dryly.

Ben laughed softly. "I don't doubt it a minute."

"Nor I," Babs teased, before adding seriously, "I hope it's not eight months before we see you two again. As a matter of fact, we'd like to have you for Christmas."

"Well, we'll see," Sam hedged, then nearly jumped as Babs gave her a kick under the table while turning a sweet smile on Morgan. "Do you think you could make it?"

"I don't see why not." Morgan's white teeth flashed in a grin as he answered blandly. "Let us know what time, Babs."

"I will," came the emphatic reply.

They waited until Babs and Ben had finished eating, then made their way out. As Morgan stashed their suitcases and Ben brought Sam's car from the garage, Babs whispered, "Have you told him?" Sam shook her head. "Well, do it as soon as you get home," Babs ordered. Sam hugged Babs, whispered, "I will and thanks for being my friend." Babs kissed Sam lightly on the cheek. "Always, you know that, Sam."

Sam, feeling tears too close, nodded and slid behind the wheel. Giving a quick wave, she drove out of the driveway, the Jaguar right behind her. Halfway to the ranch Sam began to resent the short distance Morgan kept between them. *As if I can't be trusted behind the wheel,* she thought peevishly, her foot pushing the pedal to the floor. The Miata shot ahead and in no time had put some distance between them. Her satisfaction was short-lived, however, as glancing in the rearview mirror, she saw the Jag gaining rapidly on her. *I should have known better,* she was thinking when the car hit an oil slick and went into a spin. Sam gripped the wheel, but going with the spin, not trying to halt it, and by some quirk of fate, the car didn't roll over. She finally managed to bring it to a stop facing in the same direction she'd been going. She was still clutching the wheel, shaking all over, when the door was flung open. "What kind of a stupid trick was that?" It was the closest thing to a shout she'd ever heard from Morgan. "You crazy woman, are you trying to kill yourself?"

It was the wrong side of enough. Sam refused to listen to this cowboy speak to her like this any longer. The engine was still idling, and forcing her shaking fingers from the wheel, Sam did two things at once. She reached out far the handle and slammed the door shut, seeing Morgan straighten in surprise as she did so, then she floored the pedal again. She kept it floored until she reached the road to the ranch property, thankful of the sparse traffic, and then only slowed down a fraction until reaching their driveway. She crawled along the driveway sedately, parked in front of the garage, jumped from the car, and ran to the back door of the house, rummaging in her bag for the kitchen door key.

Inside the kitchen she stood breathing deeply, shaking all over with reaction. Her body jerked when she heard the Jag purr to a stop in the drive and she ran from the room through the house to the bedroom. She flung her jacket and purse onto a chair and sat on the side of the bed fighting for control. *I must leave him, get away from here,* she was thinking wildly when he walked into the room in a cold fury. Wincing at the slam of the door, she repeated her thought aloud, "I'm going to leave you, Morgan, get a divorce."

His eyes glittered like two pieces of wet coal and his voice was icy.

"What kind of games are you playing? What the hell did you come back for?"

At the end of her rope, her voice rose. "I'm not playing games."

"No?" Morgan's eyes narrowed as he walked slowly toward her. "You didn't drive all the way out here just to see the scenery. Or to tell me you were going to divorce me. So let's have it."

"It doesn't matter." Sam had to fight to keep her voice even.

"What doesn't matter?" He stopped in front of her "What aren't you telling me?" At Sam's helpless shrug his tone lowered threateningly. "Tell me, Samantha."

"I'm pregnant," Sam whispered starkly.

Cold eyes in a rock-hard face raked over her. "Is it mine?"

"Oh, God," Sam's whisper held pain, anguish. "Oh, *God.*" Feeling nausea churn upward from her stomach to her throat, Sam brought one hand up to cover her mouth, moved to get up, away from his cold eyes. His hand grasped her shoulder, held her still as he sat down beside her.

"I'm sorry," Morgan grated harshly. "I had to know. When?"

"What?"

"When is the baby due?" he snapped.

"Late spring," Sam whispered. "The end of May."

"I see." He had finished his mental calculations; his deductions were only partly correct. "And you drove all the way out here just to watch my face when you told me?"

Sam's eyes widened. He really believed she'd come to lay some sort of guilt trip on him, torment him, because of his actions on the night she'd conceived. His opinion of her hurt unbearably. Blinking quickly against the hot sting in her eyes, Sam looked up at him. His face was set in hard, rigid lines; his eyes studied her coldly.

"You really hate me," she whispered brokenly, "don't you, Morgan?"

The hand gripping her shoulder tightened painfully while his other hand grasped the hair at the back of her head and forced her face close to his.

"Hate you?" he grated. "You redheaded witch, I love you."

His crushing mouth smothered her gasp of disbelief. Had he really said he loved her? Wild hope mingled with the fire surging through her veins. The smothered gasp came out as a low moan when he lifted his head.

"Morgan."

"No." His lips teased hers. "Don't talk. You can add my scalp to all the others on your belt," he groaned against her mouth. "But don't talk. Not now. It's been so long, Sam."

In between deep, hungry kisses their clothes were abandoned and then, as their hunger grew urgent, it was the two of them that gave in to their abandon. Driven to the edge of delirium by his hands, his mouth, Sam clung to Morgan, moaning softly deep in her throat, begging him to make her a part of him.

He came to her almost hesitantly, but that hesitancy was soon lost to the need to possess and be possessed. As their shudders subsided to gentle tremors, Sam's hand lightly caressed Morgan's warm, moist back.

"Don't go, Sam." The words were muffled against her hair. "These last weeks have been hell. The idea of spending the rest of my life without you is unbearable. Stay with me. Bargain with me one more time."

"Bargain?"

Morgan sighed, then the sweet weight of his body left hers and he lay beside her, his fingers lacing through hers as if he couldn't bear the thought of breaking all physical contact.

"I want my baby," Morgan said softly. "Your baby." His fingers crushed hers. "I want you. I'll match the amount that was laid on the line last March, if you'll stay with me."

"Match the amount?" Sam repeated incredulously.

"Yes," he answered flatly. "I can't give it to you in one lump sum, but I'll put one million a year, for the next five years, in an account in your name."

"But how?"

"I don't need your money, Sam. I never have," he went on in the same flat tone. "And I haven't touched it."

"But Babs said—" Sam began uncertainly, but he cut her off.

"I know what my friends think and I've let them think it. It's kept the cats away. But I was never as broke as they thought and I've made a lot of money over the last ten years. I'm a fairly rich man, Samantha, and I worked like hell for every cent of it."

Confusion kept Sam quiet for several minutes. His tight

grip on her hand was causing her ring to dig into her finger and that sparked a sudden thought.

"My jewelry and the plane and the Jag?"

"I paid for them. Your charge accounts too." His flat tone grew an edge of amusement. "That's why your lawyers wanted to see me. They couldn't understand why we hadn't drawn on the money."

"But when you bought the plane and the car you consulted me!" Sam exclaimed.

"Of course." All traces of amusement fled. "You're my wife."

"I don't understand, Morgan." Sam spoke slowly. "If you didn't need the money then why did you—"

"Marry you?" Morgan finished for her. "I wanted you," he added bluntly.

"Physically?" Sam whispered.

"Yes."

His head turned on the pillow and Sam found herself looking directly into unreadable black eyes.

"I wanted you physically," he said clearly. "From the minute I looked up and saw you framed in the doorway of Ben's living room." His eyes roamed over her face, a small fire springing to life. "I've wanted many women, Samantha, and I had most of the ones I wanted, but I had never wanted a woman on sight as badly as I wanted you." The fire leaped a little higher in his eyes. "I had to fight the urge to tear your clothes off and throw you onto the floor."

"But you seemed to dislike me," Sam gasped, the flame in his eyes igniting a similar one inside her body.

"What I disliked was the intensity of my own feelings." His free hand came up to touch her face, his long index finger traced the outline of her upper lip. "But believe me, I'd decided there and then that I'd have you. And when Ben outlined your proposition, I agreed at once. If I hadn't fallen in love with you by the time we got married

I'd have taken you a lot sooner than I did." The tip of his finger slid between her lips, brushed the edge of her teeth. "And when I did take you, it was because I could no longer control myself."

His eyes, watching the play of his finger, darkened with fresh desire. His other hand loosened, moved to caress the inside of her arm as his head moved closer to hers.

"Will you bargain one last time, Sam?" he asked huskily.

"You want to *buy* me, Morgan?" Sam murmured tremulously.

"If that's the way it must be, yes," he said bluntly. "You and our baby."

"Who was conceived in violence."

The moment the words were out, Sam wished them unsaid. Raw pain flashed in Morgan's eyes before he rolled away from her to sit up on the edge of the bed.

"Yes, who was conceived in violence," he repeated harshly, long fingers of one hand raking through his hair. Sam barely heard the whispered words that followed. "But welcomed with love."

He turned back to face her again, his hard, muscular shoulders gleaming darkly in the late afternoon sunlight slanting through the window. The golden mellow rays brought into relief the harshly defined features of his face.

"And he *will* be welcomed with love, I promise you that." His hand massaged the back of his neck and his voice grew husky again. "I've hurt you badly and I know it." He paused, his hand dropping to his side, before adding roughly, "I wanted to hurt you."

"Why, Morgan?" Sam asked softly, then wished she'd been still as she lay and watched the fire of desire explode into a blaze of fury.

"Why? Because I had been bought and paid for, that's why."

"But you just said you didn't need—"

"But you didn't know that, did you?" Morgan's harsh

voice slashed across her protest. "You wore my ring and you shared my bed and then you calmly told me you'd sleep with anyone you wanted to."

"Morgan, please," Sam cried, suddenly frightened. "I never meant it. I was lashing out in jealousy."

"Jealousy?" Morgan looked completely stunned. "Jealous of whom?"

"Carolyn." At his totally blank expression, Sam cried, "I saw you with her in the garden the night of the party. I saw you take her into your arms." The anger she'd felt that night returned to jab at her. "Did you take her with you the first time you left Long Island?"

"I did not." The denial was prompt and emphatic and held the unmistakable ring of truth. "And I did not take her into my arms in the garden. She had a few suggestions along that line but I politely declined." One black brow arched sardonically. "I figured I had enough to handle with a fiery-tempered, green-eyed redhead. The last thing I needed was a doll-faced, simpering blonde."

"And what about a white-faced, black-haired, ex-mistress of an Italian shoe merchant?" Sam shot back forgetting her nakedness as she sat up to glare at him.

"What about her?" Morgan returned easily.

"Do you deny you were with her in Italy and London?" Sam almost screamed at him. "Or that you damned near crawled all over her last night?"

The light of devilment jumping into his eyes, Morgan studied her for long moments before he dropped back onto the bed, his body shaking with laughter.

Staring at him in impotent rage, Sam was struck with two conflicting urges. The first was to slap his laughing face. The second was to caress his smooth dark skin. Trembling with anger and the longing to be in his arms, Sam snapped, "Damn you, Morgan, answer me."

With the swiftness of tightly coiled springs suddenly released, Morgan's arms shot out and his hands, grasping her shoulders, hauled her down with a jarring thud on top of him.

"No, you answer me," he demanded. "Do you love me?"

"Morgan, let me go." Sam struggled wildly, gasping softly at the sensations the feel of his hair-roughened chest against her breasts sent splintering through her body.

"Do you love me?" One hard hand released her shoulder to grip the back of her head and force her lips to within a whisper of his.

"Yes." His lips touched hers briefly. "Yes." Another touch. "Oh, yes." With a sigh Sam sought the searing brand that was his mouth.

Sam surfaced to the pearl-gray of predawn, reaching for Morgan before she opened her eyes. When her searching hands found nothing but empty sheets beside her, she opened her eyes, called his name unsteadily.

"Coming." The reassuring sound of his voice and the fragrant scent of freshly brewed coffee preceded him into the room.

Sam was sitting up, covers draped around her shoulders against the chill morning air, when he sauntered into the room, a mug of coffee in each hand.

"Good morning."

A light shiver rippled over Sam's shoulder at the husky timbre of his voice, the altogether male look of him. He was freshly showered and his taut, dark-skinned cheeks gleamed with an attractive, just-shaven sheen. Dressed in tight jeans and a finely knit, longsleeved white sweatshirt, merely looking at him did crazy things to Sam's senses.

Morgan saw her shiver and, after setting the mugs down on the nightstand beside the bed, he strode to the closet that ran the length of the far wall, pulled out a white terrycloth robe, and walked back to the bed, holding the robe for her as he would a coat.

Unsure of him still, Sam hesitated, but when one black brow went up slowly in a ark she drew a deep breath, scrambled off the bed, and slid her arms into the sleeves of the robe. As her trembling fingers pulled the belt tight, his hands tightened on her shoulders then were removed.

"Drink your coffee before it gets cold."

Turning quickly, Sam took the mug he held out to her then sank onto the side of the bed, her eyes fastened on his back as he walked to the window, stood staring through the glass, his face set in brooding lines.

His strangely cool, withdrawn attitude, following so swiftly on the heels of his hot, passionate lovemaking, sent a shaft of fear through Sam's heart. Sipping the hot brew she watched him nervously, trying to steel herself for whatever he had to say.

"Do you still want to leave me, Samantha?" He did not turn his head to look at her and Sam shivered again, this time at the flat emotionless tone of his voice. "Do you still want a divorce?"

Sam's mouth went completely dry. Was he trying to tell her he wanted her to go? After the night they'd just spent together? She considered using delaying tactics in an effort to draw him out, find out exactly what he wanted. For herself, well, she knew what she wanted but, if he wanted his freedom, her pride dictated that she should give it to him, walk away from this debacle with her head still high. Her sigh of surrender could be heard across the room more clearly than the whispered words that followed it.

"No, I don't want to leave. I don't want a divorce." Sam drew a deep breath. "I love you, Morgan. I want to stay here with you."

She couldn't see his face, but she heard his breath expelled slowly, as if he'd been holding it a long time. Then he turned to face her, his knuckles white from gripping his coffee mug.

"About Stacy," he said quietly. "I was with her in Italy and London."

Panic crawled through Sam's mind. Had he deliberately waited for her to commit herself before telling her about Stacy? She was suddenly sure she didn't want to hear any more, but before she could tell him he asked, "Who told you, Dudley?"

"Yes."

"I see." His tone was so cold Sam shivered again.

"No, Morgan, you don't." Sam stared unflinchingly into those cold, black eyes. "What I told you in London was true. Duds is like an older brother to me, nothing more. He is protective of me, he always has been. That's the only reason he told me you had been seen with her."

"I see," Morgan repeated, but in a different tone. "It seems I owe the both of you an apology for what I was thinking about your relationship." He finished his coffee and placed the mug on the wide windowsill behind him before going on calmly. "I ran into Stacy in Spain. She told me bluntly that she had had a violent argument with her shoe merchant friend and that, as he had acquired another to replace her, he was kicking her out."

"But what was she doing in Spain?" Sam asked in confusion.

"She said she was paying a last visit to some close friends," Morgan replied dryly. "When I mentioned that due to a change in business plans I was flying to London in two days, she begged me to take her with me." He shrugged carelessly. "We flew to Italy the next day. She collected some of her things and made arrangements for the rest to be sent to her parents' home here in Nevada. We flew to London the following morning."

"Did you bring her with you when you came back to the States?" Sam asked hoarsely.

"Yes," he answered flatly. "I also gave her some money. In Spain, in London, and again, two days ago, in Vegas."

Sam closed her eyes against the sudden hot sting of tears, swallowed with difficulty against the dryness in her throat. The sharpness of his tone brought her eyelids up again.

"I did not touch her. Not in any personal way. I wasn't even tempted." His lips curved in self-derision. "Even if I had been, I doubt if I'd been able to do anything about it. She doesn't have red hair."

"Morgan." A different kind of shiver slid down Sam's spine and her heart gave a wild double thump. "She seemed very sure of herself at Babs's," she said carefully. "Did you make any—promises?"

"Are you out of your beautiful red head?" Morgan grated. "I just finished telling you I can't see any other woman—" He broke off suddenly then added softly, "I wanted you to assume there was something between Stacy and me." His voice dropped to a ragged whisper. "I thought that if I couldn't get at you any other way, maybe I could hurt you through your pride." He laughed harshly in self-mockery. "You were so cool, so untouched by it all. I was sure the only one I'd managed to hurt was myself, again."

"Again?" Sam repeated. "But when—?"

"The night of the party," Morgan answered her question before she'd finished asking it. "I was so damned mad. I've been mad ever since."

"But, I—"

"Not at you," he interrupted again. "At myself."

"Why?"

"Why?" He barked. "Good God, Sam, I'd never physically harmed a woman in my life and I'd savaged you." His lips twisted in a grim mockery of a smile. "And I'd done it deliberately. I walked into that bedroom knowing I was going to hurt you in some way."

"Morgan, stop."

His smile, the harsh lines of self-disgust that edged his

face, clutched at Sam's heart. The punishment he had meted out to her was as nothing compared to the punishment he'd obviously inflicted on himself.

"You were so magnificent," Morgan went on as if he hadn't heard her. His black eyes grew warm with admiration. "You are some woman, Red, and I handled you badly." His smile turned self-derisive. "It was a new experience for me—the jealous lover. I'd never cared enough about any other woman to feel jealousy."

"Jealous?" Sam breathed, wide-eyed. "You, Morgan?"

"Funny, isn't it?" Morgan shrugged, as if uncomfortable in a too snugly fitting coat. "Want to hear something even funnier? I was scared. Deep down gut scared."

"That I find impossible to believe."

"It's true all the same." Morgan's eyes caressed her face. "The scary feeling began soon after that first night we slept together. It got worse every time I had to go away. I was so damned scared that one day I'd come home and find you'd gone." He smiled ruefully. "Last summer when you first started to lose weight I grasped at the idea you might be pregnant."

"You wanted me to be pregnant?" Sam cried in disbelief. "But I was positive you'd be angry if I was."

Morgan's head moved sharply in the negative. "I was praying you'd become pregnant. I thought—I hoped that might keep you with me." Again that rueful smile curved his lips. "Stupid, I know. But, as I said, I was running scared and willing to grasp at any straw."

Wide-eyed, stunned, Sam stared at Morgan as if at a stranger. Where was the cold-eyed, unfeeling, arrogant man she had thought she'd married? A series of scenes flashed through her mind. Morgan, Benjie clasped firmly in his arms, laughing down at Mark. Morgan, his eyes soft, his voice gentle, asking Deb to be his sister. Morgan, his eyes filled with contrition, giving her his word that he'd never hurt her again. Suddenly she knew that if this man was a stranger to her, she had no one to blame but herself. Drawing a deep breath, Sam decided to get to know this stranger better.

"Of course"—Morgan's eyes skimmed her body possessively—"I dreaded that trip to Long Island. I felt sure that once you left the ranch you'd never come back. You'd been jetting around the world all your life." He waved his hand to indicate not only the room but the whole property. "After the world, what could this place offer you?"

"You."

All the harshness drained out of his face at her whispered reply. His eyes, flaring with rekindled passion, set off tiny explosions of pure joy all through Sam's body. She shivered deliciously as he walked slowly to her.

"I love you, Sam."

Cradling her head in his hands, he tilted her head back. As he lowered his head she chided, "You said I was your woman."

"I also said you're my wife." His lips brushed hers tantalizingly. "I want you to remain my wife. Tell me you love me, Sam."

"I love you, Morgan."

His mouth touched hers, the pressure increasing as he slid his body onto the bed. His arms, closing around her, drew her body alongside his. His mouth left hers, sought the tender skin behind her ear.

"I could bear not being your wife, Morgan."

"Samantha!"

Morgan's head jerked back and his black eyes pinned hers, narrowed at the teasing light he found there.

"But I don't think I could bear not being your woman."

Sam swam the length of the pool slowly, reveling in the delicious feel of the water on her body. It was the first time she'd been able to go into the pool and the July sun had quickly pinkened her pale skin. Pulling her body through the water, Sam was grateful for her renewed energy, the strength in her arms. For so many weeks after she'd left the hospital she'd been so damnably, stupidly weak.

Movement along the side of the pool caught her eye and she turned her head to see who it was. The sight of her husband's tall form sent all thoughts of her health out of her head. Dropping her feet to the floor of the pool, Sam watched as Morgan walked to the edge of the pool and stood, hands on hips, watching her. He was incredibly dusty and incredibly sweaty and incredibly beautiful.

"Come here, Red."

Sam was galvanized into action by the soft order. When she reached the side of the pool, she raised her hands for him to help her out. Ignoring her hands, Morgan bent down and caught her firmly under the arms and lifted her out of the water as he straightened. When she stood, dripping, in front of him, his hands dropped to circle her slender waist.

"Do you have permission to go in the water?"

Morgan's eyes, searching her face, warned her she'd better have.

"Yes," Sam replied softly, knowing full well the importance of her answer. "I gave the doctor a verbal report on my condition by phone this morning," she went on to explain. "He told me I could resume swimming and all normal activities."

The pressure of his hands on her waist increased. Bending his head, he brushed his lips across hers.

"*All* activities?"

The pulse in Sam's neck fluttered wildly. "Yes." She breathed softly around her excitement-tightened throat. Taking a step nearer to him, she brought her hands up to cup his face, draw him closer. His hands held her body firmly away from his.

"Sam, stop," he groaned against her lips. "I'm filthy and sweaty."

Lightly her hands slid over his taut jaw, down his neck to the front of his cotton work shirt. Her mouth still touching his, her fingers began opening the buttons.

"What are you doing?" Morgan murmured.

"Unbuttoning your shirt."

"I *know* that," he rasped. "But why?"

"I want you to swim with me."

"Sam," Morgan groaned hoarsely. "I've got to get cleaned up."

"The chlorine in the pool will clean you," Sam said complacently, tugging the shirt from his jeans. When the shirt was free, her hands went to his belt buckle, flipped it open. When the belt hung open, she opened the snap of his jeans and caught at the zipper pull. One hand left her waist and covered her fingers, stilling their movement.

"Sara will see."

"No, she won't," Sam denied. "Both she and Jake are at home—playing grandparents." Her teeth nipped his lower lip. "We're alone till bedtime, Morgan."

She heard his sharply indrawn breath, then her hand was brushed aside. He stepped back, shrugging out of his shirt. He glanced up at her when his hands moved to complete the job she'd started on his zipper. Eyes dancing with deviltry, he teased, "Are you prepared to yank off my boots?"

"At your service, sir." Even in a bikini Sam's curtsy was graceful. "But I'd think it would be easier if you sat down."

Abandoning the jeans, Morgan dropped to the grass and lifted a very dirty booted foot. After much tugging and exaggerated grunting the boots were removed and his socks followed swiftly. Springing to his feet, Morgan released the pants zipper and stepped out of his jeans. His thumbs slid under the elastic of his enticingly form-fitting underwear, then he paused, black eyes skimming her bikini.

"The suit's got to go," he decided, laughing at her shocked face. "If I'm skinny dipping, so are you. Will you take it off," he grinned, "or will I?"

"Mor—gan," Sam pleaded.

"Either you take it off"—he took one step toward her—"or I will."

He dropped his briefs, kicked them aside, then waited, a small smile on his lips, while Sam removed the two skimpy pieces. As soon as they were gone, he held out his hand, grasped hers, and jumped into the pool.

"God that feels good," Morgan sighed when he surfaced. "How about you amusing yourself while I do a few laps, sluice the grime off my hide?"

"Be my guest," Sam waved a hand to encompass the pool. "Just don't be gone too long."

"I won't," he promised, shooting away from her.

Doing a slow sidestroke, Sam watched as Morgan's powerful arms cut cleanly through the water. After the fourth lap he came toward her. With hardly a break in motion his one arm caught her around the waist and he drew her with him to the side of the pool. Pinning her back to the smoothly painted wall, he growled, "I want my kiss."

"What kiss?" Sam asked, her eyes innocently wide.

"The kiss you've been teasing me with ever since I got home, you witch."

Planting himself firmly in front of her, he brought his mouth crashing onto hers. His lips were cool from the water and tasted slightly of chlorine. His tongue was hot and hungry. Excitement splintered through Sam's body, sending tiny, sharp shards of pleasure along her veins. Her hands moved slowly up his chest, over his shoulders, loving the feel of his cool, wet skin.

"Let's get out of here."

Moving away from her, Morgan pushed himself up and

over the edge of the pool, then turned to lift her out. She was no sooner on her feet than she was off again, swept up into Morgan's arms. Holding her tightly against his body, he strode to the house, his clothes and her bikini forgotten.

Once inside the bedroom, he kicked the door closed, dripped across the carpet, tossed her, soaking wet, onto the bed, and dropped down beside her, his mouth urgently seeking hers. Sam moaned a protest when his mouth left hers, then her face was caught, held still by his hard hands.

"Is it safe, Sam?" he grated harshly.

"Morgan, please," Sam whispered, her arms tightening around his neck, trying to bring his mouth back to her.

"Is it safe?" he demanded.

"Yes," Sam sighed, then, "Morgan?"

It was all the assurance, or plea, he needed. His hand moved, slowly, arousingly, from her face to her breasts, to her hips and back again to her breasts where they lingered, his fingers gentle, but exciting. His mouth demanded, his tongue searched, until she cried out with her need for him.

Their union, after so many weeks of abstinence, was wild and sweet and totally satisfying.

Her breathing returned to normal, and Sam lay in Morgan's arms, unmindful of the damp sheets. A soft sigh, almost a purr, escaped her lips at the delightful sensations Morgan's hand, stroking her thigh between hip and knee, created in her. Shifting his body, Morgan buried his face in the curve of her neck.

"You don't like taking those pills, do you?" he asked quietly.

"Morgan."

"Do you?" he insisted.

"No, I don't," Sam admitted reluctantly. "But it's all right, really, I—"

"Goddamnit, Sam," he grated roughly. "You should have let me have the vas—"

"No." Sam's tone was soft, but sharp with finality. "You'll change your mind some day, you'll see." She felt the movement of his forehead against her jaw as he shook his head.

"I need you, Sam," Morgan whispered close to her ear. "Not just for times like this, but all the time. I need to know you're mine, that you're here, that you're alive."

"Morgan, don't," Sam urged. "Don't talk about—"

"I must," he cut across her plea, "I must talk about it. Dear God, Sam," he groaned. "If it hadn't been for Babs and Ben, I'd have torn that hospital apart."

"Morgan, stop."

"I was so damned scared," he went on as if he hadn't heard her. "I felt that I had to get to you, help you, hold on to you to keep you from slipping away from me."

His arms jerked convulsively, crushing her to him so tightly Sam had to bite her lip to keep from crying out in pain. Her own arms held him fiercely, protectively, her hands smoothing over his tension-bunched muscles.

"I know, darling," she soothed softly when he shuddered. "I know."

I know now that this is some kind of man I married, she mused wonderingly. The gentle way he'd taken care of her through the long winter, into the spring, had amazed her. If Sara had fussed and clucked over her like a mother hen, Morgan had guarded her like a watchdog. In March, when she had cried and stormed at him that she was enormous and ugly, he had teased her out of her bad mood by declaring he liked the round, full look. And it had been such a bad winter. And he had worked such terribly long hours.

From their first meeting she'd thought he was unfeeling and hard. Over the winter she'd found out she'd been right on one count. He was hard. Hard and tough. The amount of hard, physical work he did appalled her. And as if that wasn't enough, he'd had to make several business trips. Each time he'd come home looking exhausted, and she'd found out, through Ben, by way of Babs, that he drove himself tirelessly in an effort to get home to her sooner.

The knowledge had induced feelings of guilt and she'd stared morosely at her steadily growing, increasingly clumsy body.

When she'd gone into labor four weeks before her due date, Sam had panicked, Morgan had not. Talking to her quietly to calm her down, he'd made her comfortable in the Jag and driven at his usual high speed to the hospital. It was later, Sam learned from Babs, after they realized there were problems, that Morgan began pacing like a caged animal.

She had come very close, too close, to dying and although Sam was beyond the point of caring at the time, Babs later told her that they all knew and what the news did to Morgan was terrible to watch.

His eyes, Babs had said, were frightening and on several occasions he'd actually snarled in reply to what anyone said, even Ben. His long, rangy frame had measured the room countless times before the door had opened to admit Sam's doctor. And that poor man, Babs had laughed afterwards, had looked terrified when Morgan's head had snapped around to him, his eyes narrowed dangerously, his teeth bared like a hungry dog's.

That, to Sam, was all hearsay. All she knew of those long hours was of crying out in agony for Morgan, and hanging on to life with all the will she possessed. When it was finally over, and she lay in a bed in a private room, her body spent, but her mind strangely alert, Morgan came to her.

The door opened and he stood there staring at her for long seconds. The same Morgan who was capable of endless hours of hard, physical work. The same Morgan who had promised to "drop" Jeff and would have. The same

Morgan who had threatened to kill Duds and could have. That same Morgan stood staring at her, then walked to the bed, dropped to his knees beside it, lay his head on her breast, and wept. Wept with the release of bottled-up fear, as only a man, strong in himself, can weep.

"Have you seen them?" Sam's hands, looking white and fragile, smoothed his hair.

"No." His head moved from side to side in her hands.

"Go see," she urged softly. "They were worth it."

His head jerked up, his eyes luminous, but fiery, pinned hers.

"Nothing was worth it."

"They were."

Now Sam trembled in Morgan's crushing grip. Her convalescence had been so long, how good it felt to be with him like this again. Loosening his hold, Morgan lifted his head, his eyes, sharp with concern, studying her face.

"What's the matter? Are you cold?"

"No, I'm not cold." A becoming pink tinged her cheeks. "In fact just the opposite. Oh, Morgan, I want you to make love to me again before Sara brings the boys back."

"Our boys," Morgan chided softly, an enticing smile on his lips. "Our redheaded twins," he murmured. The smile twisted. "I love them so much, Sam. And they nearly killed you getting into the world."

"But they didn't," Sam whispered, the tip of her tongue teasing the corner of his mouth. "I'm alive, I'm here, and I'm yours."

Her words were stilled by the pressure of his mouth, her tongue was caught, entwined with his. When his tough, hard body moved against, then over, hers, she moaned in surrender. His mouth left hers to seek, tantalize, the gem-hard tip of her breast and she gasped, crying, "Yes, please, Morgan, make me your woman again."

NIGHT STRIKER

For my live-in lover of thirty-three years—my husband, Marv. Thanks for all the memories, hon.

Chapter One

"Who *is* this man, Morgan?" Samantha Wade stared at her husband, a frown marring the perfection of her smooth brow. "Is he an undercover agent for the government or something like that?"

"No, darling, he is not an undercover agent or even something like that—at least not anymore." Standing by his desk, his hand grasping the telephone receiver, Morgan Wade smiled reassuringly at his wife.

"Not anymore!" Samantha exclaimed—in a very lady-like shriek. "What do you mean—not anymore?"

"Calm down, my love," Morgan soothed, a smile teasing his sharply defined lips. "As I told you. His name is Rio McCord. He and I were at Texas A&M together. Rio owns a horse ranch in West Texas. In fact, he's one of the best horsemen I've ever known." The smile on his lips grew reminiscent. "One of the best damned trackers too."

Walking to him, Samantha curled her fingers around one of his tightly muscled arms. "But, darling," she protested softly, "don't you think it would be better to leave this in the hands of the FBI and the local authorities?"

"The FBI surely," Morgan agreed—partly. "Your uncle has already notified them. But"—he shrugged—"what local authorities? We're not even certain exactly what locale they have Courtney in by now." His prominent features locked in anger. "Just because the van was spotted near the Texas border certainly doesn't prove they're actually *in* Texas."

Samantha revealed the depth of her concern by biting on her full lower lip. "I know that. That's why I don't understand why you want to involve this friend of yours. A friend, I might add, whom I've never met." Her oval nails dug into the long, hard muscle in his forearm—another indication of the tension gripping her. "I . . . I can't help feeling that you should leave it alone."

"Leave it alone!" Morgan's nostrils flared angrily. "Dammit, Sam! Until two weeks ago Courtney was a guest in this house! She is *your* cousin!"

"I know that!" Releasing her grasp on his arm, Samantha spun away to pace the braided rug on the hardwood floor, the fingers of one hand raking through the strands of mahogany-shaded hair that fell to the middle of her back. "And all I want is to have her returned safely!" As she pivoted to face him, her eyes pleaded for understanding. "Morgan, I'm terrified that these people will hurt Courtney, possibly even . . ." Samantha's voice trailed away, as if she couldn't bear putting her fears into words.

His expression softening, Morgan crossed the floor to her in three long strides. "Don't even think of it, love." He slid his arms around her slender waist and drew her trembling body close to his "We'll know more when they make their demands," he murmured into her hair, gentling her with long strokes down her spine. "Until then you must keep control of your emotions and imagination."

"I know." Breathing deeply, Samantha rubbed her face

against the smooth cotton shirt that covered his warm, muscled chest, drawing strength from the solid feel of him. "But I'm so frightened. You don't know her, Morgan." Raising her head, she gazed helplessly into his concerned eyes. "Courtney is so very much her own person. She is so very"—she shrugged—"so very arrogantly independent."

"A family trait?" Morgan inquired dryly, his dark eyes alive with teasing mockery. "I seem to remember another young, very, very arrogantly independent woman from the Tremaine-Smythe branch of the family tree."

Samantha laughed softly. "Horrible creature, wasn't I? Five years later I wonder whatever attracted you to me in the first place."

A blatantly wicked smile curving his hard lips, Morgan stepped back to gaze at her tall, elegant figure. "After all this time words shouldn't be necessary," he drawled, his smile widening at the color that washed her cheeks. "You know damn well what attracted me. Not only were you the most beautiful woman I'd ever laid eyes on," he admitted seriously, "but that same arrogance was a challenge I couldn't refuse." More than a hint of arrogance crept into *his* tone. "Come to that, I met the challenge very well— didn't I?"

Her laughter easy now, Samantha hugged him fiercely. Morgan's ploy to calm her had worked, as, indeed, *all* of the ploys he'd ever used to control her always had!

"About as well as I met yours," she concurred, arching one perfect eyebrow. "All right, darling, I'm ready to listen now." Her even tone was assurance of her renewed confidence. "Why do you feel this friend of yours can help us?"

Grasping her hand to keep her by his side, Morgan moved back to the desk as he answered her. "Two reasons," he said tersely, flipping open a leather-bound phone directory. "First, as I said, he's an expert tracker—of people as well as animals." Ignoring her soft gasp of dismay, he went on steadily. "And, second, he knows Texas, especially

West Texas. *If* they are holed up somewhere in that state, Rio is the one to find them." His tone conveyed absolute belief in his assessment.

Samantha frowned. "Why haven't I ever met this Rio, Morgan?"

"Because he very recently decided to stop wandering the world and settle down." Morgan grinned. "Rio is like quicksilver, damn near impossible to pin down. Hell, I only found out that he was back in Texas by accident!" His long forefinger moved through the *M*'s in the phone directory. "I hope he's still there."

"All right, Morgan." Samantha gave in when he lifted one black, questioning eyebrow. "Do whatever you think is best."

Morgan was lifting the receiver before she'd finished speaking.

Stark terror choking her, Courtney Tremaine-Smythe slowly emerged from the drug-induced sleep. Her temples were throbbing, her throat was parched, her nerves were frayed, and every muscle in her body was screaming a protest against the rough treatment that had been inflicted upon her for the last countless number of hours. In fact, the only relief during those horrendous hours had come when she'd finally been removed from the back of that bouncing van. And Courtney only vaguely remembered that!

Her mind still fuzzy from the drug, Courtney strained her eyes as she moved her head carefully. The exercise was useless; the darkness was complete. Swallowing in an effort to relieve the dryness in her throat, she tentatively jerked at the bindings securing her wrists. The leather bonds merely cut more deeply into her tender skin. Sighing in defeat, Courtney relaxed as much as was physically possible against the lumpy surface on which she was so awkwardly lying. If only she knew where she was, and why.

As the effects of the tranquilizing drug wore off, Courtney attempted to keep herself from falling completely apart by replaying the sequence of events of the previous hours over again in her fear-rattled mind.

It had begun with that phone call—which, of course, had been a trap, as Courtney now knew full well. . . .

On her own for the day, and happy to be so, the British socialite had gone to the brightly decorated restaurant in the Las Vegas hotel for an early lunch. Vacationing with her father, Courtney was enjoying the exciting resort. Male heads turned as she made her way across the dining room. Her tall, slender body, long blond hair, and classic features added up to aristocratic good looks. Unaware of the gentlemen's gazes, she ordered a lobster salad for lunch.

Having finished her salad, she was sipping a fresh cup of tea when the waiter brought a phone to her table. Frowning at the instrument, wondering who in the world would be calling her in Las Vegas, and why, she lifted the receiver and spoke into it briskly.

"Courtney Tremaine-Smythe here."

"Miss Smythe, this is Don Carleson." The unfamiliar, edgy-sounding voice deepened her frown; she didn't know a Don Carleson! "The golf pro out at the club," the man added with clarifying swiftness.

A shiver of apprehension slid down Courtney's spine; her father had gone out to the club to play golf hours earlier.

"Yes?" she responded in a clipped tone that masked her sudden uneasiness.

"I'm sorry I have to be the one to tell you this," the man said apologetically, "But I'm afraid your father has had a heart attack." At her soft, involuntary gasp, he hurried on. "He was stricken on the course a little while ago."

The apprehension coalesced into a tight knot of fear.

"Where is he?" Courtney's cool tone reflected her control and breeding.

"He's been taken to a private hospital not far from the club." There was a brief pause, as if the man were short of breath. "The ambulance left here just a moment ago. I ran right into the pro shop to place this call as they drove away."

"I appreciate your consideration, Mr. Carleson." Though her voice held steady, Courtney's fingernails slashed into the palm of her free hand. "Would you direct me to the hospital, please?"

"Yes, of course." Slowly, distinctly, he told her the name and exact location of the private hospital, ending with: "I'm sure you'll have no difficulty finding it."

After scrawling her name and room number at the bottom of the check the waiter presented to her, Courtney scooped up her bag and hurried from the restaurant and through the hotel lobby.

As she pushed through the wide plate-glass entrance doors a taxicab shot in front of several others that were in line to pick up passengers, and came to a screeching halt inches away from the hotel doorman.

Frowning his displeasure at the breach of professional etiquette by the eager cabdriver, the uniformed doorman then turned to Courtney, smoothing his face into a polite smile.

"Cab, miss?" he asked respectfully.

"Yes, thank you." Sliding a bill into the man's hand, she stepped into the cab, instructing the driver where to go as the door closed beside her.

"I know where it is, lady," the driver assured her as soon as he'd heard the name of the hospital. "I'll have you there in no time flat."

Expecting something of a wild ride, Courtney was vaguely surprised when he drove the vehicle well within the speed limit. It wasn't until much later that she realized that her driver had no intention of being stopped for an infraction of highway safety laws.

The ride lasted well over a half hour and they had long since left the city limits behind before the driver turned the cab onto a private road. Riddled with concern for her father, Courtney glanced repeatedly at the diamond-encrusted watch encircling her slim wrist.

"Is it much farther?" she asked impatiently, glancing around at the desolate desert terrain.

"No, miss. We'll be there in a few minutes," the driver assured her tersely.

Too worried about her father to notice the nervous edge to the driver's tone, Courtney closed her eyes, breathing deeply to calm herself for whatever she'd have to face on arrival at the hospital. When the cab came to a sudden, jarring stop, she opened her eyes, expecting to see the clean lines of a small hospital. The sight that met her shocked gaze was a very ordinary looking, rather battered blue van and three men as nondescript as the tired-looking vehicle.

"Why have you stopped?" Courtney demanded imperiously.

Ignoring her question the driver pushed his door open. At the same instant the door beside Courtney was flung open.

"Out, lady." The harsh order came from the man holding on to the door.

"I certainly will not get out!" Courtney exclaimed, an altogether different type of fear rising in her throat. What did these men want? she wondered wildly. Money? God! Were they modern-day highway robbers? Infusing a coolness she was far from feeling into her voice, Courtney raised her chin haughtily. "I have very little money with me, if that's what you're after!" she lied coldly.

The man laughed nastily. "Wrong on both counts, lady." Leaning into the car he caught Courtney's arm in a bruising grip. "You most certainly *will* get out," he snarled, pulling her off the seat as he backed away. "And we're after a hell of a lot of money." With a final, brutal tug he yanked her from the car.

The moment her feet were steady on the sandy ground, Courtney began to struggle against the man's painful hold on her arm. "Let go of me at once!" she cried through the fear swelling in her throat. "I must get to the hospital! My father is very ill!"

With the help of the other men Courtney's struggles were swiftly subdued. Dragging her gleaming patent leather shoes in the yellow dirt, cursing and screaming all the way, she was forcibly moved to the back of the van. She twisted and fought frantically as the back panel doors were wrenched open. Rough hands brought her struggles to an end and a grimy hand was clamped over her mouth, sealing her protests inside her head.

"If it's any consolation, lady," one of the men growled at her ear, "your old man is probably having a drink with his golfing buddies in the club bar right this minute." As he finished speaking, he grasped her around the waist and literally tossed her into the back of the van.

The breath was knocked out of Courtney's chest as she landed on the metal floor of the vehicle. A frightened moan burst through her lips along with the expelled breath as her forehead scraped the rough metal. Before she could regain her breath, her arms were yanked behind her back and her wrists tied securely. Seconds later her ankles received the same rough treatment.

"You—you can't get away with this!" Courtney panted, kicking out with her tightly bound feet and receiving a measure of satisfaction on hearing a curse when the spike heel of her shoe scraped against a body. But her satisfaction was short lived; she was struck across the face for her trouble.

"You bitch!" The man who'd forced her from the car

yelled close to her face. Courtney cringed at the rank odor of onions on his breath. "If you even try anything like that again, I'll—"

"Shut up and give her the injection!" a new voice ordered coldly from outside the van.

Sheer terror welled inside Courtney. "An injection!" she yelped. "Don't you dare inject me with anything!"

Hard hands grasped her around the hips, and Courtney began to wriggle wildly in an effort to get away.

"Get on with it, dammit!" the cold-voiced man snapped. "I want to get the hell out of here."

Though Courtney fought against it, cursing in an unlady-like, violent way, all her efforts were in vain. The needle was plunged into her soft skin, and moments later she was plunged into oblivion.

The lucid moments Courtney had after that all contained a nightmarish quality.

Now, lying exhausted on a lumpy surface she assumed was some sort of bed, Courtney concentrated on remembering those brief moments of awareness.

She had awakened from the drug slowly, disoriented and wondering where she was and why she was so very uncomfortable. Memory had rushed back as her mind cleared. Slowly opening her eyes, Courtney had glanced around cautiously.

A man, obviously asleep, judging from the tenor of his loud snores, sat hunched against the door panels at the back of the van. By raising her eyes to the two small windows in the panels, Courtney could tell it was just about dusk outside. When she shifted her eyes to the front of the van, her gaze encountered two more even smaller windows, beyond which were outlined two heads, that of the driver and the man in the passenger seat beside him.

Who were these men and where were they taking her? Courtney wondered dazedly, blinking her eyes in an effort to clear her mind. Then, beginning to feel the strain on her shoulder muscles, she eased herself into a sitting position. Balancing awkwardly with the sway of the rapidly moving vehicle, she groaned aloud as she tumbled sideways into the metal side panels.

"Look alive, Ben!" The order came from the driver. "Our guest is awake."

As he straightened from his hunched position against the rear panels, the man the driver had called Ben stared at Courtney with calculating, beady eyes.

Biting her lip to contain the shudder of revulsion his avid stare produced, Courtney averted her eyes from his.

How long she sat there, her lips compressed, her body shuddering as it absorbed the jolts and bumps of the swaying van, Courtney hadn't the vaguest idea—it seemed to go on forever. Fear was a constant, a living entity that throbbed throughout her being. Speculation was her steadfast companion.

Where were they? Where were they taking her? What would they do to her when, if ever, they arrived at their final destination? The questions haunted Courtney through that wild ride, and through the hours of the night. She didn't consider asking them what they wanted. Although she had no idea of the terms, she knew she'd been kidnapped and would be held for ransom. Courtney didn't doubt that her father would meet their demands, whatever they were. The question was: Would they allow her to live after he'd met them?

She was cold: deep down cold, in her bones and in her mind. Shivering, Courtney huddled beneath the thin, scratchy blanket covering her. Fully alert now, she was struck by the realization that she'd been stripped of everything but her flimsy panties and lacy bra.

Damn them. Damn them. Damn them. Courtney's outraged mind condemned her abductors. Hadn't she been humiliated enough by being tossed around in that van and subjected to drug-induced sleep? Had they really thought it necessary to strip her of her clothing as well as her dignity?

All concept of time had deserted her. Although it seemed she'd bounced from floor to side panels for days, it had probably been no more than a few hours, perhaps less. Tired, frightened, and beginning to feel vaguely sick to her stomach, Courtney braced her aching shoulders against the side of the van and rested her head on the shuddering metal. Closing her eyes in an attempt to escape the unreality of her situation, she began to float in the nether world between wakefulness and sleep. Then all hell seemed to break loose.

There was a loud bang, followed by the wild lurching of the van. Courtney was thrown from one side of the vehicle to the other. Stunned but not unconscious, she lay listening to the driver spew out a string of obscenities as he brought the careening van to a quaking stop. Compressing her lips to contain the bile rising in her mouth, she closed her eyes as a storm of angry voices swirled around her.

"God damn it!" the cold-voiced driver cursed, "I thought you said all the tires were new!"

"They were! They are!" beady-eyed Ben shouted back. "You musta run over somethin' that slashed one of them!"

"We damned near bought the highway that time!" As the voice was a new one, Courtney assumed it was from the man in the passenger seat. "God! What were you doin', eighty-five?"

"Shut up and get out," Cold Voice snarled. "We gotta change the damned thing."

Courtney heard the sound of the two doors being angrily flung open; then Cold Voice called back, "Stifle the broad, Ben."

Keeping her eyes closed, Courtney concentrated on breathing evenly. Tension tautened her spine; she heard

Ben scramble to her side and felt his moist breath feather her cheek.

"She's out cold," he shouted. "I think she rapped her head when the tire blew."

"She's not dead, is she?" Fear edged the tone of the cold-voiced man.

"Naw," Ben yelled. "She's breathing okay."

"You just keep an eye on her," Cold Voice directed from the front of the van.

Intent on her ruse of appearing unconscious, Courtney forced her tight muscles to relax. Lying in a limp heap, she felt the body of the van lift as the jack handle was cranked to the accompaniment of grunting curses. Then a new element of horror was added to the ongoing nightmare as she felt a hand slide along her thigh.

Biting down hard on her tongue to keep from crying out in revulsion, Courtney cringed inside as the hand moved over her hip and up her ribcage.

"So pretty, and so rich," Ben muttered thickly. "And I bet those legs only spread for rich men too."

Her flesh shrinking from his touch, Courtney endured the disgusting feel of his hands on her body until she felt his fingers groping for her breasts. A moment before she would have betrayed her supposed unconsciousness by flinging herself away from him, the unmistakable sound of a stopping vehicle startled him into snatching his hand away.

"Damned truckers!"

Even as Ben cursed Courtney recognized the grinding and wheezing of a semi being brought to a halt.

"You guys need some help?"

As Courtney had not heard the sound of a door being opened, she assumed the trucker had called the offer from inside the cab of the truck. She was slowly drawing breath into her lungs when Cold Voice responded.

"No, we've just about got it. Thanks anyway."

Her nerves humming with tension, she released the hoarded breath in a pleading rush.

"Wait! Help me, plea—"

A sweaty hand was clamped over her mouth and a snarling voice hissed close to her ear.

"I'll strangle you, you stupid bitch!"

Her eyes wide, panic beating a mad tattoo in her pulse, hope and fear running in equal measure through her mind, Courtney strained to hear the masculine exchange outside.

"What the hell was that?" The trucker's voice held both amazement and suspicion.

"Nothin' important," the cold-voiced man replied in a surprisingly indulgent tone. "My old lady's sleeping in the back." His tone hinted at a shrug. "She gets nightmares."

Willing the trucker to ignore the excuse and investigate, Courtney sagged in defeat when she caught his uncertain response.

"Well, if you're sure . . . ?"

"Hey, fellah." Cold Voice actually laughed. "I've been married to her for over ten years. That's about as sure as I want to get!"

Hope shriveled and died inside Courtney when the trucker returned the laughter.

"I know what you mean. I got an old lady with some strange habits too. Ten four, buddy."

Everything inside Courtney went cold as she listened to the truck lumber back onto the highway. Would they kill her now? Terror ballooned in her mind. Dear God! Would they kill her and toss her body in some ditch alongside the road?

No. No, a tiny voice of logic argued. *If they kill you, they won't be able to collect the ransom.* Hanging on to that last glimmer of reason, she stared up at the man bending over her in threatening silence until she heard the other two men return to the cab of the van.

"That damned bitch nearly ruined everything!" Cold Voice snapped as he slammed the door. "Knock her out again, Ben."

Even though Courtney knew she should feel relieved at having escaped retaliatory punishment, she didn't. For all her cool sophistication, she abhorred the use of drugs to the point of obsession.

Once again she had struggled like a wild thing against the sleep-inducing injection. And, as before, she lost the struggle.

Now, many hours later, deprived of her clothing, Courtney huddled beneath the poor excuse for a blanket, waiting for the light of day, yet fearing what morning might bring.

Rio McCord was standing by the corral, his whipcord-lean body propped indolently against the railed fence, when the old Jeep came barreling into the yard, a plume of tan dust swirling in its wake.

Lids narrowed over brown eyes so dark they appeared black, he observed, from under the concealing brim of the well-worn black Stetson that was pulled low on his forehead, the man and woman who stepped from the Jeep and began walking toward him.

Lord, that is one gorgeous woman! Rio mused, deciding that everything he'd heard about Morgan's wife had been an understatement. Most men would likely forfeit half their remaining years on earth for one night in bed with that tall, strikingly beautiful redhead.

Most men perhaps, but not all men, and certainly not Rio McCord. Rio was very definitely *unlike* most men. In his opinion there wasn't a woman alive worth half of *his* remaining years.

The speculative thoughts inside Rio's mind were not revealed in his shuttered eyes or on his thin, harshly etched face. Rio had learned at an early age to guard his thoughts more greedily than everything else.

As Morgan and Samantha Wade came to a stop before him, Rio lazily eased himself away from the corral fence, straightening to his full height of six feet one inch. Lifting two fingers to the brim of his hat, he nodded respectfully at the woman, then shifted his dark eyes to stare levelly into Wade's even darker pair.

"Morgan." Extending his hand, Rio registered the startled expression that sprang into Samantha's face. The reaction to his voice seldom varied, yet it still amused Rio. One woman had claimed his voice sounded as if it came out of a throat filled with jagged-edged stones.

"Rio," Morgan murmured, returning the brief, firm handshake. Sliding his left arm around his wife's waist, he continued, "Sam, meet Rio McCord. Rio, my wife, Samantha."

"Mr. McCord." Sam smiled easily, thrusting out her slim right hand. As Rio slid his callused palm over hers, she said, quite seriously, "So, you're Night Striker."

The surprise that rippled through Rio's body was not betrayed by as much as the flicker of an eyelash.

"So I've been called," he grated softly. "Morgan's been talking, has he?" One black, neatly arched brow rose quizzically. "What did he tell you about me?"

"Very little, actually." Sam laughed softly. "And I must admit I had to badger that out of him." Her laughter ceased abruptly. "Courtney is my cousin, Mr. McCord."

"The name's Rio, Sam, and I understand." Releasing her hand, he glanced at Morgan. "Come into the house and tell me everything you know."

Rio led the way to the Spanish-style ranch house and first entered the walled patio through an archway, his boot heels clacking sharply on the flagstone flooring. Passing through another archway, he strode into the cool interior of the house, removing his hat as he called, "Maria, coffee for three in the sala, please."

Rio led them across a wide, hardwood-floored entrance foyer and down two steps to a large, square living room. The room was comfortably elegant, Spanish-Mexican in decor, with splashes of brilliant, jewellike colors relieving the somber, intricately carved hardwood furniture. A huge natural-stone fireplace took up most of the far wall.

"Make yourselves comfortable," he invited with the absent wave of one broad hand. After Morgan and Sam were seated side by side on the ornate sofa, he stretched his length on the matching chair opposite them and fixed a calm gaze on Morgan's face.

"Okay, let's hear it."

"The woman's name is Courtney Tremaine-Smythe," Morgan said quietly. "Her father, Charles, is Samantha's late mother's brother."

"Money?" Rio inserted.

"Of course." Morgan shrugged. "Old money, new money, and a lot of money in between."

"Go on," Rio drawled.

"She left the hotel in Vegas sometime around noon yesterday, directly after receiving a phone call. The call's a dead end. It went through the hotel switchboard, she took it in one of the restaurants. The hotel doorman was the last person to see her; he put her into a cab but did not hear what address she gave to the driver."

"FBI, local authorities?" Rio shot the question at him.

"Charles called them immediately," Morgan replied, "even though the contact gave the standard warning against doing so."

"Where did they get the make on the van?" Rio continued, "and how?"

"Through a flat tire, of all things." Morgan smiled faintly. "A trucker saw the disabled vehicle and stopped to offer assistance. The men working on the tire told him they had everything under control. He was about to pull out again when he heard a woman scream for help. When he questioned it, one of the men told him his wife was sleeping in the back and that she was prone to nightmares."

"It's possible." Rio shrugged.

"Sure," Morgan agreed, shrugging as well. "At any rate, the trucker wasn't about to argue, not with two men outside the van and who knows how many more inside. But he was suspicious."

"So he got the hell out of there," Rio guessed correctly.

"Right." Morgan nodded. "As soon as he got into a more heavily traveled area, he got on the CB and notified the authorities."

"And the van was heading for Texas." Rio sighed.

Morgan smiled. "Actually, it was already *in* Texas. The trucker placed it right over the state line." Raising his hand, he ran long fingers through his jet-black hair. "Rio, I've got a gut feeling that Courtney was the woman who screamed for help, and I believe the kidnappers are holed up right here in your bailiwick."

Reclining lazily, his overall appearance indicating sublime disinterest, Rio gazed at Morgan expressionlessly. Slowly, he shifted his gaze from Morgan to Sam, who had remained silent through Morgan's briefing.

"Your uncle's British?"

"Yes."

"Of *the* influential Tremaine-Smythe family?"

Sam smiled. "Yes."

Rio's unrevealing gaze sliced back to Morgan. "Are there political overtones here?" Before Morgan could respond, he added sharply, "As in the possibility of some international repercussions?"

"No." Morgan's reply was prompt and decisive. "This is not the work of some terrorist group trying to gain political leverage. As a matter of fact, the experts theorize that this is the brainstorm of rank amateurs.'' His sigh was short on patience and long on disgust. ''From what they've pieced together, they've concluded that this was a spur-of-the-moment snatch—the entire plan was so goddamned simple!''

''But effective,'' Rio retorted. ''And the motive was . . .''

''Good old-fashioned greed,'' Morgan finished for him.

''A demand has been made?'' Rio grated.

''They want three million dollars . . . in cash of course.''

''Who doesn't?'' Rio's lips tilted up at the corners in the closest he'd come to a smile since entering the house. He regarded Morgan for several seconds, then shook his head slowly.

''You've got the Federal Bureau of Investigation,'' he said in that soft, not unattractive, gravelly voice. ''And you've got state and local authorities. What do you want with me?''

Morgan's smile was both chiding and dry. ''You know damned well what I want. I want to hire the legendary skills of the man known in *un*known circles as the Night Striker.''

Chapter Two

Fear, like the night, blanketed everything. Panic clawing at her throat, Courtney shivered, her senses straining for the slightest sound, the faintest flicker of light.

Nothing. Nothing. And then, intensifying her shivers into bone-shaking shudders, came the mournful cry of an unidentified animal. Her throat working spasmodically, her teeth digging relentlessly into her bottom lip, Courtney cringed into the lumpy mattress.

Dear Lord, would morning never come?

Terror tightened her chest, stiffened her limbs; Courtney was fighting a losing battle against choking sobs. Now, here, under the cloying blanket of darkness, she could allow herself the release of tears. Morning would come, as it always did, and with it her abductors.

Courtney's memory of the three men was sketchy. Eyes tightly closed in concentration, she conjured an image of the men as she'd first seen them.

Everything had happened too quickly for any lasting impressions. Courtney vaguely remembered the one man who'd sat up front and said little, as average in every way; average height, average weight, average face. Then there was the driver with the cold voice—that one she instinctively knew was the most dangerous of the three. Cold Voice was rather small, and wiry, with detached, dead-looking eyes set in a ferretlike face. But it was the third man Courtney was most frightened of; the man the others had called Ben. Ben with the overweight, lumbering body and avid, beady eyes terrified Courtney at a basic level. She knew if he was set free of all restraint, Ben would rape her. The knowledge of the threat Ben posed to her body chilled Courtney's blood.

First light was heralded by the twittering and rustling of small wildlife. Calmer now, Courtney lay listening to the sounds that preceded morning in unpopulated areas. The noises were not unfamiliar to her. She had grown up on a country estate, had accompanied her father on several photo-safaris. She was versed on the predawn murmurings of the wild.

As Courtney catalogued the morning arguments of the birds and the scurrying of tiny rodent feet, the complete blackness receded before creeping gray, which in turn dissipated into pearlescent pink. Surrounding features emerged from shadowy forms into solid objects.

Resentfully grateful to whoever had rearranged her bound wrists from back to front, Courtney shifted position on what she could now see was a narrow cot. Struggling to sit up, she shivered in the cool dawn air when the threadbare blanket slithered off her shoulders and onto her lap. Her eyes now clear of the blurring effects of the tranquilizing injections, Courtney examined her immediate surroundings.

The room was small and boxlike, measuring no more than eight feet by eight feet. The cot she lay on was shoved into one corner of the room, head-end below and to the left of a small, paper-shaded window. The shade was old, and torn, and thick with years of accumulated grime, which explained the absence of moonlight during the long night.

The furnishings in the room consisted of the cot, one straight-backed chair, and a chest of drawers that looked like it had been old when it came over on the *Mayflower*. In the opposite corner from the cot sat a paint-blistered, boxlike contraption with a hole cut out of the top surface. A delicate shudder washed over Courtney as she recognized what it was—an out-of-date, rickety-looking commode.

Wrinkling her nose, Courtney ran her gaze over the two door frames set into joining walls, the one opposite the cot, and the one facing it. The badly hung, warped doors were tightly closed. One of the doors, the one facing her, had an old-fashioned lock plate beneath the curved metal latch.

By simple deduction Courtney concluded that the lockable door led to the outside, and the other connected to another room in the structure. There was no way she could determine the size of the building, but by the fact of its crude construction, she surmised it to be quite small.

In contrast to the animal activity outside all was quiet inside. Not for an instant did Courtney entertain the optimistic idea that she'd been dropped off and abandoned. Those men who had forced her into the van—had it been the day before?—were around somewhere, probably still asleep. And, for all she knew, their numbers had increased.

What were their plans for her? The question created goose bumps on Courtney's shoulders and arms. Grasping the blanket with fingers numbed by the tight bindings on her wrists, she drew it up as she slid down on the cot, seeking warmth and rest. When her hands were level with her breasts a choking gasp broke through her compressed lips.

Her ring! Eyes wide, Courtney stared at her naked left hand. Her engagement ring was gone! Her gaze slid from her finger to her wrist; her watch was there! Lifting her arms awkwardly, she brushed her fingers over her earlobes; the diamond stud earrings were in place. Had her ring slipped off her finger during the scuffle when she'd fought against being loaded like so much baggage into the van? She frowned. Or had one of those men removed it while she lay unconscious?

The mere thought of being touched, even briefly, caused a sick, burning sensation in Courtney's stomach. Why take the ring and not the watch and earrings? It hurt to even think, but still, the questions persisted in teasing her mind.

Where was her handbag?

Fully aware she had not missed a thing in her initial perusal of the room, Courtney nonetheless sent her gaze over the area a second time. There were no signs of her clothes or handbag.

In addition to traveler's checks she'd had over four hundred dollars in cash in her purse. Was the money gone as well? Courtney felt positive that it was. So then, why leave the watch and earrings? Odd. Certainly, the ring was of much greater value than the other pieces, but the stones in them were flawless and worth quite a bit.

Very odd indeed!

Conscious of the ring's loss now, Courtney tentatively moved her fingers, her feelings mixed. She had grown used to the weight of the three-carat gemstone. The emotions that should have been attached to the symbol were simply not there. Courtney was not in love with the man who'd placed the ring on her finger seven months previously.

Her delicate eyebrows drew together above her aristocratically straight nose as she stared broodingly at her naked finger. Had Phillip been notified of her disappearance? she wondered. Was he, perhaps, en route to the States at this very minute? An image of her fiancé, frantic with worry, distracted her if only momentarily from the very real danger of her present predicament.

Dear Phillip. Courtney sighed. Dear, dear Phillip, so doggedly attentive, so very single-minded in his pursuit of her, and so obviously upset and alarmed at their last meeting before she'd left England for the States.

Memory swelled of their last meeting, crowding all other considerations from Courtney's consciousness. It was a self-defensive mechanism, of course, a means of temporary escape from a reality too frightening to contemplate. Courtney grasped at the mechanism in silent desperation.

The meeting had taken place in the elegantly decorated morning room in her father's equally elegant house in Berkeley Square.

"Darling, you can't mean it!" His slender, impeccably attired body quivering with tension, Phillip leapt from his chair.

Courtney's smile conveyed compassion and sadness. "But I do mean it, my dear." The endearment had not been used as a sop to his sensitive male ego; Courtney genuinely liked Phillip Barrington. "I don't love you in that way, Phillip." Removing the diamond-and-platinum ring he'd given her at Christmas, she held it out to him.

"Dammit, Courtney!" Phillip exclaimed. "I thought we'd resolved that particular bone of contention!" Crossing to where she sat, he caught her hand in his. "You haven't met someone else? Some man for whom you do feel *that* way?"

"No, I haven't, but—" Courtney began impatiently.

"Well, then," Phillip interrupted forcefully, plucking the ring from her hand and sliding it onto her finger again. "I'm afraid I don't quite understand what this is all about, darling." Being very careful of his trousers, he knelt down before her. "I knew you were not in love with me when you accepted my ring, didn't I?" he murmured chidingly.

"Yes, of course, but—"

"Darling, nothing's changed," Phillip again interposed. "We've known each other forever, and what's more, we like each other." He arched light-brown brows. "Hmmm?"

Courtney had no choice but to smile and nod her agreement.

"All right, then, there you have it!" Phillip's own smile was utterly charming. "Love will come after we're married," he said persuasively. His argument and tone were the same as when he'd finally talked her into accepting the engagement over half a year before. "And you know the parents want it, don't you?"

As there was no denying that truth, Courtney nodded again.

"Then what is this all about, my sweet?" Rising gingerly, Phillip went back to the chair he'd been occupying when Courtney announced her intention of breaking their engagement. After meticulously straightening the crease in his trousers, he frowned questioningly at her.

"Oh! I don't know!" Now it was Courtney who jumped up to pace the floor. "I'm restless and"—she lifted her shoulders in an eloquent shrug—"and rather bitchy, I suppose." Raising a long-fingered, slender hand, she smoothed the gleaming mass of pale blond hair that fell well below her shoulders. "I thought that if I broke it off," she went on in a level tone, "I'd be freeing you to have a look around for a better deal." Courtney didn't bother to add that she'd feel easier about the whole thing also.

"But, darling, I don't want a better deal!" Phillip protested. "I'm quite happy with the status quo." Easing to his feet he intercepted her as she retraced her pacing steps across the Aubusson carpet. "As long as you drop me a postcard now and then from points of interest, I'll be perfectly fine while you're on holiday in the States with your father." Smiling benignly, he drew her into an undemanding embrace.

Closing her eyes, Courtney sighed.

* * *

As she shifted on the lumpy mattress, Courtney's chest expanded and contracted in memory. Then, suddenly alert and very much in the present, she inhaled again, deeply, her mouth watering with the scent she'd detected.

Coffee! Courtney's nose twitched and her stomach rumbled. Suddenly famished, she drew in a deep breath, savoring the aroma of—oh, heavens—not only coffee, but bacon as well!

How long had it been since she'd eaten? Salivating, Courtney wriggled her body into an upright position. She clasped the blanket to her chest, her nose twitching again. Oh, God, toasting bread! Her stomach issued a low growl and she waited in hungry anticipation. Were her captors planning to feed her?

The query chilled her. What if no one came with food for her? But surely they would not starve her? Or would they? Courtney moistened her lips. The action made her acutely aware of a growing thirst. A sudden pressure in the lower half of her body made her uncomfortably aware of another bodily function needing attention.

Courtney's glance sliced to the decrepit contraption in the corner. Ugh! A delicate shudder rippled the length of her spine. The . . . the thing didn't look too clean. Still . . . Courtney shrugged—the need definitely *was* there! Now, how to get someone's attention. Lifting her chin regally, she opened her mouth and yelled.

"Help!"

A moment later the door was flung open and beady-eyed Ben came lumbering in, Ferret Face at his heels. Both men stopped dead at the sight of her sitting calmly in the bed, the threadbare blanket held primly to her determinedly set chin.

"What the hell's all the yelling about?" Ferret Face

demanded, his sharp-eyed gaze ricocheting off the four walls. Beady Eyes merely stood there, looking stupid.

"I'm hungry," Courtney announced succinctly. "And I need to use the facilities."

"You're going to need medical attention if you yell like that again," Ferret Face snarled, moving toward her menacingly.

Though she cringed inside, Courtney raised her chin higher in defiance; she'd be damned if she'd show these men how frightened she was! "I'm not being deliberately difficult!" she snapped—if a trifle weakly. "The situation is growing desperate!" She squirmed uneasily to give added proof.

His eyes narrowing on her wriggling form, Ferret Face came to a halt. "Ben, escort our guest to the—ah—facilities." A sneering smile revealed uneven teeth as he observed the horror filling Courtney's face.

"Your coffee, señor."

Rio smiled his thanks to the soft-spoken woman, then returned his attention to the man sitting across the kitchen table from him.

"You're positive it was them?" he asked in his raspy voice, eying the small, wiry man intently.

"Yeah, the stupid sons of—" the man broke off, shooting an apologetic glance at the placid housekeeper. "They left the end of the van sticking out of the lean-to." He blew noisily on his steaming coffee. "The trail leads into the hills."

"Figures." Rio grunted. "All right. Bring the Jeep and Hot Foot around in about fifteen minutes. I'll take off as soon as I've finished eating."

"Right." The wiry man nodded, gulped the last of his coffee, then, scraping his chair back, got quickly to his feet. He was at the kitchen door when he paused to glance back at his boss. "Ah, Rio, what about Tracker?"

"What about him?" Rio cocked one uneven eyebrow at his ranch foreman.

"He's gettin' a mite restless." Cleat Jamison grinned. "I think he's tired of being confined to sick bay."

Rio frowned. "The leg?"

"Good as new," Cleat assured him.

"All right, I'll take him along." A wry smile played over Rio's thin lips. "He's come in handy a time or two."

Fifteen minutes later Rio walked out of the ranch house and into the chill Texas predawn. His torso was covered in a faded blue cotton shirt. His narrow hips and long legs were encased in well-worn Western-cut jeans. His tan boots were scuffed and dusty. His Stetson had seen better days — much better days. He was wearing the typical uniform of the working cowboy, with one important addition. Riding low on his hips was a gun belt, the holster anchored to his taut thigh by a knotted thong. Nestled in the holster was a lethal-looking, long-barreled pistol.

A low whine greeted Rio's emergence from the house. With an easy, loping gait, he walked to where Cleat stood beside the Jeep, horse reins in one gloved hand, a dog's lead in the other.

"Ready to ramble, are you?" Rio murmured, reaching out with one leather-gloved hand to caress the narrow head of the quivering Doberman at the end of the lead.

The dog was large, for a Doberman, and sleek, its black hide gleaming in the defused light from the kitchen. At his master's touch another low whine trembled from his salivating jaws. Though he didn't lift one paw from the tan earth, his body moved with the excitement rippling through him.

"I think you have your answer," Cleat observed dryly, stepping away from the Jeep. Bending, he disconnected the lead from the dog's collar. "In, Tracker," he ordered mildly.

With a fluid bound Tracker's body left the earth, then landed dead center in the front passenger seat.

"How does he do that?" Cleat marveled, not for the first time.

Rio chuckled softly. "Beats the hell out of me." He laughed as he got into the Jeep and slid behind the steering wheel. "But I think he's demonstrated the soundness of that leg quite effectively," he drawled. "Don't you?"

"Yeah." Nodding, Cleat tied the horses' reins to the back of the Jeep. "He's too damned smart for an animal by half," he muttered, backing away from the vehicle. "You know where you're goin' now?" Cleat asked.

Rio paused in the act of turning the key in the ignition to cock his head and level a dry look at his foreman.

"Your directions were very concise," he chided mockingly. "If I get lost, I'll send up a smoke signal." The smile that curved his lips as Cleat turned beet-red could only have been described as wicked.

Before shifting around to the front again, Rio slowly ran a narrow-eyed glance over his horse, Hot Foot, dancing behind the motionless Jeep. The beautiful animal stood at least fifteen hands high. Rio knew that Hot Foot, hand picked and hand trained, would respond immediately to his command in the same fiercely loyal way that Tracker would.

Rio trailed his gaze from Hot Foot to the back bench seat in the Jeep, his glance encompassing the bedroll propped against his own saddle and the rifle lying under the bedroll. His perusal of gear completed, he shifted position and started the engine.

"Might as well get comfortable, ole buddy," Rio advised the avidly panting dog. "We've got a long ride before going to work."

As if he understood his master perfectly, Tracker circled

the seat, then curled his slender body into a ball on the worn leather.

"Good hunting," Cleat called as Rio set the Jeep into motion.

"Thanks." Rio tugged the Stetson lower on his forehead.

With the trotting horse in mind, Rio teased the gas pedal with his booted foot, all his concentration centered on the bumpy, dusty, unpaved road. He hesitated briefly when he came to the intersection of his own and the county owned road. He paused, then drove under his SHADOW C RANCH sign that marked the entrance to his property.

Though he accelerated slightly after pulling onto the secondary road, the ride became smoother on the macadam and required less of Rio's attention. Controlling the Jeep with casual expertise, he mused on his direction and his own crews' investigative work in pinpointing the location.

Rio had dispersed the four separate crews the previous afternoon, after accepting Morgan Wade's request for help in finding his wife's kidnapped cousin. One of the teams had scoured the area from the air with the ranch helicopter. Two others had set off in four-wheel-drive vehicles. Cleat and two other men had gone out on horseback. All had communication devices.

The helicopter crew had spotted the van. The pilot had relayed the location to the driver of one of the Jeeps, who, in turn, had alerted Cleat—who just happened to be closest to the designated area.

On investigation Cleat had observed the van from a discreet distance. As reported, the van had been driven into the ramshackle lean-to attached to an equally decrepit abandoned ranch house situated in a fold of the mountain foothills. The kidnappers had literally taken to the hills. Darkness was already settling in by the time Cleat confirmed the make of the van so any attempt at scouting out a trail had to be put off till morning.

Morning was now sending tentative shades of pink into the eastern horizon as Rio tooled the Jeep in the direction of the ranch he knew well as the Henderson property.

Sadistic bastard!

Trembling with the rage searing her body, Courtney clutched the blanket to her breasts and screamed curses at both men while refusing to move.

The man was an absolute sicko, she fumed, and she wasn't going to allow his foul mind to derive amusement from humiliating her this way.

Ferret Face's twisted form of early-morning fun and games was over, because Courtney's screams showed him that she insisted on privacy while seeing to her body's hygiene. She'd been screaming since Ben had actually put his grimy hands on her to 'escort' her to the commode, and now the boss issued his order in that chillingly cold voice.

"Enough, Ben. Cut her bonds and get her some hot water." That sneering smile tugged at his lips at Ben's grunt of disappointment. "We don't want to soil the merchandise, do we?" Arms crossed over his narrow chest, he stood watching her implacably while Ben carried out his order. After Ben returned to the room with a basin of steaming water and a towel, and set both on the rough surface of the rickety chest of drawers, he motioned Ben out of the room again with a jerk of his head. Before following Ben, he favored Courtney with another of his sneering smiles.

"You have exactly ten minutes to wash up before 'Hot-to-Trot' there brings your breakfast. Better rustle your rump, honey." Chuckling in what Courtney thought was a decidedly evil way, he strolled from the room.

Shivering in her panties and bra in the morning chill, Courtney performed the fastest sponge bath of her life.

Take 4 FREE Books!

Zebra created its convenient Home Subscription Service so
you'll be sure to get the hottest new romances delivered
each month right to your doorstep — usually before they
are available in book stores. Just to show you how
convenient Zebra Home Subscription Service is, we would
like to send you 4 Zebra Historical Romances as a FREE
gift. You receive a gift worth up to $24.96 — absolutely
FREE. There's no extra charge for shipping and handling.
There's no obligation to buy anything - ever!

Save Even More with Free Home Delivery!

Accept your FREE gift and each month we'll deliver 4 brand
new titles as soon as they are published. They'll be yours
to examine FREE for 10 days. Then if you decide to keep
the books, you'll pay the preferred subscriber's price of just
$4.20 per title. That's $16.80 for all 4 books for a savings
of up to 32% off the publisher's price! What's more…$16.80
is your total price…there is no additional charge for the
convenience of home delivery. Remember, you are under no
obligation to buy any of these books at any time! If you are
not delighted with them, simply return them and owe
nothing. But if you enjoy Zebra Historical Romances as
much as we think you will, pay the special preferred
subscriber rate of only $16.80 each month and save over
$8.00 off the bookstore price!

We have 4 FREE BOOKS for you as
your introduction to
KENSINGTON CHOICE!

To get your FREE BOOKS,
worth up to $24.96, mail the card below.
or call TOLL-FREE 1-888-345-BOOK

Take 4 Zebra Historical Romances FREE!

MAIL TO: ZEBRA HOME SUBSCRIPTION SERVICE, INC.
120 BRIGHTON ROAD, P.O. BOX 5214,
CLIFTON, NEW JERSEY 07015-5214

YES! Please send me my 4 FREE ZEBRA HISTORICAL ROMANCES (without obligation to purchase other books). Unless you hear from me after I receive my 4 FREE BOOKS, you may send me 4 new novels – as soon as they are published – to preview each month FREE for 10 days. If I am not satisfied, I may return them and owe nothing. Otherwise, I will pay the money-saving preferred subscriber's price of just $4.20 each... a total of $16.80. That's a savings of over $8.00 each month and there is no additional charge for shipping and handling. I may return any shipment within 10 days and owe nothing, and I may cancel any time I wish. In any case the 4 FREE books will be mine to keep.

Name _____

Address _____ Apt No _____

City _____ State _____ Zip _____

Telephone ( ) _____

Signature _____
(If under 18, parent or guardian must sign)

Terms, offer, and price subject to change. Orders subject to acceptance.

4 FREE

Zebra Historical Romances are waiting for you to claim them!

(worth up to $24.96)

See details inside....

KENSINGTON CHOICE
Zebra Home Subscription Service, Inc.
120 Brighton Road
P.O.Box 5214
Clifton, NJ 07015-5214

Being careful of the red welts inflicted on her wrists by the leather cords she'd been bound with, she scooped water into her cupped hands and splashed it over her face, moistening her lips and mouth with the hot water.

Even though her watch had stopped sometime during the night, she was certain no more than six or seven minutes could have elapsed when Ben came lumbering back into the room, bearing a tray of food and a leering grin.

Feeling every bit as exposed as if she were completely naked, Courtney dived for the cot and the concealment of the threadbare blanket.

"Have you ever heard of knocking?" she snapped icily, glaring at him.

"Why bother?" Ben's beady eyes crawled over her form outlined clearly under the thin covering. At the evidence of a shudder she couldn't repress, his grin widened. "I've seen it all before," he said thickly. "I undressed you." He laughed as Courtney blanched. "Got a few good feels in while I was doing it too," he continued tauntingly, lumbering to where she now crouched on the cot. "You're the first woman I ever touched whose skin felt like silk."

Courtney had the sensation that tiny bugs were cavorting under her skin. In an instant's flashback of memory she could feel his hand roving her body during the minutes she'd pretended she was unconscious in the van. Knowing he had touched her again while removing her clothes created an empty, sick feeling in her mind and stomach.

"You had no right to touch me!" Courtney exclaimed fiercely, hate blazing from her glittering blue eyes.

"Sez who?" Ben retorted smugly. Holding the tray of food just out of her reach, he licked his lips and taunted, "I'll let you have this food for another feel."

"Go to hell, you bloody swine!" Courtney spat, drawing her legs protectively to her chin. "I'll starve first!" As he began moving closer to the cot, she warned, "I'll scratch your eyes out if you touch me again!"

Ben's beady eyes actually seemed to light up with anticipation. "You want to fight, huh?" he jibed hopefully. "I
like when a woman fights me, it gets me all kinds of
excited."

Disgust and fear ran in relays along Courtney's nerves.
Eying him warily, she watched as he headed for the chest
of drawers to free his hands of the tray. "Don't you dare!"
she croaked—her throat had gone suddenly dry. His only
response was a frightening laugh. A coldly snapped order
from the doorway wiped the look from his face and the
laughter from his lips.

"Let her the hell alone, Ben." There was an edge to
the words that stopped Ben in his tracks. "The food's
getting cold, give it to her and then get out of here."
Confident that he would be obeyed, Ferret Face turned
away from the doorway.

"You're not going anywhere," Ben said in a tone pitched
for her ears only. "I'll get a feel, more than one." He
lowered the tray to the foot of the cot. As he straightened,
he smiled in a way that sent an icy chill down Courtney's
back. "I'll get more than a feel. We're gonna have us a
real wrestling match." Chuckling nastily he shuffled out
of the room.

Oh, dear God. Motionless with dread Courtney stared at
his retreating back. A violent shudder ripped through her
trembling body. What was she going to do? Her mind
racing in circles, she sent her gaze on a frantic search
around the room for a means of escape.

Inching stealthily from the cot, she tested the window.
It was not only locked but nailed shut as well. Dragging
the thin blanket with her like a toga, she crept to the other
door in the room. That also was securely locked. A fine
film of perspiration sheened her body as she crept back
to the cot. Her stomach lurched as her gaze collided with
the food on the tray.

There were two pieces of unbuttered toast, now cold.

On a paper plate lay three strips of undercooked bacon, the edges thick with congealed fat. There was a chipped earthenware mug of coffee as black and thick as tar. Swallowing bile, Courtney drew the tray closer to her; she had to eat to keep up her strength—which she felt positive she was sorely going to need.

Courtney was longing for a cup of hot tea; with a grimace she sipped at the rancid coffee. If nothing else, the brew was wet and quenched her now raging thirst. How long had it been since she'd had anything to eat or drink? she wondered, gingerly picking up the greasy bacon strips and hiding them from view between the two slices of toast.

In between chewing each bite methodically and washing the mess down with swallows of cold coffee, Courtney recalled what had happened the day before. She now had a flashing memory of surfacing from the drug to the realization of being tied to the back of a mule. Even in her groggy state of mind she'd been aware of the intensity of the heat and her own raging thirst. She recalled crying out for water, and then the sweet coolness of liquid trickling down her throat. A reflexive shudder moved her body as she felt again the plunge of the hated needle that sent her tumbling back into oblivion.

Fortified by the food, Courtney pushed the tray to the foot of the cot and stared defiantly at the partially open door to the other room. She was trapped and she knew it. There would be no escape. Her only hope was that her abductors would release her after her father had met their demands, but even that hope held only a very dim glimmer. She could identify and describe in detail every one of her abductors, including the man who'd driven the cab.

As the summer sun rose in the eastern sky, bright rays pierced the grimy windowpanes, flooding the small, airless room with stifling heat. Wrapped in the blanket, crouched at the head of the narrow cot, Courtney stared fixedly at the doorway.

Intellectually, she knew her chances of ever being released were slim. Even if she were released, Courtney didn't allow herself the luxury of believing she'd be set free in the same mental and physical condition she'd been in when she'd entered that cab.

Through the four-inch opening between the door and warped frame, she could hear the men talking in the other room. Although their voices were too low for Courtney to make out more than a word here and there, she knew they were discussing her. The knowledge increased the tremors quaking through her slender body.

The unpleasant sound of Ben's laughter wafted into the room, reinforcing the decision Courtney had reached while eating.

The unhealthy glow deep in Ben's eyes as he'd taunted her before leaving her to eat, convinced Courtney of his determination to possess her physically—and soon. Not for one minute did she delude herself. When he took her, Ben would be brutal.

Swallowing the brackish coppery taste of fear, Courtney shuddered outside while resolution set into concrete in her mind.

She would die rather than suffer that man's invasion of her body.

By the time the sun was high enough and warm enough to scorch his skin through the soft material of his shirt, Rio had been in the hills for well over an hour.

He had not been on the road long before he'd deserted the macadam to shoot across country, cutting his actual traveling time almost in half. After his arrival at the Henderson property, which was literally falling down, Rio had ascertained within minutes that it was completely deserted; the van and its driver were gone. Not many minutes more and very little of his tracking ability were required for Rio to pick up the kidnappers' trail into the hills.

Sitting easily in the well-worn saddle, Rio held the reins loosely in one hand, allowing Hot Foot to pick his way delicately as he bore his rider up the uneven terrain. Tracker, his pointed ears at attention, trotted tirelessly by the side of the horse.

"Morgan was right, old friend," Rio confided to the bright-eyed dog.

Tracker tilted his sleek head to gaze adoringly up at Rio, jaws opening slightly as he panted, for all the world giving the impression that he was grinning in agreement. Rio grinned back.

"These clowns *are* rank amateurs," he continued softly. "A first-year Cub Scout would have little trouble following this trail." A derisive smile played over his thin lips. "Or in reading it either."

Rio himself had read the signs at once. Five animals had entered the hills from the back of the Henderson property: three horses and two mules. If the woman was astride one of the horses, that meant two men and two pack animals. On the other hand . . . Rio opted for the other hand. If he was reading the signs correctly—and he invariably did—that meant there were three men on horseback, and two pack animals, one of them packing supplies, the other packing a hostage.

Though he'd kept his own speculations to himself while questioning Morgan Wade the previous afternoon, the possibility that the kidnappers had crossed the border into Mexico had occurred to Rio. Now he strongly doubted it. They were close, Rio could feel it in his bones . . . and though he'd often wondered where these intuitions of his came from, Rio never questioned them anymore.

An hour later Rio's shirt was clinging damply to his back and Tracker was panting for real. Leaning forward in the saddle, he ran his palm over Hot Foot's sweaty coat. The animal trembled in response to the caress.

"We'll rest soon," he murmured, positive in his own mind that he could follow through on the promise.

Following a trail that looked as if it had been made by a stampeding herd of buffalo required very little of Rio's concentration, so he amused himself by thinking about his friend Morgan's wife.

Samantha. Rio rolled the name around in his mind. Beautiful—the name and the woman. A sardonic smile teased his lips. A cool, controlled man could happily kill for the right to call such a woman his.

Tracker cocked his head at the soft chuckle that whispered from the throat of his master. Catching the dog's action from the corner of his eye, Rio chuckled again.

"Of course, you do realize that if I had serious designs on that ravishing creature, I'd have to knock off Morgan to carry them out?" he asked the eager-eyed animal solemnly. "And knocking old Morg off would be no minor accomplishment." A shadow of a smile twitched his lips. "Not impossible, mind you, but a long way from minor." Tracker's head swiveled around when Rio chuckled again. "Lucky for Morgan that I don't have designs on his woman. Knocking him off would put a hell of a strain on our friendship." A frown drew his dark eyebrows together. All Samantha had told him by way of a description was that Courtney was tall, slender, and blond. "I wonder what the cousin looks like?" he said reflectively.

God, if my skin looks as bad as it feels, I very likely resemble a harridan by now, Courtney thought despairingly as she drew her palm down one cheek. Though her skin was wet with perspiration, drawn from every pore by the intense heat in the closed-off room, it still felt gritty. *What it needs,* she wailed mutely, *is a drink of moisturizer.*

She slid her fingers into her hair, grimacing at the feel of the lank strands. She could do with a brush as well! Dropping her hand to the cot, she wriggled uncomfortably under the now heavy-feeling, scratchy blanket. If the covering had failed miserably to keep her warm during the night, it was making up for the omission now! Still, the threat of bodily injury or death wouldn't have made her relinquish the threadbare protection.

Sighing, Courtney fought the leaden pull of her eyelids. The heat was making her extremely sleepy, and she longed for the blessed relief of oblivion. Stark terror kept her from seeking escape in sleep.

Since serving her breakfast, and warning, Ben had come into the room twice to torment her. The first time he'd come on orders from the cold-voiced, ferret-faced man, who was obviously the head kidnapper, to rebind her wrists and ankles. Ben had taken full advantage of his assignment by running his filthy hands over her arms and shoulders after he'd secured her wrist bindings, and stroking the length of her legs after he'd fastened the leather cords to her ankles.

The second time Ben entered the room, Courtney wriggled into as tight a ball as humanly possible, glaring her hatred and loathing for him out of fiery blue eyes. He was carrying a metal cup of water in one bearlike hand.

"The boss says it's time for your midmorning tea, your highness," he taunted, lumbering to the side of the cot. "Can't have you dry up and blow away from us, can we?"

The water had a brackish, mineral taste. Courtney gulped it down greedily, longing for more when the cup was empty. As she'd lowered the cup from her lips, Ben had grasped her by the hair to hold her steady and, swooping like a bird of prey, fastened his thick lips onto hers.

Gagging, Courtney had twisted her body violently, raising her bound wrist to hit him with the cup. All her resistance had earned her was the degrading action of his fleshy hand clutching at her body through the thin blanket. She was spared further debasement by a shout from the other room.

"Hey, Ben, Dub says you're to get out here and help with the damned animals!"

As the voice was only vaguely familiar to Courtney, she had to assume it belonged to the man she thought of as average, and that "Dub" was the given name of Ferret Face. Regardless, she was thankful for the call, whomever it came from, for it freed her of the obviously aroused Ben. Muttering a string of obscenities, Ben shuffled heavily out of the room.

Courtney kept her eyes open, fighting sleep by replaying the two nerve-shattering scenes over and over in her mind.

"Well, well, look at what we've got here," Rio murmured to himself, sitting statue still on the back of the heaving horse. Eyes narrowed, he scanned the crude two-room cabin that was nestled in the bush slightly beyond a small, narrow canyon. The place appeared deserted but the bray of a mule betrayed its occupancy.

From his concealed observation point Rio studied the lay of the land carefully, imprinting every rock, bush, and cranny on his memory. Then, his reconnaissance complete, he withdrew to the far end of the canyon. Selecting a spot safe from detection, Rio dismounted and prepared to wait out the daylight.

After the animals were cared for, and watered at a small pool formed from a trickle of water that ran over the rocks, he opened the bedroll, ate the cold beef sandwich and crisp apple his housekeeper had packed for him, sipped appreciatively at the tepid coffee, and stretched out.

Less than thirty minutes later, the rifle by his side, the holstered pistol within reach of his hand, and Tracker curled up on his other side, Rio tilted his Stetson forward to cover his eyes, and promptly fell asleep.

For Courtney, simply surviving the noon meal was an ordeal she never wanted to repeat.

The ritual of the morning—release wrist and ankle bindings, use disgusting receptacle, wash hands and face, eat revolting food—was carried out to the letter. The only difference was that this time Dub didn't bother tormenting her with the threat of surveillance during her toilette. Ben was dispatched immediately after he'd removed her bonds; the "average" man brought the food tray to her.

It was after she'd finished eating the garbage Dub had called a sandwich that the horror began all over again. The horror entered the airless room under the guise of the lumbering Ben.

Even applying all the considerable self-control Courtney possessed, she could not contain the shudder that shivered through her at the sight of his thick, leering lips and gleaming, avid eyes. The visual evidence of her revulsion drew a snicker from his throat.

"You're afraid of me," he muttered, halting near where she cowered at the head of the cot. "That's good, I like that." Bending awkwardly, he grabbed her by the hair, jerking her upright painfully. His thick, wet lips peeled back to reveal small, yellowed teeth. "Tonight," he whispered on a heavy breath, "after the others are asleep, we're gonna get it on."

Fear vied with fury in Courtney s mind and fury won. Ignoring the sharp pain it caused, she shook her head violently. "If you don't let me go, I'll scream for Dub!" she warned in a dry squeak.

"Dub, is it?" Ben snarled, yanking her head back to expose her arched throat. "When the time comes, I can take care of Dub!" Bending lower, he fastened his open lips on her vulnerable neck. "I can't wait to get at you!" he mumbled against her cringing skin an instant before he sank his teeth into it.

Arching her body frantically, Courtney bucked like a horse gone berserk. Nausea rose to burn in her chest, nearly choking the scream that burst from her throat.

"No! No! Get away from me!" When Ben's dirty hand grasped one breast, she shouted shrilly, "I can't stand it! Somebody please help me!"

There was the pounding of feet against the plank floor, then a command: "Dammit, Ben, I told you to let her alone!"

Courtney kept the wracking sobs at bay until Ben had left the room and Dub had angrily pulled the door closed behind the both of them. Then, burying her face in the smelly, lumpy mattress, she surrendered to the hot tears and shattering chills that tore through her body.

By God, if I get the opportunity, I'll kill him, I swear it! Courtney repeated the vow over and over again like a litany.

"Phillip, will you please sit down! Pacing the room will not get her back any faster." Charles Tremain-Smythe frowned at the young man circling the spacious sitting room in the opulent hotel suite.

"I know that, but I feel so bloody useless!" Phillip Barrington came to a halt at the wide window that overlooked the swimming pool fourteen floors below. Slanted rays from the glaring afternoon sunshine struck sparks off the stone set into the ring he held between his thumb and forefinger. "Shouldn't we have heard something by now?" The face he turned to the older, calmer man was scored with lines of strain. He had not slept since leaving London the previous afternoon.

"I'm positive we'll hear any and all news immediately the authorities find her," Charles replied soothingly. Rising from his chair with unstudied elegance, he crossed the room to the window. "That is, unless this Rio McCord finds her first." A brief smile touched his lips, easing the austerity of his aristocratic face.

"Who is this Rio McCord? What do you know of him?" Phillip questioned suspiciously, his frown darkening into a scowl.

"I know nothing of him," Charles answered candidly. "But Morgan not only trusts the man implicitly, he has a great deal of faith in the man's ability to find people. And"—he held up a detaining hand when Phillip would have spoken—"*I* have a great deal of faith in Morgan."

"That may well be," the younger man murmured sourly. "I for one think you'd do well to put your faith in the authorities." As the beginnings of a frown drew Charles's brows together, Phillip forestalled an argument by continuing, "I hope, since you've agreed to the kidnappers' demands, they'll release Courtney as soon as they get their money."

"I hope the same." Charles sighed. "Yet I'm not encouraged that they will."

At dusk a built-in alarm went off in Rio's head. He came fully awake at once, alert to his surroundings and the slightest of rustling noises. By the time darkness had shaded the hills from deep purple to near black, he was ready to move. Hot Foot was saddled, the bedroll was tied in place, the gun belt was buckled securely around Rio's narrow hips, soft moccasins had replaced the scuffed slanted-heeled boots.

"Time to go to work, boy. The key word is *quiet.*"

Tracker pricked his ears at the soft command; then, quivering with readiness, he followed his master as he silently blended into the night.

Employing all the expertise he'd acquired in Asia and

South America, Rio approached the cabin with the silent stealth that had earned him the nickname "Night Striker" from his covert contemporaries. Shaking his head in disbelief at finding the entrance door to the cabin wide open, he knelt beside Tracker.

"Stay." Rio covered the dog's bony head with his palm as he whispered the command. "Wait." He was gliding away again as Tracker's bottom made contact with the ground.

Reconnoitering, Rio circled the cabin, coming up to the far end of a crudely-knocked-together, three-sided structure that housed the animals.

At the first uneasy movement by one of the animals he slipped silently inside the manger, murmuring in a shaman's chant, soothing and settling them before they had time to become alarmed.

There were five animals in the crude manger, three horses and two mules—exactly as he'd figured. That meant there were three men to contend with. Pleased with the odds, Rio was smiling grimly when he heard the murmur of conversation from beyond the far end of the structure. Whispering past the last two animals, he came to a noiseless halt at the rough board wall.

"What do you think Ben's doing in there?" a slurred voice wondered aloud.

"Huh!" The snort came from another equally slurred but cold voice. "I know damn well what he's doing. If I know Ben, by now he's got his fat hands all over that high-class dame's body."

"Lordy, she's somethin', ain't she?" The first voice slurred away to a sigh. "But don't you think we ought to get Ben off her?"

"Hell, yes!" The one with the cold voice agreed. "And we're gonna too." There was a pause and a gurgling sound. "Just as soon as we finish this bottle." There was another pause, and a different sound to the gurgle, and then the voice heated up on a string of curses. "What the hell do you think you're doin'? You jerk! Go into the trees to do that!"

There was a whining mumble, then the shuffle of booted feet stumbling drunkenly over the uneven ground. The smile on Rio's lips turned feral as he melted back into the darkness; the animals didn't make a nicker of protest as he whispered by them. Slipping around the end of the manger, he followed the direction the kidnapper had taken into the trees.

Rio came silently up behind the man as he was zipping up his pants. A moment later the inept kidnapper dropped like a stone to the pine-needle-cushioned ground, felled by the stiffened edge of Rio's chopping hand.

Using the tape he'd slid into his pocket earlier, Rio securely bound the unconscious man's wrists and ankles. Not many minutes later he was performing an instant replay on the other man. Then, his lips twisting with disdain, he quietly saddled one of the horses and led it to the front of the cabin. Kneeling once more beside the quivering dog, he slipped the reins between Tracker's powerful jaws.

"Hang on to the leather, boy, and stay put."

Even as he issued the soft order, Rio was blending into the darkness of the open doorway. The brief exchange he'd overheard by the lean-to had given him an inkling of what he'd find inside. Every muscle in his body tensing, Rio cursed to himself in several languages in a bid to keep his mind clear of conjecture.

Tension humming along her nerves and tautening her muscles into painful knots, Courtney crouched on the cot staring wide-eyed at the closed door. The evening meal had passed without incident, despite the fact that the food offered had been every bit as revolting as the preceding two meals. Fortunately for her sanity the cold-voiced Dub had stood guard outside the bedroom door throughout the reenactment of the morning and noontime ritual.

But full darkness had now settled on the land, and revived terror stalked through Courtney's mind with the memory of Ben's muttered threat.

"Tonight, after the others are asleep, we're gonna get it on."

Courtney's midriff ached from the clenching and roiling in her stomach. Her head pounded from the effort of straining to hear every tiny noise. Her eyes burned from maintaining an unblinking gaze on the door. At least, she thought wearily, she'd had the foresight to raise the window shade while free of her bonds. In contrast to the night before, pale moonlight lent some illumination to the shadowy room. The waiting was making her ill.

How long before the others turned in for the night? The question revolved in her mind sickeningly. How long before that slimy creature slithered into the room? Merely speculating about the odious Ben sent waves of horror washing over Courtney's entire being. Then, with a barely noticeable scraping, the door was slowly opened, and the waiting was over. Ben's low growl reached her even as she opened her mouth to scream for Dub.

"You might as well save your breath—they're both outside."

"But they'll be back!" Courtney's high-pitched voice betrayed her fear.

"Not for a good long while." He snickered, moving closer to the cot. "They're halfway into a bottle I just happened to have with me." Grabbing the blanket, he tore it from her and flung it aside.

Resolution covered Courtney's mind like a shroud; she would have to die—but not without a fight!

Courtney struggled against Ben with all the strength of a demented person. It was a losing battle, and a painful one. Her resistance only served to make Ben more brutal than he'd been before. Concerned only with his lust, he would maul her, inflicting bruises on her tender skin and scars on her mind.

Tearing the bonds from her ankles with vicious fingers, he clutched at the delicate flesh of her inner thigh. "You're gonna learn what it feels like to have a man between your legs, Miss High-and-Mighty," he snarled, forcing her thighs apart to kneel between them. Grasping her bound wrists with one hand, he drew them up, over her head, laughing nastily as she twisted and arched her hips to get away from the disgusting feel of him. "Yeah, you're gonna bump and grind for me, sister." Courtney jerked violently, crying out in protest when he pushed the heel of his hand between her thighs.

They were both breathing heavily, Courtney from fear and inflamed rage, Ben with consuming lust. Neither one heard the soft click of a pistol being cocked. Courtney became aware of a change in the situation when Ben froze. A soft, raspy voice chilled the air.

"Take your grimy hand off the woman, you scumbag."

Chapter Three

Ben snatched his hand away from her body as if from a red-hot stove plate.

"Now let go of her hand." The quietly rasped command was obeyed instantly.

Her body bathed with the sweat of exertion, her breathing ragged and uneven, Courtney lay absolutely still while her rattled mind grappled with this new, and possibly even more dangerous, threat.

The intruder stood just beyond the pool of moonlight that washed the cot with its pale glow. All that was visible of him was the lower half of his arm and his hand, which was wrapped securely around the butt of a long-barreled pistol, glimmering a deadly blue-black. The tip of that barrel was touching the back of Ben's oversized head!

Motionless, fighting a fresh surge of panic, Courtney felt the muscles in Ben's legs tense, as if to spring. Somehow, someway, the intruder felt or sensed the tensing also.

"Yes, do it," the raspy voice coaxed softly. "Give me an excuse for killing you." When Ben again froze in place, the intruder laughed—unpleasantly. "No? I didn't think so. Pity." He jerked the revolver. "All right, slob, back away from her and get off that cot . . . very slowly, and very carefully."

Ben carried out the order to the letter. Barely breathing, Courtney strained to see the intruder as Ben withdrew, instinctively positive the man was infinitely more dangerous than all three of her abductors. The ensuing action had Courtney boggling in disbelief.

The moment Ben cautiously backed away from the cot, the intruder's arm arced up, and then down with incredible swiftness. The pistol struck Ben's skull with a dull thunk; Ben's body struck the floor with a loud crash.

The panic ballooned inside Courtney's mind, tightening her chest, blocking her air passages. Without conscious thought she began moving, inching back on the cot into a crouching position. Her movements did not go undetected.

"You have nothing to fear from me, Ms. Smythe." For all its softness the raspy voice reached Courtney's ears clearly. "I've come to take you out of here."

The rush of relief was weakening. Hanging on to the last of her composure by a very thin thread, and sheer will, Courtney dragged a calming breath into her constricted lungs.

"You . . . you're from the FBI or police?" she finally whispered.

"No, ma'am."

"But—" Courtney swallowed, almost afraid to continue.

"I'm Morgan Wade's friend," he inserted soothingly. "Morgan . . . ah, asked me to look for you."

"Morgan!" Courtney could have wept with relief. "Oh, thank God! I . . . I . . ." Searching her mind for adequate words, she fell back on the trite but sincere. "And thank you, Mr. . . . ?"

"McCord. Rio McCord. And you're welcome." A trace

of humor lightened his tone. "Now I think we'd better get out of here." His leg came into view in the moonlight as he nudged Ben's unconscious body with a moccasined toe. "I don't know how long fatso here will be out of it."

With his observation the tension was back. "There are two more of them!" Courtney informed him, her gaze flashing to the open doorway as she scrambled off the cot.

"Not to worry," Rio murmured, turning away as she scooped the blanket from the floor. "The other two are in the same never-never land as that thing on the floor." Even in the darkness Courtney could see his head move, as if he were searching for something. "I don't suppose you have any idea what they did with your clothes?"

"No." Beginning to shiver in the chill night air, Courtney drew the blanket around her. "They are not important. I just want to get away from this place.

"Right." His movements silent, Rio glided toward the doorway. "Let's move. I have a horse saddled and waiting for you."

Rio shot one look around the room, then stepped through the doorway. "I'll have a look in here for your things," he called back softly from the other room. She was about to follow him, but a mere moment later he stepped through the doorway, a neatly folded bundle in his arms.

"I found your clothes and handbag." Crossing the room, he cast a wry glance at the unconscious Ben as he dropped the articles on the bed. "That animal will likely be out for a while," he observed dryly. "But I think I'll immobilize him just the same." Moving with that swiftness Courtney could barely follow in the dimly moonlit room, he secured Ben's ankles and wrists with tape he removed from his pocket. "Be as quick as possible, please," he advised softly as he left her to dress.

For a woman who never dressed in less than an hour, Courtney set a record for herself, pulling on the silk blouse, stepping into the badly crushed suit skirt, and shrugging into the matching jacket. Ignoring her pantyhose, she slid her feet into the leather pumps, scooped up her purse, then hurried from the room. Rio was standing at the entrance door, his back to the room.

"Ready?" he asked without turning.

"Yes." Courtney's eyes darted around the trash-littered room as she walked to the door. The curl of disgust on her lips eased as she strode from the cabin into the cold night air. A low, menacing growl stopped her in her tracks.

"Behave yourself, boy," Rio murmured from beside the patiently waiting horse. "Come on, Ms. Smythe, Tracker won't hurt you."

Courtney moved toward Rio cautiously and was practically on top of both man and horse before she could discern the large dog. The dog was standing at the right front leg of the horse, reins clamped tightly in his long jaws, tethering the animal securely. Prudently Courtney gave the canine a wide berth as she circled around to Rio.

The cleared area in front of the cabin gleamed silvery white in the glow from a melon slice of moon. Coming to a stop less than a foot from her rescuer, Courtney got her first real look at him. The sight of him provoked contrasting feelings of reassurance and trepidation.

He was taller than he'd appeared in the shadows of the small bedroom, and he had the type of lean body that indicated hard strength. In the watery illumination his hair was an indescribable dark color, as were his eyes. But it was his face that gave Courtney pause. The features were sharply defined, the lips thin, the jaw unrelenting, giving the impression of rocklike hardness and fear-inspiring ruthlessness. Unthinkingly Courtney took one step back. A shiver ran the entire length of her body as he swept it with a narrow-eyed glance.

"You can't ride dressed like that," he said flatly, indicating the straight skirt hugging her hips and thighs.

"I'll manage," Courtney replied stiffly, imagining herself hiking the garment up around her hips.

"Like hell you will." Moving with the mercurial quickness he'd displayed in the bedroom, Rio leaned forward to grasp the hem of her skirt at the side seam. With one sharp tug of his long fingers the seam came apart to the top of her thighs.

"What are you doing?" Courtney gasped. She tried to step away, but was not quick enough. With a ripping noise that sounded loud in the stillness, he tore open the seam on the other side of the skirt.

"Freeing your legs," Rio drawled laconically—after the fact. Moving to the side of the horse, he cupped his hands. "Come on, I'll give you a leg up. We've got to move."

"That won't be necessary," Courtney said tightly, ignoring his cupped hands as she approached the animal. Out of the corner of her eye she saw him shrug and step back as she stepped into the stirrup and swung gracefully into the unfamiliar feel of the Western-style saddle. As she reached forward to gather in the reins, Rio plucked them from Tracker's mouth.

"I'm afraid you're going to have to keep your seat by hanging on to the saddle horn." Rio's voice came to her even more softly as he walked away. "I need the leather to lead your horse out of here." He gave a gentle tug on the reins to start the animal moving.

Courtney was an excellent horsewoman and at any other time would have had little difficulty in "hanging on" to the horn to retain her seat. But now, very close to the edge of both mental and physical exhaustion after her ordeal, she had little choice but to hold on for dear life.

The going was far from easy over rough terrain in the meager light from a moon playing hide and seek with a few errant clouds. Holding her nerves together, and her body erect in the saddle, became a challenge Courtney was determined to meet. Traversing the canyon was a test she very nearly failed. She was relieved when Rio brought his horse to a halt.

Courtney frowned in confusion. Where were they? she asked herself bleakly. She could see no signs of habitation anywhere. They were still in the hills. A low murmur and a shadowy movement to her right attracted Courtney's attention.

Rio stood beside his horse, gentling the animal with crooning murmurs.

"Steady, boy, we're going home now." Stroking the arched, quivering neck of the horse with one hand, Rio lifted a wide-brimmed hat from the saddle horn and put it on his head, settling it low on his forehead with one swift tug. As he turned to face her, he scooped a garment from on top of the bedroll. "You'd better put this around your shoulders," he advised, walking toward her horse. "The nights can get pretty cold in these mountains."

Though Courtney was already feeling the truth of his statement, she shook her head. "I'm fine," she insisted, noting the lightweight shirt he was wearing. "You keep it, my jacket is quite warm enough," she lied evenly, hoping he could not discern the goose bumps coating her thighs— what good would his jacket do her legs, at any rate?

"Suit yourself." Shrugging into the waist-length jacket, Rio unfastened a coil of rope from the saddle before turning back to her. "I don't want to lose you on the way down," he murmured dryly, tying an end of the rope to the harness. "Ready?" Tilting his head back, he stared directly into her eyes.

"Yes." Though her voice was faint, it held steady.

Rio turned away at once. Sliding his moccasin into the stirrup, he literally stepped into the saddle in one smooth, blurring motion.

"Okay, Tracker. Get us the hell out of these hills."

As if he understood his master perfectly, Tracker loped to a few feet ahead of Rio's horse. Alternately sniffing

the ground and lifting his long head to glance around
watchfully, he led the way down the trail they had made
early that morning.

Her insides cringing at every noise, Courtney could not
prevent herself from glancing over her shoulders periodically in fear of seeing her abductors in hot pursuit. At
regular intervals scenes from her captivity flashed through
her mind, especially those terrifying moments when Ben
had tortured her with his lecherous and sickening atten-
tions. Less than an hour after they'd taken to the trail,
Courtney was trembling violently from cold and reaction.

Incredible! A smile tugged at Rio's thin lips as the observation shot through his mind for perhaps the tenth time.
If he had thought Samantha was some kind of woman—
and he most definitely had—her cousin Courtney was absolutely incredible.

Following Tracker's lead with automatic ease, Rio
savored the memory of the way Courtney looked as she'd
stepped into the revealing glow of moonlight. Her skin
had the shimmer of white satin. Her hair, unbrushed and
tangled, had the sheen of gleaming gold. Her mouth, free
of artificial color, and trembling, had the allure of luscious
wild strawberries.

Now, as he had then, Rio was filled with an urgent need
to crush the wildness out of those trembling lips, making
them his. The one need spawned another, hotter need in
the part of his body that pressed against the saddle.

Damn! he reflected, acutely uncomfortable. How had
one family managed to produce two such ravishingly beautiful women? No wonder Morgan had worn that oddly
amused expression on hearing Samantha describe her
cousin simply as tall, slender, and blond!

Rio's eyes narrowed dangerously at the memory of the
scene he'd witnessed on entering that bedroom. How many

times had that scene, or one similar to it, been enacted during Courtney's captivity? Rio tensed, experiencing again the scorching fury he'd felt in the cabin. Even in the pale moonlight he'd seen the sweat that slicked her body from her struggle with the would-be rapist.

Had that fat slob succeeded in violating Courtney's beautiful body? The speculation locked his features into granite. In the hours she'd been held hostage in that stifling room, had he, or possibly all three of the kidnappers, raped her?

Closing his eyes briefly, Rio felt an angry regret at having left the kidnappers alive. For one flashing instant he was tempted to go back and finish the job as he would have in the jungle.

Rio shifted in the saddle to check on Courtney and raged inwardly at the kidnappers as his sharp glance noted the rigid set of Courtney's jaw and spine. Experience told Rio that she was hanging on to both the horse and her composure by a very thin thread. How long would it be, he reflected, before that thread snapped, leaving her dangling and exposed to the buffeting winds of reaction and shock?

A low, whining sound from Tracker's throat drew Rio around in the saddle just as the dog was leading them into the back of the Henderson property. Rio felt like whining with joy himself.

As Rio had confidently expected, the Jeep was exactly where he'd parked it early that morning. He reined in Hot Foot and dismounted, then bent to run his palm rewardingly over the dog's head and down his quivering neck.

"Good work, Tracker," he congratulated softly, turning to grasp the reins of the other horse.

As he gazed up at Courtney, Rio felt a tightening in his chest. Her eyes were drooping with weariness and her face was dead white with shock. When she shook herself alert valiantly, the tightness spread to his throat. This cousin of

Samantha's was some gutsy woman, Rio decided in admiration.

By the time the horse stopped jostling her aching body around in the unfamiliar saddle, Courtney's mind had long since lost any notion of where she was or why she was there in the first place. She was so very cold, and so tired, that, at that moment, she would gladly have died—just to get the rest.

"Where are we?" she asked dully, focusing her eyes and attention on Rio.

"Not much of anywhere." He reached up to grasp her around the waist. "But at least we're out of the hills," he added encouragingly, sliding her effortlessly from the saddle into his arms. He felt the chill on her skin the instant her body touched his. "Damn, you're freezing!" he muttered, cursing under his breath.

Carrying her to the Jeep, he settled her onto the front passenger seat, then reached into the back for the blanket that was always kept there.

"This isn't too clean," he said in a rough but concerned tone. "Still, it will warm you." Tucking the blanket around her, he demanded impatiently, "Why didn't you call out . . . tell me how cold you were?"

Snuggling into the sweet warmth of the scratchy old Army-issue blanket, Courtney managed a weak smile. "I was too busy clinging to that saddle horn, and clamping my teeth together to keep them from rattling out of my head," she retorted as he slid into the seat beside her.

Rio's soft laughter flowed over her like a soothing balm, sparking a curious curl of response deep inside that Courtney was beyond understanding in her muddled mental condition. All she comprehended was that the feeling was rather pleasant.

"I like your style, lady," he observed seriously, firing the Jeep's engine. "You'd do to ride the river with."

"Thank you," Courtney murmured, surrendering to the

pull of her weighted eyelids; reflection was simply too much for her to handle at the moment. "I think," she added in afterthought, in a fuzzy, half-asleep mumble.

Rio's soft laughter was the last sound Courtney heard before drifting into a semiconscious fog.

Courtney was floating on swiftly moving clouds that kept colliding with other, jagged clouds, jarring her, tossing her to and fro. Sinking deeper into the strangely scratchy cumulus, she drew herself together in an attempt to ride out the buffeting of atmospheric pressure. As she broke through the clouds' flat bottom she jerked erect, eyes flying wide at remembered terror.

"Steady." Rio's voice, as scratchy yet comforting as the blanket around her, chased away the demon of memory. "You're safe, Ms. Smythe." The assurance was backed by a strong arm that shot out protectively, preventing her from flinging herself against the windshield.

"I was falling!" Courtney's breath was expelled on short, ragged puffs. "I had no control!" A shudder tore through her body. *"I had no recourse!"* Courtney knew as well as the man sitting beside her that she was no longer referring to her dream.

"I know the feeling." Rio grunted in understanding. "I've been there."

"I hated it! I hated the feeling of helplessness. And I detested the feel of that man's hands!" Hearing the growing note of hysteria in her voice, Courtney clamped her lips together; feeling the tremors increasing in her shuddering body, she hugged herself to contain them.

But reaction had taken over and the shudders overpowered her clasped arms, and the need to purge in words broke the barrier of her lips.

"I was so frightened," she babbled on. "I've never been so very frightened. I wanted to kill!" Courtney closed her eyes, agonized by the remembrance of the bloodlust she'd felt. "I was actually consumed with the need to kill that disgusting man!"

Courtney was no longer aware of riding in the Jeep. In her mind she was back in the mountain cabin, experiencing all the sensations and emotions that had terrified her throughout her captivity. A sharply voiced command snapped her back into the here and now.

"Stop it, Courtney!"

Her breathing stabilizing, Courtney opened her eyes, unconscious of the fact that her rescuer had used her given name for the first time.

"I'm sorry." Swallowing convulsively, she imposed control over her screaming nerves by sheer strength of will.

"Don't be," Rio grated softly. "But don't let it destroy you either." Bringing the Jeep to a stop, he turned to face her, an understanding smile softening the harshness of his set features. "We're here in *my* territory. You are safe now."

Not knowing Courtney had been rescued, the fourth kidnapper placed a call. What little color there had been on Charles Tremaine-Smythe's face drained as he listened intently to the muffled voice over who knew how many miles of telephone wire.

"You're stalling, Smythe, and we're not waiting any longer."

"No, really!" Charles protested, slicing an anguished look at the FBI agent standing with his back to the wide window. "My people cannot get the money to me before noon tomorrow!"

"Okay," the filtered voice snarled. "I'll get back to you sometime tomorrow morning with instructions for the drop."

"Wait! Don't hang up!" Charles's tone was edged with panic. "I insist you let me talk to my daughter!"

"You insist!" The caller laughed nastily. "The ring was proof that we have her. But you want more proof?" The caller laughed again, sending an apprehensive chill down Charles's spine. "How about one of her earrings?" he asked insinuatingly. "Still attached to her ear?"

"God, no!" Charles gasped, grasping the receiver to prevent it from slipping from his sweat-slicked palm. "I'll have the money by noon, I swear it." His aristocratic features tautened at the snicker that preceded the dial tone as the line was disconnected.

Standing on the other side of the telephone table Phillip seemed to have readied himself for a physical blow. "For heaven's sake, what is it, Charles?" he demanded hoarsely. "What did he say?"

His appalled eyes fixed on the watchful gaze of the agent at the window, Charles repeated the conversation. The agent crossed the room to Charles as he spoke, gently removing the receiver from his clutching grasp. The instrument rang an instant after the agent had dropped it onto the cradle.

Charles's stricken gaze flashed to the phone, then back to the agent.

"Answer it," the agent directed quietly.

Snatching up the receiver, Charles brought it to his ear and drew a deep breath before saying, "Tremaine-Smythe here." After listening intently a moment he sighed. "I'm sorry. Yes, I'll tell him."

"The tap?" The agent guessed correctly.

"Yes." Charles nodded in a defeated manner. "He couldn't get a trace. The call wasn't long enough."

"Dammit!" Phillip exploded, in a way that was completely out of character. "You people must do something!"

Unaffected, yet sympathetic, the agent smiled gently. "We are doing everything possible, Mr. Barrington. There are teams of our people scouring the area where the van was reportedly spotted. There are other teams chasing down every clue we've received on the phony cabdriver, and still more pursuing every lead we've picked up, regardless of how far-out or far-fetched." The agent shrugged helplessly. "A phone trace would have been of inestimable help . . . but, these men are obviously wise to that."

"Well, I still say—" Phillip argued doggedly; Charles cut him off in midbluster.

"Leave it, Phillip, please." Looking as though he'd aged ten years within the last few days, Charles walked slowly to the couch, lowering himself heavily to the cushion. "My brave, beautiful girl," he murmured, as if to himself. "Oh, Phillip, I only pray God I get to see her beloved face again."

It was close to midnight when the phone rang in the office-study.

"Wade here," Morgan snapped tensely into the receiver, clasping the trembling hand Samantha stretched out to him.

Rio came directly to the point. "I have her, Morgan. She's here at the ranch."

Relief washing through him, Morgan tugged on Samantha's hand to draw her close to his work-toughened body. "Courtney's safe with Rio, darling. They are at the ranch." Morgan felt his own throat thicken at the sob that was wrenched from his wife's. Holding her tightly to his side, he returned his attention to his silent, patiently waiting friend.

"What's her condition, Rio?" Morgan asked in the same terse tone.

"Shaky," Rio replied briefly. "Reaction has set in and she's in a mild state of shock."

"I'll leave as soon as I've notified her father," Morgan said briskly, smiling reassuringly into Samantha's tear-brightened eyes.

"No, Morgan." Though soft, Rio's tone relayed flat adamancy. "She's out on her feet, and not up to traveling. I'm going to put her to bed and let her sleep until she wakes naturally. Then I'll bring her to you." A hint of humor touched his voice. "Delivery is part of the job."

"Hang on, Rio," Morgan requested, lowering the receiver and covering the mouthpiece with his palm; Samantha had demanded to know what was going on.

"Rio says that Courtney's exhausted," he explained quickly. "He thinks it would be best if we let her sleep. He'll bring her here when she has slept herself out." When Samantha frowned her disapproval he shrugged. "We know she's safe now, love. We can wait one more day."

"I want to talk to her at least," Samantha insisted, reaching for the receiver. Smiling in understanding, Morgan handed it to her.

"It's Samantha, Rio," she said in a tear-clogged voice. "May I speak to Courtney, please?"

"I'm afraid not, Samantha," Rio responded gently. "She's in the shower. She insisted on it the minute I brought her into the house. Said she had to be clean. Under the circumstances, I think that's understandable, don't you?"

"Yes, of course, it's just that I . . ." Samantha's voice wavered. "You're positive she's all right, Rio?"

"She's all right, Samantha," he responded confidently. "I give you my word."

Though she had no previous knowledge to go by, Samantha knew instinctively that Rio's word was all that anyone ever needed. Sighing softly she accepted the added day's wait. "All right, Rio we'll look for you sometime tomorrow."

"We'll be there," he promised. "Now, would you put Morgan back on, please?"

"Shoot, Rio," Morgan said as he raised the receiver to his ear once again.

"I've got some directions for you to pass on to the authorities, friend. I left some garbage in the hills for them to pick up."

Briefly but concisely Rio gave Morgan the exact location of the Henderson property and the trail he'd followed into the hills, detailing guiding landmarks. "Got that?" he asked when he'd finished.

"Got it," Morgan replied. "But will the garbage still be there when the collectors arrive?"

Rio laughed softly. "They won't be going anywhere."

"Rio, you didn't . . . ?"

"No, Morgan, I didn't." Rio's sigh was heavy with self-disgust. "I wish I had, but I didn't."

His expression thoughtful, Rio replaced the receiver. Then, shrugging off the nagging certainty that he really should have eliminated the kidnappers, he strode from his in-home office. Let the authorities handle them, he mused. He had a shocked, exhausted houseguest to worry about.

Courtney had been so very intent on cleaning herself off that she'd barely noticed Cleat when he'd stepped from the shadows as Rio brought the Jeep to a stop. Indulging her pleas for an immediate bath or shower, he'd left Tracker, Hot Foot, and the other horse in his foreman's capable hands and escorted her into the house and directly to the largest guest room. Courtney had homed in on the bathroom like a missile. That had been approximately fifteen minutes ago.

Running a hand around the back of his neck, Rio decided he could do with a shower as well. But he wanted to reassure himself first that Courtney was comfortable. Dragging a velour robe for her from the depths of his closet, he left his own room to stride across the hall to the guest room. The door he'd deliberately left open still remained so. Even before he entered the room Rio heard the sound of water rushing from the shower head.

A frown drawing his dark brows together, Rio stood

statue still, staring at the closed bathroom door. Was she all right? As the question sprang to mind, Rio wondered at the sharp stab of alarm it elicited. Dismissing the tension that suddenly gripped him, he turned abruptly and strode from the room, tossing the robe on her bed from the doorway.

Rio was not the man to tarry in the shower—he believed one bathed to become clean, not shriveled. Even so, prodded by the pale, desperate-eyed image of Courtney as she entered the bathroom, he knocked three or four minutes off his usual shower-and-shave ritual time.

With his damp hair lying in sculpted waves around his face and neck, and belting a midthigh-length terry robe around his otherwise naked body, Rio crossed the hall, eyes narrowing at the open door.

Damn, what was the woman doing? he railed inwardly. Though the sound of running water had ceased, the bathroom door was tightly closed. The velour robe was still lying where he'd tossed it. Picking it up he moved to stand less than a foot from the door, ready to hand the robe to her the moment she opened it.

"Ms. Smythe?" he called softly. When his call was met by silence, Rio grew really apprehensive.

"Ms. Smythe." His voice was stronger now, serrated with concern.

There was silence. Nothing. And then, a soft, whimpering sound, like a small animal in pain. Rio stepped to the door and yanked it open. The sight that met his eyes turned his spine to ice.

"Courtney!" The exclamation exploded from his constricted throat. "What in God's name . . . ?"

She was standing in the center of the floor, her wet hair gleaming in the glow of the indirect lighting, the water dropping off the ends mingling with the flow of tears coursing down her cheeks. She had wrapped a bath sheet around her slender body and, with one corner of it, was rubbing her shoulders and arms with wild-eyed determination. Where she'd rubbed her beautiful, pale skin was already dark pink and abraded.

A strange twist of emotion very like fear clawed at Rio's insides, and cursing softly, he dropped the robe and closed the space between them in one stride, stilling her action by grasping her wrist.

"What are you doing to yourself?"

"I've got to rub it away," Courtney mumbled distractedly, pulling against his hold. "Don't you understand?" She sobbed. "I've *got* to rub it away!"

"What?" Rio demanded, frowning darkly. "What do you have to rub away? There's nothing there!"

Flinging her head back, Courtney glared up at him from sapphire-bright eyes. "The feel of that beast's hand on me!" she shouted. "I must get it off!"

"Oh, Courtney." Sympathy and compassion gave Rio's naturally raspy voice a jagged edge. "It's gone," he murmured soothingly. Drawing her hand back, he exposed the irritated flesh. "You see? You've washed it aw . . ." Rio's voice trailed off. Eyes narrowing dangerously, he stared at the purple bruises on her shoulders and upper arms. He tore the towel from her hands, cursing viciously at the sight of the ugly marks Ben's brutal hands had inflicted on her perfect breasts and satiny thighs.

"That son of a—"

"Are you sure? Is it off?"

Amazed at the intensity of the fury raging in him, Rio draped the large towel around her and led her from the bathroom. His voice a husky whisper, he murmured assurances.

"Yes, it's off." He brushed the wet strands of hair from her cheeks with incredibly gentle fingers, marveling at the tremor that ran the length of his arm. "There are bruises," he murmured. "But they will fade in time." Giving in to temptation, he allowed his fingers to drift to her eyes to brush at the tears flowing over the red-rimmed edges of her eyelids. "As will the memory of it all," he promised.

Courtney shook her head sharply. "It will never fade. Never!"

Her vehemence spawned the question that slipped past his guard. "Were you violated, Courtney?" With a confusing sense of shock, Rio held his breath as he waited for her answer.

"No!" Her head moved again in that sharp, negative way. "I wouldn't be here, alive, if I had been."

Rio didn't pretend for an instant that he didn't understand. "Don't talk like that!" he snapped, fury racing through him again. "You have everything to live for. You're a beautiful woman." Reflexively he grasped her arms, drawing her to within inches of him.

"Am I?" She sobbed. "Am I, Mr. McCord?" Sniffling, she brought her hands up between them to swipe ineffectually at the increasing flow of tears. "I don't feel beautiful. I don't even feel real." She gulped for breath around the wrenching sobs. "I feel like a thing, Mr. McCord. A *thing!*"

"You are not a thing, dammit!" Rio grated, tightening his grasp to steady her. "You're a woman, an exceptionally lovely woman."

Courtney stared at him with anguished eyes. "Would . . . would you kiss me, Mr. McCord?" she pleaded. "And make me feel like a person instead of a thing?"

In the subdued bedroom lighting Rio's narrowed eyes sketched her face. Even with the puffiness around her eyes from weeping, and the strain of exhaustion pulling at her pale face, she was unbelievably beautiful. She had gnawed at her lips while rubbing her arms, drawing a flush of color to their fullness. The wash of tears lent an inviting slickness to her trembling mouth.

Wild strawberries. Rio shivered with the effort of imposing his will against the hot need rushing through his veins.

"You're tired," he rasped thickly. "You'll feel differently after twelve solid hours of sleep."

"No! I won't feel different!" Courtney closed her eyes as if in acute pain. "I feel subhuman. Do you have any idea what that feels like?"

Her anguished cry set a reel of memory spinning in Rio's mind. For an instant he was back in that bamboo cage in the jungle, teeth bared and snarling like an animal at his torturing, tormenting captors. Oh, yes, he knew what it was like to feel dehumanized. After his escape he had coldly meted out slow, agonizing death to cleanse and reclaim his soul. All Courtney was asking was to be kissed and caressed as a woman instead of a "thing."

And Rio wanted to kiss her, had in fact been aching to since his first glimpse of her in the moonlight. His fingers flexing into her soft flesh, he fought the temptation with an effort that extracted moisture from his brow.

"Mr. McCord, please, help me." Courtney was begging now, begging in a soft, sobbing tone that stabbed at his heart "Oh, please, kiss me, love me the way a man loves a woman he thinks of as beautiful."

The lure of her soft, begging lips proved stronger than even Rio's considerable willpower. Lowering his head slowly, he touched his mouth gently to hers.

Chapter Four

The soft, comforting kiss Rio had thought to bestow singed his lips like a branding iron. Courtney's mouth was both the promise of heavenly attainment and the hell of unattainable satiation. One kiss was a joyous torment. A million kisses would never be nearly enough.

With a low groan Rio released her arms to slide his hands down her back, pressing against her delicate spine to urge her closer. A sighing whisper fluttered through Courtney's parted lips to tease his mouth and senses as her pliant body melted and flowed into his.

Muttering a curse against his own weakness, Rio crushed her soft lips with his hard mouth, drinking the essence of her in like a man with an uncontrollable thirst. She was wild strawberries, and warm honey, and sweet, exotic, forbidden fruit. Defying reason, Rio nibbled hungrily.

Driven by need, he slid his lips from hers to test the satiny texture of her cheeks and ears and the secret spot behind the delicious lobe. Courtney's whimper of pleasure

as she curled her arms around his taut neck caused a flare
of pain in his loins.

"Oh, you are beautiful, Courtney," he murmured into
the curve of her neck as he trailed a string of moist, biting
kisses from her ear to her arched throat. "And you are
every inch a woman—never doubt it."

Berating himself for having taken advantage of her in
her shocked, exhausted state, Rio moved away. As his crushing hold loosened, Courtney's tightened. Clinging to him,
she arched her body into his.

"Don't stop, Mr. McCord, please don't stop." Breathing
raggedly, Courtney skimmed her parted lips over his tension-
tightened cheekbone.

"Dammit, Courtney! The name's Rio." Pulling his head
back, Rio glared down at her with eyes burning like coals
in his strained face. "And I must stop. You need rest
and—"

"I don't need rest!" she cried angrily. "Damn you! I
need to feel alive, vital, real!" Tugging on his hair, she
drew his face to hers. "Make me real, Rio. Breathe your
life into my dead body."

"Oh, God, Courtney, forgive me," he groaned molding
his mouth and body to hers.

Digging his fingers into her hair, he kissed her deeply,
parting her lips wider and still wider, feeling a desire unlike
anything he'd ever experienced before.

With her soft moans urging him farther into madness,
Rio plunged deeper and deeper, extracting the flavor of
her and drawing it into himself. His hands, restless and
damp with sweat, roamed her back over the soft nap of
the terrycloth towel, until he grasped the material and
dropped it to the floor.

The creamy warmth of her skin set a torch to Rio's body,
and to the last of his good intentions. Fired by a demanding
desire to know her, to love her, he skimmed his palms the

length of her back, stroking her hips, her thighs, then lifting her to his naked body.

Fully expecting Courtney to withdraw in renewed fear from the intimate contact, Rio was shocked into momentary stillness when, murmuring encouragement, she parted her thighs while seeking his mouth with hers.

This time it was her mouth that ravished, her tongue that sought the smoky taste of his, her hands that grasped to feel all of his body.

Crazily spinning pinwheels of flashing lights exploded inside his head, and groaning in triumph and defeat, Rio drank the fire from her mouth as he urged her back, onto the bed. Even as she settled on the smooth bedspread, Courtney was holding out her arms, grasping hold of him to drag him down to her.

Sprawling half over her, Rio went again and again to the wellspring of desire that was her mouth. Sometimes sweetly tender, others deeply passionate, he kissed her over and over in a desperate attempt to smother a fire that only raged more wildly out of control.

As the passion consumed him, Rio learned every inch of Courtney's body with his hands and his mouth and his tongue. Spurred on by her whimpering murmurs of pleasure, he kissed and tasted her from her hairline to the slender arch of her foot and back again, feeding his own needs while building hers.

His breathing reduced to harsh gasps, his body slick with perspiration, Rio banked his own raging need in his determination to make Courtney feel "alive."

When Courtney came to the realization of how very much alive she was, she became every man's dream of the perfect love partner. Writhing beneath him, exciting him to the edge of endurance with her softly moaned pleas, she was all woman.

Rio brought her to completion the first time with his mouth. Grasping her by her hips, he absorbed the shudders that rippled in cascading waves through the length of her body with his own, making her pleasure his as well.

Refusing her rest now, he returned to her mouth, to tease and torment, until she was a gasping, pleading flame, burning for him, breathing for him, begging for him.

Anticipating the luxury of thrusting into the velvet softness of her, Rio slid between her legs, thrilling to the sensations sent through his body by the brush of his hair-roughened thighs against the satin smoothness of hers.

Watching her flushed face and cloudy eyes through passion-slitted lids, Rio lifted her hips with his splayed hands and began entering her slowly, savoring every nuance of pleasure. When she shifted suddenly under him, Rio assumed it was for her own fuller enjoyment, not because of any discomfort. Then, the need to bury himself in the softness of her overwhelming his control, he thrust his hips into hers.

Courtney's sharp outcry of pain froze Rio deep inside her, and brought an oath of amazement to his lips.

"Sweet Lord! Courtney, am I the first man?" Rio knew the answer, of course. Even though he had disregarded the instant of resistance, he had recognized it for what it was.

Courtney Tremaine-Smythe was a virgin—or at least she had been until a moment before Rio's deep thrust.

"Courtney, baby, I'm sorry!"

Hearing the note of self-condemnation in Rio's softly spoken apology, Courtney opened her eyes and smiled up at him. Besides coming after her in the mountains, he had given her so very much. He had given her both pleasure and pain—but the pain as well as the pleasure had proved to her that she was not a frozen creature, but a warm, attractive woman.

And, in the deepest reaches of her mind, Courtney knew

the frozen creature had existed long before the brutish Ben had ever touched her. Ben had merely added another layer of ice. Warmer now than she'd ever been, she likened herself to the fairy-tale sleeping princess, only she'd been wide awake, watching the world go by in a virginal state, waiting, waiting, for the one person capable of making the physical expression of love the perfect act of her expectations. Until now she had waited in vain, arrogantly determined to have all or nothing.

Her smile fading, Courtney studied Rio's harshly etched features. His was certainly not the face of a Prince Charming. But his face revealed character, and strength, and compassion, and vibrant, exciting life. Her drifting gaze settled on his strongly defined lips.

How could she have known? She wondered in awe, basking in the heat radiating through her. When she'd asked him to kiss her to reaffirm her identity as a member of the human race, however could she have known that the frozen woman inside would go up in flames at the first touch of his fiery mouth?

At her lengthy silence Rio started to withdraw. Startled out of introspection, Courtney reacted to his movement by clasping her legs around the long, hard muscles of his thighs.

"No, Rio, don't!" Raising her arms, she cradled his frowning face in her hands, drawing him down to her parted lips. "The pain is gone," she whispered, outlining his lips with the tip of her tongue. She smiled as he drew his breath in on a soft hiss. "Would you now deny both of us the pleasure?"

As if he could not stop himself, Rio lightly kissed her lower lip. "But you're so damned beautiful," he said with a groan. "And I hurt you."

"Yes, you did," she admitted. When he stiffened she stroked his tongue with hers. "But I'm alive Rio. Really alive."

"You are that." Rio smiled with the release of tension. "Oh, God, baby! You are the most alive woman I've ever met." His kiss sent the sexual tension swirling through her again. "This man," he murmured excitingly, "could happily burn to a crisp in the fire of your very alive body."

Courtney smiled as his breath warmed her lips, then gasped as his hand found her breast, then moaned as his slowly undulating hips moved his body more deeply into hers.

"Pain?" he asked roughly, jerking his head back to study her expression.

"Pleasure." Courtney sighed. Gazing up at him she frowned in confusion. "Unbelievable pleasure," she murmured wonderingly.

Rio laughed softly, excitingly, heating her lips and her skin and her desire with his warm breath. "For me too," he whispered sexily, gliding his tongue along the sensitive spot on the inside of her lower lip. "Being inside you is like being sheathed in hot, wet velvet."

"Ohhh," Courtney moaned, closing her eyes to better enjoy the stabbing motion of his teasing tongue. "I never . . . never thought it would be like this!"

"Like what?" Rio prompted, sinking his teeth delicately into her lip. "Talk to me, beautiful woman, tell me what you're feeling."

Even though his hard body was on top of her, Courtney was experiencing the oddest, most delightful sensation of flickering, like a flame, inches above the mattress. Raising her heavy eyelids, she gazed in bemusement into the corresponding flame that leapt in the depths of Rio's midnight-dark eyes.

How strange, she mused, mesmerized by his compelling face, taut with desire. This man was a virtual stranger to her, and yet she felt not the slightest shame or embarrassment at sharing this most intimate act with him. Raising her hand lazily, she caressed his harshly etched features with her fingertips, absorbing each bone, every mark, into her skin. There was a thin white scar that arched his dark eyebrow, and was picked up again in a short, scoring line along his prominent cheekbone.

How had he gotten that scar? Even as she formed the question, the answer slammed into Courtney's mind. A knife! Someone had slashed out at Rio with a blade! Good Lord! How had it missed his eye? An image of Rio with one eye scarred into uselessness flashed into her mind. Responding automatically to that image, her fingers clenched on his dark skin.

"Feeling remorse, Courtney?" Rio asked tightly, turning his head to press his lips to the fluttery pulse beat at the inside of her elbow.

"No! Oh, no!" Courtney denied hoarsely. "That scar . . . Rio . . . ?"

"The scar is old, and forgotten," Rio murmured, stroking the now hammering pulse with the tip of his tongue. "Do you find it repulsive?" he asked, too quietly.

"Repulsive?" Courtney frowned. Then, indignantly, "Certainly not! But, what if it had caught your eye?"

"But it didn't," he chided, "so forget it." Stroking, stroking with his tongue, his mouth moved up her arm and over her shoulder. "Are you feeling shy with me, beautiful woman?" he murmured into the curve of her neck.

"Shy?" Courtney's frown deepened. "No." Her fingers speared into the silky strands of his hair. "Why do you ask?"

"Do you have any idea at all what you're doing to me, remaining still with my body inside yours?" he countered softly, raggedly.

"Oh!" Courtney gasped. "I'm sorry!"

"I'm not." His lips moved in a sucking action up the side of her neck and over her cheek to her mouth. "I'm rather enjoying the agony of anticipation."

Her humor sparked, Courtney laughed freely, and moved her hips invitingly. His low groan stilled her movement.

"Oh, Lord! Don't stop, beautiful woman." As she resumed the motion, Rio moved his body rhythmically with hers. "Now make it perfect, Courtney," he ordered coaxingly. "Talk to me. Tell me what you're feeling."

"Hot, so very hot!" Courtney said with spontaneous honesty. "And tense—inside, outside—an exciting tension. Free, and loose, yet strangely tight."

"Hmmm, yes." Rio's lips played touch-and-go with hers. "Yes, you are wonderfully loose, and excitingly tight." A low groan whispered into her mouth as he slowly increased the rhythm of his body. "It gets better," he promised.

"How—how could it possibly get better than this?" Courtney gasped, fighting for breath. Tension was mounting unbearably along her every nerve ending as he steadily increased the measured strokes into her body. "I don't know if I could bear it if it gets much better!"

Blindly following impulse, she raked her nails down his back, marveling at the steellike cords of muscle her fingers skimmed over.

"Yeah," Rio groaned into her mouth. "Oh, yes, I like that!" He was quiet a moment as he synchronized the rhythm of his tongue with his body. When she quivered in response, he laughed softly. "Better and better, hmmm?" he murmured in a darkly sensuous tone.

"Oh, yes! Oh, God, yes!" Clinging to his now slick back, Courtney sought his lips with hers. Their mouths fused, they melted together to reach perfect harmony, perfect union.

As Rio increased his rhythm in that final drive toward completion, Courtney sank her teeth into his shoulder to keep from crying out with the intensity coiling ever tighter inside. Yet, when ecstasy gripped her, she flung her head back to cry his name hoarsely.

"Rio!"

Rio's answer was silent, yet eloquent. His body shuddering, his breathing harsh, he crushed her mouth with his.

In the long, long moments after passion, while the earth slowly righted itself on its axis, and thumping hearts and gasping breaths returned to normal, Courtney and Rio lay entwined, stroking each other softly, not yet ready to give up the afterglow of loving.

When he felt her shiver, Rio tightened his embrace. "You're cold, and you're tired." With the gliding motion she'd come to recognize as natural to him, he sat up, taking her with him. "Let me put you under the covers. You must rest."

Feeling wonderfully taken care of, Courtney smiled at him sleepily. "What I really *must* do is use the bathroom," she murmured, inhaling the musky, all-male scent of him appreciatively. "If you'll hand me that towel, please?" Even as she spoke of moving, she snuggled into the warm strength of him.

"Not the towel," Rio corrected, reluctantly disentangling himself from her. "There's a robe here somewhere." Sliding off the bed, he moved to the foot end. "Ah-ha," he grunted, bending to scoop the velour robe off the floor. Straightening, he held it open and shook it lightly. "Come put this on, Courtney," he ordered softly. "I can hear your teeth chattering from here."

Courtney obeyed him instantly, scrambling from the bed without giving a moment's consideration to the fact that she never obeyed orders from anyone. Closing her eyes, she leaned back against him as he wrapped her in the smooth material that, for all its warmth, was not nearly as comforting as his embrace. Her sigh of contentment was met by his delightful, gravelly laughter.

"Go," he commanded, grasping her shoulders and aiming her toward the bathroom. "I'll straighten the bed."

This time Courtney's sigh was heavy with disappointment. She was practically out on her feet, and she knew it, yet she wanted nothing more than to stand there indefinitely, anchored to the lean hardness of Rio's body. When it became obvious that she was not going to move on her own, Rio escorted her to the bathroom door.

"Don't set up house in there, beautiful woman," he teased. "And don't close your eyes." Pushing the door open, he gave her a gentle shove. "Because if you do, I'll probably have to sweep you off the floor." Rio met her frown of confusion with a chiding smile. "You're nearly unconscious now," he explained. "If you close your eyes, you'll be asleep before your body hits the floor. Your lovely body has too many bruises now," he said harshly, reaching out to stroke her cheek with one long finger. Concern deepened the lines scoring his face from the edges of his nose to the corners of his mouth. "Don't be shy, Courtney," he urged tightly. "If you need help, yell."

Feeling absolutely cosseted, and loving it, Courtney favored Rio with a breathtakingly tender smile. "I will," she promised, shutting the door quietly.

The smile in place, she turned, then gasped in horror at the bedraggled urchin reflected in the mirror that ran the entire length of the bathroom wall. Was this the woman Rio had referred to as every inch a beautiful woman? Appalled, Courtney stared at the less-than-beautiful vision in the silvered glass.

Her hair was a wildly tangled mass framing her face and spilling onto her shoulders. Staring into the dreamy eyes in the mirror, Courtney frowned at the indigo-shaded smudges under her eyes and, now that the flush of passion had faded, the excessive lack of color in her cheeks. Rio was correct in his judgment, she mused wryly. If she should close her eyes, she very likely would be asleep before her body hit the floor!

* * *

Thoroughly captivated by Courtney's smile, Rio stood staring at the bathroom door in bemusement. Despite the ravages of exhaustion from her recent ordeal—*and* intense lovemaking—she remained the most stunningly beautiful woman he had ever gazed upon—or wanted.

And want her he did! Even now, after what was the most powerful sexual experience of his life, Rio could feel the stirrings of renewed hunger in both body and mind.

Approaching the bed, he stopped, narrowed gaze riveted to the rumpled, sea-green spread. The stain was small but glaringly obvious, the once bright-red color of life darkening as it dried.

Blood. Courtney's blood. Proof positive of her chastity prior to his invasion.

As he stared at the coin-sized spot, Rio's body swayed with the overwhelming urge that swept through his mind. Irrationally, unreasonably, he felt compelled to tear the spread from the bed and display it in triumphant pride.

The compulsion was ridiculous, if not downright crazy; yet, even as Rio attempted to convince himself the compulsion was crazy, he had to curl his hands into fists to keep from performing the act.

Lord! It wasn't as if Courtney had been his first woman or virgin. A man did not number his years to near forty without knowing both, even a man as selective as Rio. And, though it was true he had always had a particularly soft spot in his heart for the virgins he'd known, Rio had never before felt this overwhelming urgency to possess and protect.

The sound of the opening bathroom door snapped him out of the muddled confusion of his thoughts. Coming to an instant decision, Rio whipped around, strode to Courtney, and swinging her into his arms, walked purposely from the guest room to the sanctuary of his own bedroom across the hall.

Long after Courtney's breathing confirmed her state of exhausted sleep, Rio lay awake, holding her relaxed body close to his, glaring at the window that faced east as if daring morning to come one second sooner than scheduled.

A frown of concentration drawing his dark brows together, Rio studied Courtney's face as if to imprint her features on his memory.

When daylight came, and she woke, he would escort her to the Wade ranch in Nevada. Rio had never, even as a child, attempted to avoid facing reality. Now his reality was that Courtney Tremaine-Smythe was not only of a different country, but a different world, from a working horse-ranch west of the Pecos. Come daylight he would take her back to her own people. Until then he would hold her close, and yet closer, in an effort to fill the unfamiliar emptiness yawning inside him.

Dawn was encroaching on the horizon and Rio was losing the battle against the weights tugging on his eyelids when he was brought to alert awareness by the arousing feeling of Courtney's slim fingers hesitantly exploring the swirls of dark hair on his chest. Angling his head, he pressed his lips to her golden hair.

"What woke you?" he murmured into the silky strands that tickled his mouth—and fancy.

"I haven't the vaguest," Courtney responded sleepily. "Perhaps it was the need to touch you." Sighing, she rubbed her cheek over his chest. "Just to make sure you were still here."

Enduring the near pain of contracting muscles in his chest, and his stomach, and parts due south, Rio inhaled the sweet female scent of her. "I'm still here," he assured her huskily. "Go back to sleep." A ripple of sensation rushed through his body when her fingers caught on a few hairs as she fingered, then lifted, the medal he always wore around his neck.

"A talisman?" Her cheek slid excitingly over his skin as she moved to get a closer look at the coin-shaped medal.

"Not altogether." Rio smiled. "It has some sentimental value."

The chain holding the medal scraped his neck as she twisted it to examine it. "From a lady?" she demanded curiously.

"No." Rio laughed softly. "My father—the secretly superstitious Irishman."

"What does it represent? I can't make it out."

"St. Patrick."

"St. Patrick?" Courtney pulled back to stare up at him. "Why would an American wear a talisman of the patron saint of Ireland?"

"To keep the snakes out of the hair on my chest?" Rio asked innocently.

"Indeed!" Courtney arched one perfectly shaped brow elegantly, but the twitch of amusement at the corners of her lips ruined her effort at haughty disdain.

"It works too," Rio continued seriously. "There hasn't been a viper in the bush since my father slipped the chain over my head the day I left for the army."

"You were in the service?" Courtney asked interestedly, prudently ignoring the bit about vipers.

Rio smiled sardonically. "Like every red-blooded American boy. I served my time right out of college and ROTC."

"Hmmm, fascinating."

As Courtney's fingers had now discovered the quickly hardening male nipples hidden within the springy curls, Rio wasn't sure whether she was referring to his statement or his body—but then, since a much more vital part of his anatomy was hardening just as quickly, he didn't really care much. Gliding his hands down her back, he gripped her enticingly rounded derrière.

"Courtney"—Rio's breath was expelled on a groan—"do you know what you're doing?"

Raising her head, Courtney gazed at him with the same innocence he'd shown her moments before. "Searching for hidden vipers?"

"You keep on and you're going to find something a lot more dangerous than a viper," he teased.

"I was so hoping you'd say that." Slowly, deliberately, she lowered her mouth to the hardened nipple.

The touch of her lips to his body sent a shaft of sheer pleasure rocketing through Rio's nervous system. He drew her slender hips into line with his, making her aware of the physical reaction she was eliciting from him.

"Maybe you should have gone back to sleep when you had the chance," he suggested thickly.

Courtney jerked her head back to stare at him in amazement. "Do I appear stupid to you?" she demanded imperiously.

"Not likely," Rio drawled. "Why do you ask?"

"I would have to be utterly stupid to prefer lying unconscious to this." Watching him closely, Courtney slowly rotated her hips, grinding her body into his.

"Oh, Jesus . . . Courtney!" Rio's body arched in reflex. "I . . . I . . . oh, Lord, yes!" The words were torn from his throat as, parting her thighs, she moved to straddle him.

Conflicting emotions stormed Rio's mind while sweet hot passion surged through his body. What was it about this particular woman that she could arouse him so very quickly, so very urgently? he wondered in a fleeting instant of lucidity. Then, as her silky thighs caressed the bunched muscles of his, rational thought retreated before the hot advance of rampaging need. Grasping her hips, he attempted to impale her, only to be frustrated by her quickly shifting body.

"Want to play games, do you?" Rio growled, releasing her hips to bring his hands up to capture her face.

"Yes, please." Her smile sensuous, Courtney allowed him to draw her face to his.

The gently cradling hold of Rio's hands changed dramatically the instant Courtney's mouth settled on his. With a convulsive kick he felt painful power surge into his manhood. Reacting instinctively, he tangled his fingers in her hair to anchor her mouth to his. When she moaned and opened her mouth in response, he thrust his tongue deeply into the sweetness of her.

As had happened earlier, wild erotic lights danced behind Rio's eyelids before deciding to take a swim through his racing bloodstream. Despite his attempt at restraint, the urgency overpowered his control. He lifted her, then slowly settled her over him as he arched his body to thrust into the moist, sheathing velvet of hers.

"Rio! Yes, please!"

Courtney's outcry was a delicious spur to his urgency. Responding to it, he thrust up while pulling her hips down.

"Lean to me, Court," he ordered harshly, straining to drive his body more deeply into hers. As she lowered her slender torso to him, Rio shuddered with intense excitement at the sight of the desire flushing her face and clouding her eyes. "Yes, like that," he rasped encouragingly as her dusky nipple brushed his lips. "I want to taste you," he murmured thickly, closing his lips around the diamond-hard bud.

Giving in completely to the rioting clamor of his senses, Rio lavished attention on her perfect breasts, kissing, gently biting, suckling, first one, then the other, in equal measure. And all the while his body arched rhythmically into hers to the inflaming music of the sounds of pleasure she was making deep in her throat.

Fighting to hang on to the last shred of control to ensure her pleasure, Rio was quivering on the edge of ecstasy when he felt her tighten around him.

"Give in to it, beautiful woman," he urged roughly. "Let

go and soar with me." Gasping for breath, he gave one final thrust that raised his hips high off the mattress, attaining his own satisfaction at the exact instant he speared into hers.

His body shuddering, his teeth tightly clenched, Rio drank in Courtney's cry of repletion, and absorbed her rippling tremors into his own throbbing completion. When her trembling body collapsed onto his, he held her to him with an embrace at once fiercely protective and tenderly possessive.

How long they lay locked together physically and spiritually, he had no idea. For himself, he felt he could remain buried in the satin warmth of her forever. But, concerned for her comfort, he lifted her from on top of him to ease her onto the bed beside him, drawing her close.

"Go back to sleep now, wild lover," he advised softly. "You need more rest."

Courtney was quiet for so long, Rio believed she'd drifted back to sleep. Surrendering to the weariness dragging at his mind, he closed his eyes, only to have them flip open again when, seconds later, she spoke.

"Was I a wild lover, Rio?" she asked in sleep-slurred tones.

"Excitingly wild, satisfyingly wild," he replied in a voice husky with remembered pleasure. Amazingly, excitement curled in him again as Courtney, murmuring contentedly, stroked his chest with the tip of her tongue. His hands had begun moving in a reciprocal stroke down her spine when her voice froze him, inside and out.

"Then would you be willing to pay for that wildly exciting satisfaction?" she asked with stunning calm.

"What form of payment would you demand if I were willing, Ms. Smythe?" he inquired in a cold, remote tone.

With a convulsive jerk of her body Courtney reared back into a sitting position, her face pale, her eyes wide with shock.

"Rio, you misunderstand!" she cried.

"Then educate me," he half snarled, refusing to give in to the urge to fill his palm with her heaving breast. "What do you want?"

"Food, you odious beast!" Courtney articulated loudly. "Rio, I'm positively famished!" As if she had the uncanny power to read his mind, she grasped his hand and drew it to her breast.

"Oh, Jesus . . ." Rio cursed in an undertone for long seconds, all the while caressing her satiny skin with infinite gentleness. "Courtney, I'm sorry. Of course you're hungry." Reluctantly sliding his hand from her breast, he rolled away from her and sprang from the bed. "Come to that, my stomach is beginning to feel as if my throat's been cut! Sit tight, beautiful." Grinning at her, he pulled a pair of faded jeans from a dresser drawer and stepped into them. "I'll forage around in the kitchen and see what I can rustle up for us."

"But, Rio, wait!" Scrambling off the bed Courtney followed him to the bedroom door. "Can't I help you in some way?"

"Sure," he drawled lazily, swinging the door open. "You can get back into that robe, and take my brush to that mop of yours." At the startled expression widening her eyes he explained, "That tangled mop is every bit as inviting as your sexy body. Tame it, honey." Stepping over the threshold he shot her a blatantly sensuous smile. "Or I'll just have to tame it, and you, myself."

As he strode to the kitchen a burst of soft laughter rumbled in Rio's chest as Courtney's sweetly voiced rejoinder wafted back to him.

"I sincerely hope you're the type of man who keeps his promises, Mr. McCord."

Rio and Courtney ravenously devoured the hastily gathered repast of slices of cold roast chicken wrapped in warmed tortillas and chunks of canned pineapple, and washed it down with large earthenware mugs of darkly rich, steaming hot coffee.

Sitting cross-legged on the bed opposite her, the remains of the meal between them, Rio drank the last of his aromatic brew while his gaze drank in the incredible beauty of her. In the now bright morning sunlight, Courtney's hair gleamed with varying shades, from ash blond to bright gold, all the way to the curled ends that tumbled over her shoulders to cover her breasts. Her eyes sparkled like many-faceted gemstones. Her cheeks glowed pink and dewy fresh from the shower she'd indulged herself in while he'd been in the kitchen. Her body curved invitingly, even through the luxurious pile of the velour robe.

Throughout his perusal of her, Rio was acutely aware of Courtney's eyes slowly taking his measure. When he raised his gaze to hers, she met it directly.

"Were you pleased with what you saw?" she asked boldly.

Rio's lips parted in a rare, teeth-flashing smile. "You are one fantastically beautiful woman, Courtney Tremaine-Smythe," he praised softly. "Beautiful in appearance. Beautiful in spirit. And beautifully wanton in bed." His smile growing dangerously sensual, he watched a flush of pleasure tinge her soft skin.

"Now it's your turn, wild lover," he taunted when the color had begun to fade from her cheeks. "Were *you* pleased with what you saw?" Before she could respond, he added, "And don't feel you have to be kind." His smile tilted into a devil grin. "My shaving mirror never lies."

"I'm rarely kind," Courtney retorted cuttingly—then spoiled the effect by grinning back. "And you are certainly not a matinee idol," she observed candidly.

"Thank God!" Rio laughed outright.

"Be quiet, it's my turn," Courtney scolded. "But there is a rugged who-gives-a-damn aura about you that intrigues, and goes well with your rather harshly delineated features . . . you know?"

Rio's deep laughter exploded in the early-morning quiet. "Only the British!" he gasped. "Only the British can manage such a left-handed compliment so elegantly—and make you love hearing it!" He met her gaze with shrewd intensity. "That is no aura, lady. I don't give a damn about a hell of a lot."

Courtney wet her swollen lips and smiled softly. "Has life been hard on you, Rio McCord?"

"No harder than I've been on it," he returned cynically. "Has life been easy on you, Courtney Tremaine-Smythe?"

"Up till recently, yes," she admitted. "I've had the usual number of bad moments, you understand, but hard?" She shook her head. "No, I'm afraid life has been extraordinarily easy on me."

"And then, so soon after 'recently,' I storm your defenses into the bargain."

"Oh, but the storm was beautiful, Rio," Courtney protested. "And long overdue." With a cool disregard for the food tray separating them, Courtney leaned forward to caress his cheek with her fingertips, following the creases from nose to mouth. "You were so gallant, and so very understanding of what I was feeling, and I do thank you most humbly, Rio McCord."

The realization that she was dead serious galvanized Rio. Sweeping the tray from the bed, he gathered her into his arms, taking her with him as he sank to the mattress.

Before his head touched the pillow, Rio had her mouth open under his, devouring her with a hunger that put his appetite for food to shame. In the back of his mind was the knowledge that before many more hours had passed he would be relinquishing Courtney into the care of her family.

Just once more, he promised himself. He would make love to her just one more time, and then he would let her sleep. Not comprehending the sense of desperation gripping him, Rio skimmed every inch of Courtney's body with his hands and mouth, knowing her—in every sense—more intimately than he'd ever known any other woman.

Curiously, Courtney's hands and lips moved every bit as avidly over his body, arousing him to a point almost beyond endurance, and answering a need, buried deep inside, that Rio wasn't even aware he'd had.

As their lovemaking flared into a pulsating inferno, all Rio was aware of was his gut-wrenching response to her, a response that drove him on and on in a quest to wring every ounce of sweetness from her.

Even before their breathing had leveled off, still clinging to each others' perspiration-bathed bodies, they finally slept. The harsh West Texas sunlight was powerless against the depth of their satiated slumber.

Less than four hours later Rio came awake instantly to the touch of his housekeeper's hand on his shoulder.

"I'm sorry, señor," she murmured, her eyes strangely sad. "It's the phone for you. Mr. Morgan Wade." Her lips curved in a soft smile as she ran a shy glance over Courtney's form, held within his possessive embrace. "Shall I tell him you are still asleep?" she asked hopefully.

"No." Rio's tone conveyed firm conviction. "Tell him I'll be there in a moment."

Sighing, but nodding her head in understanding, the sad-eyed woman retreated from the room.

Moving away from Courtney carefully, Rio slipped silently from the bed, then paused to stare at her regretfully a long moment. A smile played at the corners of his mouth; he realized she was everything he could ever ask for in a woman. But she was not for him. He had seen too much of the wrong side of the world, committed too many unforgivable acts. And yet that was not the reason he would be returning her to her family.

Courtney Tremaine-Smythe belonged in the drawing rooms of the privileged class. Rio McCord belonged to the earth—most especially the dry, West Texas earth. Except for a physical hunger for each other, that would, if indulged, probably fade swiftly, they had little in common.

With a final sweeping glance at her sleeping face, Rio turned from the bed, his movements soundless as he stepped into his jeans. Without a backward look he strode from the room.

Chapter Five

When Rio left the bed, Courtney awoke with a start and, for a moment, panicked. Then she remembered Rio—strong and loving—and she smiled as she headed for the shower. When Rio returned to the bedroom she was completely dressed, her weariness disguised by expertly applied cosmetics.

Entering the room silently, Rio came to a dead stop at the vision of her, bathed in the sunlight streaming through the windows. Her glorious hair was pulled back off her face and coiled into an intricate French chignon. The hairstyle exposed her aristocratic bone structure to advantage, lending an elegant, sophisticated image that was in direct contrast to the wildly disordered picture Rio carried in his memory. He disliked it at once.

In the seconds before Courtney detected his presence in the room, Rio skimmed her tall figure with an encompassing glance, his sharp-eyed gaze missing nothing.

Her suit, restored by Maria, made a bold statement for the advantages of exquisite taste and an unlimited bank balance. Everything about her, from the neat coil of her hair to the hand-worked leather of her classic pumps, spoke eloquently of cultivated refinement. Courtney Tremaine-Smythe was a lady, in the purest definition of the word.

The smile Courtney bestowed on him, when she caught sight of him, took Rio's breath away—along with something else—something he was not yet ready to examine or identify.

"Good morning," she said softly. Her smile widened. "Or should I say, good afternoon?"

"Afternoon, I'm afraid," Rio murmured, frowning. "But not late enough in the afternoon. You should have slept longer." He went to his closet and was reaching his hand inside when her response momentarily froze him in place.

"I was cold . . . after you left the bed."

The simplicity of her statement caused a gentle ache in the depths of Rio's soul. It was past noon, in summer, in West Texas, and already the temperature was flirting with a higher-than-hundred-degrees reading. His eyes closing briefly, Rio accepted her admission for what it was. Courtney had confessed to missing the warmth of *him,* not his body.

Ruthlessly blocking the rush of emotions her confession generated, Rio calmly chose a suit and shirt before turning slowly to face her.

"I left the bed to answer the phone." His smile was as remote as his carefully controlled expression. "The call was from Morgan. Your father is at the ranch, waiting anxiously for your arrival."

"Oh! Oh, good Lord! I haven't given a thought—haven't even considered . . ." Courtney's voice trailed away, along with what little color there was in her cheeks. "Poor father! He must be frantic by now." Guilt stricken, she looked at Rio imploringly. "We must leave for the ranch at once."

"Not quite at once." Rio's smile revealed none of the

feelings churning inside him. "Maria has breakfast ready for you. You can eat while I shower and dress."

Though it was obvious Courtney felt impatient about the delay, she gave in gracefully. "Yes, of course." Her elegant body erect, she started for the door, then paused to glance at him over her shoulder. "Have you eaten?"

"Yes." It was an outright lie that didn't bother Rio in the least. Suddenly the appetite he'd awakened with was gone—just as the woman he'd awakened next to was gone, replaced by an exquisitely beautiful stranger.

"You go ahead, I'll be with you in a few minutes." Tossing his clothes onto the rumpled bed, he walked to the bathroom. "The kitchen is at the end of the hall." Stepping inside, he closed the door quietly.

Hours later, Rio watched Courtney as she slept peacefully on a seat inside Morgan Wade's private Learjet. In repose, Courtney's body revealed the weariness eating up the last of her reserves. Her skin gleamed with an unnatural, whitish color and there was a defenseless, vulnerable look about her that caused an ache of conscience in Rio's mind.

After her ordeal in the mountains, Courtney had needed rest, many hours of rest. Instead, she'd had brief periods of sleep between bouts of sexual calisthenics and now, here, on a less-than-comfortable seat in a small airplane.

The plane had been waiting for Courtney and Rio at the landing strip Rio maintained on his ranch; Morgan had dispatched it to Texas early that morning. To Rio's mind the Learjet was unnecessary. Rio owned his own plane—a good one, if not a Lear. But Morgan had insisted and Rio gratefully accepted the jet.

What he could not accept was the news of the absence of any human or domestic animal presence at the cabin in the mountains when the authorities had arrived there early that morning.

Rio was no novice to the art of immobilizing a man. He had known that, without assistance, the kidnappers were not going anywhere under their own power. All of which indicated a simple conclusion: There was a fourth kidnapper—and Rio McCord should have known it.

Damn! Self-disgust left a bitter taste in Rio's mouth. How had he overlooked such a simple factor? There *had* to be a fourth man—because there had to be a contact.

Good thing you retired when you did, ole son, Rio chided himself scathingly. *If you hadn't, you'd probably have had your ass shot off by now.* To overlook the rudimentary element of a contact! Jesus! His expression grim, Rio shook his head in wonder. Then, understanding that hindsight was as useful as self-pity, he closed his eyes and went immediately to sleep.

The light touch of Courtney's hand on his forearm woke Rio a short time later.

"We'll be landing in a few minutes, Rio," she said softly when he opened his eyes. "The pilot is circling the air strip at the ranch."

Moments later they were on the ground, taxiing toward the small building that housed the sleek plane. As the plane approached the hangar, Rio could discern a group of people standing in front of it. Rio spotted Morgan immediately, simply because he stood a head taller than the others, and was the only one wearing the flat-crowned, flat-brimmed Andalusian hat Morgan preferred. And then he identified Samantha by the bright beacon of her flaming red hair. The other two members of the group, both men, were strangers to Rio, but obviously not to Courtney.

"That is my father, standing beside Sam," she said quietly. Then, with a sharp gasp, "And Phillip!"

Although Rio had a gut feeling he knew the answer, he asked the question anyway. "Your brother?"

Courtney turned from the miniature window to his expressionless face. "No." Her tone steady, she went on, "My fiancé."

A shadow of a curl he could not contain played over his lips. "I see."

"No! Rio, you must understand, I—"

"But I do understand, Ms. Smythe." Rio's voice rasped harshly. "The circumstances were more than a little unusual." His shrug effectively halted the argument she had opened her mouth to launch. The plane came to a smooth stop, and flipping the lock on his seat belt, Rio stood with lazy grace. "They're waiting." Stepping back, he executed a courtly bow. "After you, Ms. Smythe."

Before Rio's eyes, Courtney underwent a complete metamorphosis. Gone was the smiling, soft-spoken, wild love partner of the night and morning hours. In that woman's stead was the cool, haughty daughter born of the manor.

Like a creeping disease the gentle ache in Rio spread outward, encompassing his vital organs, interfering with his breathing process.

Imposing his will over emotion, Rio straightened his spine and followed Courtney from the plane. In the emotionalism of reunion Morgan was the only one of the group to note Rio's presence. The smile that quirked Morgan's lips spoke eloquently of appreciation and relief. Rio accepted the smile with a barely perceptible nod.

Standing on the fringes of the group Rio coolly observed the tall, distinguished man who was obviously Courtney's father draw her into his arms.

"My dear, my dear," Charles murmured, unabashed by the tears evident in his eyes. "I was so dreadfully afraid for you." There was a muffled response from Courtney, then Charles studied her face. "You are unharmed?" he asked anxiously.

"I am fine, Father," Courtney assured him gently. "Really."

"Courtney?"

Rio's eyes narrowed on the slender, fair young man who had spoken her name uncertainly.

"Oh, Phillip!" Turning to him, Courtney stepped unhesitatingly into his open arms. "How wonderful to see you."

Every muscle in Rio's body tightened as Phillip embraced Courtney, and an instinctive urge for violence threatened to outweigh his common sense when the young man's lips took hers. Fortunately Samantha chose that moment to greet her cousin.

"Oh, please, Phillip, let me get a hug in!" Samantha chided, laughing and crying at the same time.

The tension in Rio's body eased as Phillip relinquished his fiancée into the arms of her cousin.

From Samantha, Courtney was turned over to Morgan, who gathered her close to murmur his delight at having her back.

While his attention was centered on Courtney, laughing up into Morgan's face, Rio was aware of her father moving toward him.

"Mr. McCord?"

"Yes?" Reluctantly, Rio shifted his narrow-eyed gaze from Courtney to the man responsible for her presence on the earth.

"Charles Tremaine-Smythe, sir." The clipped British accent didn't quite conceal the emotion woven through his tones. "I fear I owe you a debt of gratitude I'll never be able to repay," the older man continued, offering his hand.

Clasping the pale, delicate-looking hand, Rio was surprised to discover a handshake of solid strength. "You owe me nothing, sir. I'm glad I could be of assistance, Mr. Tremaine-Smythe," he added dryly.

"Charles, please, Mr. McCord," the older man urged sincerely.

"Rio, please"—Rio's lips tilted at a hint of a smile—"Charles."

"Why are we standing around here?" Morgan demanded, planting an avuncular kiss on Courtney's brow that shot sparks into Rio's dark eyes. "Let's get out of the sun and back to the house." Draping his arm around Courtney's shoulders, he caught Samantha's waist with the other. "I've got a case of champagne chilling to celebrate the occasion." Flashing the devilish grin that had melted many a female heart, Morgan led the group to the two cars parked to one side of the hangar.

Rio was about to announce his intention of returning to his ranch immediately when Charles, reading his attitude with amazing accuracy, forestalled him in a firm tone.

"Please, join us, Mr."—Charles smiled warmly—"Rio. It is due to you that this celebration is possible."

On the point of adamantly declining Charles's invitation, Rio caught sight of the infinitesimal spasm of annoyance that scurried over Phillip's face. Smiling sweetly—an expression that would have instilled a dread of warning into the heart of anyone who knew him well—Rio graciously accepted, lazily falling into step with the older man.

As they approached the vehicles, a brand-new Range Rover and a five-year-old Jaguar, Samantha said, airily, "I'll drive the family back in the Rover, darling. You can bring Rio in the Jag." Sliding away from his encircling arm, she turned, her hand held out for the car keys.

The expressive look Morgan gave his wife was a curious mixture of indulgence and admonition. "Play light-foot on the pedal, Red," he cautioned softly, dropping the keys into her palm.

"Morgan, really!" Exasperation heightened the trace of a British accent in Samantha's tone. "I have no desire to knock off my family by running us into a damn ditch!"

The accent, coupled with the American slang, drew soft laughter from Morgan. "I'll follow behind you, just the same," he taunted, motioning Rio toward the Jaguar.

"Sam isn't a good driver?" Rio probed softly as Morgan tailgated the larger vehicle.

"Sam is an excellent driver," Morgan corrected, slanting

a grin at Rio. "But, she is also a fast driver." He shook his silver-salted dark head. "I don't know what comes over her, but whenever she slides behind the wheel of any vehicle, whether it's this beauty or the oldest four-wheeled heap on the property, she imagines herself on the track at Indy."

Morgan's observation elicited one of Rio's rare, breath-taking smiles. "I've been hearing things about Sam for some years now." Rio offered the information casually, watching his friend closely.

"What 'things'?" Morgan's black eyes narrowed as he sent Rio a warning, sidelong glance.

Rio grinned. "Oh, mostly how very beautiful Morgan Wade's woman is." He chuckled softly. "On inspection I'd say it was a bit of an understatement."

"More than a bit." Morgan returned the grin, while keeping his eyes on the road and the vehicle in front of him.

"I also heard that you nearly lost her a few years back," Rio went on. "Childbirth, wasn't it?"

"Yes." The change in Morgan was instantaneous and almost frightening. Tension tightened the smooth skin over his high cheekbones and added a serrated edge to his tone. "I was never so damned scared in my life, Rio," he confessed hoarsely. "Not before or since." A visible shudder rippled down his spine at the memory. "I felt a bloodlust to kill—doctors, nurses, everyone separating her from me." Collecting himself by inhaling deeply, he smiled with wry self-amusement. "I was ready to tear that entire hospital apart with my bare hands."

"You love her very much, don't you?" Although Rio posed it as a question, it was not one; he knew the answer.

"No, old son, I don't love her." The tension eased from his features as Morgan smiled. "Trite as it probably sounds, I absolutely worship the ground that lady walks on."

They were quiet for some minutes, each with his own thoughts. Morgan's musings were pleasant, for a gentle smile teased his chiseled lips. Rio, on the other hand, frowned with the effort of comprehending a love so strong and deep. Was that kind of romantic love really possible? he wondered cynically. Or was his friend living in a fool's paradise? Unbidden, an image, too sharp, too clear, of Courtney, her hair wildly tangled around his fingers, her mouth hot and eager on his, rose to cloud Rio's thinking. In an attempt to banish the vision, and the resultant physical reaction to it, Rio spoke abruptly.

"Twins, weren't they? Boys?"

"Hmmm." Morgan nodded, then laughed. "And sometimes I feel positive they have the devil's blood in them. Of course," he tempered, "I can't say they're solely to blame. Sara has spoiled them outrageously since the day Sam and I brought them home." Morgan thus serenely indicted the woman who'd been the Wades' housekeeper from the day Morgan's mother married his father. And, after Morgan's mother, Betty, died in a car accident, Sara had taken on the role of surrogate mother to the two-year-old Morgan.

"How is Sara?" Rio asked, smiling in remembrance of the only woman who'd ever had the temerity to take him to task for his lifestyle.

"Bossy as ever." Morgan's smile was tinged with sadness. "Although a little of her fire dimmed when Jake died."

Rio nodded in understanding; Sara had been devoted to her husband Jake. "Jake was a good man."

"Yes, he was." Morgan sighed soundlessly. "At least he went quickly. The doctor said Jake was dead from that hemorrhage before his body hit the ground."

"There are worse ways to die," Rio agreed.

"And you've seen most of 'em, haven't you?" Morgan shot him a knowing look.

Rio smiled cynically. "I've looked at death a time or three. It's never pretty. And sometimes it's downright messy. But, either way, it's final as hell." He was pensive a moment, then rasped with soft violence, "I should have made it final for those bastards in the hills."

"Was she raped, Rio?" Morgan asked, very softly.

"No." The steel of conviction laced Rio's tone; no one knew better than he how chaste Courtney had been when he'd found her. "She'd been pawed and she was bruised and shaken, but she hadn't been violated."

With his mind's eye, Rio could see the bruises on Courtney's slender arms and legs, and on her silky breasts. Impatient with the memories that persisted in teasing his mind and tormenting his body, he spoke.

"So, what's the story on our inept kidnappers?"

Morgan shrugged. "There was a fourth man, of course."

"Don't remind me," Rio drawled disgustedly.

"You did what you were asked to do, Rio." Morgan, aware of the portent of fury in his friend's oversoft tone, continued evenly. "The authorities can handle it from here."

"I suppose." Tension eased as Rio exhaled slowly. "Any theories?"

"Yeah." Morgan paused as he turned onto the drive to the house, shifting as the Jag began climbing the slight incline in the wake of the Range Rover. "They figure that, for whatever reason, the fourth man went into the hills sometime before dawn and, after he'd freed his trussed-up partners, they lit a shuck for the Mexican border." As he finished speaking, Morgan brought the car to a smooth stop in the driveway behind the Range Rover. "Hopefully the authorities will round them up before long, once they have descriptions from Courtney."

"Hopefully," Rio repeated vaguely, his gaze clinging to the woman under discussion as she alighted from the vehicle. Even pulled back into a chignon, Courtney's hair gleamed like gold in the late-afternoon sunlight. Rio felt his hands itch with the desire to yank the clips from her hair and slide his fingers through the silky strands.

"Rio?"

Morgan's voice jerked Rio out of the forming fantasy. Tilting his head, he smiled wryly at the discovery that Morgan was out of the car, frowning in at him. "I'm right behind you, Morgan," he assured him, pushing the door open and stepping out onto the paved driveway.

"I was afraid you'd drifted off to sleep," Morgan jibed as they approached the entrance to the large L-shaped ranch house. "I know your habit of grabbing *z*'s when the opportunity presents itself."

"I could use some," Rio admitted blandly. "I'm about out on my feet." He shrugged as he preceded Morgan into the house. "I wanted to go directly home. Mr. Tremaine-Smythe insisted I stay."

"The authorities are going to want to talk to you," Morgan said, ushering Rio into the living room.

"They know where to find me," Rio responded laconically, his manner belying the tension riding him again at the sight of Courtney once more enfolded in Phillip's embrace. *If he kisses her again,* he's *going to find himself on the floor, hurting like hell,* Rio vowed silently, sauntering into the room as if he hadn't a care in the world.

Courtney felt exhausted, and on the verge of tears. Rio had not so much as glanced at her since they'd deplaned.

Well, what had you expected? she charged herself bitterly, squirming delicately inside Phillip's possessive embrace. Rio was an unlikely candidate for avowals of deep affection on the basis of a one-night stand—or even an extended affair! Nevertheless, he might at least *look* at her!

"Champagne, darling?"

Startled out of her reverie Courtney forced a smile for Phillip. "Yes, thank you." Accepting the glass she sipped at the wine before asking, "When did you arrive in the States, Phillip?"

"Early yesterday morning." He grimaced. "Very early yesterday morning."

Cognizant of Phillip's propensity for sleeping until mid-morning, Courtney made a soft sound of commiseration. "Poor, darling, such a bother."

"But not at all!" Phillip had the grace to flush. "I mean, naturally I had to come over!"

Courtney patted his glowing cheek. "There's a dear. Now, I think I'd like to sit down." Turning toward an inviting couch she missed the glittering, narrow-eyed glare drilling her from the other side of the room.

"But, darling, wait! You're not completely dressed." Phillip halted her with a touch on her arm.

"I beg your pardon?" Though Courtney's tone was pitched as low as his had been, Phillip could not help but note the edge of hauteur in it.

"Your ring." Displaying her missing engagement ring he grasped her left hand.

"But how . . . ?" Courtney began, then smiled dryly. "Of course. They sent it to Father, didn't they?"

"Yes," Phillip responded, slipping the ring onto her third finger.

An urge, a compulsion, something, made Courtney glance up. A gasp rose to clog her throat when she found herself caught by a flame leaping in the depths of Rio's dark eyes.

He's angry . . . no, he is furious! Courtney thought, a rush of excitement heating her body. Does the idea, the very meaning, of the engagement ring bother him? Breathing slowly, she glanced at Rio again and felt all the energy drain out of her. Rio had turned away.

What was left of the afternoon and the evening hours dragged intolerably for Courtney. All through the endless questioning by her family, and then by the FBI agent who arrived after dinner, Courtney longed for solitude and sleep. When, finally, Samantha escorted her to the guest bedroom and left her with a hug, Courtney flung her clothes off and dropped like a stone onto the bed. She was dead to the world within minutes.

And it seemed mere minutes later when a knock drew her from a dream in which a pair of dark eyes smiled instead of glared at her. Courtney was struggling into a sitting position when the gentle knock sounded again on the door.

"Yes?" she called softly, smothering a yawn with her palm.

"It's me, Courtney." Samantha peeped around the door. "I wanted to make sure you were still breathing. It's after one."

"In the afternoon!" Courtney exclaimed.

"Yep." Samantha grinned. "I've brought your breakfast," she announced unnecessarily, bumping the door wide with her hip and entering the room, a large silver tray in her hands. "Would you like it in bed or over there?" Sam indicated the small table placed before a wide window.

"On the table, please." Yawning again, Courtney slid off the bed. "The coffee smells delicious." She inhaled appreciatively. "I hope you brought two cups."

"I did." Samantha laughed.

"Good. Pour out, then, I'll be with you in a moment." Pulling on her satin robe Courtney headed for the bathroom. After splashing her face with cold water, and brushing her teeth, she exited the room, a soft smile for her cousin curving her lips.

"Thanks again for unpacking my things, Sam." With a flick of her wrist Courtney indicated her nightgown and robe.

"It kept me busy while we were waiting for you," Samantha said, returning the smile.

Silence fell in the room while they sipped at the hot coffee; then Sam glanced directly at Courtney. "You are all right," she asked carefully. "Aren't you, Courtney?"

"Yes, darling, I am all right," Courtney assured her firmly. "There were a few bad moments when I was positive I'd never leave that disgusting cabin alive," she went on candidly. "But I was not raped, Sam."

The breath whooshed out of Samantha in relief. "I was an absolute basket case," she admitted. An expression of wonder widened her eyes. "And to think I didn't want Morgan to call Rio." She shook her head in self-despair. "If it weren't for him"—a delicate shudder moved her shoulders—"who knows what might have happened!"

"Yes," Courtney whispered, forcing composure to features that ached to crumble with tears. "If it weren't for Rio." *I would still be a virgin. I would still be innocent. I would never have known the rapture of his lovemaking,* she added to herself. Fixing a smile on her dry lips, she asked brightly, "Where is Rio, by the way?"

"Oh, he left for Texas this morning, long before anyone else was awake." Samantha paused to swallow her coffee, then corrected herself. "Anyone but Morgan, that is. Morgan drove him to the plane."

"I see." The sense of desolation was shocking in its intensity. Wanting to cry out in pain at his desertion, Courtney lowered her gaze to her breakfast because Samantha would surely detect the agony in her eyes. In a bid for time to collect herself she automatically lifted, then lowered, her fork, methodically chewing the food she didn't taste.

The plate was almost clean when Courtney decided her composure was as solid as it was going to get. "Tell me about Rio, Sam," she requested coolly, amazed at the steadiness of her hand as she refilled the cups. "I really didn't have a chance to get to know him." That is, if one could overlook sharing the most intimate acts with him—and not merely once, but numerous times, she anguished silently. The first time could possibly be excused; the circumstances had been unusual, as Rio had pointed out. But what of the subsequent acts? What excuse could she manufacture for those? Courtney suddenly felt exhausted again.

Pressured, stressed, she shivered with relief when Samantha's cultured voice drew her from introspection. Later, Courtney promised herself; she would deal with the examination of self later. Her tone low with inner strain, she apologized for her inattention.

"I'm sorry, Sam, but would you repeat what you said? I . . . I'm afraid I was distracted and didn't hear you."

Samantha's smile held a depth of understanding only another woman could feel for Courtney's mental state. Replacing her cup on the saucer she reached across the table to grasp Courtney's hand.

"Please, don't," she said softly. "Darling, there's no need to apologize to anyone, least of all me. I'm family, remember? And so is Morgan. We want you to feel free here, to rest and try to put the memory of it behind you." Blinking suspiciously she squeezed Courtney's hand. "Will you do that?"

Forget? Good Lord, she would never forget! Courtney's mind raced. That frightening ride through the night. That filthy cabin in the hills. Those horrible men. That beastly Ben. Rio! Dear God, Rio! Why had he returned to his ranch so quickly? She needed him! Didn't he know how very badly she needed him now? Or did he simply not care?

The muscles working in her throat, Courtney closed her eyes, fighting desperately to reassert her composure.

"Would you like me to leave?"

"No!" Courtney's eyes flew wide. She couldn't be alone, not yet, and Rio had gone. Turning her hand, she clasped Samantha's in a crushing grip. "No, don't go. Talk to me, Sam, please," she pleaded. "Just keep talking. I can't bear my own thoughts at the moment."

Samantha launched into a monologue before Courtney had finished her plea. Her tone light and airy, she com-

menced chattering on every and all subjects that sprang
to mind, from the antics of her sons to the vagaries of
Wall Street. The even cadence of her voice was balm to
Courtney's nerves, and slowly the tension lessened in her
chest. The coffee had long since grown cold in the china
cups when Samantha wound down, then stopped speaking
altogether.

Calm now, if not serene, Courtney again pressed her
fingers against Samantha's. "Thank you," she murmured
simply.

"Better?" Sam studied her anxiously.

"A great deal, actually." Courtney managed a brittle
chuckle. "At least I no longer have the terrifying feeling
that I might shatter at any moment."

Setting her chin determinedly Courtney slid her chair
back and stood up. Following her example Samantha rose
also, a questioning arch peaking one dark red brow.

"I'm going to dress," she answered Sam's mute query.
"I'm sure Father is worrying by now."

"And Phillip?" Samantha asked, in a carefully modu-
lated tone.

Courtney sighed. "And Phillip," she concurred wearily.

Samantha stared into Courtney's troubled eyes; then,
shrugging, she asked, "You aren't comfortable in the
engagement, are you?"

"No." Courtney raked her fingers abruptly through her
sleep-tumbled hair. "I tried to give the ring back to him
before coming over here." She smiled piquantly. "He
wouldn't have it. Why do you ask?"

"Because it's obvious you're not in love with him," Sam
said bluntly.

"But I am fond of him . . . deeply fond," Courtney countered.

Samantha smiled pityingly. "Oh, Courtney—fond?
You're willing to settle for *fond*?"

"I've never met anyone else. . . ." Courtney's voice faded, became faint, as her conscience chanted: *Liar, liar.*

"But that hardly means you won't!" Samantha objected strongly.

Courtney's nerves were quivering. She could feel Rio, *taste* him, as if her senses had absorbed the essence of him into her system.

"Is love so very important?" she cried, consciously denying the ache of longing inside. "Phillip and I grew up together. We've been friends forever. We understand each other. Isn't that enough?" she demanded, more of herself than of her cousin.

"Is it?" Samantha chided gently. Circling around the table she drew Courtney into an embrace, murmuring, stroking, in the same way she comforted her children when they were hurting. "Darling, I'm sorry. I have no right to question or badger you, especially now, after what you've just gone through." She sighed. "But, oh, damn, I want you to be as happy as I am, and Phillip . . . well . . ."

"Phillip is a long way from being another Morgan," Courtney finished for her. *And even farther away from being another Rio,* she acknowledged to herself.

"Yes." Stepping back, Samantha smiled.

"And does Morgan share your less than enthusiastic opinion of Phillip?" Courtney managed a weak smile in return.

Samantha's smile dissolved into trilling laughter. "Morgan hasn't offered an opinion. He does have this frustrating habit of keeping his own counsel! That's the reason I couldn't answer your question about Rio."

"What?" Courtney was suddenly alert.

"Right after we sat down," Samantha reminded her. "You asked me to tell you about Rio, and I said I really didn't know all that much about him *to* tell." She lifted her shoulders in a helpless shrug. "Morgan is about as communicative as a dead telephone line!" An impish glow flared in her green eyes. "I'm dying of curiosity about Rio myself. Maybe, just maybe, if we both work on Morgan, we can pry some information out of him."

Tilting her head Courtney stared at Samantha. "I can't get over the change in you, Samantha Denning Wade. You are so completely different from the Samantha I knew before you married."

"I hope the difference is an improvement," Samantha teased.

Courtney pursed her lips. "It is, rather. Even in your early twenties you were so regal, so"—she shrugged—"so very self-contained and impervious to everything and everybody."

"Somewhat as you are now?" Samantha suggested softly.

Courtney stared at her in startled blankness a moment; then she laughed, the first easy laughter Samantha had heard since her return.

"You know, you're right!" Sliding her arm around Samantha's waist, she hugged her briefly. "Being the younger by almost four years, I always tried to emulate you, be exactly like you." Removing her arm, she started for the bathroom. "It would appear that I've succeeded." She laughed, pausing at the doorway.

"Not quite," Samantha chided. At Courtney's arched look she taunted, "I'm desperately in love with the man I married."

The verbal dart hit home. Reflexively Courtney glanced down at the sparkling diamond on her finger. Samantha was right, of course, she thought tiredly. She had no choice but to return the ring to Phillip.

A frown marring her smooth brow, Samantha crossed the room to Courtney. "Forgive me," she urged contritely. "I've upset you, and I never meant to."

"No, no." Courtney shook her head, sending the gold strands of her hair flying like spangled sunbeams around her shoulders. "I know you're right. I've always known it. I can't possibly marry Phillip.

Especially not now, she thought pensively, stepping into the bathroom; *not since Rio.*

Rio. Even with the hot water cascading over her head in the shower, Courtney shivered at the thought of his name. Rio, with his raspy, nighttime voice. Rio, with his silent, shadowy movements. Rio, with his rangy, long, muscled body, and his hot, searching mouth.

Tasting his hunger, feeling the stroke and thrust of his tongue, Courtney parted her lips with a sigh of longing. The rush of water into her mouth quenched the heat rising in her body and drowned the too real dream.

What a fool she was! Sputtering, she switched the water off and stepped out of the shower. Patting her body dry, she lectured herself bracingly.

She was looking at Rio through newly misted eyes, seeing him as the hero, bigger than life; her knight in shining armor. It had to stop. Rio McCord was a man, if not quite like other men. So he had been gentle with her, so he had been compassionate and understanding—so what?

What did she expect of the man? Hadn't he given her enough?

The towel dropped from Courtney's hands. Her eyes stinging with hot tears she skimmed her reflection in the mirror. Rio had given her much more than compassion and understanding. Rio, a man she had never seen before that night, had proved to her that every secret hope she'd held about the possibility of beauty in the act of making love was true.

No, Rio had taken nothing from her, he had given. And then only after she had begged him to make love to her! She, Courtney Tremaine-Smythe, the arrogant young woman who had breezed through life with the best of everything, now felt bereft of everything.

She had no earthly right to expect anything from Rio

McCord, no right at all. She knew that, and the knowing hurt like hell!

The young woman grew pale, while her eyes brightened with the threat of tears. Staring at her own reflection Courtney shook her head in mute denial. She rarely ever wept! What was happening to her? She didn't feel like herself! But if she wasn't herself, who was she? She needed to be around people—people who knew her, knew Courtney Tremaine-Smythe! Swallowing a sob she forced herself to dress very slowly, very carefully, in exactly the manner Courtney was known to do.

She was all right. Of course she was all right! She'd had a bad time of it, but now it was over. *I need time, that's all, time,* she thought, buttoning the silk shirt she had pulled out of the closet. *The memory will fade,* she insisted silently, stepping into raw silk pants, even as the bruises on her body were already starting to fade.

Bruises. Ben. His hands, grabbing, kneading, her breasts, her thighs! Oh, God! *Rio, take me out of here, away from him! I'm so cold, so frightened!*

The harsh, uneven sound of her own breathing startled Courtney out of her trancelike state. In amazement she realized that she was cradling her body with arms wrapped tightly over her breasts. Her teeth were clenched, and she was shivering uncontrollably.

How long would it continue to haunt her? How many times would she be caught like this, unaware, unprotected? An urge to run, somewhere, anywhere, swept through her. But where could one run to get away from the images of memory?

Panting as if she'd already run to the point of exhaustion, Courtney sent her haunted gaze scurrying around the room. There was nowhere to hide, no corner to crawl into. Her glance collided with the bed—and held. She had felt safe in *his* bed. The memories had receded in *his* bed. Terror was held at bay in *his* bed.

Courtney's arms tightened around her breasts convulsively. His arms had given haven. His mouth had banished fear. His body had been the tutor of memory-blanking pleasure.

Rio.

Chapter Six

The stain was gone.

His stance rigid, his expression grim, his eyes narrowed into slits, Rio stared at the pale-green bedspread. There wasn't the faintest trace of the coin-sized spot. Maria took her role of housekeeper very seriously.

Yet, with his mind's eye, Rio could still see the red stain, and feel again the riot of sensations he'd experienced at the sight of it. And the sensations were awesome in their power. Foremost of the emotions bedeviling him was blatant masculine pride. He, Rio McCord, had accomplished the feat Courtney's fiancé, the elegant Phillip, had not managed to pull off!

The back side of the heady emotion was chagrin; Rio was all too cognizant of the mental state Courtney had been in at the time of her initiation into full womanhood.

And there were myriad other emotions vying for recognition: anger, contrition, frustration, and the oddest sensation that felt very similar, too similar, to grief.

Rio was not by nature introspective. He'd come very

early in life to an understanding of self. Acceptance had followed understanding. What he was, he was—and what he was not, he was not—until Courtney Tremaine-Smythe. The advent of Courtney into his life had created inner conflict Rio was positive he could easily live without. Yet the conflict was there, riding him as tenaciously as a cowboy hell-bent on winning top money at the rodeo.

Frowning, Rio walked to the bed and tore the spread from it; then, turning abruptly, he strode across the hall and into his own room. As neatly as Maria had, he smoothed the covering over his bed.

The work completed he stepped back, a derisive smile pulling at his lips. An empty gesture, perhaps, and yet, in his mind, the spread and the lovemaking were connected. He wanted her, wanted her so badly his bones ached, and until the wanting ceased to torment him, he'd sleep wrapped in the spread of their first time together.

"By some he's called Night Striker."

Courtney was too much of a lady to gape, yet now she sat openmouthed in surprised reaction to Samantha's calmly delivered statement. One week had transpired since Rio had escorted her to the Wade ranch. Within that week she had been to Las Vegas for further debriefing by the authorities, had returned her engagement ring to a disgruntled Phillip, had assured her father she would be fine if he remained in the gambling city for some relaxation, and had returned to the ranch the day before.

Now, stretched out on a lounge chair by the Wade pool, Courtney gaped at her serenely smiling cousin.

"Close your mouth, darling," Samantha teased. "You're creating a draft."

"Night Striker?" Courtney repeated softly, envisioning Rio the first time she'd seen him, standing in the shadows in that boxlike room in the cabin.

"Night Striker," Samantha reiterated, grinning at the wary expression stealing over her husband's face. Her statement had been in response to a question from Courtney about Rio. Courtney's query had not been made casually; it had been the opening move in the game plan contrived by the two women to pry information out of Morgan.

"But why on earth would anyone call him that?" Courtney's gaze turned in unison with Samantha's to pin Morgan to the lounger he was sprawled upon.

"Why do I have this nasty suspicion that I've been set up?" His eyes shuttered, Morgan glanced from Courtney to Sam.

"Very likely because you have," Samantha retorted sweetly. "We are both consumed with curiosity about your friend, my love, and you are the only person at hand who can satisfy that curiosity."

Impatient, yet cautious, Courtney forced herself to relax while avidly observing the byplay between Samantha and Morgan.

"Samantha," he said warningly, "I told you before, several *times* before, that Rio's business *is* Rio's business."

"There, you see?" Jerking into a sitting position Samantha swung her gaze to Courtney. "Didn't I tell you?" Her eyes beginning to glitter like gemstones, she whipped her head around to glare at Morgan. "For heaven's sake, Morgan, we aren't asking you to divulge state secrets, you know! You claim the man is your friend, yet I never even heard his name mentioned until a little over a week ago! And we've been married for over five years!"

Morgan shifted his deeply tanned, leanly muscled body on the padded lounger. Again his gaze flashed from his wife to her cousin. Both countenances were set in lines of determination. His hands lifted slightly off the lounger, then dropped back.

"Okay," he muttered. "What do you want to know about him?"

"Everything!" Courtney and Samantha demanded simultaneously.

"Oh, Lord!" Morgan closed his eyes and groaned. "As if I didn't have my hands full with the redhead! Now I get her blond counterpart!"

"Stop stalling, darling." Settling back comfortably, Samantha favored her husband with a dazzling smile. "Spill your guts," she ordered pleasantly.

Morgan's expression grew pained at Samantha's terminology. His black eyes glowing like hot coals, he observed, "I think you and I are going to have an in-depth discussion about your language very soon, Mrs. Wade."

"Everything I know, I learned from you," Samantha reminded him serenely. "Now let's hear all about Rio."

A spark of pain ignited in Courtney's chest at the loving banter between her host and hostess. Samantha and Morgan were so blatantly, so very unself-consciously, in love! The unconcealed evidence of their love had struck Courtney at once, on her first arrival at the ranch a month previously. On that initial visit she had cynically decided that Samantha and Morgan were putting on an act, a performance designed to impress Samantha's British relatives. Now Courtney knew better.

Courtney also realized that the spark of pain she'd felt at odd moments while in Samantha and Morgan's company contained elements both of envy and longing. Sighing for an unnamed something she'd missed in life, she riveted her attention on Morgan as he began to reminisce.

"I met Rio at Texas A&M," Morgan commenced, a faraway look on his face. "I think we gravitated together naturally because neither one of us had any interest in sports." He grinned. "At least not as participants."

"I would have thought the opposite to be true," Courtney commented, skimming his well-knit athlete's body with unabashed admiration.

Morgan laughed softly. "Well, it wasn't really that neither one of us wasn't interested exactly, we simply didn't have the time. Both of us were carrying schedules heavy enough to break an elephant's back." He settled back, as if for the duration. "And, as many of our courses coincided, we kept running into each other in lecture halls. Then one afternoon, after one particularly boring session, we left the hall griping about the professor and wound up in a bar off campus." A smile twitched the corners of his mouth as his voice trailed away.

"Morgan!" Samantha drew him into the present sharply. "What happened then?"

"We both got smashed," Morgan answered, laughing, "and sealed our new friendship with Jack Daniel's, a lot of Jack Daniel's. It didn't take us long to discover we had much more in common than a few college courses," he went on soberly. "The most important thing being our land."

Though his statement was obviously old news to Samantha, Courtney, fully aware of Morgan's many and varied business interests, shot an inquisitive look at him.

"I'm a cattleman first, Courtney," Morgan answered her mute question. "I always have been. And, that day I learned that Rio was, first and foremost, a horseman. And, also like me, he had taken on the backbreaking study load to get through school in the shortest amount of time possible." A reminiscent smile tugged at his lips. "You might say we were drawn together at that time because we were both homesick for the range."

"But what does that have to do with the nickname 'Night Striker'?" Samantha asked, clearly exasperated.

"Shut up, darling," he ordered mildly. "You badgered me into this true confession, now let me tell it my own way."

Courtney silently supported Morgan's position; she personally was soaking up every word. When Morgan continued, Courtney was thrown into confusion by what she considered an unrelated observation.

"His father is Patrick McCord, you know."

Courtney frowned but not Samantha.

"Patrick McCord!" Samantha exclaimed, bolting upright on the lounger. *"The* Patrick McCord?"

"The Patrick McCord," Morgan repeated with relish, grinning in satisfaction at having stunned his wife.

"Ho-ly mackerel!" Samantha muttered in an awed tone.

"Have I missed some vital bit here?" Her frown deepening, Courtney glanced from Samantha to Morgan. "Who, exactly, is Patrick McCord?" Even as she voiced the name, memory stirred, not of a person, but of a medal, nestling in the dark curls on Rio's chest. And of Rio's soft laugh as he told her the medal was a gift from his father, the secretly superstitious Irishman.

"Oh, I'm sorry, Court," Samantha responded for Morgan. "Of course you wouldn't know. Patrick McCord's name is synonymous with oil in Texas," she explained.

"And quite a few other places," Morgan inserted dryly. "He is known affectionately as 'the flamboyant Irishman,' " he added on a chuckle.

Rio's father? Courtney smiled vaguely in bewilderment, attempting to equate *flamboyant* with the silent, self-contained Rio.

"Rio doesn't look at all Irish!" she blurted when the equation proved impossible for her.

"That's for damn sure!" Morgan laughed. "He's got more the look of his Conquistador ancestors than he does the leprechaun."

"His mother is Spanish?"

"Was," Morgan corrected Courtney gently. "His mother is dead, but yes, his mother had undiluted Spanish blood." His lips tightened into a grim line. "When she ran off with Patrick, her family declared her dead. She had no contact with them until the day she actually did die, six or seven years ago. Patrick adored her, so did Rio.''

In the small moment of silence that followed Morgan's explanation, Courtney achingly wondered what being adored by Rio would be like. Heaven, she decided, sheer heaven. Morgan's voice, as he resumed his narrative, drew her from longings of celestial perfection.

"Luz was beautiful," Morgan mused, a smile softening his lips. "I met her at graduation. She had creamy skin, and dark, soulful eyes, and a soft, caressing voice. And all Patrick's millions were useless against the illness that ravaged her lovely body." A sigh moved his chest. "After her funeral Patrick went on a two-week rip. Rio finally dragged him, roaring drunk and sobbing, out of a bordello in a dusty little town across the border." The smile that touched his lips held more sadness than humor. "The funny part was, one of the girls told Rio that Patrick hadn't bedded any one of them, but that he'd talked of Luz incessantly to *all* of them."

Courtney's heart contracted at the picture Morgan's words drew so clearly. How sad that a man who could have afforded the most expensive of counselors, had paid prostitutes to listen while he'd poured out his grief for his wife! With sudden sharpness the thought hit Courtney that Rio probably did indeed favor his father, in temperament, if not in appearance. The only difference being their methods. Instinct assured Courtney that Rio would suffer the loss of a loved one as deeply as his father, if not more— only Rio would suffer in silence and solitude. Morgan confirmed her belief when he continued speaking.

"It was an extremely bad time for Rio as well as Patrick," he told them solemnly. "I'll never forget how shocked I was when I saw Rio at the funeral. He had aged ten years in two." Morgan was quiet a moment, then he amended, "Of course, the change in him wasn't all due to his mother's death. His occupation was beginning to take its toll."

"Night Striker." Samantha's murmur was not a question.

"Yeah," Morgan concurred.

"Well, for heaven's sake, go on!" Samantha voiced the plea hovering on Courtney's lips.

"I know very little about it." Catching sight of the utter disbelief mirrored on their faces, he added earnestly, "I really don't! Hell, I doubt if more than a handful do."

"Mor-gan!"

"Samantha, all I can tell you is that Rio was employed by private corporations in a covert capacity."

"Private corporations! Covert capacity? I don't under—"

"What he means is," Courtney interrupted softly, "Rio earned his probably exorbitant salary by getting a corporation's employees out of any trouble they might have got into in some foreign country or"—Courtney smiled wryly—"created the trouble himself, whichever way his employers wanted it. Right?"

"That about sums it up," Morgan drawled. "And, as Rio preferred to do his 'thing' at night, his—ah—companions dubbed him Night Striker."

Night Striker. Courtney rolled the sobriquet around in her mind. Yes, it fit him; hadn't he struck in darkness up in those hills? Instinct assured Courtney that there were probably deeper connotations to the nickname than Rio's penchant for working in the nighttime hours—*striker* hinted at acts she didn't even care to think about.

"By comparison, designing haute-couture clothes for wealthy women seems rather dull and dilettantish," Courtney murmured at length, unconscious of the sigh that whispered through her lips.

"Dull and dilettantish! Really, Courtney!" Samantha exclaimed. "There is absolutely *no* comparison. I mean, who would even want to be some sort of female James Bond!" Morgan's bark of laughter earned him a glaring glance from Samantha. Then, ignoring his continuing chuckle, she went on, "I think your work is very exciting. And don't frown," she scolded as Courtney's brows drew together. "Do you have any idea how many women envy you your talent? You are an exceptionally gifted designer!"

"If you'll pardon the opinion," Morgan inserted. "Of what importance is this discussion? As he is officially retired from the cloak-and-dagger game, Rio is now merely a horse rancher." He grinned. "By comparison, designing haute couture sounds rather exciting."

"Morgan's right, you know," Samantha agreed promptly. "What brought on this feeling of inadequacy, Court?"

"Oh, I don't know." Courtney sighed. "I suppose I had an attack of the guilts. I was so utterly helpless, and Rio handled everything so effortlessly. Masculine envy, perhaps."

"Understandable," Morgan grunted. "Rio is something."

How extraordinary! The observation was still ringing in Courtney's mind long after she'd retired to her room for the night. The conversation had ended shortly after her explanation to Sam when the twins—the Wades' version of the dynamic duo—came tearing onto the patio, raring to go after their nap.

Though delightful, watching Morgan roughhouse with his sons increased the twist of envy and longing in Courtney's heart. By anyone's definition of the word Morgan was all male. Yet, with his wife and sons, he was gentle and tender, revealing a sensitive understanding of their emotional as well as physical needs.

Courtney readily admitted that she was jealous of the life her cousin had wrought for herself. She was not jealous of Morgan, the man, though she had grown very fond of him already. No, Courtney was jealous of the deep love and rich companionship Samantha had realized from marriage. And Courtney no longer felt even a twinge of regret for having broken her engagement to Phillip. After the past week at the Wade ranch she decided that, unless she could have a relationship even remotely close to what Samantha and Morgan shared, she would rather not marry at all.

As Courtney's father had an unprecedented run of luck at the craps table in Las Vegas, her visit with Samantha and Morgan was extended several times. After the second phone call from Charles begging for "just a few more days," Courtney turned to her hosts with an apologetic smile.

"He's still running hot," she explained wryly. "If you'd prefer, I could join him there."

The vigorous objections made by both Samantha and Morgan brought a thickness to Courtney's throat and a sting to her eyes. And, as events unfurled, having Samantha close proved not only beneficial to Courtney, but necessary.

As the hot summer days melted one into another, and Courtney and Samantha became closer friends, the residual trauma of Courtney's recent experience lessened. There were, of course, the odd moments when the memory—too sharp, too clear—flared and she found herself cold and shivering. At those moments Samantha was there, talking to her, drawing the coldness out, instilling warmth and confidence. One of those moments came on an extremely hot afternoon when Morgan came storming into the house, his black eyes glittering, his expression frightening in its fierceness.

"That son of a—"

"Morgan!" Samantha's startled yelp drowned his string of curses. "What or who put a burr under your saddle?" she demanded, releasing the twins into the care of the housekeeper, Sara.

"The law has picked up one of the kidnappers," he said, in the closest thing to a snarl Courtney ever wanted to hear. "The bastard worked for me!"

"One of *our* men?" Sam fairly screeched.

"Not one of the permanent crew, no." Morgan's abrupt movements betrayed the rage searing his lean body. "It was one of the extra men I hired for spring roundup." Sheer amazement left his face blank for a moment. "And do you want to hear what his name is?" he asked, unnecessarily. "Henderson! Henderson, for Crissake!"

Sitting stiffly, as if glued to her chair, Courtney was feeling both associated fear and fuzzy confusion. Why had learning the man's name so enraged Morgan, she wondered vaguely, rubbing her hands up and down her suddenly chilled arms. Samantha partially answered Courtney's mute question.

"Henderson," she repeated musingly; then, eyes widening, "The Henderson property was the name of the place where Rio's men spotted the van!" she exclaimed.

"Exactly," Morgan gritted. "And where the kidnappers went into the hills. The Las Vegas police got a positive identification on him. Henderson was the man driving the bogus cab that picked Courtney up at the hotel. He was also the man who stayed behind to make contact with Charles."

"And the man who set the kidnappers free," Samantha inserted.

"Hell, yes," Morgan snorted disgustedly. "No wonder he had no difficulty finding that cabin in the dark. His family built the damn thing! And he probably grew up crawling all over those damn hills!"

"Wh—What about the other men?" Courtney asked starkly, an image of the leering Ben looming large in her mind.

Morgan stopped pacing and gave a concerned glance at the sound of terror lacing Courtney's voice. Moving to stand in front of her, he placed his hands over hers to halt their chafing movements.

"There is nothing to be afraid of, Courtney," he said

softly. "You are completely safe here." A hint of steel underlined his soft tone. "I protect my own." A smile eased the harshness as he added, teasingly, "And that includes my own's relatives."

Gazing into his now smiling black eyes, Courtney chastised herself for cowardice. She had to put the memory of that time behind her! Forcing herself to relax, she smiled back at him.

"But is there any information about the other men?" she asked with hard-fought-for calm.

"No." Morgan shook his head as he straightened. "Henderson claims they split up after they crossed the border. The authorities are inclined to believe him. But don't worry, the other three will be found; stupid outlaws usually are. And talk about stupid!" Swinging around, he cocked an eyebrow at Sam. "Do you know where the Rangers picked him up?" Since he obviously didn't expect an answer, he didn't wait for one. "That jerk was hiding in that pile of rotting lumber on his property! I suppose he figured the law would never dream of looking for him there—at the scene of the crime, so to speak." Shaking his head, Morgan strode out of the room.

"Are you all right?" Samantha asked softly after the dust had figuratively cleared from Morgan's passage.

"Yes, I'm fine." Smiling at Samantha, Courtney repeated aloud the dictate she'd silently given herself. "I must put the memory of it behind me."

A few days later Courtney came to the jolting realization that putting the memory behind would be not only difficult, but impossible.

On awakening, Courtney lay in the deliciously air-cooled room, staring at the open beamed ceiling. She had fallen in love with the place—not just the apricot-and-cream bedroom she now occupied, but the entire ranch. The ambiance, the casual, easygoing pace of the ranch, appealed to her, after the more formal setting she was used to.

But it was time to go home. Courtney had reached the decision the night before. Now, her smile fading, she reiterated it. If she could extract her father from the gaming rooms and golf courses, she planned to be back in England before the week was out. She had work to do; it was time to start on next year's fall line—even if it was frivolous and unimportant.

Disturbed by her thoughts, Courtney shifted restlessly. It was not the realization that her work was less than world shattering that made her uneasy, but the man the thoughts brought to mind.

Courtney did not want to think of Rio. Most of all she did not want to remember the haven and heaven she'd discovered in his arms. Intellectually, she understood the traumatic needs that had initially driven her to seek reassurance of her worth as a woman by begging him to love her. Emotionally, she felt shattered by the effects and after effects of their lovemaking.

Which was precisely why Courtney did not want to think of Rio.

Secretly, to herself, Courtney could admit that she was very close to obsessed with the man. No matter how often she told herself her feelings had more to do with hero worship than any deeper emotion, she continued to think of him constantly, and with painful longing.

And so Courtney knew it was time to go home, to put the distance of miles as well as culture between them. Rio had walked away from her without a word or backward glance; it was past time she did likewise.

She was, Courtney reminded herself, the daughter of a very wealthy, prominent man. And though she had gained her reputation as a designer working for her father, it did not lessen her talent. She was good at what she did, and she knew it. It was time to get back to her life.

Her decision reaffirmed, Courtney swung her legs out of the bed and stood up, only to sit down again immediately. The room, or her head, was spinning and her stomach churned warningly. Clutching the edge of the bed she drew a deep breath; then, her eyes flying wide, she sprang to her feet and dashed for the bathroom. When the roiling in her stomach ceased, she hung over the sink, shaking her head slowly in silent denial. She couldn't be pregnant! She simply could not be! Yet even as she rejected the idea, Courtney faced the very real possibility that she was indeed pregnant.

Courtney was well aware that only one mating was required to create a baby. She had also duly noted the absence of her flow at the completion of her normal cycle earlier that week. Optimistically she had assured herself that the missed period was a direct result of the trauma she'd suffered. The wrenching sickness had ripped away the veil of optimism.

The condition would have to be confirmed, of course—but only to make it official. In her own mind Courtney needed no official confirmation; she knew she had conceived Rio's child.

After brushing her teeth and showering, Courtney dressed in comfortable summer-weight linen pants and a brightly patterned cotton shirt—one of her own designer outfits—and stepped into a pair of wedge-heeled sandals that bore the mark of an equally famous Italian designer. Smoothing her hair back into a simple braid, she applied a light covering of makeup, then left the bedroom, all traces of her earlier nausea gone.

Courtney announced her decision to spend the day in Las Vegas while she sat across the kitchen table from Samantha as they breakfasted together, Sam on bacon, eggs, toast, and coffee, Courtney on Sara's delicious home-made biscuits and herbal tea. Samantha took Courtney's announcement enthusiastically.

"It will do you good to get out and mingle with other people," Samantha said in a mother-hen tone. "I'd offer to go with you, but I just spoke to Babs Carter on the phone and agreed to meet her for lunch in Ely. I was going to ask you to join us, but . . ." She shrugged. "Do you remember Babs, Court?"

"The madcap?" Courtney laughed softly. "Of course I do. Who could ever forget her?" Sipping her tea, she imagined the bubbly young woman as she'd looked the last time Courtney had seen her. "How is she?"

Samantha grinned. "Babs will be forever Babs. And her husband is still head over heels in love with her. They have three children now, two boys and an adorable little girl." There was a wistful sound to Samantha's tone as she mentioned the girl.

Sam's wistfulness was echoed mutely inside Courtney's mind. How had both Sam and Babs, who had been best friends from their teens, managed to find men—wonderful men—who obviously adored them? Into Courtney's mind came a vision that brought a sting to her eyes. She could actually see a small child, a girl, with dark hair, and dark eyes, and the occasional smile that stole one's breath and heart.

"Courtney?"

Courtney reluctantly surrendered the vision for reality. Her dream-clouded eyes clearing to deep sapphire, she smiled at Samantha, who was staring at her with concern.

"Yes?" she asked brightly.

"Are you all right?" Samantha demanded suspiciously. "You had the strangest expression for a minute there."

"Yes, I'm fine." Courtney infused a carefree note into her tone. "I was remembering some of the outrageous stunts Babs used to embroil you in," she lied blandly.

"Babs *was* a scorcher!" Samantha laughed. "As a matter of fact it was Babs who embroiled me into this marriage with Morgan!"

"She did what?" Courtney's eyebrows peaked into an arch.

"Uh-huh." Samantha grinned, rising to fill their cups. "It was shortly after my father died," she explained, sliding onto her chair. "I don't suppose you ever heard anything about the terms of my father's will?" she asked wryly.

"No." Courtney frowned. "Were the terms unusual?"

"You might say that," Samantha drawled—in much the same way Morgan did regularly. "The terms stated that I had to marry, an American citizen, mind you, before my twenty-fifth birthday—which was only five months away at the time." A tiny smile hovered on her lips as she waited for Courtney's reaction.

Courtney's cup hit the table with a thump. "But that's ridiculous!" she exclaimed in shocked tones. "Surely you challenged the terms?"

"I had planned to, until my lawyers informed me the challenge would come to nothing." Samantha drank deeply from her cup, then leaned back lazily in her chair and smiled. "Needless to say, I was furious."

"Well, I should say so!" Courtney exclaimed. "But, love, what does that have to do with Morgan?" she asked, frowning. "And Babs?"

"Only everything." Samantha laughed. "But in reverse. It was Babs first, then Morgan."

"Sam, really!" Courtney cried in utter exasperation. "If you don't explain, I'm going to take an absolute fit!"

"Well, if you're positive you won't be bored?" Samantha said teasingly.

"Samantha!" Courtney fairly screamed. "If you don't tell me at once, I'll murder you!"

"What a grouch!" Grinning, Samantha settled herself more comfortably in her padded chair. "Okay, here goes . . . and no interruptions, please. As stated, the terms of the will could not be broken, and I was frantic and cursing mad!" As she spoke, her beautiful eyes grew opaque with memory. "I *could* have married any number of eminently suitable young men. The problem was, I didn't *want* to marry any one of them. I was worrying the situation to death when I received a letter from Babs asking if I'd stand as godmother for her second child. I agreed at once, for several reasons. For one, I simply gave in to the urge to run away—and put some distance between my bad temper and my family. And two, I'd missed out on being godmother to Babs's first baby, because I'd been out of the country at the time."

"Are you getting to the part about Morgan soon?" Courtney inquired politely when Samantha had paused to drink.

"Actually, the whole thing is about Morgan, as you'll soon see ... if you'll be patient?" Samantha taunted sweetly.

"Oh, carry on, please," Courtney rejoined with equal sweetness. "You won't hear another croak out of me!"

"I'll bet," Samantha muttered. "Now, where was I?" she asked in a tone of contrived innocence. "Ah, yes, the christening. Well, as Babs was and is my dearest friend, I cried out my tale of woe to her immediately upon arrival at their home. Babs, being not only the mother of her children, but of hare-brained ideas, came up with—in her words—the perfect solution to my dilemma."

"Morgan?" Courtney interposed in surprise.

"Morgan," Samantha concurred softly. "Lord, we were antagonists from our first sight of each other!"

"You and Morgan?" Sheer disbelief laced Courtney's tone.

Samantha smiled gently. "Oh, yes. I suppose I must have recognized my match—or master—in him at once." Her smile became misty. Then, straightening abruptly, she went on. "At any rate Babs hatched this dubious idea of an arranged marriage between me and Morgan." She grinned at Courtney's shocked face. "The exchange being, my money for his name," she said, deliberately adding to her cousin's shock.

Courtney looked at Samantha in disbelief. "Morgan was broke?"

"No." Samantha shook her head. "But he allowed his friends to *believe* he was, for reasons we won't go into. And, of course, I believed it also. In truth, it did seem like the perfect solution; I could continue with my world-trotting existence, and Morgan could continue to work himself to death on this ranch; I with his name, he with my money." Samantha laughed easily. "In theory it sounded perfect. The catch came when Morgan informed me that he expected a real marriage—in every sense of the word."

"He—ah—asked you to sleep with him?" Courtney asked in carefully couched words.

"No, he never *asked!*" Samantha's laughter filled the spacious room.

"Oh!"

"You might well say 'oh.' " Samantha grinned. "Of course, as I was already in love with him, I didn't offer too much of a struggle."

"Incredible" was the only comment Courtney could rake out of her stunned mind.

Samantha wore a wondering expression. "Yes, it is, rather. You can't imagine how many times I've thanked God for the urge that brought me to Nevada at the time. *Time!*" she repeated in a ladylike yelp. "Good heavens, will you look at the time! I've got to meet Babs!" Jumping out of her chair she dashed to the sink to deposit her cup. "Darling, you don't mind if I run, do you?" she asked anxiously.

"Not at all, Sam," Courtney responded absently, still caught up in her cousin's story. "I'll see you when I get back from Las Vegas."

Samantha started from the room, then paused in the doorway. "I'll arrange for someone to fly you into Vegas in the Cessna, Courtney, and for somebody to drive you to the airstrip." Sam smiled, then waved her fingers. "Good luck at the tables, love."

I would do better to hope for luck on the examining table! Such was the silent retort that rang in Courtney's mind as she entered the plush office of a prominent Las Vegas obstetrician some hours later.

Lady luck must surely hate blondes, Courtney decided still later—after hearing the results of the pregnancy test. The test had proved positive—which really came as no great surprise to Courtney, as she'd been positive since being sick to her stomach early that morning. The question that tormented her now was: What in the world was she going to do about it?

There were several options open to her, and Courtney was aware of every one of them. As she was only approximately three weeks into the gestation period, she could marry at once and have no one the wiser at the time of the baby's birth. Or, she could remain single, have her baby in due course, and thumb her nose at traditionalists. Then again, she could go off somewhere on her own and have an abortion.

The mere thought of the third option gave Courtney the shudders, so she immediately discounted it. That left marriage, in all probability to Phillip, or single parenthood. Strange as it might seem to anyone else, Courtney was positive Phillip would still want to marry her even knowing she was carrying another man's child. But Courtney did not want to marry Phillip, even if it did mean upsetting her father, which she knew she unquestionably would.

As there was no blazing necessity for an on-the-spot decision, Courtney left the doctor's office. She mentally played with the pros and cons of her situation as she physically played the various games of chance in Las Vegas. And if her father at times looked at her oddly, wondering at her more-than-usual reserve, he attributed it to her recent ordeal and spoke even more gently to her than before.

The following afternoon Courtney left her father with a kiss, an embrace, and an admonition that he join her at the Wade ranch by the beginning of the next week at the latest.

"It may even be sooner." Charles smiled ruefully, returning her embrace. "It would appear that luck has deserted me."

Must be a family trait, Courtney thought with sudden tiredness, smiling in defiance of the tears that brightened her eyes. With a final wave of her hand she stepped into the cab that would deliver her to the airport and the waiting Cessna.

By the time Courtney returned to the Wade ranch, she was completely exhausted from her day. Never could she remember having felt so utterly weary, not even after her sojourn into the Texas hills. Courtney spent some time talking to Sam and Morgan; then, as soon as she deemed it decently possible, she excused herself and went to her room.

After standing listlessly under the shower Courtney blow-dried her hair, then tugged a lace-and-satin nightgown over her head. She was brushing her teeth when a light tapping sounded on the bedroom door.

"Yes?" she called softly, rinsing her mouth.

"It's Sam, Courtney. Are you in bed?"

Patting her lips dry, Courtney left the bathroom. "No, come on in, Sam," she invited, crossing the room to open the door.

"I hesitated to disturb you," Samantha admitted as she entered, studying Courtney's face with concern. "But you looked"—she shrugged—"well, odd. Is there something wrong, Court?"

The strange weakness swept over Courtney again, bringing a warm mist to her eyes. Determined not to lay any more of her troubles on her cousin's shoulders, she turned away quickly with a husky denial. "Nothing I can't handle."

Circling around her, Samantha confronted Courtney with her hands resting firmly on her slim hips. "There's nothing you *have* to handle alone!" she exclaimed. "Are we not family?" At Courtney's brief nod she demanded, "Are we not friends?"

"Yes! Of course we are!" Courtney had to swallow against the sudden thickness in her throat. "But . . ." she began.

"But nothing!" Sam overrode her objection with a vigorous shake of her head. "Something is obviously troubling you, and I want to help if I can."

Courtney stared into Samantha's compassion-filled emerald eyes for several seconds; then she caved in . . . inside. Lifting her chin with unconscious pride she met Samantha's gaze directly.

"I went into Las Vegas to consult with a physician," she said evenly. "I'm pregnant, Sam."

"Oh, Courtney!" Samantha murmured sympathetically. "Phillip?"

"No." Courtney shook her head, a wry smile shadowing her tremulous lips.

Frowning, Samantha stared at her an instant, then her eyes flew wide with horror. "My God! Was it one of the kidnappers? Were you afraid to tell us?"

"Oh, no! Sam, I was telling the truth when I said I was not raped!" Courtney hastened to relieve Samantha on that point.

Now Samantha's eyes widened with confusion. "But then, darling, who?" she asked in bewilderment.

"Rio McCord." The name came off Courtney's lips distinctly.

Chapter Seven

"Rio?" Samantha repeated the name in a whisper. Then, very clearly, "Rio!" she exclaimed. "But, Courtney, you were only with the man one night!"

"Exactly." Courtney wet her suddenly parched lips, and she moved to sit down on one of the comfortable chairs at the window facing the patio.

Her expression revealing bemusement and confusion, Samantha moved to drop onto the matching chair she'd occupied that morning, opposite Courtney. "Courtney," she began slowly, "I know it's really none of my business, but what in the world happened between you and Rio?" Before Courtney could respond, she pleaded, "And please don't tell me *he* raped you!"

"No, of course he didn't rape me!" Courtney said adamantly.

"But, dammit!" Samantha exploded with frustration. "Then, what happened?"

Briefly Courtney explained to Samantha—or attempted to explain—her feelings of that night. As Samantha listened, her expression softened with understanding and compassion, and she nodded encouragingly several times.

"I ... I felt like an object, Sam! Like an inanimate thing!" Courtney had to pause to swallow repeatedly. The panic was clutching at her chest again with the restored memory, tightening her throat and chilling her bloodstream.

Leaning across the table that separated the chairs, Samantha grasped Courtney's cold fingers. "You don't have to continue if it causes you pain, Court," she said anxiously.

"I'm all right." Courtney drew a shuddering breath. "But you see, Rio was so kind, so gentle with me, so very *real* and human, not beastly like that Ben!" She lifted her shoulders helplessly. "I suppose I needed his very realness to make me feel real too."

"Yes," Sam whispered in understanding. "Yes."

Lost in their own thoughts they were quiet for some minutes; then Sam asked gently, "What are you going to do, Court?"

Courtney's chuckle had more the sound of a sob than of laughter. "I haven't quite decided," she admitted. "Except that I'm going home next week."

"What?" Samantha cried, her eyes wide with shock. "Courtney, are you saying you're planning to leave this country without telling Rio?" she demanded in amazement.

There was no need for a verbal response; the answer was clear on Courtney's face. Springing to her feet, Samantha paced the room, then spun to face Courtney challengingly.

"I am not going to let you do it," Samantha threatened decisively. "Half—hell, more than half—the responsibility lies with Rio," she declared. "Besides which, the man has a right to know that he is going to be a father."

Naturally, Courtney had given considerable thought to the question of Rio's right to know. But how the devil to go about telling him? And, more unnerving still, how the devil would he react to the information? Courtney certainly didn't relish the idea of facing an exasperated Rio McCord! Unaware of doing so, she began shaking her head slowly back and forth.

"Courtney, you must tell him! He *does* have rights here!" Samantha's sharp tone snapped Courtney to attention. "And even if he didn't, you simply cannot have this baby single!"

"Why not?" Courtney demanded, feeling cornered. "It's done all the time these days."

"Yes, it is—but not by us! I will be the first one to admit that our family can lay claim to more than one skeleton tucked away in closets in an assortment of town houses and country estates," she argued heatedly. "But every one of them was legitimate!"

Courtney winced, as if physically struck. Realizing her advantage Samantha charged on bluntly.

"Up until now you have gone your own way with impunity; defying all advice to the contrary by financially backing every nonviolent cause going; flaunting convention by living precisely as you chose; lifting your chin imperiously to any detractors. And I've applauded you for it." Samantha smiled at Courtney's startled look. "Oh, yes, I've kept track of your career and exploits. But in this instance you are wrong."

"But you don't understand!" Courtney protested.

"I understand perfectly," Samantha countered. "And I understand even more. *I* understand and accept the ramifications. Do you wish to see your child grow up with the handicap of speculation about his parentage?" Samantha shook her head, red mane flying like angry flames around her shoulders. "Dammit, Court! The child will be referred to as the Tremaine-Smythe bastard, and you know it!"

"Yes, I know, but . . ." Courtney closed her eyes, and her voice dropped to a whisper. "I—I can't tell him, Sam."

"Why not, for heaven's sake?" Samantha retorted in exasperation. "Court, what the devil happened to you up there in those hills? You are simply not the same person anymore. The Courtney I knew was not afraid of anything or anybody."

"I'm not afraid of Rio!" Courtney denied at once. Not in a physical sense, at any rate, she amended silently.

"Well, then, what is this nonsense about not being able to tell him?" Samantha demanded, frowning.

How could she explain, make Sam understand the weight of responsibility she was feeling? Courtney shrugged her shoulders in an uncharacteristically vulnerable way.

"I feel it simply would not be fair of me to burden Rio with what is, in all honesty, the result of my own precipitous action." Lifting her chin, she faced Samantha squarely. "Sam, what I failed to mention in my recounting was that I literally begged Rio to make love to me."

Samantha quickly swallowed the gasp of shock that rose to her lips; she found it impossible to imagine Courtney begging for anything! Then again, Samantha reminded herself, she had never been exposed to the traumatic events that her cousin had been forced to endure. Breathing deeply, she fought for a calm tone. "I really do understand your position now, love, but it doesn't change the fact of your pregnancy, or Rio's right to be informed of it."

Courtney closed her eyes as if in pain. "I . . . I simply cannot tell him, Samantha." As she opened her eyes again a curl of uneasiness shot through her at the confident expression stealing over Samantha's face.

"All right," Samantha murmured, too easily. Her emerald eyes betrayed nothing of her thoughts: *Maybe you can't, but Morgan can.*

The dawn was heralded by a freshening gust of cold air. Lying opposite the open window, wrapped within the folds of the sea-green bedspread, Rio stared sightlessly into the grayness beyond the broad pane of glass.

After a total of three and a half hours of sleep Rio had wakened over an hour before, and had been staring out, while looking in, ever since. The regimen was not unfamiliar; it had been the standard every night since he'd returned from Nevada.

The lack of sleep, and the work pace Rio set for himself during the daylight hours, were beginning to show. The fuse to his temper grew shorter with each successive sunrise. He had dropped some weight from his already finely honed body, and his increased physical activity had hardened muscles and sinews into rippling cables of steel. His features had sharpened and were set into a mask of austere remoteness. Rio was fully aware that the majority of his men actively avoided contact with him.

Impatience rode him relentlesssly; impatience with his crew, impatience with Cleat, impatience with prevailing weather conditions, but most of all, impatience with himself.

Never having known the mental and physical discomfort of emotions tied in knots by thoughts and memories of any one woman, Rio was at a loss how to deal with it. Being in a near constant, almost painful, state of sexual arousal was another previously unknown irritant.

"Dammit all!"

Rio threw back the spread and rolled off the mattress, unmindful of the cool air rushing over his naked flesh. He was tired both physically and psychologically, a combination he had experienced only once before in his life—during the weeks he'd spent caged up like an animal after he had been captured in the jungle in South America.

Now, free as he was to roam at will over the land he loved, Rio's cage was mental, and of his own devising, the bars constructed of silken threads, the memory of a woman with the taste of wild strawberries on her softly sculpted mouth.

How was she? Rio had grown used to speculating about Courtney's well-being—it nagged at him on the average of twice an hour. Was she still at the Wade ranch, or had she returned to England . . . with the ever-so-handsome Phillip? Rio's jaws had developed a constant ache from grinding his teeth over the thought of Courtney—with Phillip.

Courtney with Phillip. The connotations contained in the coupling of the two names seared Rio's mind and body like a branding iron straight from the flames.

If he touches her he is dead! Rio made that vow, and other promises of a lethal nature, concerning Phillip, when he was at his most tired, and thus vulnerable, moments. The intensity of these feelings shook him to the core.

This particular morning, with the cool air coiling around his body, Rio felt extremely tired, annoyingly vulnerable, and eager to destroy . . . anyone or anything with the temerity to look at him sideways.

As he thrust his legs into well-worn jeans, and stomped his feet into scruffed boots, Rio concluded that he was feeling almost mean enough to reenlist in the hired-gun business. And *that* thought shook him as much as his lethal feelings against Phillip.

Maria greeted him with a tentative smile as he entered the kitchen. "Good morning, señor." Having been born and raised in West Texas, Maria spoke English without a trace of an accent, yet she persisted in addressing Rio as "señor."

"Good morning." Rio's raspy tones contained a gentleness he was far from feeling. Yet no other kind of response would have occurred to him. The sun had never risen on the day Rio could force himself to be less than gentle with Maria—the woman who had cared so lovingly for his mother throughout Luz's ravishing illness.

"Mr. Wade is on his way in to the ranch, señor." Maria offered the information with the mug of steaming, dark coffee she set before him as he seated himself at the table.

"Morgan?" Though he felt a shiver of alarm, Rio's expression remained closed, his tone mildly inquiring.

"Yes. Frank, the mechanic on duty, called from the airfield when Mr. Wade's plane landed"—she glanced up at the wall clock—"twenty minutes ago." Her coal-black eyebrows arched slightly. "Would you like your breakfast now, or would you prefer to wait for Mr. Wade?"

"I'll wait," Rio murmured absently, sipping at the hot brew. Musing, he swallowed the coffee without really tasting it. Morgan would be arriving shortly, especially if Frank was driving him in, because Frank drove as if the devil were breathing down the Jeep's exhaust pipe!

Frank was driving—Morgan sauntered into the kitchen while Rio was nursing his second mug of coffee.

"I wonder if Frank could be distantly related to Samantha," Morgan quipped, as he dropped into the chair Rio indicated opposite his own. "Morning, Maria," he continued. "Thanks, that smells good," he added, inhaling the scent of the coffee she had placed on the table in front of him.

"Good morning, Mr. Wade." Maria smiled softly. "What would you like for breakfast?"

"Oh, whatever ole blabbermouth over there is having." Flashing white teeth in a grin, Morgan nodded at Rio. "That is, unless he's having bent rusty nails and sweaty saddle leather."

"Humph," Rio snorted into his mug.

Slanting an amused glance at her employer, Maria turned to go to the gleaming stove. "The señor always eats the same breakfast," she said blandly, "a steak so rare it yells ouch when he cuts into it, covered by two eggs, over easy, and refried beans on the side."

"Now you're talkin'." Morgan gave an appreciative sigh.

"Please, throw those steaks under the broiler, sweetheart. I've been up and moving since three this morning, and my stomach's beginning to feel like a deep well at low water."

"How's the family?" Rio drawled sardonically when Morgan flashed his laughing gaze to him.

"Fine." Morgan matched the drawl exactly.

A tiny warning smile curled one corner of Rio's upper lip. "And your houseguests?" he inquired politely.

Acknowledging Rio's tone, Morgan changed his own. "One of them has a problem," he murmured for Rio's ears only. "That's why I'm here now." Sliding smoothly to his feet, he relieved Maria of the two large plates she was carrying to the table, letting a smile suffice as an answer when she murmured her thanks.

While the small exchange went on, Rio was busy fighting a welling sense of panic. Was Courtney ill? Had she been hurt? Surely not the kidnappers again? At the thought of the kidnappers rage swelled to smother the panic. In his mind Rio could see the overweight Ben, slobbering all over Courtney as his hands clutched at places Rio now thought of as his exclusively.

His expression revealing nothing of the emotions exploding inside, Rio fixed Morgan with a glittering stare as he slid the plate in front of him.

"There's been more trouble from the kidnappers?" His cold, remote tone was as unrevealing as his expression.

"No." Morgan shook his head. "As a matter of fact, the law has one of them behind bars." The slice his knife made into the rare piece of beef was a clue to the anger he felt at the felon. "Wait till you hear it," he said sourly, forking the meat into his mouth. Between bites of his breakfast he related the events of Henderson's arrest.

"Stupid bastard," commented Rio when Morgan had finished speaking. Then, calmly, as if his patience wires weren't frazzled and humming dangerously, he nudged

Morgan verbally. "So, what then is the problem *one* of your guests has now?"

"After we've finished eating," Morgan murmured. "Privately."

The ice broke on Rio's features; he frowned. What the hell was all the mystery about? He didn't like it. Morgan's whole attitude bothered him. With enforced coolness, he slowly ate his food.

Closing his office-study door quietly Rio crossed to the intricately carved, Spanish-style credenza and withdrew a black-labeled, square-shaped bottle. Holding it aloft, he raised his eyebrows at Morgan.

"Why not?" Morgan agreed.

Dropping two ice cubes into two short glasses, Rio splashed amber liquor over them, then handed one of the glasses to Morgan. Without fanfare or toast both men drank deeply from their glasses. As he lowered the glass from his lips, Rio's dark eyes stared levelly into Morgan's.

"Okay, what's the story?"

"Courtney's pregnant," Morgan responded bluntly. "She claims that you're the father. Are you?"

"It's possible." Rio's tone betrayed none of the thoughts rioting in his mind. He had been the first man with Courtney; he *knew* that as an irrevocable fact. But . . . had she slept with that pretty boy after she'd returned to Nevada? Rio raised his arm to sip at the whiskey he now really needed. "It's even probable," he added softly. "So?" He was feeling none of the iciness coating his tones.

"So, she'd like her child to have a name." Morgan was relaying Samantha's words to him exactly.

"Mine?" Hoping the fire in the drink would banish the tremors in his insides, Rio drank again.

"If not yours, it will have to be some other man's," Morgan observed curtly, obviously losing patience with his friend. "If it is your child, don't you want it to have your name?"

"Hell, yes!" Rio ground out the agreement fiercely, breaking the chill barrier for the first time.

"That's what I thought." Morgan smiled easily as he raised his glass in a silent salute.

Courtney and Samantha were lounging on the patio after a late-afternoon dip in the pool when Morgan called Sam into the house. Frowning at the edge of command in his tone, Courtney watched Samantha jump to her feet and hurry toward the sliding glass patio doors. Mildly surprised at her cousin's display of wifely docility Courtney let her heavy eyelids droop with a sigh. Morgan had been away from the house all day; perhaps Samantha had some news about their sons to impart to him.

Mentally shrugging off speculation, she shifted into a more comfortable position; why *was* she so listless and sleepy lately? In the next instant her speculations and her laziness were swept from her mind by a chill tingle of awareness. There had not been the faintest murmur of sound, yet she knew she was no longer alone. His very silence announced his presence.

Rio! Here? Frozen, almost afraid to breathe in case she'd conjured him in her mind and not in substance, Courtney slowly raised her long, gold-tipped lashes. Inching, devouring, her gaze crawled up the imposing length of his long, muscled body, almost indecently clad in the briefest of navy-blue swim trunks. Her eyes caressed his slender waist, then moved to the dark hair on his chest. Struck by the sunrays, the metal nestled among the curls seemed to wink at her wickedly.

Startled by her own imaginings, Courtney glanced up abruptly and found her gaze ensnared by the steady regard of Rio's dark, contemplative eyes.

Strangely nervous, wildly excited, Courtney blurted the first thing that came to mind.

"You came all the way from Texas for a swim?"

Rio's quiet laughter brought a tinge of pink to her cheeks. What an absolutely asinine thing to say! She was searching her mind for something a little more intelligible when he saved her the effort.

"I came to claim what's mine." His tone was unusually low, the rasp unnaturally heavy.

For one wild, improbable moment sheer joy leapt in Courtney's heart and mind. As Rio continued speaking the joy died a painful death.

"It is my baby, isn't it, Courtney?"

Controlling her expression with every ounce of will she possessed, Courtney met his stare directly. "Yes. The child is yours."

At her admission a light appeared to click on in the depths of his dark eyes; then it was quickly doused. "What are we going to do about it?" he asked in a maddeningly even tone.

"We?" Incensed, Courtney stared at him arrogantly.

With the agile swiftness natural to him, Rio dropped to kneel beside the lounge chair. "Yes." His voice contained an angry hiss. "*We.*"

Her own flash of anger was subdued by the sudden flare of fury from him.

"What—what do you suggest *we* do?" she inquired unevenly.

Obviously pleased at having the advantage, Rio lifted one hand to trail the tips of his fingers over her flushed, warm cheek. A hint of a smile touched his lips at her involuntary tremor of response.

"I suggest we get married at once." The hint of a smile tilted cynically. "And make the little one nice and legal."

Courtney bit her lip to keep from crying out in protest

against his cynicism. A moment later she was glad she'd kept silent as he went on in an excitingly dark tone:

"We are worlds apart, Courtney, *literally* worlds apart. But we do share the life now inside your body." Watching for her tiniest reaction, he slid his thumb over her lips, smiling again when they parted with her indrawn breath. "And we do share this electrifying physical attraction."

Before she could refute or even argue his assertion he was on his feet in one fluid motion. "Would you like me to take care of the arrangements?"

"If you like," Courtney murmured, frustrated by her inability to glance away from his hard body. "You're more familiar with the proper procedure."

"Right, I'll set the legal wheels in motion tomorrow morning." His rare grin flashed momentarily. "But right now I'm going to have a swim." With a minimum of body action he moved to the edge of the pool. He stood perfectly still for a moment, preparing his dive, then slanted a glance at her over his shoulder. "Who knows," he whispered. "We might even make it work."

With a pretense of deferring all and any suggestions to Courtney, Rio went about making simple plans, then executed them with a like simplicity The legalities were dealt with with a swiftness that aroused Courtney's suspicions. It was obvious, at least to her, that Rio had called in favors from some high places.

Without flair Courtney, with Charles, Samantha, and Morgan in tow, was ushered into the private study of a very prominent Texas judge. Less than fifteen minutes later the judge, smiling benignly, ushered them all out again, and on exiting Courtney was no longer a single woman.

From the judge's home they all went directly back to the ranch for the party Maria had arranged for them. Never before in her life had Courtney witnessed the sort of exuberance Rio's crew displayed. But the absolute highlight of the entire day came with the sudden and unexpected arrival of Rio's father, the legendary flamboyant Irishman, Patrick McCord.

The man was a veritable giant! Well, perhaps he merely looked like a giant, due to the muscular width of his shoulders and the breadth of his burly chest. At any rate Rio, her father and Morgan all appeared reed thin beside Patrick.

Patrick lived up to his name on his very entrance onto the walled patio where the party was being held. Courtney, breathless from being swung in an incomprehensible dance in the arms of one of Rio's slightly drunken men, heard the lilting bellow of Patrick's voice before she caught her first glance of him.

"Where is she?" he demanded in a tone that easily carried above the clamor of the festivities. "Where's my new daughter?"

The music stopped so abruptly, Courtney's senses reeled. As the spinning world settled, her gaze focused on the remotely amused expression of her husband as he sauntered toward her, the giant by his side.

"Courtney, I'd like you to meet your new father, Patrick." Rio's dry voice was in variance with the hawklike watchfulness of his eyes. "Pat, my wife, Courtney."

"Well, now, she is a beauty!" Patrick exclaimed—loud enough to be heard in El Paso, Courtney felt sure.

Not in the least intimidated by his size or booming voice, she smiled and extended her hand. "Mr. McCord, I'm delight—" That's as far as she got before she was swept off her feet and into a bear hug that expelled the breath from her body with a whooshing sound.

"Not nearly as delighted as I am to meet you, girlie!" The big man laughed, swinging her around as if she had no more substance than a rag doll. "I'd just about given up hope of a grandbaby from ole Silent-in-the-Saddle there." He flashed a grin at Rio as he set her on her feet. Had Rio told his father that she was pregnant? Even as the question registered in her whirling mind, Patrick bellowed the answer.

"I only hope he doesn't fool around too long. I ain't getting any younger, you know!"

"You ain't getting any quieter, either," Rio remarked, saving Courtney the effort of a suitable response.

Patrick's laughter seemed to bounce off the patio walls, enveloping everyone in its merry, echoing waves "What the hell is there to be quiet about?" he roared. "Is this a wedding or a wake?"

"Would it make any difference?" Rio inquired wryly.

"Not a lot," his father shot back, along with a grin.

Feeling like a spectator at a tennis match, Courtney shifted her gaze from father to son as the exchange continued. Within seconds Courtney decided that for all Rio's austere attitude, and Patrick's audacious verbal shots, the two men loved each other fiercely. For some unknown reason the knowledge pleased her greatly. They were still exchanging mild insults when Samantha and Morgan joined the trio.

"Hey, Morgan!" Turning with incredible swiftness for a man of his size, Patrick flashed hard white teeth in a breathtakingly beautiful smile. "How the hell are yah?" But before Morgan could open his mouth to do more than return the smile, Patrick spied Samantha. "Well, hot damn!" he said in a subdued, awed tone, his sky-blue eyes darting from Samantha to Courtney to Morgan and then Rio. "Leave it to you two throwbacks to corral the most beautiful women I've laid these tired old eyeballs on in years!"

"You didn't do too badly for yourself." Rio's observation was voiced in a near whisper, and had an immediate sobering effect on his father.

The change in Patrick was startling, and for an instant Courtney could see the son in the father, as the older man appeared to freeze emotionally before her eyes. Then a gentle smile relieved the tightness of his lips.

"No, son," he murmured softly. "I didn't do too badly. I just didn't have her with me long enough." For a millisecond Courtney witnessed pure anguish in Patrick's face. "Love her well, son," he advised quietly. "You never do know how much time you've got."

Later, sitting in the quiet bedroom, Courtney thought back to the scene. What an extraordinary man her father-in-law was, she mused, smiling mistily. And how very startling was his ability to leap from one emotion to another with no effort. For, immediately after charging Rio with her care, he'd created that smashing smile for Samantha while demanding Morgan introduce them.

The party had continued for what seemed like ages to Courtney, who'd been twirled around the patio at least twice by every man there—excluding her own husband, who stood back watching everything through shuttered eyes. Amazingly, by the time the party finally wound down to a natural death, Patrick had retired to a corner with, of all people, her father! Shortly after Sam and Morgan had left to go back to Nevada, Patrick took his leave also— bearing Charles with him!

Shaking her head in bemusement, Courtney kicked her slim-heeled sandals off her aching feet and stood up to begin undressing. A light tap on the door stilled her fingers on the side zipper of the ice-blue, raw-silk sheath she'd chosen to be married in. The sound of the knock forcefully reminded her that this was her wedding night. But would Rio knock on his own bedroom door? Courtney seriously doubted it.

"Yes?" she called softly, padding in stocking feet to the door. "Who is it?"

"Maria, señora," the older woman said quietly. "I have a message that was just delivered for you."

Swinging the door open Courtney muffled a surprised

gasp at the sight of Rio gliding silently down the wide
hallway toward her bedroom. Tearing her gaze from him,
she fought to control the sudden tremor in her hands as
she accepted what appeared to be a greeting card from
the housekeeper.

"Thank you, Maria, and good night," she said softly,
turning back into the room as Rio came to a halt beside
the woman.

"Good night, señora, señor," Maria murmured, a smile
hidden in her tone, as she started back down the hall.

Clutching the large white envelope, Courtney retreated
to the far end of the room as Rio shut the door with a
muffled click.

"Another card of congratulations?" He stalked her to
the window chair.

"Apparently so." Keeping her back to him Courtney
skimmed her tongue over her tension-dried lips.

"Are you going to open it?" Supreme indifference laced
his tone.

"Yes, of course." With ridiculously shaky fingers Courtney broke the seal on the envelope and, frowning, withdrew a single square of paper, folded once. Flipping the
fold open she began to read the blocked, hand-printed
message, her eyes widening with horror as they skimmed
the lines.

So, the big horse rancher is going to ride you now,
is he? Is your body his reward for rescuing you? Well,
that's okay because all he'll be doing is warming you
up for me. But you best tell him to watch his back
because I'll get him. And I'll get you too. Only I don't
plan to shoot you. I plan to ride you to death.

There was no signature, of course, but then none was
necessary; Courtney knew who had written it. With a low,
frightened moan she reached out blindly for the chair

back to steady her trembling body. Her hand was caught and held firmly in Rio's hard grasp.

"What is it?" Plucking the paper from her nerveless fingers Rio shot her a sharp stare before glancing down at the message. Eyes narrowing, he scanned the lines, cursing from the first words his glance encountered.

"How—how did that thing get here?" she choked, fighting the urge to run, anywhere. The panic was back, chilling her blood, numbing her reason. "Rio!" she cried wildly. "That man is going to kill you! And then . . . and then . . ."

"Stop it, Courtney!" The soft command was accompanied by a sharp shake as he grasped her by the shoulders. *"You are safe here."*

Courtney moved her head from side to side frantically. Her eyes had a haunted look. "But how did he know I was here?" she cried. "Rio, the note is from that Ben. I *know* it! How did he know I was here?"

Biting off another curse Rio circled her shoulders with one arm and drew her with him to the door. He shouted for Maria as he urged Courtney into the hallway with him.

"Yes, señor?" Maria's voice revealed her concern; Rio never shouted at her.

"Get Cleat up to the house at once," Rio instructed, leading Courtney to his office. "And make a pot of coffee, please." Not waiting for a response he practically carried Courtney's trembling body into the office.

"What . . . what are you going to do?" Stark terror broke through the restraint Courtney was trying to impose on her voice.

"The first thing I'm going to do is pour a brandy into you." Suiting action to words, he crossed to the credenza. Grasping the brandy bottle, he released her to fill a pony glass to the rim. "Sip," he ordered as he handed the liquor to her.

Courtney obeyed him instantly, welcoming the warmth

that spread from her throat to her chilled insides. "Rio, how *did* Ben know I was here?" she asked in a strained whisper, as she handed the empty glass to him.

"Not by any mysterious method," he chided, refilling the glass and tossing the fiery drink back neat. "Whew!" Rio expelled his breath sharply as the drink hit his throat. "It's sacrilegious to drink this stuff like that." But even as he spoke the words, he tipped the bottle to fill the glass with more of the aged brandy. After taking a small swallow he held the glass out to her. "We'll share this one," he said, his lips curving up at the corners.

"Rio . . ."

"Drink, Courtney." The tone he used left little doubt in her mind that he meant to be obeyed; still shaking, Courtney complied—convincing herself it was *only* because she was still shaking.

"Now," Rio said as he led her to the leather sofa in front of the fireplace, "as to how he knew you were here." After seating her he went to stand before the grate, leaning indolently against the mantelpiece. "I don't know, but I can think of several ways he might have found out."

"How?" she demanded tremulously.

"If you weren't so rattled, the answer would be obvious, babe." If Rio hadn't glanced down into the brandy glass at that moment, he'd have caught the spark of hope that lit Courtney's eyes at his casual endearment. By the time he looked up it was gone, replaced by the fear crawling through her. "I told you you're safe here, Courtney. I can and will protect you."

"I know that, but—" Courtney began.

"Will you trust me?" Rio rapped the question out with unusual impatience. Courtney was too scared to notice the tension tautening his lean body; she merely responded automatically and with complete honesty.

"I'll trust you with my life." Courtney was also too distracted to notice the tension ease out of him, or even the softening of his tone.

"Good." Savoring her admission, Rio was quiet a moment, then went on. "As to how that slob knew you were here"—he shrugged—"although we were married quietly, for all I know there could have been a notice of it in the papers." His lips twisted wryly. "I am Patrick McCord's son; and Patrick McCord is news."

"I like your father, Rio." Courtney offered the information softly, earning for herself a genuine smile.

"So do I, as a matter of fact." His smile disappeared as he returned to his subject. "Then again, Ben might have picked up the information in town. Maria began planning our party over a week ago. She needed some supplies and, well"—he shrugged again—"men talk—even my men."

"Sad, but true." The observation came from the doorway, from Cleat Jamison, who stood there waiting respectfully to be invited into the room. "You sent for me, Rio?"

"Yeah." With a motion of his hand Rio indicated the sheet of paper he'd dropped onto his desk. "Have a look at that—ah—charming note. But handle it carefully, there may be prints on it."

Frowning his confusion Cleat sauntered into the room and to the desk. Bending over he read the note without touching it at all. His reaction reflected Rio's of a short while before: Cleat began cursing softly. Then, finished, he glanced up, a stain of red flowing from his neck to his cheeks.

"Excuse me, ma'am," he apologized gruffly.

"She's heard the words before, Cleat," Rio drawled. "My reaction was the same."

"You call the authorities?" Cleat asked.

"Not yet." Rio smiled. "I'm giving Pat and Courtney's father time to get back to Odessa. I want to inform them first."

"Father is going to insist that I immediately return to

England." Courtney said dully, fighting an overwhelming weariness.

"Insist?" Rio repeated, too softly. "Charles can insist until the Big Bend is underwater," he added in a hard tone, referring to the desert area west of the Pecos. "You are *my* wife, and I'll protect what's mine."

Inside Courtney's tired mind echoed Morgan's voice of a few weeks previously as he'd made the same ironclad statement. *Patrick was absolutely right,* she mused sleepily, *Rio and Morgan are "throwbacks."*

"Did you hear me, Courtney?" Rio demanded when she failed to respond. Sighing, she forced her heavy eyelids up.

"Yes, Rio," she murmured. Losing the battle against fatigue, she closed her eyes again. "Whatever you say," she added in a sleepy mumble. She never saw the tender smile that briefly softened Rio's hard lips.

Listening to, but really not absorbing, the conversation between Rio and Cleat, Courtney clung to consciousness for a few minutes longer, then curled more comfortably into the corner of the couch and dropped into oblivion. She stirred restlessly sometime later as she felt herself lifted, then carried a short distance. Her lashes fluttered at the intrusive sound of a door closing sharply, and she murmured incoherently as she was swiftly divested of her clothing. But she didn't fully awaken, and slid back into deep slumber the instant she was carefully placed on the bed.

Fortunately, Courtney was beyond hearing the frustrated mutter from her new husband as he left the room.

"What a hell of a way to spend my wedding night."

As always Rio came awake instantly, every one of his senses fully alert. He was lying on his side and he frowned at the dark, rich-looking paneling on the wall he was facing.

It was still the middle of the night, yet something had wakened him. What had it been? Motionless, he waited, then it came again, and a shiver feathered the length of his spine as Courtney's warm breath caressed his naked skin.

A sensuous smile curving his lips, Rio luxuriated in the feel of her as she curled closer to him, seeking his warmth. Courtney needed the rest, he thought, trembling as her breath whispered over his flesh once more. She needed the sleep, but, oh hell, he needed her! Giving in to the demands of his hardening body, Rio carefully turned and drew her into his arms.

"Rio?" Courtney murmured sleepily, moving instinctively, sweetly, into his embrace.

"Yes." His pulses beginning to hammer, Rio inserted a hand between them to stroke her naked, silky skin. "Courtney?" he whispered urgently against her sleep-warmed lips.

"Oh, yes!" Lifting her head, she parted her lips for him.

Tiny explosions flared throughout Rio's body as he took her mouth forcefully and sought the honey inside with his thrusting tongue. The explosions created a river of fire that ran through his veins as, murmuring deep in her throat, she gave herself up to his hungry mouth and stroking hands.

The warm satin feel of her tested the bounds of Rio's control. Desire clawing at him, he slid his lips from hers, tasting her neck, her shoulders, her breasts. Taking her puckering nipple inside his mouth, he brought it to tight arousal with his flicking tongue, and felt his own nipples tighten with excitement when Courtney gasped and arched her body into him, silently demanding yet more pleasure.

Murmuring in both English and Spanish, Rio praised her beauty as he explored every inch of it. His own tension mounting, he dipped the tip of his tongue into her navel before gliding his burning lips over her abdomen. Suddenly remembering the life unfurling inside her beautiful body, Rio pressed his open mouth against her skin to whisper, "Rest easy, my child, I will keep you and your mother safe."

So intensely protective did Rio feel at that moment, so awed by the reality of *his* child inside Courtney's body, that the tight coil of passion gripping him began to cool; but the delicate movement of Courtney's arching hips rekindled the fire into a blaze and his mouth greedily sought the moist heat of her.

Courtney was a living flame against his hungry mouth, a flame feeding the fire inside him. With openmouthed kisses and flickering tongue Rio loved her until he felt her entire body grow taut; then, grasping her tightly with his hands, he absorbed the shudders that rippled through her body as his senses drank in her throaty cries of satisfaction.

And now it was his turn. Passion throbbing through him, Rio retraced his trail of kisses back to her mouth, his pleasure increasing as she began to move sensuously against him again. With his hands caressing her soft breasts, he brought his open mouth to hers, nudging her lips farther apart as he parted his wider, and yet wider.

A shudder tore through his already trembling body as Courtney went wild beneath him, urging him with low moans and hot, wet kisses. His mouth fastened to hers, he positioned himself between her thighs, groaning in pleasure when her soft fingers curled around his pulsing arousal.

"Yes," he growled, "bring me to you, Courtney."

Spreading his long fingers over her slim hips, he lifted her, and then, his body following the urging of her hands, he slowly moved inside her. Closing his eyes, Rio hesitated an instant, savoring the velvet sheath of her. But then, driven by the heat scorching every inch of him, he began a rhythmic stroke, moving faster and faster until, like shattering glass, his senses spun out of control and he cried

her name through gritted teeth an instant after she gasped
his own.

Dawn was turning the sky to mauve when Rio woke again.
This time it was a numbness in his arm that woke him.
Shifting carefully, he freed the arm, then resettled Courtney's relaxed body even more closely to him, amazed at
the sense of possessiveness gripping him.

But though he was amazed by it, Rio accepted it calmly.
Courtney was his. And after the weeks of aching for her,
longing for her, he fully intended to keep her.

Though Rio had been deeply infatuated before, he had
never truly been in love. Now, at daybreak on a morning
in early July, Rio wondered curiously if he could possibly
be in love with his wife.

It might help if he knew who exactly his wife was, he
thought. Was Courtney the scared but fiercely determined
young woman he'd brought out of the hills? Or was she
the cool, remote aristocrat he'd delivered to Nevada? Then
again, was she the pleasant, easy-to-get-along-with person
he'd come to know during the short period of time before
their marriage? Rio sighed. Perhaps she was really the
warm-blooded, sensuous woman who had twice shared his
bed.

Tilting his head, Rio glanced down at his sleeping wife.
Merely looking at Courtney heated his blood. He wanted
her again, wanted her exactly as she'd been with him the
night before, hot and eager and ready for him, and only
him.

Hell, maybe he was in love with her! Rio gave a mental
shrug. Time would tell. Meanwhile, he would keep her,
and protect her, and maybe, someday, she would even
come to love him.

The consideration sparked another, exciting trend of
contemplation. What would it be like to be loved by Courtney? What would it be like to know that all her arrogance
and fierceness and fire and love were there just for him?

The answer sprang into his mind instantly. It would be like all the heaven he had ever hoped to find. And, Rio mused, after all the hell he'd known in Asia and South America, he could happily wallow in Courtney heaven! He was laughing softly to himself when the celestial body woke up.

"Rio?" Even as she murmured his name, Courtney wriggled closer to him.

"Umm?" Rio caught his breath at the picture she made with her lips swollen from his kisses and her hair wildly disarrayed by his tangling fingers.

"What time is it?"

"Early. Too early. Time to go back to sleep." Rio silently damned the betraying huskiness of his tone; she was pregnant, for heaven's sake! The last thing she needed after a few hours rest was more sexual action!

"I don't want to go back to sleep," she said adamantly.

"Are you hungry?" he asked, belatedly remembering how very little she'd eaten the day before. "Should I ask Maria to get some breakfast for you."

"Yes, I'm hungry." Courtney yawned prettily; Rio experienced an odd, anticipatory thrill. "But you don't have to bother Maria," she continued in an exciting purr, raising her arms and curling them around his neck. "You'll do nicely, thank you."

At the touch of Courtney's lips on his, Rio exploded all over again. Yet deep inside the heart of the explosion echoed the sound of his father's soft voice. "Love her well, son. You never know how much time you've got."

An unfamiliar fear urging him on, Rio loved Courtney with the fire of near desperation.

Chapter Eight

Courtney rose from the depths of deep, restful sleep, her mind refreshed, her body replete, and her stomach complaining of a lack of nourishment. Warm beneath the covers, she moved slowly with the sensuous grace of an awakening feline. Drawing a deep, contented breath, she opened her eyes—and froze.

Rio was standing before the wide window looking larger than life in the glare of the midday sunshine, his expression veiled by the smoke rising from the cigarette between his compressed lips.

In an instant the dreamlike memory of the night was shattered, exposing her mind to the stark reality of her situation. She was a woman with a husband who had been pressured into marriage and, because of it, was now a hunted man.

Courtney felt a sudden longing to roll over, bury her face in the pillow, and escape back into unconsciousness, preferably with Rio's warm body next to hers under the covers.

"Hungry?" he asked with his usual taciturnity.

Afraid to trust her dry throat to speech, Courtney nodded, refusing passage to the sigh that rose to her lips. Rio had not been spare of words under the blanket of darkness, she remembered achingly. His gravelly voice had whispered exciting, erotic phrases in English and Spanish.

How many others before her had thrilled to those exact same erotic words?

Appalled by the pain induced by speculation about Rio's previous partners, Courtney sat up abruptly, then immediately wished she hadn't. Color tinged her cheeks at the realization that her nude body was bathed in sunlight and exposed to his narrow-eyed gaze.

"I've seen it all," he reminded her coolly, moving to scoop her robe from the foot of the bed. "You didn't seem to mind at all last night," he observed wryly, handing the garment to her.

"I . . . I . . ." Was she supposed to respond to his taunt? she wondered, hastily shrugging into the robe. What could she say, other than the truth? She hadn't minded his searing gaze on her body; she had reveled in it! Avoiding a reply, she headed for the bathroom, tossing over her shoulder, "I'll be ready for breakfast in a few moments."

"Don't let it throw you, Courtney. Most mornings I'll be long gone by the time you wake up."

Courtney halted her headlong rush in the center of the large bathroom. Did Rio consider her a slugabed? A pampered socialite, whiling away her days in mindless pursuits? Well, he obviously did! Anger and frustration vied for supremacy over her emotions. Frustration won.

Stepping under a steaming shower, Courtney expelled a sharp breath in a sigh of agitation. What had she expected, for heaven's sake? Until now Rio had only viewed her in one light—that of the daughter of the brother of an English lord, on extended holiday in the States. Good grief! Pictured in the light of the British aristocrat, Rio's conclusions about her were understandable, if rather insulting.

Well, she decided briskly, twisting the faucet shut, she would simply have to educate her husband as to her usefulness as a human being. Hadn't the man heard that most females, even of the British elite, were holding down meaningful jobs these days? Practically all the young women she knew worked, and not merely as charitable volunteers, either, even though they did that as well.

Would her occupation as a haute-couture designer alter Rio's opinion of her? Probably not, Courtney decided, fighting a swamping sense of despair as she patted herself dry. Would any man who lived close to the earth give genuine credence to the work of creating expensive clothes for wealthy women? Not bloody likely, she admitted ruefully, slipping into the robe again, and most especially not a man like Rio.

Courtney my girl, she mused, *I'm afraid your upper lip is going to atrophy from stiffness, for you are surely in for a long, uphill battle if you hope to make this marriage work.* She was reaching for the doorknob when Rio's voice filtered through to her.

"Breakfast, Courtney."

Closing her eyes for a moment she rested her forehead on the smooth oak panel, giving in to a longing to hear him call her *querida* in the passion-filled voice he'd used during the night.

"Courtney!" The morning sound of Rio's impatience held not a hint of that passion.

As she straightened away from the door a self-mocking smile feathered her lips. The nighttime Rio was one person; the daytime man was apparently someone else altogether. And, in truth, hadn't she had fair warning about the man who struck at night?

Courtney's meandering thoughts stirred memory, and a shiver skittered down her back. That note! How had she ever forgotten it? Yanking the door open, she rushed into the bedroom and straight to the table at the window where Rio had placed their breakfast.

"Rio, the note!" she panted. "What did my father and yours have to say?" The sight of him stole the little breath she had left.

He was sprawled lazily on the chair, a pair of faded jeans his only concession to convention. The medal lying on his chest reflected glittering sparks back at the afternoon sunrays, and drew her gaze to the swirls of dark hair on his sun-browned skin. Courtney had to sit down quickly in the opposite chair to prevent herself from melting at his feet.

Rio frowned as she abruptly plopped into the chair. "Are you feeling all right?" he demanded, easing himself erect to stare across the table at her.

"Yes, of course," Courtney assured him too swiftly, earning herself another frown. "I—ah—just now remembered that disgusting note. I can't imagine how I ever forgot it!"

"Can't you?" he murmured. "I can."

Oh, dear! Courtney moaned silently, beginning to ache inside at his gravelly, sexy tone. Quite suddenly she was famished, but not for the food beneath the covered dishes neatly arranged on the table. Feeling hot, and cold, and incredibly *ready*, she sputtered into speech.

"But what did our fathers say? And did you notify the authorities? And—"

"They said plenty, and yes." Rio's obvious amusement at her expense instilled a needed dose of reserve in her mind.

"What exactly did the parents say?" she asked very coolly, curiously lifting the lid off the plate in front of her; her mouth watered at the aroma of broiled steak and eggs.

"About what we'd both expected," Rio replied, lifting a Thermos pitcher and pouring dark coffee into their cups. "Pat was all for making a direct call to the FBI in

Washington." A smile twitched his lips, then faded abruptly. "As you predicted, your father was all for rushing you onto the next plane to England." His mouth flattened, as if from a sour taste.

"Well?" Courtney asked in exasperation when he failed to continue. "What did you tell them?"

In the process of slicing into his own steak, Rio glanced up at her, a slow grin tugging at his lips. "I told them to butt out." Calmly ignoring her shocked gasp, he slid the beef laden fork into his mouth.

"Rio, really!" she exclaimed angrily, positive she would be hearing from her very irate parent before too long.

"Courtney, really," he mimicked. "I don't need or want my father throwing his weight around, either here in Texas or in Washington," he said coldly. "And I definitely don't need or want *your* father's suggestions on how to protect *my* wife." And he infused steel into the possessive pronoun.

Men, and their blasted egos! Courtney was suddenly furious with him. Rio had received a threat to his life and all he could concern himself with was his pride! Forcing back her anger she methodically chewed the bite of delicious homemade biscuit she had in her mouth. When she swallowed, she decided to take the tack of reason.

"Perhaps it would be wise to allow your father to do as he suggests," she opined reasonably.

"No," Rio said flatly. "The proper authorities have been informed, Courtney. Cleat left this morning to deliver that note to them." Revealing cool unconcern, he continued to make inroads into his breakfast.

"But what if Ben should come here?" she asked softly, suddenly short of breath. *To kill you and rape me,* she added to herself fearfully.

"Here? To the house?" Rio's laughter warmed the chill seeping into Courtney's bones. "If he does he's even more stupid than I thought." His laughter subsiding, Rio shook his head slowly. "I told you you are safe here and I meant it. My men have been alerted, security measures have been taken, and even if I should be gone overnight for some reason, you will—"

"Gone!" Courtney's mind got tangled up in the word. "What do you mean, gone?" she cried.

"This is a working ranch, Courtney," Rio explained patiently. "And I have other business interests that need looking after. There will be times when that business necessitates my absence from the ranch for several days to a week."

"But—"

"But," he went on insistently, "even when I'm away you'll be completely safe here. Sal Alvarez will see to that."

Sal Alvarez? Courtney blinked as he tossed the unfamiliar name into the argument. Who the devil was Sal Alvarez? Rio answered the question hovering on her lips before she could ask it.

"Sal is the best horse handler on the place, and second in command to Cleat." His patience was clearly thinning.

Courtney frowned in concentration; she couldn't remember having been introduced to anyone named Sal. "Have I met him?"

"No." Rio shook his head. "Under normal circumstances you would have met him at the party last night, but there was a mare ready to foal and Sal opted to stay with her." Rio smiled sardonically. "As stated, you have nothing to fear if I have to be away. Sal is part Italian-American and part Mexican-American, and all mean when he's riled." His smile smoothed into a grin. "As he is also Maria's live-in lover, he is also in the house at night."

Courtney's head jerked up in surprise. Maria? That quiet, unassuming woman had a live-in lover? she thought in amazement. Of course, Maria was also still quite attractive at fifty-odd, yet . . . Courtney stared at Rio—who took exception to her reaction.

"Maria is a warm, loving, God-fearing, good woman,"

he said very softly, "who lost her husband and only child to a renegade horse over ten years ago. Sal fulfills more than a physical need."

"Rio!" Courtney protested through fear-dried lips; Rio's tone had had an absolutely terrifying edge. "I don't condemn her!"

"It's a good thing." Courtney could actually see the tension ease out of him. Then he smiled—well, almost. "I'm all mean, too, when I'm riled."

Courtney felt a twinge of sympathy for the renegade horse. "What did you do?"

Rio didn't pretend to misunderstand her. Cradling his fresh cup of coffee he leaned back in the chair. "I tracked the stallion for two weeks, and when I found him I castrated him with my hunting knife." He shrugged "He died, of course."

Blanching, Courtney swallowed convulsively against the nausea burning her throat. Her eyes wide with disbelief, she stared at him mutely.

"I told you I was mean when I'm riled." Watching her over the rim of his cup Rio's eyes began to gleam devilishly. "Maybe you'd better be careful not to rile me . . . umm?"

He was teasing her, surely? And, dammit, who did he think he was to threaten her? Courtney's fear subsided as her fighting spirit rose. How dare he taunt her? she thought in cold fury, reflecting his actions as she picked up her cup and leaned back in her chair. Wretched man!

"I was unusually riled once," she said mildly, smiling sweetly, "by a charging rhinoceros while on a photo safari with my father. I shot the beast, dropped him in his tracks. I'm an expert shot, you know." She arched both delicate eyebrows. "Your hide isn't quite as thick as a rhino's—or is it?"

Rio nearly choked on the laughter that erupted from his throat. "Are you really an expert shot?" he finally managed.

"Yes, actually, I am." Glancing down she reflected his action by placing her cup on the table. "Does that amaze you?"

"No, actually, it doesn't," he mocked softly; then, standing abruptly, he leaned across the small table to grasp her chin, tilting her face upward. "You know, I'm beginning to think we just might be well matched, Courtney." Bending smoothly he fastened his mouth to hers.

Courtney was instantly spun into the sensuous realm that Rio's hard mouth had the power to create. Within that molten realm there were no fears or differences or even the tiniest thought of her barely touched breakfast. In that realm was a hunger of a different sort. Curling her arms around his taut neck she clung with helpless need, her lips parting eagerly for the bold thrust of his tongue.

Rio lifted her effortlessly and carried her back to the rumpled bed, settling her gently in the midst of the disorder. Releasing her mouth lingeringly, he stepped back, hands going to the waist snap on his jeans.

"Rio, it's the middle of the day!" Courtney gasped as she emerged from her kiss-induced fog.

A smile eased the strain of desire tightening his lips. "Yes," he purred sexily, stepping out of the jeans. "And all the more exciting in full daylight."

Courtney didn't require his assurance; her eyes gave her the evidence of that. Her lips parted slightly, her breathing shallow, she gazed in fascinated wonder at his hard, naked body.

Lord, he was beautiful! And the same even nut-brown color from head to toe. Out of her control her gaze traveled slowly over the lean, muscular length of him from his neatly knit ankles to his well-formed calves to his hard-looking, long-muscled thighs and beyond until her gaze came to a startled halt on the rigid evidence proclaiming him all male. Then, acutely aware that she was staring in awe, Courtney hurriedly raised her glance to his face.

"I could feel your gaze on me like the touch of fire, *querida,*" Rio said in a tight, husky murmur. "It felt incredibly erotic. Take off your robe and lie back, I'll show you what I mean."

Middle of the day or not, Courtney was long past resistance. His use of the Spanish endearment was an added inducement. She removed the silky garment with unstudied sensuality and her pulse rate went wild at the leap of excitement his eyes flashed when she tossed the robe aside and eased onto her back on the bed.

Within seconds Courtney came to an immediate understanding of Rio's claim. The flame seemed to leap from his eyes to lick hungrily over her trembling flesh everywhere his gaze touched, igniting a responsive heat in her that quickly raged out of control, consuming her entire being.

Following an urge that refused to be disobeyed, she lifted her empty arms in invitation.

Murmuring words that she couldn't really hear, yet understood nonetheless, Rio slid into her embrace and into her body like a brilliant pillar of fire.

"Yes, *querida*, there are differences between us," his raspy voice crooned against her mouth, "vast differences. But in many ways, especially this one, we are well and truly matched."

The afternoon was lost to the delicious discoveries of conjugal bliss.

On awakening near sunset Courtney felt absolutely marvelous, except that she was alone, not only in the bed but in the room.

"Rio?" she called softly, testing to see if he was in the bathroom. Her own soft voice echoed hollowly around her.

Missing his nearness with an intensity that startled her, she scrambled from beneath the tangled covers. Where was he? she grumbled silently, striding into the bathroom.

Why had he gone off like that, leaving her alone and cold in that huge bed?

Her thoughts stopped Courtney dead, one foot in the shower stall, the other on the floor. Good heavens! How was it possible? It was inconceivable even to imagine that Rio had become so very important to her feeling of well-being! Wasn't it?

Stepping into the stall she turned the hot water on full blast; merely thinking his name sent a thrill dancing crazily over her body!

Rio. Rio. Rio. Like a litany, a prayer, a longing, his name reverberated inside her head.

She loved him! Surprise parted her lips, and Courtney sputtered as water rushed into her mouth. She was in love with her husband. Backing up, she stood numbly watching the water cascade over her body. Was it possible, really possible, to fall in love so very quickly?

Without conscious command her hand slid protectively over her flat belly. Her child. Rio's child. Theirs! Oh, dear Lord! She was carrying *their* child—the child they had created! Not until that instant had the full meaning of her pregnancy hit her. Her reaction was stunning. Wild, riotous joy coursed through her, singing to her of the richness of her womanhood. She was carrying Rio's child in her body—the body he had loved so exquisitely.

Euphoric, Courtney was barely aware of turning off the water or leaving the bathroom minutes later. Still floating in a self-induced "in-love" high, she dressed in a haze of baby-blue and pink, by sheer instinct pairing a silky jewel-toned green shirt with slim-legged, buff-colored jeans.

Courtney was humming to herself as she brushed the tangles out of her hair when his low, gravelly voice crept to her from the doorway.

"Afternoon loving appears to agree with you. I'll have to remember that."

Glancing up quickly, Courtney's gaze collided and

meshed with his. Rio! *Her* husband! The singing joy was back, brightening her eyes, painting her cheeks an apricot hue. Her lover!

Rio's soft laughter had the sound of contentment. "Have I embarrassed you?" he asked teasingly.

"No," Courtney said softly, honestly. "I think the term is 'pleasured' me." To reinforce her statement she allowed her glance to drift slowly over his relaxed body as he leaned lazily against the door frame.

"Come over here, Courtney," he commanded in an enticing drawl. "I want to taste the heat coloring your cheeks."

The hairbrush clattered to the dresser surface from her suddenly nerveless fingers, and without pause she walked to him, her eyes cloudy with expectancy.

Lowering his head Rio caressed her warm cheek with parted lips and tasted her skin with the tip of his tongue. "Humm," he breathed, "you smell good." Lingeringly he slid his palms up her body. "Feel good too," he whispered raspily. "Like a woman made for loving . . . at night, at dawn, at the height of the day."

Her body softening to his touch, Courtney melted into his exciting hardness, seeking closer and still closer contact with him. Every thing she'd been yearning for all her adult life was waiting for her inside his embrace. She willingly surrendered everything female in her to everything male in him by offering her mouth to his, and with it her heart and soul.

Rio kissed her deeply but without the crushing, hot demand she had come so easily to crave. As he reluctantly raised his head his dark eyes smiled into hers.

"Maria has dinner ready," he told her by way of explaining the briefness of his caress. Looping one arm around her shoulders he drew her from the doorway. As they started down the hall he spread the fingers of his other hand over her abdomen. "You must nourish the little one."

Feeling cosseted, Courtney allowed him to seat her at the large, oval dining room table. Quite used to elegant furnishings, she was nonetheless impressed with the heavy, exquisitely carved dark wood table and chairs, which were padded on the seats and backs with wine-red leather. The spacious room was bathed in soft light from a hanging lamp of Moroccan design. Courtney adored the room on sight.

The table was set with exquisite china and sterling silver on a delicate lace tablecloth. The deep grooves of the heavy crystal glasses reflected a rainbow of colors in the glow of the gently swaying lamp.

Maria entered the room—through a filigreed door set into the archway into the kitchen—just as Rio was pouring wine into their glasses. With smiling, silent efficiency she arranged the food on the table, then disappeared behind the door with a murmured "Enjoy your meal, señor, señora," leaving Courtney in no doubt who ranked first in the house.

Fingering the stem of his glass, Rio raised the scarred eyebrow at her. "Would you like a toast to commemorate our first real dinner together?"

Surprised, Courtney smiled fleetingly. "Yes, that would be lovely," she murmured a trifle breathlessly.

He frowned in concentration as he lifted his glass and said quietly, "Then let's drink to the few qualities we do share: a determination of character, a mutual physical attraction, and the life growing inside you. It's not nearly enough, but it will have to do . . . for now." His lips curved cynically as he brought the glass to his mouth after tipping it slightly in her direction. "Salud."

As he spoke those words, he broke the euphoric bubble Courtney had been floating in. The song of joy was stilled in her veins. Deflated, she raised her glass listlessly.

It will have to do . . . for now.

At that moment Courtney felt positive that his bleak-sounding words would ring in her mind for the remainder of her life. Had she actually begun to believe their marriage might have a chance of survival? Afraid she'd cry out in protest, she swallowed whatever it was she'd unconsciously bitten into. The bit of food was hot and spicy, a fact that she was grateful for, as it excused the tears shimmering in her eyes.

"Too hot?" Rio commiserated, holding a glass of iced water out to her. "It's Tex-Mex." He grimaced. "I should have thought—"

"No, it's fine." Courtney conjured a smile from somewhere. "I like the taste. I'll get used to it." She forked another, bigger portion into her mouth to prove her claim, rather amazed to find she really did like the taste. Conversely, her action annoyed Rio instead of reassuring him.

"You don't have to prove anything to me, Courtney." Hard, discouraging impatience serrated his tone. "If you'd prefer something milder, say so. Maria will prepare it for you."

The flare of anger inside soothed the sense of dejection weighing on Courtney. Obviously Rio considered her finicky as well as a layabout do-nothing! Flinging her head up she angled her chin haughtily and glared at him.

"This meal will do fine," she said distinctly.

Rio seemed to be on the point of argument, and where it all would have ended Courtney couldn't imagine; but fortunately the low sounds of another dissension filtered to them through the filagreed door.

"The señor is having dinner," Maria said softly but adamantly.

"But this is important!" The voice was low, intense, and unfamiliar to Courtney.

"It will keep until after—"

"Come on in, Sal," Rio called, overriding Maria.

Sal? Courtney shifted her gaze from Rio's tautly set face to the door separating the two rooms. The man who pushed through the door, battered Stetson in hand, was something of a shock to her.

He was about the same as Maria's slightly below-average size, his slim frame wiry and compact. If pressed, Courtney would have guessed his age to be in the vicinity of forty-five, while admitting he could be anywhere between forty and fifty. His head was covered by a mass of black curls, badly in need of trimming. His skin was swarthy and smooth over a lean face with a defiant jaw. His eyes were the deepest, softest brown Courtney had ever seen on man or woman.

This man is mean? she thought at once, shifting a disbelieving glance at Rio. Reading her expression, Rio nodded briefly, but firmly, as he waved one hand at the chair to his right.

"Sit down, Sal," he invited tersely. "Wine?"

"No, thanks." Startling white teeth flashed against his dark skin. "But I sure could use a beer," he added, tilting his head back to smile at the woman who'd followed him into the room.

"Sal Alvarez!" Maria hissed, her eyes sparking with warning.

"Get the man a beer, Maria," Rio ordered gently. "And a plate, too, if he's hungry."

"No, sir!" Sal shook his head. "I've had supper." A soft smile touched his lips as he ran a caressing gaze over Maria's hips, swaying gently as she swept into the kitchen.

Studying the glow in Sal's eyes, Courtney felt a jolt of emotion rush through her. Why, he loves her, really loves her! She admitted sadly that she was feeling the envy she'd experienced earlier while in Sam and Morgan's company. At that moment Courtney was relieved that Rio's gravelly voice snagged her attention.

"So, what's so all-fired important?" Rio demanded calmly.

"The law has made a positive ID on the note writer," Sal replied, smiling his thanks as Maria handed him an open can of beer. "His name is Benjamin Colten. He fits the description your wife gave the authorities a couple weeks ago." He glanced at Courtney with a fleeting smile. "Seems the bad-ass is wanted for just about everything: armed robbery, assault with intent, parole violation, *and* attempted rape." His lips twisted sourly. "A real sweetheart."

"Yeah." Rio's eyes narrowed. "I should have put him away when I had the chance."

Courtney's gasp rang loud in the silence that fell after Rio's disgusted statement. "You—you mean kill him!" she choked, biting her lips when he turned a cold-eyed stare at her.

"Yes, Courtney, I mean I should have killed him." If possible his eyes grew even colder, deadly cold. "It would have saved the law the trouble of rounding him up." Glancing away dismissively, he fixed that cold stare on Sal. "The authorities have anything on the other two men?"

"Nothin'." Sal shrugged. "And no leads as to their present whereabouts. Looks like they've gone to ground." Lifting the can to his lips he finished the beer in a few deep swallows.

"This Colten from the Pecos?" Rio asked softly.

Sal shook his head. "From Nevada originally."

"Figures." Rio snorted. "That's probably where he hooked up with Henderson."

"That's what the tin stars figure too," Sal concurred. "They theorize that Henderson was the brains behind the plan. That son-of-a . . ." He flashed a chagrined glance at Courtney. "Sorry, ma'am. Anyway, Henderson was working as an extra hand for the spring roundup when your wife was visiting the Wades. Mr. Wade has grilled every one of his regular men and it appears that Henderson was overly curious about your wife's actions.''

"Why the hell wasn't that reported to Morgan?'' Rio exploded angrily, ignoring Courtney's low moan of dismay.

"He wasn't obvious about it and''—Sal lifted his shoulders in a helpless gesture—"well, the men put his interest down to natural curiosity over foreign visitors.''

Rio's smile was not pleasant. "Something like that had better not happen on *this* property.'' He raised his voice, which, for some inexplicable reason, now seemed sinister to Courtney.

"I don't think you have to worry on that score,'' Sal said quietly. "But I'll pass the word around anyway.''

"I'd appreciate it,'' Rio drawled, his rasp more pronounced. "Anything else?''

"No.'' Pushing back his chair, Sal got to his feet. "Cleat and I will be keeping lines open to the law. If there is anything, you'll know as soon as we do.''

"All right, and thanks, Sal.'' Rio dismissed him with a sharp nod of his head.

Sal nodded back before shifting his gaze to Courtney. "Sorry I interrupted your dinner, ma'am.'' Without waiting for a reply from her he strode from the room, leaving a constrained silence behind.

Courtney finished eating the now almost cold food. The conversation about the disgusting Ben had unnerved her, yet she admitted to herself that Rio's flatly cold statement that he should have killed the man had unnerved her more. She had always had an absolute abhorrence for violence, and the very idea that Rio could talk so calmly about taking a life, a human life, chilled her blood. Her feelings were evident to Rio.

"You're shocked?'' he asked coolly, sipping his wine.

"Yes.'' Courtney was beyond dissembling. "I hate the thought of killing.''

"Yet you told me you'd shot a rhino,'' Rio taunted softly.

"The beast was charging!" Courtney insisted. "It was either the animal or me!"

Rio smiled. "It may come to that with Ben," he reminded her smoothly. "I could have prevented all the hassle we're having with him now."

"By killing him in cold blood?" Courtney cried.

"But you admitted to wanting to kill him." He shrugged. "I don't see the difference."

"At the time he had hurt me, Rio!" Courtney argued. "He never actually gave you reason to kill him." Without thinking through her charge she rushed on, "Is that how you acquired the name Night Striker . . . by killing?"

Rio withdrew, closing himself off from her completely. If Courtney had thought he'd been cold before, she now learned the true meaning of the word.

"What do you know about the Night Striker?" His voice had the consistency of ice crystals forming into words.

Courtney gathered her composure around her like a shield and met his frigid stare with deceptively cool eyes. "Very little, actually. Morgan was not exactly forthcoming."

"Morgan?" His quiet, almost pleasant, tone had a sinister ring. "I never knew Morgan to be overtalkative."

Courtney squirmed in her chair. Had she seriously been afraid of Ben for Rio's sake? she thought wildly. Now, mesmerized by the deadly stillness of her husband, she almost pitied Ben for having "riled" Rio.

Her husband! Courtney's thought reverberated in her head loudly. The connotations connected to the phrase were too overwhelming to consider at the moment. Slowly inhaling a calming breath, Courtney attempted to thaw some of his ice.

"Rio, Morgan was *not* overtalkative," she placated. "I was naturally curious about the man who rescued me." She lifted her shoulders in what she hoped was a light is-it-really-so-important shrug. "I questioned him; his answers were sketchy at best."

"Umm."

What was "Umm" supposed to mean? Dammit! Rio was no more enlightening than Morgan had been! She was his wife. She had entrusted not only her future but that of her unborn child into his care. Feeling as cold as he looked, Courtney decided she deserved some answers.

"Rio, how did you get the name Night Striker?" Courtney would not have believed it possible, yet he seemed to withdraw even more. Suddenly fury born of uncertainty seared through her, and flared from her trembling lips. "Damn you! Did you earn the name by taking human life?"

"Yes." Rio's response was devastatingly calm, and shatteringly remote.

Slumping against the chair, Courtney unconsciously slid her palm over her abdomen. Rio observed her action through eyes devoid of expression—or even life.

"I did what I was paid to do, Courtney. I was tagged with the stupid title simply because I preferred to execute my assignments at night." Rio's tone was as devoid of life as his eyes, which flickered only once—when Courtney shuddered at his use of the term *execute*.

"And . . ." Courtney wet parched lips. "And those assignments were to . . . to kill?" she choked out.

Rio's lips curved sardonically. "If necessary." The smile faded. "And it usually was."

Courtney felt sick to her stomach; still she kept on, inflicting deep pain on herself while lashing out at him. "You were paid to execute?"

"I was paid to rescue," he corrected her in a jagged-edged tone. "In much the same way I was hired to rescue you." Rio smiled naturally for the first time since their confrontation had begun. "Even though taking a leisurely ride into the hills was a piece of cake compared to crawling through some damned jungle.''

Though spare, Rio's description was enough to set her meal rumbling in her stomach. Grasping her wine she swallowed convulsively in an effort to drown the nausea stinging the back of her throat.

"You—you were no more than a hired gun," she accused.

"There you're wrong." Rio studied her pale face unemotionally. "The companies I worked for had the wherewithal to hire any number of guns. *I* was hired, and paid very well, for my expertise." Not a hint of conceit or ego colored his even tone.

"But why?" Courtney cried.

"Why what?" he queried softly.

"Why did you ever even consider *that* kind of work?"

"I've already told you," Rio replied. "I was more than adequately compensated for my skills."

"But your father is a wealthy man!" she exclaimed, feeling at the end of endurance.

"And I'm my own man."

Emotionally spent, her stomach upset, Courtney closed her eyes and rested her head against the back of the chair. His own man. Of course, she really should have known. Out of all her male acquaintances Rio was, with the exception of Morgan Wade, unquestionably *the* most definite "man."

"I almost feel sorry for that beastly Ben." Courtney murmured her earlier thought aloud, her eyes flying open when Rio laughed quietly.

"Would you like my word that I won't kill him?"

He was serious! The evidence of her probing gaze left Courtney in no doubt whatever that Rio was dead serious. And, without questioning how she knew, she was positive that once given, Rio's word was unshakable.

"Yes, I want your word on it, please," she pleaded.

"You have it," he promised unhesitatingly. Then a dry

smile tilted his lips. "I might bend him a mite, but I swear I won't break him."

"Thank you for that, at least." Courtney could not know that the excessive weariness shading her tone came across as disgust to the man sitting opposite her, and so could only wonder why when the shutters were again drawn over his expression.

"Like it or not, you are going to have to learn to live with it, and me, Courtney." The ice was back, double thickness. "At least until the child is born."

"What?" Her mind and body beginning to succumb to the effects of too little food, too little rest, and an abundance of sexual activity, Courtney shook her head in confusion.

Rio misinterpreted the gesture as one of rejection. Fluidly surging to his feet he rounded the table to her. "You heard me," he said grittily, bending to lift her out of her chair and into his arms. "You wanted a name for the child," he growled, carrying her along the hall to his bedroom. "We both wanted the correct name for the child," he amended grimly.

The bedroom door swung shut at a short, backward kick of his foot. Intent on his purpose Rio crossed the deeply piled carpet to the large bed.

"Okay," he grunted, settling her gently on the bed. "You've got what you wanted; you'll take what goes with it."

Snuggling into the mattress Courtney sighed as she closed her eyes. She was so very tired; what was Rio talking about? With an effort she roused herself enough to open her eyes a smidgen. Rio's face, set into unrelenting lines, sent a shiver over her arms. He seemed so terribly intense.

"Rio, I don't—" Courtney started to tell him she hadn't understood what he'd said, but he cut her off harshly.

"It's too late now, Courtney." His light touch in variance with his rough voice, he began to remove her clothes. *"You*

set the rules by sending Morgan to me. And now you'll
live with them. When you accepted my name you accepted
everything that entails." He stepped back as he stripped
her last piece of clothing from her and began divesting
himself of his own garments. Moments later he slid onto
the bed beside her.

"You are my wife, *querida*. The marriage has been con-
summated." Gathering her into his arms he drew her to
the hardness of him. "And you'll be my wife in every way,
including—no, especially—in the bedroom." He paused,
then repeated his earlier remark. "At least until after the
child is born. Do you understand?"

Courtney didn't, not fully, yet she was so sleepy, she
breathed, "Yes, Rio. May I go to sleep now?"

"Yes, Courtney," he returned, mockingly.

Chapter Nine

Holding Courtney captive in a close embrace, Rio lay awake long into the night. Although the night was warm and the house comfortable, he shivered from the chill of his thoughts.

Courtney thought him a killer, probably of the same ilk as the lumbering Ben and his buddies. No. Rio's lips twisted. She considered him even worse than the men who'd kidnapped her. She considered him a cold-blooded killer, a hit man, a hired gun. And Courtney of the social elite hated violence and killers.

Feeling suddenly old and used up, Rio sighed. For a few brief hours he had seriously begun to believe their marriage might have a chance of working. Now he knew better.

The loving had been so unbelievably good, it had bordered on the perfect.

Damn! Why had Morgan—Rio cut off the condemning thought abruptly. If Morgan hadn't said word one it wouldn't have made any difference, and he knew it. Courtney would have learned the truth about him at some point, and her reaction would have been the same.

It was as he'd known from the beginning: they were from two vastly divergent worlds. Now Courtney had suffered the trauma of emotional shock as well as of cultural shock. Added to the hard-baked earth of West Texas, she found herself with an equally hard-baked man.

Shifting, Rio inched onto his side to gaze on Courtney's sleeping face. Why did she have to be so very special? he reflected achingly. Why couldn't she have been like any other of the many nice, pleasant, yet ordinary women he'd known? What made Courtney special, anyway?

She *was* stunningly beautiful—but it was more than her surface beauty that appealed to him. Outwardly caressing her features with his brooding gaze, Rio examined images of Courtney with his inner eye.

There was the image of the first time he'd seen her, after stepping into that bedroom in the cabin. Even then her physical beauty had stopped the breath in his throat. But it had been her expression that had caused a cold, murderous rage in his body. Her expression had revealed a variety of emotions, the uppermost being stark terror. Yet, even in the watery light from the moon, he had been able to read revulsion, hatred, and fierce determination in her face as well.

Rio had known instantly what she'd been determined about. It was as plain as if she had shouted it aloud; she would die before enduring the rape of her body by the animalistic Ben.

Courtney's resolution had been quixotic perhaps, possibly even foolish, but Rio had understood it at a gut level.

Then there was the image of her tenaciously holding on to the horse, and holding herself together, while he'd led her out of the hills. Though suffering from shock, reaction, sheer exhaustion, and physical discomfort from the cold, Courtney had clung to the saddle and her composure grittily, without complaint, arousing in Rio regret for not having eliminated the kidnappers, and thus any future threat from them.

On arrival at the ranch Rio had discovered yet another Courtney: a vulnerable woman pleading for reassurance about her attractiveness and realness as a person. That woman had stirred compassion in him.

But it had been the woman he had held in his arms, the passionate, giving woman, who had stamped a tormenting image in Rio's mind and senses. It was that Courtney who compelled his body and lured his thoughts.

Of course, there was also the Courtney he had observed for a few enlightening hours after he'd returned her to the haven of her father's arms and her cousin's home. That Courtney was arrogant and haughty, a true representative of the British aristocracy.

Gazing bleakly at her shadowed features, Rio sighed; damned if he wasn't intrigued by every facet she'd revealed to him. In truth he couldn't even fault the woman who deplored violence . . . even though it meant she naturally deplored him, and the way he'd earned his living as well.

Shifting position again Rio cradled her form closely to his own, feeling the warmth of her in the depths of his body and soul. He wanted her. God how he wanted her! But he wanted all of her. He wanted every facet of her attuned to every facet of him. The muscles off his throat tightening, he spread his open hand over her flat belly. His child. The concept awed Rio. *His* child! If they could never share anything else, they would forever share the living proof of their time together.

Lowering his lashes, Rio kept his eyes shut tightly as a spasm of pain moved over his rigid features. Damn! Falling in love was a bitch!

As the chill of dawn pervaded the room, Courtney snuggled against him, seeking warmth. The silky skin on her cheek teased the hair on Rio's chest and tangled his libido and emotions.

Once again his hand sought her abdomen. However deep her antipathy for him, he would keep Courtney with him until her pregnancy was over, Rio decided. He *would* see his only child come into the world!

Living with Rio McCord was like trying to set up housekeeping on a seesaw, Courtney concluded after a month of the up-and-down relationship. To all appearances Rio had donned the role of husband with aplomb, wearing it with the ease with which he wore his faded jeans and scuffed boots. And, to the casual observer, the marriage would seem to be working very well, Courtney felt positive. But appearances aside, she knew their marriage was a sham; there simply were no lines of communication open between them.

Courtney and Rio lived in the same house, ate at the same table, slept in the same bed, and monitored the growth of the child they had created. And they were still strangers to each other.

By the time the merciless summer sun softened its grip on the parched land, Courtney knew Maria, Sal, Cleat and most of the rest of Rio's employees better than she knew him. In his silence Rio remained an enigma.

As the weeks accumulated into months Rio maintained a consistent attitude toward Courtney. He was considerate, he was polite, he was often kind, he was remote—except in the bedroom, in the bed. When he made love to her, as he did most nights, Rio was a living, breathing flame, a flame that burned away every trace of the reserve Courtney used as a defense during the daylight hours.

Despite a growing sense of futility Courtney never considered refusing his nighttime advances. She loved him, and against all her attempts at rationalizing her feelings away, her love for him deepened with each successive day. Even on her most depressed nights it was always the same. Rio had but to reach for her and her resistance melted like an ice cube exposed to the Pecos summer sun.

With an eerie sensation of existing somewhere in limbo land, Courtney drifted in the ebb and flow of Rio's tide, her chin angled regally, her sapphire eyes cool, her upper lip stiff as the starched collar on Sal's Sunday go-to-church shirt.

There were many times when Courtney longed for the release of tears, but she never once gave in to the temptation. She was a Tremaine-Smythe, and she'd be damned before she'd ever again betray her weakness to Rio McCord!

Fortunately Courtney had her work. The week following their marriage she requested transport into El Paso to do some shopping. When he found out what she wanted to shop for, Rio himself flew her to Houston, where, within a few hectic hours, she was able to purchase all the materials she needed to set up her own studio in the ranch house. The work was her only means of escape from the reality of the situation.

Through the weeks that followed, Courtney worked long hours in the room Rio allocated to her. It was only while working that she could lose herself, and the pressing sense of failure that haunted her waking hours.

Curiously the line of clothes she eventually sent off to her father was the best she'd ever designed. Utilizing mainly the tweeds and soft wools that were produced at the mills owned by her father, Courtney poured out her soul onto the detailed drawings that came to life under her talented hand.

While sitting, standing, pacing, before her drawing board in a ranch in West Texas, Courtney never dreamed that the exquisite fall and winter fashions she created from her own unhappiness would electrify the entire world of

haute couture when they were unveiled the next spring.
At the time all she thought of was surcease from her own
conflicting emotions.

If there was any bright spot at all during those never-
ending weeks and months, it was the apparent disappearance of Ben and his cohorts.

The arrest of the man named Henderson had necessi-
tated several trips to Las Vegas for Courtney for the purpose of identification and depositions. Rio accompanied
her, supplementing her story with his own.

Henderson had absolutely refused to name his accom-
plices, and was languishing in the county prison awaiting
trial.

In early November Courtney was again called back to
Vegas for additional (in Rio's words) "legal red-tape
unwinding." As her body was beginning to show the proof
of the child growing within, Courtney was uncomfortably
aware of the speculative glances she received from the
representatives of the law. Though the question was delicately couched, she was once again asked if she *had* been
violated by one of the kidnappers.

The connotation was not lost on either Courtney or Rio;
the authorities believed that she *had* been raped but, as
often happened, was too ashamed and embarrassed to
admit it. And though every man who spoke to her was
gentle in approach, the speculative gleam was there in the
glance that shifted from her body to her husband.

By the time Courtney was told she was free to return to
Texas, Rio was icily furious. He bluntly informed them that
he would not allow Courtney to travel to Nevada again
until after the birth of *his* child. Amazingly Rio's dictate
was met with sheepish agreement.

Strangely, with each successive trip away from the ranch,
Courtney felt more like coming home on her return. The
realization that she was coming to regard the desolate, dry
Pecos as *home* instilled in her both happiness and grief,

for not at any time had she forgotten Rio's words to her on the evening of their first full day of marriage:

"You'll be my wife in every way—at least until after the child is born."

Courtney didn't want to love the land any more than she wanted to love the man. But there it was, she was caught up in love for both.

The week before Thanksgiving, Courtney came to the dinner table with her mind set on a purpose. She broached the subject before Rio had finished his fruit cup appetizer.

"I would like to go shopping."

Rio's hand paused midway between the fruit cup and his mouth.

"In Houston," Courtney added coolly.

His gaze remote, Rio slowly lowered his hand to the table. "You know the doctor said no long trips before the baby comes," he said in a deliberately reasonable tone. His too cool, too calm attitude set a spark to her temper.

"Houston is not a long trip, Rio!" she exclaimed in exasperation.

"What do you need that you can't buy in Marfa?" he demanded, referring to the picturesque town in Presidio County that Courtney had fallen in love with at first sight.

"Problably nothing," she responded honestly. "But I want to shop at the Galeria."

His lips curved wryly. "Nieman-Marcus," he murmured.

"Yes," Courtney admitted, glancing down at her blossoming abdomen. "I'm growing out of even the loosest of my clothes. But that isn't the only reason I wish to shop in Houston," she went on. "With both of our fathers coming for the Christmas holiday there are some specialty foods I want to purchase."

"I don't like the idea," Rio said flatly, picking up his fork again. "Make a list of the things you want and I'll have them sent out from Houston." He resumed eating

as if the subject were now closed. Courtney quickly disabused him of that notion.

"Rio, I really don't care whether you like the idea or
not." Straightening her shoulders, she favored him with
her most haughty look. "Nor am I seeking your approval,"
she continued cuttingly. "I am going to Houston, with or
without you." She shrugged. "One or the other, it doesn't
make the slightest difference to me." The last was an outright lie, but Courtney certainly was not about to let him
know that.

Rio flew Courtney to Houston the Monday after Thanksgiving, and booked them into the city's most expensive
hotel. Then he proceeded to confound her utterly by being
the most considerate, charming companion she ever could
have wished for.

For four lovely days and five ecstastic nights it was as if
she and Rio were on the honeymoon they had never had.
Stunned by his attentiveness, Courtney drank in his sudden
warmth. Not only did he accompany her on her shopping
binges, he offered his opinion on each and every selection.

As Rio had insisted she take her shopping in small doses
due to her condition, Courtney made four separate lists,
determined to eliminate one list per day. The first morning
after their arrival she set off, Rio by her side, with the list
containing the items of clothing she'd decided to purchase
to see her through the remainder of her pregnancy. Fully
expecting Rio to stand by, bored to the nines, Courtney
was delightfully surprised when he took an active part in
choosing the garments.

That evening as he escorted her into the very elegant
restaurant in the hotel, Rio brought Courtney to a full
stop by complimenting her on her appearance in the clev-
erly cut maternity dress he had particularly admired in the
shop.

Calling herself a fool, Courtney nonetheless bloomed

with his praise. As she had very recently begun to feel awkward and ungainly, Rio's timing was perfect.

The dinner they were served was delicious and satisfying; the loving that came later that night was even more so.

The first day in Houston set the precedent for the three that followed. Together Courtney and Rio crossed off every item on her Christmas list on the second day. On the third day they shopped for the special foods and wines she wanted for the holiday. On the fourth morning, filled with trepidation, Courtney led Rio into the infants' department in a very exclusive shop.

Later she asked herself why she'd ever entertained the fear of Rio's displeasure; hadn't he made it abundantly clear from the beginning that he wanted the child? On entering the gaily decorated department Rio had merely smiled and drawled teasingly:

"What color are we going to buy—pink or blue?"

Set free of constraint Courtney indulged in an absolute orgy of shopping for the nursery she had secretly planned. But even though she went a little wild, at least her purchases were all practical. Rio, on the other hand, chose such vital items as enormous stuffed animals, a crib mobile, and a huge, hand-carved rocking horse in a dark wood that was tagged with an equally huge price sticker—discreetly hidden, of course.

By the time they flew out of Houston the next morning, Courtney was tired, but pleasantly so. The flight was smooth and uneventful. As Rio had arranged to have all of their packages sent to the ranch, their only baggage was the hand luggage they'd left with the previous Monday.

As they deplaned, Rio saw Sal, leaning negligently against the dusty Chevrolet Blazer Rio had bought a few months before.

"What are you doing here, and where's Frank?" he demanded as he guided Courtney to the vehicle.

"Maria's orders." Sal's grin revealed sparkling white

teeth. "She sent Frank into El Paso for some supplies, and me out here to pick—"

Sal's voice broke on a high note with the zinging sound that cut through the air, and the puff of dust that burst from the ground as the rifle slug hit, missing Rio's head by less than half an inch.

"Je-sus!"

Courtney heard Sal's exclamation as Rio's body bore hers to the earth. After that the sequence of events happened so swiftly she was never quite sure of them in her memory.

Protecting her body with his own, Rio crawled, dragging her with him, to the Blazer and the shield of the large rear tire. From the corner of her eye Courtney had caught the motion as Sal dived through the open door of the vehicle just as another slug tore through the side window.

"Sal?" Rio called sharply.

"Missed me," Sal caroled back; then, "Comin' at ya, Rio," as he tossed a long-barreled handgun out through the door.

To Courtney's amazement Rio's arm snaked out and he plucked the weapon, butt to palm, from the air. The gun glinted blue-black in the harsh sunlight, mesmerizing her.

"Rio, who . . . ?" Courtney paused to swallow.

"I can make a pretty accurate guess," he muttered, checking the rounds in the chamber. "The bastards."

"B—but, I thought—" There was another whistling noise, then a thud at the impact of the shell into the body of the Blazer. Had she really convinced herself that they had heard the last of Ben and the other kidnappers? she wondered wildly.

"Stay as far down as possible, Court!" Rio ordered tersely, pushing her head down to her drawn-up knees. "And stay absolutely still!"

Before she could utter a protest he was scrambling away from her on his belly, moving toward the protection of the front wheel. Courtney bit down hard on her lip to muffle the scream that rose to choke her. Dear God! Was Rio trying to get himself killed? An instant later Courtney did scream as another bullet whizzed through the air to sear a shallow trough in Rio's thigh. Rio's reaction was a low grunt of pain followed by a string of obscenities.

As sinuous as a reptile, Sal, the rifle in his fist looking like an extension of his right arm, slithered off the front seat of the Blazer and along the ground to Rio's side to examine the bloody wound briefly.

"I'll live," Rio snarled as Sal's fingers probed carefully. "The sons of bitches are behind the hangar."

"Right on both counts, as usual," Sal murmured. "They've got us pretty well pinned. How do you want to play this, ol' horse?"

"I'd say one of us has to make a dash for the hangar door, and since you have the rifle, it looks like I'm the one." Rio's tone was so imperturbable, Courtney had to bite back another scream.

In a continuous, fluid movement Rio was up, in a crouch, heading for the hangar, and Sal was firing the rifle repeatedly in the general direction the shots had come from. Before Rio reached the hangar doorway there was a shout of pain, then the sound of an engine starting, then the screech of tires as a vehicle drove away at considerable speed.

There was an instant's pause; then Rio and Sal were both running to the corner of the hangar and around it. Scrambling to her feet with an agility that belied her condition, Courtney was mere seconds behind them. As she rounded the corner of the hangar she came to an abrupt halt, her eyes widening with shock.

Rio and Sal were kneeling beside a man lying on the ground. There was a red stain spreading over his shirt. Courtney had never heard the man's name, but without having to be told she knew that the man she'd thought of as average would never terrorize anybody again. The low, choking sound she involuntarily made in her throat drew Rio's attention while at the same moment several vehicles came to a tire-squealing stop a few feet away. Cleat was out of the Jeep and running toward them before the vehicle's engine had stopped.

Her gaze riveted on the man's bloodstained shirt, Courtney was barely aware of Rio surging to his feet to move to her side, or even the rapid-fire questions Cleat rattled off at his employer. Her breathing shallow, her body chilled, she stared at the dead man until Rio turned her away. The sun had oddly lost its glare and her vision was narrowing when she heard the distant sound of Rio's raspy, clipped voice issuing orders.

"Cleat, leave two of the men here with Sal to wait for the authorities. You take the others and see if you can pick up a trail from behind the hangar. My wife's in shock, I'm taking her home. Sal, tell the sheriff he can talk to me there if he needs to."

Even while he was speaking Rio was leading her to the Blazer. Still dazed by the unexpectedness of the attack, and the gruesome outcome of it, Courtney didn't break free of the faintness pressing down on her mind until they were halfway back to the ranch house. As the mental fog cleared, Rio's injury was the first lucid thought that sprang to her mind.

"Rio, your leg!" She gasped, berating herself for forgetting, even though she'd nearly blacked out. She was reaching across the seat to examine the wound on his right thigh when his hand flashed from the steering wheel to push hers aside.

"It's all right—only a crease. Maria will take care of it." Rio's tone was off putting. "She's handled worse—much worse."

The chill that pervaded Courtney's body was infinitely more immobilizing than the chill of shock. Feeling like a tolerated outsider, she withdrew into the protective cloak of haughty composure.

"Of course," she murmured distantly, unaware of the pained expression that flickered over Rio's face. She didn't speak again until Rio brought the Blazer to a stop at the house. Without waiting for him she flung the door open and dashed for the door, speaking even as she fled.

"I . . . you'd better see Maria immediately to have that wound cleaned. I'll be in the bedroom. I . . . I'd like to lie down." Her eyes stinging, Courtney ran—to escape Rio, but mostly to escape the realization that he neither needed nor wanted her assistance.

In the quiet of the bedroom, however, Courtney did not think of lying down. Instead she paced restlessly, worrying about Rio's wound, and wondering what had happened to the man she had been in Houston with.

She had actually come to hope that she and Rio had made strides during their stay in Houston in closing the gulf separating them. Because of his attitude while shopping with her, and his gentle, ardent lovemaking every night, she had believed they might actually have a chance of making their marriage work.

What a foolish, naïve woman she was! The four days they'd spent together were moments out of the real world, quite like the moments they'd shared after Rio had rescued her. The real world, or at least Rio's real world, was an alien, frightening place to her, a place that contained whizzing bullets and a red stain spreading over a man's chest.

How very quickly Rio slid from the out-of-time world to the harshness of his reality. The sound of gunfire and the scent of danger had instantly changed the Rio she had laughed with into the silent, narrow-eyed Night Striker, ready to face any challenge.

Was this the type of environment she wanted to raise her child in? she asked herself in frantic disappointment.

But what choice had she? she countered her own doubt.
She loved her child's father!

Courtney's thoughts soured her expression; at that
moment Rio strode into the bedroom, only to come to an
abrupt halt at the sight of her pale face.

He was carrying his boots in one hand and his jeans in
the other. His only covering from the waist down was a
swath of navy-blue. Rio did not appear ludicrous attired
in a shirt and very brief shorts; he looked heart-thuddingly
attractive, tough as old leather, and, amazingly after what
he'd just been through, ready for action—sexual action.

A long white bandage drew Courtney's eyes from his
arousal to his thigh. Embarrassed at having been staring,
she forced her chin up and her voice low, and cool.

"Is the wound dreadfully painful?" Strangely, the accent
that had softened over the last months rose to the fore
under stress. Even to her own ears her voice had that veddy,
veddy British note. Rio's face cringed at the sound of it.

"Middlin', but Maria assures me I'll survive." He drew
the West Texas drawl out deliberately.

Hurt by his taunting, Courtney spun around to walk to
the window. Why, why, had this had to happen now, when
they were at the very brink of understanding one another?
There was no answer, only the silent presence of the man
behind her, the man who reacted so naturally to danger,
and so casually to death. Courtney shivered with her
thoughts.

"You hate it, don't you?" Courtney started at the sound
of Rio's voice close to her ear; she hadn't even heard him
move! Before her rattled mind could form an answer he
was speaking again. "You kept your wits together very well
out there. You didn't panic or go all screaming hysterical.
But you hated it, didn't you?"

"Well, of course I hated it!" Courtney exclaimed, twisting around to face him. "Any normal person would have
hated it! Rio, a man is dead!"

"That's right," he agreed. "Now there are two down and two to go."

Courtney knew she went white because she could actually feel the blood drain from her head. "Rio! You're not going after them? You're not going to take the law into your own hands?" She clamped her lips together at the rising pitch of her voice. "Rio, you promised!"

A confusing sadness seemed to cloud his eyes for an instant; then it was gone and his eyes were as flat as dark stones. "And I'll keep my word," he said tightly. "I won't personally kill either one of them, but I do intend to join the hunt." He smiled sarcastically. "If it bothers you, Courtney, think of it as you might a hunt at home . . . only you kill the fox, don't you?" He turned and strode into the bathroom, leaving her staring after him, her eyes mirroring a wound that went much, much deeper than the one on his leg.

Why now? Why now? The question had been Rio's steadfast companion for the entire week he'd spent with the Rangers, fruitlessly trailing the two remaining kidnappers. Damn! Ben and the lowlife he hung out with couldn't have picked a worse time to surface!

She was his! Rio had felt it in his bones during their stay in Houston; Courtney had been all warm and loving during those four days they'd had together. And now she'd froze up on him again. And he hadn't even had the pleasure of seeing Ben and the other man run to earth.

Disgusted, Rio turned the Jeep over to Cleat and, after giving a brief account of the unsuccessful chase, strode into the house to confront Courtney. Tired of the lack of communication between them, he intended to resolve their differences, one way or the other. To Rio's way of thinking, marriage should not be a state of undeclared war. While trailing around in the hills, he'd decided it was either going to be a real marriage or none at all.

Besides, he'd had it with being regarded as little more than a cold-blooded killer. Rio had never regretted his decision to work as a private covert agent, and he wasn't about to start now. Courtney was going to be given the choice of taking him as he was, or leaving him the hell alone.

As Rio followed the sound of Courtney's voice into the living room he thought he was prepared to meet anything—anything, that is, except their respective fathers. As he stood momentarily unobserved in the threshold of the Spanish-style room, a wry smile played over his face. The way his luck had been running lately, he thought resignedly, he really shouldn't have been surprised to see Pat and Charles. Pat spotted him first.

"Well, it's about time you got back," Pat boomed, springing out of his chair. "How did the hunting go?"

Rio glanced at Courtney, his spirit sinking at the anxious expression on her face.

"Hello, my dear." Rio planted a kiss on Courtney's cheek, then turned back to his father. "As for the kidnappers, we lost them in the hills," he answered him. "I can't imagine where the hell they're holed up now." Extending his hand, he headed straight for Charles. "How have you been, sir?" Rio asked, as if he really cared.

"Somewhat concerned, I'll admit." Charles smiled. "I was rather hoping those men would be incarcerated by now."

"I was kinda hoping they'd be dead," Rio said bluntly, ignoring Courtney's soft gasp as he strolled to the liquor cabinet in the corner. "It would save a lot of time and trouble on a trial," he added, pouring amber whiskey into a short glass. As he turned back to the room, he tilted the glass to Courtney. "Your health, ma'am, and how are you feeling?'' His gaze holding hers, he raised the glass and emptied it in a few deep swallows.

"I'm—fine—thank you," Courtney murmured with quiet dignity.

"Glad to hear it." Rio favored her with a half smile, then turned back to the whiskey bottle. He was baiting her, and he knew it, and he couldn't stop. He was tired, and suddenly hurting like hell, and what he really wanted to do was pull her into his arms and beg her to love him. But he couldn't do that—so he baited her, for the entire remainder of the evening, and the length of Pat's and Charles's stay through the Christmas holiday.

Oh, thank heaven it's over! The phrase taunted Courtney as she watched the plane carrying her father and Charles east become a dot against the brazen Texas sky.

Turning to walk to the Blazer, she flinched as her shoulder brushed Rio's arm. An odd expression, part smile and part sneer, tugged at his lips, causing her to cringe inside. Averting her gaze she hurried to the vehicle, slid onto the seat, and stared stonily through the side window. Rio eased silently behind the wheel. Courtney's thoughts were her only real company throughout the drive back to the house.

The holiday she had awaited with such anticipation had been a complete debacle. Courtney would have had to be blind to miss the contemplative looks her father had leveled on Rio, or even the swift, sharp glances Patrick shot at his son when Rio's tongue had held a certain bite. In her own mind Courtney was sure that it was, without doubt, the worst Christmas any one of them had ever lived through.

Now, in early January, tense and stressed from weeks of forced gaiety for the benefit of Charles and Patrick, and coping with Rio's remote attitude and cynical comments,

Courtney felt on the very edge of shattering into tiny shards composed of bitterness and tears.

She was so ghastly tired. Staring sightlessly at the desolate terrain Courtney wondered again, perhaps for the thousandth time, why she simply hadn't left this unfriendly land and her equally unfriendly husband to return to her homeland with her father.

Because Rio would not have allowed her to leave, that's why, Courtney acknowledged wearily. Oh, he didn't want her anymore. Rio had established that fact in several ways, the most telling being his lack of interest in her in the bedroom; Rio had not touched her in any personal way since their return from Houston over six weeks before. Every night he came to their bed long after she was asleep, and was always gone when she awoke in the morning.

But Rio had a reason for keeping her at the ranch. He was determined to see his child come into the world. He had informed Courtney quite coolly that he had every intention of being in the delivery room when her time came. Courtney could not even speculate on what Rio would decide concerning their relationship—or lack of it—after their baby was born.

Two months. Sighing, Courtney closed her eyes. How could she manage to survive two more months in Rio's company? Her doctor had predicted the middle of March as her time for delivery. The mere idea of enduring Rio's remote companionship for that length of time sent a shudder through her.

"You can stop cringing away now"—Rio's raspy voice drew Courtney from the contemplation of the bleak weeks facing her. "You can run inside and escape now. We're home."

Before she could argue, or even protest his unfair analysis of her feelings and desires, Rio was slamming out of the Blazer and striding toward the stables.

As the weeks went slowly by, Courtney found herself

smiling in self-derision at her January fears. Rio had discovered a variety of reasons (she was positive they were false) to be away from the ranch for long periods of time, and she tormented herself imagining Rio in the arms of another woman. The image made *her* both physically and emotionally ill.

Pure, soul-destroying jealousy was a completely new and thoroughly uncomfortable emotion for Courtney. Born to beauty and privilege, she had never found cause to be jealous of anything or anybody. The closest she had come to it were the twinges of envy she'd felt for the near perfect happiness her cousin Samantha had found with Morgan. But that mild envy was as nothing compared to the searing pain and anger she experienced at the thought of Rio caressing and loving another woman as he'd caressed and loved her.

Fortunately Rio was in between "business" trips when Courtney went into labor three weeks before her projected time. During the pain of childbirth Courtney had not the time or inclination to consider Rio's reaction. It was only later, as she lay exhausted but proud at the tiny, beautiful daughter she had helped create that she mused that not even the agony and messiness of giving birth had the power to rattle the ever-so-cool Night Striker. The closest Rio came to revealing any emotion at all was in the huskiness of his tone when he spoke to her after it was finally over.

"Thank you for my daughter, Courtney. She is perfect."

Having murmured his appreciation, Rio walked from the pastel-painted room, shutting the door gently. Courtney had more than earned a long rest. Pausing in the hospital corridor he drew a slow, deep breath; then, straightening, he strode down the gleaming corridor. As Rio passed silently by, observers saw only the hard set of his features and missed the bright sheen of tears in his eyes.

Once in the Blazer, Rio allowed his facial muscles to relax for the first time in what seemed like ages. The strong, callused hands gripping the steering wheel betrayed the tremors rippling in waves through his tough body.

With every atom in his body Rio thanked his maker that he'd been at home when Courtney had gone into premature labor. A soft smile gentled his expression as a vision of his perfectly formed, beautiful daughter rose in his mind.

Luz. Rio's smile faded at the thought of the name he was positive Courtney would never agree to. And Courtney had her rights, he acknowledged. More than most, after his behavior of the last three months.

Flicking the ignition key, Rio drove off the parking lot and to the hotel he'd be staying in until Courtney was released from the hospital. Looking neither left nor right, yet missing nothing that went on around him, he went directly to the hotel bar-lounge. Over a double Jack Daniel's he decided he'd offer no objections to whatever name Courtney chose for their child; in his mind he would always think of his daughter as little Luz.

What would Courtney do now? Refusing to give in to the thickness that tightened his throat, Rio signaled the bartender for another drink. He had calls to make—to the ranch, to Nevada, to his father, who was presently in Dallas, and to England. How he longed to make those calls joyously, with all the pride and delight of a true husband. But he wasn't a true husband; he wasn't a husband at all except in name. During all the nights spent alone, whether at home or in some unfamiliar hotel room, he was longing, aching, for the passionate warmth and wild strawberry taste of his wife. He was irrevocably in love with Courtney, would be in love with her till the day he closed his eyes forever, and she was lost to him, if in fact she had ever been his at all.

And, though Rio granted Courtney her rights, he would allow himself none. He would abide by her decision in whatever she chose to do. What choice had he? Courtney thought him a killer.

The barren prospect of his own future had Rio motioning for the bartender to refill his glass.

She would have to leave. Rocking the chair gently with the toe of one foot, Courtney gazed down adoringly at the infant suckling greedily at her breast. The natural sensation radiating through her body by the action of the tiny lips was intensified by memories of a similar action by a strong male mouth.

Rio. The rocking stilled as Courtney rested her head against the chair's padded back. He was gone again, on yet another of his mysterious business trips. In the two months since their child's birth Rio had spent more time away from the ranch house than in it. His attitude spoke loudly enough. She didn't need the actual words to know that he wanted to be rid of her.

The sucking action ceased, drawing Courtney's attention to her daughter. Luz was sleeping soundly, her tiny lips slightly parted. She was glad she had acted on impulse in naming the child after Rio's mother. Each passing day the child grew more and more in the image of Rio, and thus like his mother. Rio's surprised and obviously delighted reaction to her choice of name had made it worth forgoing the one she had previously chosen—which she couldn't even remember anymore.

The occasion of the baby's christening had been the only time Rio had displayed any kind of warmth during the entire eight weeks following the child's birth.

Yes, Courtney decided, rising to lay Luz in the canopied

crib she'd fallen in love with in Houston, she would have to leave.

With her decision finally made, Courtney left the nursery and strode purposefully to the bedroom. For all its desolate dryness she had come to love the land that had spawned Rio. Before she said her good-byes to Maria, Sal, Cleat, and all the friends she'd made, she would say a silent good-bye to the land—from the back of a horse.

Fifteen minutes later Courtney approached Sal in the stables with all the regal bearing befitting her position. Sal merely sighed in apology when she requested he saddle a mount for her.

"I can't allow you to ride out alone, Miz McCord. Sorry, but I have orders straight from the boss."

Suddenly all the months of hurt and rejection and frustration welled up to overwhelm Courtney's innate good sense. Drawing herself up even straighter, she stared down at the sorrowful Sal out of eyes glittering glacial-blue with fury.

"I told you to saddle a mount for me," she enunciated coldly. "And, when your 'boss' returns, from wherever he is, you may tell him Courtney Tremaine-Smythe said he can go to—"

"Do as she asks, Sal, and throw a saddle on Hot Foot while you're at it," Rio's cool voice cut in. "I will accompany the lady," he drawled with just a hint of sarcasm.

Courtney was tempted to tell Sal to forget it and turn on her booted heel and walk back to the house. But, her pride somehow challenged, she stood rigid, trading Rio stare for stare.

In antagonistic silence Courtney rode beside Rio into the grasslands of the Marfa Highlands in the direction of the escarpment known as the Rimrock. In other sections of the grasslands she knew that herds of cattle grazed, but here, on McCord land, all was quiet now that Rio had thinned his own herd of horses.

As the sun moved steadily toward its zenith, and the heat rose in enveloping waves, Courtney requested a short respite near a rock-rimmed, spring-fed pool. She had not been astride a horse since the early months of her pregnancy and now her muscles were complaining painfully.

Shrugging his unconcern one way or the other, Rio reined in Hot Foot and stepped out of the saddle, standing absolutely still as he watched her move stiffly toward a flat rock.

Her leg muscles protesting, Courtney carefully lowered herself to the rock. A soft "Oh" whispered through her lips at the sight of a small flower valiantly lifting its blossom to the light of the sun from beneath the rock. She was bent over, reaching down to touch one tiny petal with her fingertip, when Rio's low, raspy voice froze her in place.

"Don't move, Courtney."

Although she automatically obeyed his command, Courtney glanced up, eyes widening at the taut, coiled look of him.

"W-what?" she croaked, suddenly frightened.

"I said don't move. Don't talk." His motion fluid, Rio raised his right arm and carefully slid the rifle from the saddle scabbard. "Don't even breathe." Seemingly in slow motion he turned to face her while bringing the rifle butt to his shoulder.

Every living cell inside Courtney ceased functioning as she found herself staring fixedly at the tiny black hole at the end of the rifle barrel.

"Steady."

Panic exploded inside Courtney's head at the deadly calm tenor of Rio's whispery voice.

Oh, God! My God! Has Rio gone mad? He is going to fire that thing at me! Her dry mouth stung with the metallic taste of fear as her final thought screamed through her mind.

Rio is going to kill me!

In a frozen state of terror Courtney watched helplessly

as Rio's finger eased the trigger back. She felt the bullet zing by her ear an instant before she heard the rifle's report. Stunned, she watched as he ejected the shell casing from the weapon. Then she glanced up and saw his eyes. And Rio's eyes were more terrible than the fear she'd felt seconds before.

"You can breathe again," he said too softly as he walked to where she was sitting. "I usually hit what I aim at." With the barrel of the rifle he indicated a spot behind her hand.

Dragging her gaze from his, Courtney glanced down and around and felt sickness rise to close her throat. Partially hidden under the rock was a copperhead, minus the head. Springing to her feet she dashed for a low bush edging the small pool, into which she emptied her stomach of the breakfast she'd eaten a few hours previously. When she at last backed away from the bush Rio thrust a handkerchief, moistened in the pool, into her hands.

"If you're recovered, I'd like to go back to the ranch now." His tone was so devoid of inflection or life, it caused a thrill of dread along Courtney's spine.

What had she done? Oh, Lord, what had she done to him? The insistent question tormented Courtney all the long, silent way back to the house. Her horror at what she'd believed Rio was going to do had been transparent to him; Rio's cold, lifeless withdrawal was all the proof she needed of that. He *knew* that for an instant she had actually thought he was going to kill her. Her shame was endless, and Courtney fully realized she would live with it for the remainder of her life.

Rio walked away from her as soon as they'd dismounted at the stables. Denying the urge to run after him and plead for forgiveness, Courtney spun on her heel and retreated into the house to spend what was left of the afternoon rocking and crooning to her daughter, who slept peacefully through most of it. There was work she could have busied herself with. There were designs to be completed for the next spring line. Still she sat on, numbly rocking, rocking.

Courtney went to the dinner table freshly showered, with her hair brushed to a golden sheen. But she was devoid of makeup and attired simply in jeans and a cotton T-shirt in muted shades of blue. Her appearance was a true barometer of her distracted state, for even in Texas she had insisted on always dressing for dinner.

Rio joined her after she was seated, nodding at her but saying nothing. He was in dark pants, and a dark shirt, and an even darker frame of mind. He said little throughout the meal, and then only in response to a comment from Maria, who made no attempt to hide the glances of confusion and concern she slanted from the "señor" to the "señora."

After eating less than half of his meal, Rio pushed his chair back so abruptly, Courtney looked up at him in startled reaction. His smile was an insult.

"If you'll excuse me?" His shuttered eyes were a burden. "I have work to do in my office."

Courtney followed him moments later, after bracing herself she walked to his office to apologize. Her timid knock on the office door was answered by what sounded like an impatient grunt. Squaring her shoulders, she opened the door and entered the room.

Rio was not sitting at his desk working. He was standing by the window, a glass half full of amber liquor in his hand. At Courtney's entrance he turned and stared sardonically. Loving him until it hurt, and more than a little afraid of what he might say to her, Courtney plunged into speech at once.

"Rio, I want to apologize for my hysterical behavior this afternoon." She really couldn't blame him for the sneering smile that briefly tilted his lips; even to her own ears her words rang of the finest finishing-school correctness.

"What for?" he drawled heavily. "Your reaction mirrored your true feelings."

"Rio, no!"

"Yes, Courtney," he mocked in an oddly sad way. "You actually thought I was going to fire that rifle and watch the slug slam into your body." The eyebrow inched higher. "Didn't you?"

"But . . . but, Rio! What was I to think when I glanced up to see you pointing that thing directly at me?" she cried desperately.

"You could have immediately thought that I was protecting you," he shot back harshly. "But, no, you wouldn't think that, not when you've always thought of me as a killer." Raising the glass he swallowed three quarters of the contents. A sigh hissed through his lips as he lowered the drink. "You've said your piece. Was there something else?"

"Rio, I've apologized," she cried, chilled by his remoteness. "What more can I do? Do you want me to grovel?"

"No, Courtney," he responded tiredly. "I want you to leave."

Everything was packed. Glancing around the room Courtney bit her lip to keep from crying aloud. She didn't want to go. She didn't want to take Luz and leave Rio. Now, when it was too late, she wanted to run to him and beg him to let her stay. But it was too late, he didn't want her around any longer.

Before going to Luz's nursery Courtney gazed around the room where she had lost her virginity and found her love. She had slept in the guest room since the night Rio had told her he wanted her gone. Stifling a sob, she quickly left the room.

When Courtney discovered the nursery empty she smiled and walked along the hall to the living room; Maria had taken to laying Luz on a blanket in there the last few days.

Entering the archway into the room she came to an abrupt halt at the sight that met her startled eyes.

Propped up on one elbow, Rio was lying on the floor, talking softly to his daughter, who kicked and cooed and understood not a word of what her father was saying.

". . . and I want you to be a good girl, you hear? Eat your cereal and fruit so you grow big and strong and beautiful like your mother and grandmother." His voice dropped to a whisper. "I'll miss you, little love. I love you very much, and . . ."

Tears burning her cheeks, Courtney backed out of the archway.

Chapter Ten

"Are you sure this is wise, Samantha?" Morgan Wade asked his determined wife. "It's been almost six months now. If Rio was interested in Courtney, don't you think he'd have contacted her by now?"

"Rio? The man whose own father refers to him as Ol' Silent-in-the-Saddle?" A mocking smile curved her full lips. "You have got to be joking, darling. I feel quite certain ol' Rio would go to his grave with sealed lips before admitting he'd made a mistake by sending Courtney away." Sighing with exasperation she lifted the telephone receiver from the cradle. "The man loves her, you know?" Sam didn't look at Morgan as she speed-dialled the long-distance number.

"Well, at one time I thought so too," Morgan said, shrugging. "But now I just don't know."

"We'll see." Samantha's grim tone altered. "Yes, hello, Maria, may I speak to Rio, please?" Her chin setting determinedly, she picked a sheet of stationery off the desk. "Rio, it's Samantha. I want to read something to you."

Rio's insides clenched with apprehension the instant he heard Samantha's voice. Mutely he gritted his teeth and listened as she continued.

"This is a passage from a letter I received from Uncle Charles. Please listen carefully."

Carefully? Rio almost laughed; every nerve and molecule in his body was straining to hear the contents of the letter.

"Charles writes: *Samantha, I am deeply concerned about Courtney.*"

"Is Courtney ill?" Rio broke in, imagining all sorts of terrifying things, from a serious accident to a more serious disease.

"Rio, will you please just listen?" Samantha's tone held a suspicious note of satisfaction.

Eyes narrowing in contemplation, Rio said, "All right, but get on with it, will you?"

"Of course. Now, where was I?" Sam went on too smoothly. "Oh, yes. Though Uncle Charles is concerned, he is also relieved that Morgan and I are flying over there next week. He continues: *I pray you can talk some sense into your cousin, for I'm afraid she's got in over her head this time. As I'm sure you're aware, Courtney does have this penchant for financially backing any cause that even smacks of passive action against violence. As she has both her own mind and her own fortune, I have never interfered. But this time I'm truly concerned for her personal safety.*

"*Courtney has been sponsoring a young man lately, an Irishman named Bryan Quinn, and although the man is personable enough, there are times he's simply much too intense for my tastes. I mean, really, the man has actually told me he intends to unite Ireland into a whole nation. A worthy cause, certainly. But in my experience violence seems to always surround these would-be peacemakers, and I do not want Courtney hurt by any peripheral turbulence.*

"There is more to the letter," Samantha said softly. "But I assume you get the drift?"

"Yes, I get the drift." Somehow, from somewhere, Rio found a steady tone. The phone moved in his sweat-slick palm and, frowning, Rio glanced down and grasped it more tightly. "When are you and Morgan planning to leave for England?"

"We have seats booked on the Concorde departing from Kennedy next Wednesday."

"If I can arrange passage, I'll meet you at the airport."

The following Wednesday found Rio, sprawled with deceptive laziness on a plastic chair in the departure lounge, scanning the faces of the crowd for Sam and Morgan. As he waited for his friends to arrive, Rio mentally reviewed the endlessness of the months that had passed since he'd asked Courtney to leave the ranch. Had it really only been six months? It seemed six times that long. Every day had felt like a week, and every week a month. And the only contact he'd had with her were the pictures of Luz she sent with scrupulous regularity.

Why hadn't Courtney petitioned for a divorce? Despite Rio's assurances to her that he would not contest any action Courtney instigated, he had had no notification of a suit from his lawyers. Secretly he was glad.

Where the hell were the Wades? His indolent, relaxed appearance masking the impatience eating at him, Rio scanned the faces more closely. There were still no signs of a beautiful redheaded woman escorted by a satisfied-looking tall man.

Sighing silently, Rio closed his eyes and let his mind wander. Courtney. Immediately an image of her rose to his mind, exciting him, hurting him. God, how he missed her—and the daughter whose growth he monitored periodically through snapshots. Luz was sitting up by herself now, and he hadn't been there to observe her struggles to do so.

At first Rio had eagerly looked forward to Henderson's trial, simply because he knew Courtney would be summoned back to the States to testify. Henderson himself had dashed Rio's hopes a month and a half after Courtney had returned to England. The word Rio had received was that Henderson had become involved in a scuffle in the prison yard, and had come out of it with a crudely made, six-inch blade in his chest; he had died en route to the hospital.

How many nights had Rio lain awake, aching for her, longing to hear the cultured sound of her voice blurring into the universal sound of sensual murmurings? Rio laughed wryly to himself; he had slept in snatches every night for the entire six months. Hell, he even missed the two-A.M. squalling from the nursery.

A chill of apprehension trickled down Rio's spine. Was Courtney safe? Was Luz safe? Dammit! They belonged with him, protected and cared for, not on the fringes of some fanatic's dreams of glory!

Fear tightening his throat, Rio squirmed in the small seat. He had decided months before that he would have to go to her, beg her if necessary to give their marriage another chance to work. He wanted the marriage with Courtney more than he'd ever wanted anything before in his life. Had he waited too long? A fine sheen of sweat beaded his brow. Why had he hesitated on the most important decision of his life? Rio inhaled deeply and exhaled slowly. Had it been his stiff-necked pride or simply because it was *the* most important decision of his life? There was always the distinct possibility that Courtney would turn him down.

And now that beautiful, burning flame he'd held so carelessly in his arms, *his* Courtney, was in all probability courting danger by aligning herself with a would-be crusader!

Clamping his teeth against a shudder, Rio glanced up, sighting Sam and Morgan as his will settled into unyielding steel. He would bring Courtney and Luz home, back to Texas—at any cost.

Samantha was still unsuccessfully hiding a smug smile after the plane had reached cruising altitude. Unusually edgy, Rio continued his barrage of questions.

"What else do you know of this Bryan Quinn, Sam?"

"Very little." The mention of the Irishman's name sobered her. "Other than that my uncle is obviously very worried about Courtney's involvement with his cause. I do know that she's been introducing him to some important people, along with making large monetary donations to him."

"Dammit!" Rio's anger got the better of him. "I might just decide to end the fool's cause myself. And I will, if Court gets hurt!"

"Correct me if I'm wrong but, didn't you send Courtney away in the first place?" Morgan asked blandly.

"Yes." The admission came out with a hiss.

"Might a friend ask why?" Morgan's tone was bone dry.

"No."

"Rio!" Samantha glared at him. "We want to help! You *do* love her—don't you?"

"Yes." This time his voice was a whisper. "Yes, I love her." Rio moved uneasily in the seat; he wasn't in the habit of discussing his emotions with anyone. "I sent her away because of the way she looked at me," he finally admitted.

"The way she looked at you?" Morgan and Samantha exclaimed simultaneously.

"Rio, really!" Samantha shook her head in confusion.

"That's about as clear as mud, ol' son." Morgan frowned. "I don't understand."

"She questioned me about the stupid nickname you two so very helpfully told her about." Rio related the fact with a hint of accusation. "I was honest with her. I should have lied." A ripple of emotion moved over his face, hardening his features. "She considers me a killer."

"What?" Morgan barked.

"Rio!" Sam exclaimed.

"Oh, Courtney's cool," he murmured. "Her breeding shows." Cynicism tinged his smile. "But it was there, in her eyes. I couldn't miss it."

Sam stared at him in astonishment. "Couldn't miss what, for heaven's sake?"

"The waters are still muddy, friend." Morgan inserted.

"Revulsion. Disgust." Rio's shoulders lifted in a shrug. "Courtney hates violence, remember?" He tried a smile on for size; it didn't fit. "When she looks at me, she doesn't see Rio. She sees the Striker: a killer."

"I don't believe that, Rio." Sam's tone held firm conviction.

"Neither do I," Morgan concurred.

Rio sighed raggedly. "I hope you are both right. I want to bring her back with me. I want to bring my wife and daughter home to Texas." His smile hurt Sam's heart. "Even though I know my hot, dry land is as alien to Courtney as my former employment, I want her there with me."

On arrival in England, Rio found London the exact opposite of his native land—the air was chill, a misty rain was falling, the sky was pewter gray.

During the long drive into the city and his father-in-law's home near Berkeley Square, Rio's nerves tautened and his stomach muscles clenched. How would Courtney react to his sudden appearance? he wondered, retreating still farther into himself with each passing mile. Would she object to having him show up unannounced? Come to that, how would Charles react? Might both father and daughter frown at his uninvited visit?

The hell with it. Rio dismissed conjecture with a mental

shrug. Courtney had never attempted to deny him his rights as a father. Rio longed to hold his baby in his arms while she still *was* a baby.

Charles welcomed his niece with open arms, her husband with a strong handshake, and Rio with a blatant smile of relief.

"I cannot tell you how delighted I am to see you, *all* of you." Charles looked directly at Rio. "I had not dared to hope you'd come." A smile flickered over his lips. "Even though I prayed that you would." As he ushered them into the sitting room, his smile tilted apologetically. "I'm sorry, but Courtney and Luz are not here."

Stark alarm snaked through Rio, freezing him from the inside out.

"Where are they?" The inner freeze coated his raspy voice with ice.

"In the country, at Sterling."

Rio needed no further explanation; he knew all about Charles's country estate in Kent. His eyes narrowed dangerously as Charles continued.

"I was planning to leave tomorrow"—he paused to smile at Sam—"with Samantha and Morgan, to join her there. We've invited guests for the weekend. A hunt has been arranged."

"Will Quinn be there?" Rio's tone produced an effect different for each of the other three people in the room. Sam shivered. Charles frowned. Morgan smiled.

"Yes. In fact"—Charles wet his lips nervously—"Bryan is there now."

Now Rio smiled—a sight that increased Sam's shiver, deepened Charles's frown, and widened Morgan's smile into a grin. Rio's smile was a visible harbinger of what was to come; the Night Striker was ready to prowl.

* * *

Meanwhile, in a manor house in the county of Kent, Courtney paced, crooning to the fretful child in her arms.

"If you weren't such a little pig," she murmured into her daughter's silky dark hair, "you wouldn't have a bubble tormenting your tummy."

Rubbing the child's back gently, she circled the room that had been the library and was now her workroom. All the tools and clutter of her art made dedicated pacing difficult, and as she skirted around her design board, Courtney frowned.

The design on the board was only partially complete, yet it showed exquisite promise of a breathtaking ballgown. Halting her steps, but continuing to sway easily from side to side, Courtney ran a critical gaze over her creation. A soft sigh whispered through her lips; she had so wanted to finish the design before the rest of her guests arrived. So intent was her perusal of the incomplete work, Courtney didn't hear the low click of the door opening.

"Itching to be working, are you?"

A smile smoothed Courtney's pursed lips at the sound of the lilt that all his years and schooling in England had failed to erase from Bryan's voice.

"Yes," she admitted, shifting Luz in her arms. "But this little pig has a tummy ache from gobbling up her bottle too greedily."

At that moment Luz emitted a loud burp for such a tiny thing, and immediately her eyelids began to droop sleepily.

A hint of irritation flickered over Bryan's features as he observed the child; she was much too dark and foreign-looking for his tastes.

"Why do you insist on keeping the child with you throughout most of the day?" he demanded roughly. "Taking care of her is the nanny's job. That's what you pay the woman for."

Crossing the room he came to a stop less than a foot from Courtney, staring down at her fiercely. "Everyone knows you are a devoted mother, Courtney. You have nothing to prove by spending nearly every waking moment with the babe."

Courtney was fully aware of Bryan's feeling on the subject of her method of motherhood. She was also aware of his hesitation to refer to Luz by her given name. How often had he urged her to bring two lawsuits—one of divorce, the other to legally change her child's first name? Courtney had stopped counting, simply because she hadn't the slightest intention of doing either.

"I'm not trying to prove anything, Bryan. You see, I don't feel at all as if I should spend time with Luz for appearance's sake. I *want* to spend time with her." Courtney's smile softened her firm tone; she genuinely liked Bryan, but she adored Luz, and loved Rio—another name Bryan found distasteful and foreign.

"And what of your guests?" Bryan's flash of anger revealed the rebel inside. "Are you planning to neglect them? There are some very important people coming for the weekend and the hunt; they could be of enormous help to me!" Raking a hand through his shock of auburn hair, Bryan spun away, then back to face her again. "I had hoped we would announce our engagement this weekend."

"Bryan, that is out of the question, and you've always known it. I do not have any feelings like that for you. I am still very much a married woman." Sighing, Courtney carefully carried her child to the large American-made playpen, and settled the now sleeping Luz on the padded floor of it. "I do not want to discuss the subject again. I already have a husband and my daughter has a father. You and I are just friends with the same political concerns."

"I intend to change your mind about that," Bryan argued.

"Oh, Bryan." Straightening away from the playpen Rio had had shipped to her from the same exclusive store in

Houston where they'd shopped to outfit the nursery at the ranch, Courtney smiled sadly at the fiery Irishman. "How could you hope to be a father to Luz? You can barely force yourself to either look at her or say her name."

"Her name can be legally changed," he said mulishly. "As easily as your own can," he added with a glimmer of hope.

Her movements betraying weariness with the continuing argument, Courtney walked to the liquor cabinet along the one wall, raising her brows in question as she poured wine into a fragile tulip-shaped glass.

"Whiskey," Bryan responded to her silent invitation.

After handing him his drink Courtney, sipping at her wine, studied him over the rim of her glass. In appearance Bryan represented his homeland perfectly, with his auburn hair and eyebrows, and his muscular body, and his ruddy good looks. Oh, yes, Bryan Quinn had turned more than one young, and not so young, maiden's head. It was a pity, really, that he'd had to set his sights on her, Courtney mused. For, good or bad, like it or not, she was, and always would be, irrevocably Rio's, whether he wanted her or not.

"I am not going to change my name. I will not, even if Rio decides to divorce me," Courtney responded at length. "I do not love you, Bryan. And that is that."

"I won't give up even though you insist on ending this conversation," His tone had an underlying pout.

At that moment Bryan looked quite like an overindulged young man. Courtney nearly choked on her wine as a vision rose in her mind, a vision so sharp it made her ache all over—quite the way she did each and every night when she was finally alone in her bed. The comparison between her vision and the man scowling at her was so ludicrous, she almost laughed aloud. In comparison to the dark, silent, self-confident man of Courtney's vision, Bryan appeared little more than a petulant boy.

With a harsh shake of her head Courtney swung back

to the cabinet, splashing wine into her glass with careless abandon. She didn't want to think of Rio, didn't need the proof of comparisons. Rio was the only man she wanted in her life, in her arms, in her bed; if she couldn't have Rio, she would sleep alone for the rest of her life. And, as it was patently obvious that Rio didn't want her, Courtney had resigned herself to an empty future and an equally empty bed. But she would not change her mind about Bryan and it was a pity, she mused again, raising her glass in salute to him. She really did like him.

Amazingly, Courtney did finish the design on her board before the rest of her guests began arriving for the weekend. It was a good thing, too, she reflected later that night when she'd finally bidden good night to the last of the night owls. If the evening was a sample for the weekend, she was in for a rather hectic time of it!

It was not until after luncheon the following day that Courtney realized exactly how hectic the weekend was going to be.

Courtney had joined several of her guests in a motor tour of the surrounding countryside. On her return to the house a smile lit her face at the sight of her father's Rolls-Royce parked in splendor before the wide steps. She was laughing up at Bryan as she entered the large reception hall. The living vision that met her gaze widened her eyes and dried the laughter on her lips.

Rio was sitting, lounging, on the third to last step of the grand staircase that curved majestically up to the first floor, his long, jean-encased legs stretched out in front of him, booted ankles crossed. His elbows were propped indolently on the step above the one he was sitting on, his broad, slender hands dangled over the edge of the marble riser. But most shattering of all to Courtney, for some odd reason, was the fact that he was wearing his Stetson—inside the house!—the brim tugged low over his glittering dark eyes.

"Rio!" In her shock and surprise a hoarse squeak was all Courtney could manage. But even in her shock she could feel Bryan stiffen beside her at the intimate tone of voice with which Rio responded.

"Hello, Courtney."

Moving in that boneless, effortless way that was uniquely his, Rio swept the hat from his head and surged to his feet. At the same instant the rest of the touring party came clattering, chattering, into the reception hall behind Courtney and Bryan. As if as one, the members of the group seemed to sense something awry and fell silent for a tense heartbeat of time. Then a voice, cultured, authoritative, broke the electric tension.

"Rio, my boy! When did you arrive?"

There was a collective gasp from every throat, including Courtney's. His narrow-eyed glance slicing through the dozen or so people now surrounding his wife, Rio drew another gasp from them with the grin that slashed his face and the familiar greeting that passed his lips.

"How goes it, Jamie?"

Jamie? Courtney thought blankly. He refers to her uncle, James Tremaine-Smythe, the Marquis of Ravenburn, as Jamie? Even *she* only ever called him Uncle James in private! Good grief! There were only a handful of people in the entire world privy to the affectionate family sobriquet, and her father was the single person ever to use it!

Loose-limbed and easy, his grin softening to a warm smile, Rio sauntered toward the tall, gauntly imposing figure standing near the open entrance doors. Blind to the expressions of shock and the gasped murmurs of the assemblage, he moved through them purposefully, extending his hand as he drew near the older man.

"I swear—Rio McCord!" James breathed unbelievably as he grasped the proffered hand.

"My lord Ravenburn." Rio nodded respectfully, clasping the hand firmly. "It's been a spell."

"It has indeed, seven years in fact since we met in Hong Kong." A delighted smile broke his somber countenance.

"My lord!"

The confused gathering turned to the new voice that rang from the broad staircase. As Courtney's face lighted in welcome, Samantha swept down the stairs and directly into the open arms of her mother's brother.

"Well, now, what have we here?" Ravenburn demanded, holding Samantha at arm's length to gaze into her glowing face. "Ah, I do believe it's that rebellious chit my sister brought into this world!"

"The same, my lord." Throwing back her glorious red hair, Samantha smiled up at him mistily.

"And every bit as lovely as her mother was—God rest her soul," Ravenburn murmured. Then he frowned. "Where is that cowboy you married?" he demanded arrogantly.

"Ever close to her, my lord," Morgan drawled, strolling toward them from the foot of the stairs. "Ravenburn," he greeted, grasping the man's hand with the same panache as Rio had.

"Wade." Ravenburn managed a passable drawl. "You do know Rio?" It was more a confirmation than a question.

Morgan smiled slowly. "We've spoken, a time or two."

"Quite." With a sharp nod of his white-maned head Ravenburn waved languidly toward an enormous set of double doors, while fixing a frown on Courtney. "Isn't it time for tea?"

"What?" Bemused by the incredulity of the scene she'd moments before witnessed, Courtney blinked. Then, coming to her senses, "Oh, yes!" Flustered, she spun on her heel to lead her guests into the large lounge, tugging the cord to summon the butler as she swept by.

Hanging back, Ravenburn leveled a coolly assessing glance on Rio. "In getting his man, the Night Striker's record remains unblemished." One thick eyebrow peaked arrogantly. "Will he now allow his woman to get away?"

"Can't have that." Rio smiled lazily. "It wouldn't do to blot my copybook now, would it, sir?"

Inside the lounge Courtney wondered at the cause of her uncle's sudden roar of laughter.

Chapter Eleven

"What is he doing here?"

Clamping her lips against a startled yelp, Courtney jerked around at the sound of barely contained anger in Bryan's voice. She was standing in the shadows of the draperies that outlined the wide French doors leading onto the formal rose gardens. It had been nearly an hour since she'd ushered her guests into the lounge. Although her mind was still reeling from the events in the reception hall, her training had served her in good stead as she saw to the comfort of her guests. She had only moments before slipped into the protective shadows of the draperies for a breather; the absolute last thing she needed was a confrontation with Bryan.

"And why this particular weekend?" he continued harshly.

"It's really none of your business, but I assume Rio has come to England to see his daughter," she responded with a sigh.

Bryan wasn't listening. "Damn it! Besides your uncle

there will be several men here this weekend who could be of inestimable help to me in my campaign." He brushed the hair off his brow. "I need your support to enlist their aid." Bryan pinned her with a fiery gaze.

She returned his angry stare with blue eyes flashing. "It's unfortunate that Rio chose this weekend to visit, I agree. But I cannot deny him his parental rights."

"He obviously knows your uncle very well," he observed enviously.

"Yes," Courtney murmured, distracted by the same consideration. She glanced back into the long lounge, her gaze homing in unerringly on the dark man seated in the midst of a group that included her father, her uncle, and Morgan. As if he could feel her frowning regard, Rio glanced up. His dark-eyed gaze tangled with hers, refusing to release her.

Fingers curling into her palms, Courtney silently fought the sensual intimacy flaring in the depths of Rio's eyes. Her breathing shallow, painful, she received the message he was sending to her as clearly as if he'd shouted it the length of the room.

I want you, Rio's intent gaze whispered, *and I intend having you.*

Confused, wary, Courtney started when Bryan muttered close to her ear, "Damn him! I wish I could think of some way to get him out of here."

Alarm shot through her. Suddenly concerned, Courtney whirled to face him. Was he mad? she thought wildly. If Bryan started something! Oh, Lord! Courtney's cheeks flushed with anger. Bryan was foolish to think he had any say in her private life.

"Bryan, please." The fingers she placed on his arm trembled with inner tension. "Don't make a scene. I will arrange another weekend for you." She smiled placatingly. "You must accept the fact that Rio is my husband and he has every right to be here."

"Don't you understand? Time is valuable!" Bryan ground his teeth in frustration. "Dammit! I *needed* this weekend to raise financial support!" His movements jerky with suppressed anger, he strode away from her, his face working into an expression of geniality as he approached one of his targets.

Throughout the rest of the afternoon, and the entire evening, the hours blurred for Courtney, testing her exclusive-boarding-school training in deportment and gracious entertaining.

Her adroit efforts to avoid any personal contact with Rio left her tense and jumpy. Courtney's heart ached when he joined the rest of the party for drinks before dinner to see Rio in the same pearl-gray suit he'd worn on their wedding day. Sighing with a longing that clawed at her to her very soul, she lifted her chin, smiled at her guests, and averted the dark-eyed gaze that seemed intent on consuming her alive.

Would the evening never end? Courtney had asked herself that same tiresome question countless times before she smilingly bade the last of the guests good-night. Turning from the curving staircase wearily, she stared at the closed doors to her father's study. The four men—her father, her uncle, Morgan, and Rio—had been closeted in the study since shortly after dinner.

Tired beyond belief from the strain of Rio's sudden appearance, she squared her shoulders and walked purposefully to the doors; she would tap lightly, open the door a mere crack, bid them all a soft good-night, then beat a hasty retreat.

The study doors opened even as she was reaching for the knob. As the men exited the room, they bade *her* a soft good-night. Rio wasn't one of them. Frowning her confusion Courtney trailed behind the three men as they mounted the stairs.

When had Rio retired? she wondered, turning into the

hall that led to the suite of rooms she'd redecorated for herself on her return to England six months previously.

As she did every night, Courtney walked past her own bedroom to visit the nursery before retiring for the night. Moving with extreme quiet so as not to waken Luz's nanny, she crept into the room—and stopped dead, one hand flying to her shock-parted lips.

The scene her wide eyes absorbed was illuminated by the soft glow of a small night-light. There was no sign of the nanny. The small cot upon which she usually slept had been moved from its place along the far wall and placed directly against the side of Luz's crib. Positioned exactly like his daughter's, Rio's long form sprawled face down on the cot. His upper torso was naked and one arm was thrust between two of the crib bars. His splayed hand rested protectively on Luz's tiny, vulnerable spine.

Feeling herself an intruder, as she had on the day before she'd departed Texas six months previously, Courtney fought the sting of hot tears and backed stealthily from the room.

The image of Rio and their child haunted Courtney throughout that endless night. Not at any time had she doubted Rio's love for their child. But now, for the first time, she forced herself to consider what being separated from Luz was doing to Rio's soul.

Courtney wept, for herself and her hopeless love; for Rio and his guiltless entrapment; and for Luz and the life she faced with her parents separated by half a world. Dawn found her staring red-eyed and exhausted from weeping and lack of sleep. Dragging her body from the bed, she tossed off her nightgown with a sigh.

The day would be a long one, with precious few moments for Courtney to rest. There was the hunt to get through, and then the hunt breakfast, and then dinner, followed by the traditional hunt ball.

Standing under the stinging shower spray, Courtney shuddered and wished she were back in Texas.

The din of excited voices and metal horseshoes striking cobblestones greeted Courtney as she strode onto the courtyard where the hunting party was gathered. At any other time the scene, with its noise and colorfully attired hunters, would have pleased her. This morning she tapped her riding crop against her buff-colored riding breeches impatiently; all Courtney wanted was to have the weekend over with.

Responding automatically to the greeting called to her, she walked directly to a group that included her father, her uncle, Samantha, Morgan, and several grooms, all of whom were holding the reins to horses stamping and snorting in impatience to be off. There was not a sign of Rio.

After exchanging greetings of the morning, Courtney was on the point of asking after Rio when he sauntered across the courtyard toward the family group. His concession to the traditional hunting atirre were boots that rose to his knees, breeches hugging his muscle-corded thighs, and a small cap perched on his head. In comparison to the abundance of red jackets in the yard, his snowy-white, full-sleeved shirt blazed like a beacon.

As Rio joined the group a groom led a huge horse from the stables and across the cobblestones to him. Inattentive to the conversation around her, Courtney was the first to notice the horse. But before she could open her mouth to question the groom, her father spotted the animal.

"What is this?" he demanded sharply, pinning the groom with a cold gaze.

"The horse that was ordered for Mr. McCord, sir," the groom replied respectfully.

"Ordered by whom?" Charles exclaimed, thus causing the spirited animal to dance excitedly.

"Why, I don't know, sir." The groom visibly gulped,

uncomfortably aware of the silence that had fallen like a stone in the yard.

"Take that beast back at once," Charles ordered. "And bring a suitable mount for Mr. McCord."

Throughout the exchange Courtney was fully aware of Rio's narrow-eyed gaze studying her speculatively. *What now?* she thought tiredly, facing him with defiant eyes. Rio spoke and at that instant she realized he believed she had ordered the horse.

"What's wrong with that horse, Charles?" His low voice didn't penetrate beyond the immediate family circle.

Charles could barely control his voice. "The beast cannot be broken to the saddle. I've made arrangements to sell him." He again glared at the groom. "Think, man! Who dared to order Stomper saddled for the hunt?"

"I—I—" The groom sputtered.

"He's well named," Rio murmured, running a glance over the big animal, who was forcefully living up to his name. "Isn't he, Courtney?" His glittering dark gaze came to rest on her, piercing her composure like a laser.

"Rio, I—" Courtney broke off in shock. In avoiding the accusing gleam in Rio's eyes, she'd caught sight of Bryan; his smug expression explained everything. "Bryan!" she called, intent on chastising the jealous man, but Rio overrode her voice.

"A favor, Morgan?" he asked very softly.

"Anything," came the prompt reply.

"Get that English gear off that bastard." Spinning on his low heels Rio strode back to the house.

On the edge of her consciousness Courtney heard the murmured comments from her family members and the ripple of excited questions from the rest of the crowd milling in the courtyard; she was even aware of Morgan as he relieved the groom of the reins and led the horse back to the stables; but her entire concentration was leveled on Bryan. As she stared furiously at him, his smug expression grew into a smirk. His taunting remark proved he hadn't heard the exchange between Rio and Morgan.

"Well, now"—he chuckled, mounting up—"as it would appear the Texan has an aversion to good horseflesh, I suppose we'll have to ride without him."

Some members of the party had already mounted. The others moved to do likewise. Some were up, some still standing, and some were halfway between, when Ravenburn, mounted on a gleaming chestnut, turned his head arrogantly to stare down his aristocratic nose at Bryan.

"I will decide when it is time to ride," he informed the Irishman frigidly.

Bryan's expression was an open book, revealing chagrin, and remorse, and sheer panic, at the fear of his career lost for the game of one-upmanship over a rival.

Courtney could not work up one ounce of sympathy for him. The stupid fool had actually attempted to embarrass Rio, and possibly even injure him! She turned away from the sight of Bryan's flushed face; but her eyes flew wide at the more upsetting sight of Morgan, leading Stomper back into the yard. On the animal's back was a familiar, well-worn saddle. Did Rio drag the tack with him wherever he went? she wondered, spinning to the swell of murmurs in the courtyard.

Dressed much the same as he had been when lounging on the stairs the day before, Rio retraced his steps over the cobblestones to Morgan, and the unbreakable, uncontrollable Stomper, his slanted bootheels ringing loudly on the cobbles.

"Back it up, folks." Rio issued the terse warning as he approached the large animal, who was regarding him with wildly rolling eyes.

Amid the gasps and exclamations of the assemblage Ravenburn's cold voice enforced the advice. "Pull your mounts back at once."

Fluidly, smoothly, Rio stepped into the saddle. There

was an instant of absolute stillness, during which Courtney saw a smile flicker over Rio's thin lips; then the horse exploded into action.

There were female screams and male outcries as Stomper set about living up to his name. Bucking, twisting, kicking, and stomping, the maddened animal fought wildly to dislodge his rider. Gripping the reins firmly Rio maintained his seat. When all his tricks failed him, Stomper gave up the battle. Educated by a master, the horse stood panting and docile.

As the mob closed in to offer congratulations on a superb performance, Rio glanced at Ravenburn.

"Now we ride!" Ravenburn commanded.

The hunt master's horn called the group to order, and within seconds they were dashing across the fields after the braying dogs. Giving her mare its head Courtney automatically joined the chase, grasping the reins with one hand while dashing at the tears on her cheeks with the other. A simple fact revolved around in her tired mind: Rio might have been injured or even killed. Hardening her heart she vowed that Bryan would never again receive support from her of any kind.

Then, through the jumble of chaotic emotions hammering in her head, she heard the thunder of Stomper's approaching hoofbeats. As Rio drew the magnificent animal alongside her mare, Courtney glanced at him quickly. One look at Rio's set features was enough; feeling another kind of fear Courtney kept her eyes averted for the remainder of the chase.

When it was over, and the fox cornered, Courtney surrendered to the compelling force of his gaze. Lifting her eyes, she felt a spear of ice shaft through her. Rio's dark eyes were filled with contempt and disgust as he shifted his gaze from her to the trembling fox, then back to her. His cynically twisting lips spoke with silent eloquence of his opinion of their "sport."

Shamed and unable to endure his accusing stare, Courtney wheeled the mare, startling her into a gallop with a
crack of her quirt. As she shot away from the milling group,
Bryan's head jerked up and around.

"Courtney?" he called anxiously, unaware of the narrow-
eyed man inching the big horse into position beside him.
"Courtney, wait!" Bryan called again, gathering the reins
to turn his mount. His action was stilled by a firm hand
grasping his. Feeling the pain shoot up his arm Bryan
looked up, and into a pair of dark eyes glittering with
warning.

"You've had your chase," Rio rasped icily. His Stetson
tilted in the direction of the retreating horse and rider.
"That one's mine."

Releasing the other man's wrist by flinging it from him,
Rio turned Stomper, setting him into a trot until he'd
cleared the other riders; then, loosening the reins, he set
the big animal free.

"Okay, bastard," he crooned. "Let's see what you're
made of."

Stomper's long, powerful legs stretched mightily, covering the rolling countryside in a blurring movement.
Pumping easily, steadily, he closed the distance between
Rio and Courtney's flagging mare. As Rio drew the barely
winded animal alongside the mare his arm shot out to
grasp the reins and jerk the horse to a shuddering stop.

Apprehension tightening her throat, Courtney watched
as Rio swung his leg over the horse, then slid to the ground.

"Dismount, Courtney." The coldly delivered order
snapped her out of the freezing fear.

Flinging her head up with defiant arrogance, Courtney
glared her refusal at him. An instant later she was standing
on the ground before him. Had she really forgotten how
very swiftly and silently he could move? she asked herself
in amazement. Then sheer fury at his manhandling
directed her actions. Without hesitation she raised the

quirt and brought it down and across his shoulder in one continuous, flashing movement. She cried out in pain as Rio grasped her around the wrist, twisting the crop from her fingers with one hand and capturing the back of her neck with the other.

"And you say *I'm* violent?" he demanded, drawing her face close to his by applying pressure to the back of her head.

"Rio!" Courtney gasped for breath. "Please, don't—"

His head swooped down and his open mouth fused onto her parted lips. For one mad instant Courtney struggled against his possession of her mouth. Then, with the realization that she was fighting not him, but herself, she flung her body against his.

At the inciting sound of the groan that was ripped from his throat, she speared her fingers into his hair, tugging him closer to the hungry demand of her mouth. Biting, sucking, she attempted to devour his lips, while reveling in his efforts to do the same to hers. Her tongue brushed his as it thrust into her mouth.

God! Oh, God! She loved him so terribly! She had missed him so desperately. Wanting more and still more of him, she tried to consume him with her mouth, while thrilling to the evocative thrust of his stiffened tongue and the searching grasp of his strong hands.

Unmindful of the grazing horses they moved as one, dropping to the coarse, uneven meadow grass. Courtney whimpered in protest when Rio removed his hands from her feverish body, and cried out in pleasure when his ungloved hands returned to mold her breasts possessively.

"I want you, *querida,*" Rio murmured harshly. "Right now, right here, in the sunlight, in the open." His lips sought the curve of her neck; his hands sought the flesh hidden beneath the hunting jacket; his legs sought the cradle of her thighs.

"Yes! Yes!" On fire with the need to be close to him,

be one with him, Courtney was way beyond considerations of propriety.

With frantic, trembling fingers they tore at each other's clothing. When at last they were both free of the confining material, they came together with urgency, straining with the yearning to be one person.

It had been too long, and the heights were scaled swiftly through a mist of flame. On his drive to the summit Rio arched his body into Courtney, tension exposing the tendons in his neck as he called her name aloud at the same instant she cried out his name in ecstasy.

Exhausted, stunned by the magnitude of the experience, Courtney stared at him in mute wonder. *How can I bear to give him up again?* She cried inwardly, blinking against the hot sting of tears. *I can't give him up again!*

Her eyes sparkling like rain-washed blue diamonds, she gazed up at him, silently begging for a place in his heart.

Feeling shattered by the incredible experience, Rio stared into Courtney's pleading eyes. *What is she begging for?* he wondered uneasily. *Her freedom?* A tremor of emotion quaked through his deliciously replete body. *I can't let her go!*

"Courtney?"

"Rio?"

Their voices blended in unison, and in unison they both fell silent.

I want her! he thought fiercely.

I need him! she thought achingly.

If she won't come home with me, I don't want to live! he realized with a shock.

If he doesn't take me back with him, I'll die! she faced the truth wearily.

The intensity of emotional passion reignited the flame

of physical passion. Their bodies still joined, they stared into each other's eyes as he grew inside her.

"Can you bear to love again so soon, *querida?*" he whispered around a sensual smile.

"Rio." Courtney felt the ripple that coursed through his strong body as she whispered his name.

This time there would be no groping urgency, Rio determined, causing a shudder of pleasure in her with the gliding quest of his palm. Her damp skin caressed his hand like moist satin. Her tight, aroused nipple jabbed imploringly at his palm. Feeling himself expand inside her, Rio teased her wet lips with his teeth.

"It was always fantastic with us," he affirmed, gliding his slick tongue over the edge of her teeth. "Wasn't it, *querida?*"

"Yes, always." Courtney sighed into the curve of his neck. "Even the first time, when it should have hurt, but didn't." With the tip of her tongue she tested the salty taste of his skin, her body arching to his in response to the rotating movement he made with his hips.

Hard, callused palms caressed the underside of her thighs before slowly moving to the sensitive skin on the insides. As her breathing grew shallow, then labored, he trailed his fingers upward, watching the passion on her face.

"You belong to me, Courtney," he said raggedly, his body thrusting reflexively to her arching hips. "You will always belong to me." He drove himself into her as if to underscore his assertion.

"I—I know!" Courtney gasped, trembling in reaction to his powerful possession. Her eyes were tightly closed to savor every nuance of pleasure, and when he went suddenly still she blinked in confusion. The expression on his face was impossible to decipher, but it seemed to be a mixture of incredulity, wonder, and sheer awe.

"You know?" he repeated roughly.

"Yes." There was a stillness about him that brought a fine frown line to her brow. Why was he so still? "Rio, what is it? What have I—"

"How long have you known?" he demanded.

Confused by his intensity, Courtney tried to withdraw by pressing her body into the ground.

"Answer me, Courtney."

"Almost from the beginning," she blurted, shaken by his threatening whisper. "Rio, I never really wanted any man before I met you. And—and after that night we spent together, I knew I'd never want any other man."

"You wanted a killer?" he asked very, very softly.

"You are not a killer!" Suddenly incensed, she grasped at his hair and shook his head. "Dammit, Rio McCord! You are not a killer! I would not love you if you were!"

"Whoa! Honey, hold it! Are you trying to shake my head off?" Rio's rich, full laughter rang sweetly in the clear air.

Though her hands stilled, her fingers flexed against his scalp. "I should, but I won't." Fingers pressing, she urged his mouth to hers. "But only because I like the way it looks attached to your body."

His lips brushed hers tantalizingly. "Personally, I like my body attached to yours." The tip of his tongue teased the tender skin on the inside of her lower lip, then dipped into her mouth at her responsive moan. "You're coming home with me, Court. You must. We'll work out the differences between us. Maybe it won't be all roses. In fact I'm sure it won't, but it will be good. We can make it good." Pulling his head free of her grasp, he gazed at her with eyes so full of tenderness that Courtney's throat closed. "*Querida*, I can't live alone in that barren land without you. Come home with me."

"Rio?" Courtney could manage no more than a breathless whisper. "You *are* telling me you love me—aren't you?"

"Yes, I love you." Leaning to her he kissed her fast, and hard. "Of course I love you." The action was repeated.

"I've always loved you." When she sought his mouth again he pulled his head back. "Now please tell me," he asked.

"Yes, I love you." Slipping her hand around his neck she drew him to her. "Of course I love you." Tugging him closer she brushed his lips with hers. "I've always loved you." Curling her other arm around his neck she clung fiercely. "I even love that barren land of yours. Yes, darling, we'll make it work." Her lips touched his again. "We could begin right now."

And there, beneath a brilliant midday sun, Rio proceeded to prove to Courtney how well they could work together.

Chapter Twelve

Courtney woke to cool Texas air and the feather-light brush of hard male lips over her brow. Boneless with satiation, she forced her eyelids up and smiled lazily into her husband's love-softened dark eyes.

"Is it time to get up already?" She sighed, glancing over his shoulder at the faint gray of predawn beyond the window.

"Not yet," Rio murmured, gliding his lips from her brow to her temple. "In a little while."

"What woke you?" she mumbled into the warm curve of his hard shoulder.

"Need." Demonstrating, he gripped her by the hips to slide her body over his blatant arousal.

Deliberately tormenting him, Courtney wiggled her hips, laughing softly at the groan she elicited from him. "Honestly, darling, you are the greediest man!" She gasped as his hand found her naked breast.

"Yeah." He nipped at the sensitive skin along the side of her throat. "And you love it."

"Quite true," she admitted on a satisfied sigh, shimmying her body up his to allow his mouth access to her throat, and her own lips free rein to explore the hard planes and angles of his face.

"You smell of expensive perfume . . . and a long night of loving," Rio muttered, stabbing into the hollow at the base of her throat with the tip of his tongue. "It excites the hell out of me."

"Everything excites the hell out of you," she taunted, dropping biting kisses over his high cheekbones.

"Not everything," Rio corrected gently, sinking his teeth into her silky shoulder. "Only everything about *you.*"

As if to prove his point he skimmed his hands down her sides, outlining her curves with his palms. At her responsive shiver he stroked her thighs from her knees to her rounded bottom.

Gasping with pleasure Courtney arched her back for him, fingers digging into his hair to tug him closer. "I think"—she gasped again as his teeth scraped over the sensitized bud—"I think I'd want to kill anyone who dared to hurt you!"

Releasing her breast, Rio laughed aloud. "Blood-thirsty little devil, aren't you?" he teased, grasping her around the waist to draw her down and onto the throbbing heat of him.

"Where you're concerned, yes. Now I understand how you felt about protecting me," Courtney confessed, moaning as he thrust into her.

For long moments conversation ceased. The only sound that disturbed the first morning chirping of the birds was the occasional cry of appreciative pleasure.

With the strength of ever-renewing hunger Courtney and Rio took possession of each other fiercely, wildly, joyfully.

Rio's soft laughter broke the sweet languor induced by completion.

"Whatever," Courtney queried around a yawn, "are you laughing at?"

"The memory of how you attacked Quinn that day." He grinned wickedly. "When we finally did return to the house." His grin widened. "To partake of the hunt breakfast after partaking of each other."

Courtney smiled dreamily. "That day was marvelous." She sighed, gazing into his gleaming eyes. "You told me you loved me that day."

"I've told you the same a million times since," Rio reminded her indulgently. "As you've told me."

"Yes," she purred. "We both do lap it up like kittens with cream—don't we?"

"Umm," Rio murmured, laughter erupting from him again. "Which doesn't change what you said to the crusader. You went after him like a riled rattler, hissing and striking."

"I never struck him!" Courtney denied indignantly, bolting into a sitting position to glare down at him.

"Well, no," Rio allowed, grinning again. "But you came damn close."

Courtney felt the warmth of a flush wash over her cheeks. "I was tempted," she admitted contritely. Then, raising her chin with inbred arrogance, she decreed, "But the fool deserved it, damn him! He had no idea of your expertise in the saddle when he ordered Stomper for you! For all he knew, you might have been badly injured or even killed by that beast!"

"Hey, lady," Rio chided. "That 'beast' is a damned fine piece of horseflesh."

Courtney shuddered delicately. "Let's not go into *that!*" she pleaded. "I don't even want to think of that animal taking up residence in your stables."

"Stomper is a fantastic stud," Rio maintained stoutly.

"Somewhat like his new owner?" Courtney asked sweetly, setting the spark to Rio's laughter again. "At any rate," she continued quellingly, "I really did not have to strike Bryan."

"Damned straight!" Rio choked on another bout of laughter. "Ravenburn did it for you!"

Courtney fought to control the twitch at the corners of her kiss-brightened lips. "I never thought to see the day my lord Ravenburn would raise his fist at another man." Still struck by the wonder of it, and Bryan's ignominious departure from Sterling, she shook her head slowly from side to side.

"It was a great hunt ball, though," Rio observed musingly.

Her spine stiffening, Courtney peered down the elegant length of her patrician nose at him. "For whom?" she inquired icily.

"I had thought for everyone." Rio's laughter subsided as he eyed her tenderly. "You looked ravishing," he remembered, smiling softly, "with your beautiful hair and your white skin in that delicious midnight-blue confection of a gown."

"And you were quite devastating," Courtney gritted, "in your exquisitely tailored tuxedo and that crisp white dress shirt, contrasting so appealingly with your dark skin." Her tone grew colder. "Throughout the evening, whenever I glanced in your direction, it was to discover yet another lovely woman either draped on your arm, or snuggling on your chest while supposedly dancing."

"Courtney?" Rio jerked upright to sit facing her. "Are you serious?"

Having lived with the hateful, childish jealousy for the three weeks since that wretched ball, Courtney merely stared at him. The avowal of his love had come so suddenly, she was still very unsure of herself.

"*Querida!* Has this been festering in your mind all this time?" Rio's brows drew together in a frown. Courtney's anguished eyes betrayed her. And, before those eyes, his face set into unrelenting lines. "I will say this once, and only once. You are the only woman I see, regardless of how many I glance at. You are the only woman I ever want draped on my arm, or snuggling on my chest, or in my life, or in my bed." His face seemed carved from stone. "You either trust me or you don't."

For an instant a scene flashed into Courtney's mind and she could see his face on the day he'd shot the snake to protect her. A tangle of love for him, and regret for her own stupidity, brought a rush of tears to her eyes.

"Oh, Rio, I do trust you," she sobbed, flinging herself into his chest. "I trust you with my body, and my life, and the life of our child!"

Rio was quiet for some moments; then, very softly, he asked, "Are you willing to prove your trust?"

"Yes, yes, I'll do anything!" Courtney cried, clutching his hard warmth close as if in fear he'd withdraw as he had the other time. "Tell me how I can prove it."

"Will you ride out with me again?" he asked quietly. "Out to that same spot where I killed the snake?"

Leaning away from him, Courtney lifted a trembling hand to wipe at the tears on her face. "That's all you want me to do? Ride out with you to that place?"

"Yes. Will you come?" Though his face remained closed to her, she could read traces of remembered pain in his eyes.

"I hurt you very badly—didn't I?" she whispered achingly.

"Will you ride with me?" he asked, refusing to answer her.

"Rio." Reaching out with both hands she stroked his face lovingly. "I would happily ride to the very ends of the earth with the Night Striker."

* * *

The sun had not yet made its appearance on the eastern horizon when Courtney and Rio rode again into the grasslands of the Marfa Highlands. Comfortable in the Western-style saddle, and Hot Foot beneath her, Courtney observed Rio's seat astride Stomper with appreciation. When mounted, he seemed to become one with the horse under him.

Noting her perusal, Rio smiled into her sparkling blue eyes, loving her with his gaze. Behind the glow of near adoration his mind still whirled with the echo of her fervent declaration: "I would happily ride to the very ends of the earth with the Night Striker."

Residual tremors still rippled through his body from the quake of relief her assertion had sent shuddering through him. With her soft assurance Courtney had forever banished his belief that she reviled and loathed his former occupation, and him personally.

Courtney loved him! Rio shivered with the import of the thought. *Courtney loved him!* A bubbling joy unlike anything he'd ever experienced before in his life hummed along his veins. God! Rio had to fight the urge to leap into the air, whooping and hollering like a wild cowboy on a weekend rip! Rio controlled himself by making love to her with his eyes.

Courtney's breathing went slightly haywire as she gazed into the smoldering depths of Rio's eyes. Helpless against the emotion tightening her chest, she gave in to the shivers of pleasure his caressing gaze sent tingling over her flesh. Incredible, impossible, as it seemed, she had the over-heated sensation of actually feeling his touch on her body.

Her melting reaction was slightly amazing to Courtney—considering the fact that, up until little more than a year ago, she'd had no experience and didn't understand sexual contact as an expression of love! A pleasurable warmth suffused her body as she recalled how very passionately she'd expressed her love for Rio.

Love him? Courtney restrained the desire to laugh aloud at the tame expression. The word *love* barely defined the way she felt about Rio. Searching her mind, Courtney sought a more definitive term to apply. The only word she could come up with that even came close was *worship*.

To the lullaby of creaking saddle leather, and the visual expression of mutual adoration and worship, they came eventually to the spot Courtney thought of as "the snake place."

After removing his work-scarred gloves Rio stepped out of the saddle, then held his hand out to her in silent invitation. Without hesitation Courtney dismounted and slid her palm into his. The silence easy between them, they strolled to the rock-rimmed, spring-fed pool and directly to the low, flat-topped rock Courtney had rested upon over six-months before. Courtney was the first to break the silence between them.

"There was a little flower"—she indicated one side of the rock—"looking like it was striving to reach the sunlight."

"It probably was." Rio's voice was even more raspy than usual.

Dropping to one knee Courtney peered under the rock. "It's gone." Disappointment colored her tone.

"It was a spring flower, love." Rio smiled softly, lovingly. "There will be more next spring."

Courtney glanced up to flash him a quick, understanding smile; Rio was telling her *they* would come back next spring also. "It was so very small, so valiant looking." Her tone tightened. "I had reached down to touch one tiny petal when—"

Courtney's eyes widened in disbelief and horror as a whizzing sound cut across her words and a bullet plowed into the earth on the far side of the rock. Staring at the furrow the bullet had made, she was barely aware of Rio's harshly expelled curse, or that he'd moved to shelter her between his body and the rock. As he dropped into a crouch in front of her the whizzing sound rent the air again and another bullet slammed into the earth, this time from the opposite direction.

"Two of them," Rio muttered, biting out a string of curses; his rifle was in the saddle scabbard! Reaching behind him he pushed Courtney roughly to the ground. "Stay down," he ordered. He couldn't lose her now! he thought frantically, coldly glittering eyes scanning the terrain through slitted lids. His thoughts were brought to an abrupt halt by the taunting call from beyond a gently sloping sand-hill off to Rio's right.

"Just you stay where you are, cowboy." With the instruction a man scrambled around the sandhill, rifle firmly in position. An instant later another man appeared from the back of a cluster of rocks to Rio's left.

"Ben!" The name came from Courtney's throat on a sigh of sheer terror.

With flashing anger Rio had recognized both of the men at once; the terrified sound of Courtney's voice solidified his anger into an icy, deadly rage.

No. No. The denial froze to his brain. He had waited thirty-eight long, empty years before falling in love; he wasn't about to allow any two-bit, down-at-heel punks to take her away from him. A chilling smile twitched his lips. He wasn't about to die in the blaze of an orange morning sun either—he had a date, with Courtney, and a very large, comfortable bed.

Choking with fear as Ben and the ferret-faced man warily approached, Courtney nevertheless sensed the determination settling in Rio. He was so very still . . . deadly still. In that moment *he* was infinitely more frightening than the two men cautiously moving toward them.

"Rio?" Courtney whispered through fear-dried lips. "Please, don't take unnec—"

"Be quiet," he warned through lips that barely moved. "And be very still."

"Okay, big-deal rancher," Ben sneered, coming to a stop some twenty-five feet from them. "Move away from my *puta* . . . slow-ly and care-ful-ly."

Only Courtney heard the hissing sound of Rio's indrawn breath at Ben's use of the insulting term *puta.* Impossible though it seemed, he smiled. That smile was a warning for anyone with sense enough to see and interpret. Courtney was the single person there with enough sense. The realization of how very dangerous Rio was, now that he was well and truly *riled,* set her heart thumping madly.

Obeying the beady-eyed, leering Ben, while narrowly watching the silent ferret-faced man, Rio lithely rose to his feet and walked away from Courtney with a murmured "Stay put."

Tension electrified the air around her as Courtney helplessly watched the man she loved walk to almost certain death. A blur of movement to her left caught her attention and a sigh of angry regret whispered through her lips as she observed Ferret Face move at an angle to join forces with Ben. Never having been in a position even remotely resembling this one, she'd have been astonished had she been able to feel the satisfaction that rippled through Rio.

That's right, that's right. Rio's thoughts were not betrayed by his frozen features. *That's right, you stupid bastards, close ranks—please.*

Elation zinging along his nerve ends, Rio watched Ferret Face stop beside the hulking Ben. His steps measured, Rio walked to within two feet of them before Ben had the sense to order him to stop. The order came three feet too late.

Before Courtney's disbelieving eyes her soft-spoken husband, her gentle, passionate lover, exploded into a coldly precise killing machine. Employing moves she had never witnessed before, not even in films on martial arts, Rio attacked with the edge of his slashing hands and the whipping action of his long, muscular legs.

Reveling as never before in the bloodlust for destruction, Rio slashed and kicked with deadly accuracy. The two rifles went sailing through the air from suddenly numb fingers, and then he was on them, flashing back and forth from one to the other, beating them to the ground with merciless fury.

"Puta!"

Courtney heard Rio spitting the word out with a snarl as he sank his balled fist into Ben's bloated belly. With a cry of agony Ben went down, rolling into a ball before becoming still. Not even bothering to look, Rio concentrated on the ferret-faced man. Seconds later the kidnapper was nothing more than an untidy heap on the sun-baked Texas earth.

"Courtney," he called, standing over Ferret Face's prone form. "Get me the lariat from my saddle."

Springing to her feet Courtney ran to where they'd left the horses. Her trembling fingers were tearing at the rope fastening when the hoarse sound of Ben's voice stilled their action. Spinning around, she felt a sinking sensation in her stomach. Ben was on his feet, backing away to a safe distance from Rio, one of the rifles clutched to his shoulder. Loose limbed and ready, the other rifle held confidently in his right hand by his thigh, Rio stood, calmly watching every move Ben made.

"Do you want my word that I won't kill him?" The echo of his own voice whispered in Rio's mind.

"Yes." Courtney's response followed the echo.

"You have it."

Barely winded by the scuffle, breathing easily as he monitored Ben's slightest move, Rio listened to remembered voices. He had so recently succeeded in gaining her trust. Could he afford to take the chance of losing it again now? No! He'd simply have to take his chances with Ben. The decision made, Rio acted immediately on it. Loosening his fingers, he tossed the rifle aside.

Sheer amazement washed over Ben's face . . . and widened Courtney's eyes. Ben raised the rifle and aimed at Rio.

What is he doing? she thought frantically. Then, the same voices Rio had heard moments before murmured inside her mind. *Good Lord! He doesn't want to break his word to me!* With the startling realization Courtney ceased consciously thinking and obeyed instinctive command.

Keeping her movements Spartan to avoid detection, Courtney slowly slid Rio's rifle out of the saddle scabbard and carefully brought the weapon to her shoulder. Coldly, unemotionally, and expertly, she captured Ben's large frame in the sight. Without hesitating she eased her index finger back against the trigger. Her body jerked at the buck of the report. With a surprised shout of pain Ben crumpled to the ground.

With an unnatural and jerky movement Rio turned to face her, his expression blank with disbelief as he shifted his gaze from her to Ben, and then back to her again. As if clearing away a mind-fog, he shook his head, then slowly walked to kneel by the fallen man.

Courtney was lowering the rifle when Rio straightened to his full height.

"Is he dead?" she asked tonelessly.

"No. You just got his shooting arm." Rio's voice was hoarse from the emotions clamoring through him. Courtney had actually taken a bead on another human being and pulled the trigger! And she had done it to protect *him!* Containing the whoop of laughter crowding his throat, Rio glanced at her and nearly stopped breathing. She was setting the sight on Ben again!

"Courtney, no!" Uncaring of his own safety, Rio ran to her, pushing the rifle up even as the report sounded; the slug was sent on a harmless trajectory toward the sun.

"Let me go!" Courtney demanded, struggling to maintain her grip on the weapon.

"I'm not going to let you kill him!" Rio shouted, tearing the rifle from her grasp. "No matter what he did to you in the hills," he went on more calmly when the rifle was safely in his possession, "I can't let you do this to yourself."

"To me?" Courtney stared at him uncomprehendingly. "What he did to me! What he did to me doesn't matter!" she ranted, sending a murderous glance at the man, then gazing at Rio with anguished eyes. "He was going to kill *you! He was going to kill you!*" she repeated in a raw cry.

"It's over now, *querida.*" Though his tone held firm, a smile teased the corners of his mouth. Keeping a sharp eye on her trembling figure, he slid the rifle into the scabbard, then lifted a two-way radio from a sleeve on the saddle. As he called for assistance from whoever might be closest, he drew her to him with his free arm.

Replacing the radio, he gathered her close to his hard strength just as the sobs began shaking her slender body. "It's all over. We'll let the law take care of that scum."

Sal was the first of Rio's men to arrive on the scene. An unholy gleam in his black eyes, a flashing smile on his lips, he'd assured Rio he'd be delighted to stand guard over the criminals until the law got there.

"You just take your lady away from here." Sal's grin was positively evil. "If I get real lucky, one of these dudes might start something—and give me an excuse to get nasty."

Chilled, as much by her own actions as the entire attack, Courtney withdrew behind a wall of cool composure. The ride back to the ranch was made in silence.

On their return to the ranch Rio took over. His arm around her waist clamping her to his side, he went first to the study, ordering her to drink the straight whiskey he poured out for her. When she'd finally managed to swallow the last of the amber liquid, he drew her with him into the nursery, where Luz was sleeping soundly, napping off her lunch. From the nursery he led her to their bedroom, coaxing her out of her clothes and into the shower with him. The stinging shower, combined with Rio's gentle ministrations, banished the last traces of her chill and shock. She didn't have to be ordered, led or coaxed onto the bed with him.

Now, free of self-doubt, and trembling from the tension curling her toes, Courtney shuddered in the prelude to ecstasy and whispered of her love and need.

"Rio! Darling, please . . . please! I love you . . . I love you . . . I love—"

Fusing his mouth to hers, Rio drank the sweetness of Courtney's cry. Then, watching her every expression, he buried himself in her flesh again and again in the most profound, celebratory act of life he could imagine.

As Courtney soared over the edge of impossible pleasure, she cried his name aloud.

Soaring right along with her, Rio closed his eyes in both pleasure and gratitude.

"I'm with you, love, I'm with you. I'll always be with you."

Long after twilight had crept into the room, Rio held Courtney tightly to his steadily beating heart, stroking her back with his trembling hands, and her lips with his own.

"That was an incredible journey," Courtney murmured in an awed tone.

"Ah, *querida,*" Rio laughed softly. "Now you have ridden to the very ends of the earth with the Night Striker."

Please turn the page

for an exciting sneak peek of

Joan Hohl's

newest contemporary romance

MY OWN

coming from Zebra Books in April 2000!

The scent of flowers permeated the air. The altar was adorned with tall white-and-gold tapers and garlands of white roses entwined in dark green ferns. Nosegays of dusky pink rosebuds and sprays of baby's breath were attached by white satin ribbons to the endposts of each pew.

The church was full to capacity, the ladies dressed in their spring finery, the gentlemen attired in lightweight suits or sport coats. Though the children present were for the most part on their best behavior, an occasional murmur or restless rustle of movement could be heard above the combined voices of the choir singing a traditional love song.

As the last strains faded on the blossom-fragrant air, the formally attired groom and his men entered from a door to the right of the nave.

The organist struck a signaling chord.

The groom, his attendants, and the assembled families and guests turned to face the end of the center aisle, as the organ joyfully boomed forth with the wedding march.

Seated on the right—or groom's—side of the aisle with
the members of the only family she had ever known, Kate
Quinn didn't see the tiny flower girl and four bridesmaids
in their dusky pink gowns. Nor did she see the beautiful
bride, resplendent in stiffened white silk and lace, pace
down the white runner on the arm of her father.

Kate's gaze and attention were riveted on the solemn visage
of the handsome groom, Ethan Winston, her best friend.

Ethan. The cry inside Kate's mind was wrenched from
the depths of her heart.

A flood of memories brought a rush of moisture to her
eyes, blurring the edges of his face. But the inner images
were clear, bright as the spring morning.

She had been eleven, Ethan sixteeen, the first time she
had seen him. Thirteen years had passed since that fateful
day, and yet, her memory of it was as sharp, as vivid, as if
it had been just yesterday.

Oblivious to her surroundings, the ritual of the bride's
father placing her hand in the safekeeping of the groom's
palm, the beginning of the ceremony, Kate no longer saw
the present Ethan turn with his bride to face the minister.

Looking inward, Kate saw herself, as she had been all
those years past, uncertain, shy, a little scared about her
future, her place in the new house she had come to live
in with her mother and her stepfather.

To Kate, having lived every one of her eleven years in
small apartments, the house itself was intimidating, with
its spacious rooms and half bath on the first floor, four
bedrooms and two bathrooms on the second floor, and
two big storage rooms on the third floor.

"Go, Katelyn," her mother had urged, sharing a smile
with her husband of only one day. "Go explore your new
home, the yard, and the gardens."

Needing no urging, Kate had run outdoors, to breathe

deeply in the fresh air, bask in the heat of summer sunshine, rejoice in what, at that young age, she considered the extensive lawns and gardens.

Having already seen the front lawn with its trees and shrubbery, she headed for the back of the house, thrilled with the width and depth of the property. There were flower beds ablaze with color, abundant with a variety of plants in full bloom. A hedge nearly as tall as Kate herself bordered either side and the back boundaries of the yard.

It was as she neared the far end of the yard that Kate heard a clipping noise. Curious, she wandered in the direction of the sound. She discovered the boy in the far corner, trimming the hedge with long-bladed clippers.

Either he was tall or standing on something, Kate figured, for his torso rose above the high hedge. He was young, though, not yet a man, but a kid like her, just a few years older.

Shy, unsure, she moved closer, coming to a dead stop when he glanced over the hedge at her.

He was the best-looking boy Kate had ever seen. He had dark hair and even darker eyes, and when, suddenly, he grinned at her, her heart seemed to flip-flop.

"Hi," he said, his voice friendly. "You must be Katelyn, Mr. Gardner's new stepdaughter. Right?"

Tongue-tied, Kate nodded in answer.

"Thought so." He nodded, too. "I'm Ethan Winston." He indicated the house behind him. "I live next door. My parents and Mr. Gardner are good friends. I met your mother last week." He smiled. "That's how I knew your name."

"Oh," Kate said, suddenly recalling her mother mentioning that David Gardner's neighbors had two children, a son and a daughter, both older than Kate. "You have a sister, don't you?" she asked, hoping the girl would be a little closer to her own age then Ethan.

"Yeah." He nodded again. "Sharon, but she's away at college."

"Oh," Kate repeated, sighing in disappointment.

"Well, I'd better get back to work," he said, grimacing. "See you later, Katelyn."

"Kate," she blurted out.

"Okay," he agreed, grinning again. "I like that better, anyway."

Although Kate had eventually met Sharon Winston, a pretty young woman of eighteen, she had had little contact with her. But she had seen a lot of Ethan. In truth, whenever he was around the house, she trailed after him like a puppy. He tolerated her, teased her, and a time or two, took on the big brother role of protector, most particularly when she lost her mother three years later.

But even before that awful day, before she had even turned twelve, and he seventeen, Kate worshiped Ethan like a hero.

By the time she turned seventeen, Kate knew she was in love with him.

"And now, by the powers vested in me . . ."

Hearing those fateful words, Kate blinked herself into the present.

". . . I pronounce you man and wife."

The pronouncement was like a knife in Kate's heart. *Ethan.*

Staring at him, Kate saw him gather the filmy bridal veil in his hands and begin to raise it above the beautiful face of his bride. Unable to bear watching him bestow the sealing kiss, Kate lowered her eyes.

It was done. It was over. Ethan had married another woman—he belonged to another woman.

All of Kate's hopes, her dreams, died an agonizing death. The knell rang inside her head.

Now I'll never have Ethan for my own.